Book One of The Witching

The Witching Pen

(Book One of The Witching Pen Novellas)

An exciting new world, featuring
witches, demons, magic and seduction.

A London-based,
adult paranormal romance.
Written by Dianna Hardy

The Witching Pen
(Book One of The Witching Pen Novellas)

Published by Satin Smoke Press, April, 2012
First Trade Edition
Satin Smoke Press (Slice paperbacks)
ISBN 978-0-9567192-6-3

A CIP catalogue record for this book is available from the British Library.

Cover images © Shutterstock.com
Cover design by Dianna Hardy

Satin Smoke Press
(an imprint of Bitten Fruit Books)
Surrey, UK

www.satinsmoke.com

For my sister.
Thanks for reading all my crazy stuff.

~*~

Book One of The Witching Pen Novellas

The Witching Pen

Chapter One

"*Feeeel* everything around you ... go into it ... become one with it..."

It was at these moments Elena had to try really hard to feign interest. It wasn't Amy's fault. Amy was just ... well, she was Amy, and this was a Wicca group.

Yeah, everyone's a Wiccan.

Except Elena. Elena was not a Wiccan, but she couldn't tell anyone what she really was: a thirteenth generation witch. Her lineage granted her powers that other fellow witches, whether Wiccan or not, did not have – Elena was the real deal. For the hundredth time, she had to remind herself that the reason she came to these sessions was to connect with others, to make friends. The fact that she already knew how to do what Amy was trying to teach (and knew how to do it using *actual* magic) was completely beside the point. Elena, although mostly happy with her own company, occasionally felt alone – too alone and too different.

Closing her eyes and trying hard to go with it, Elena let herself *feeeel* her surroundings. It was like slipping into a warm favourite coat and it came far too easily to her.

Elena, hold back – don't get carried away. It was her own voice of reason saving her. *No one needs to see what happens to you when you lose yourself in meditation...*

At that thankful moment, Amy's stopwatch beeped.

"Okay everyone – great session today. Don't forget your glamour spells for next week," she called out as people filed out the door and others hung back in the hope of gaining advice, maybe praise, from the group leader. They were all of mixed ages, anything from eighteen to sixty.

"Elena, can I have a quick word with you?"

Oh crap, not good...

Elena always tried very hard to stay out of everyone's way, she tried especially hard not to engage in conversation with anyone. It wasn't that she disliked people, but people invariably ended up disliking her ... or at least afraid of her. But she knew that her distance wasn't helping her cause to make friends and curb her loneliness, so instead, she put on her best I'm-one-of-the-crowd-voice, and said, "Sure."

"Elena, you've been coming here for three months now and you haven't led a session yet. I think you should, or at least think about it."

"Sure," she said again. *No way – unless you're all prepared to see me floating off the ground and accept it as reality.*

"Okay ... well, how about next week? It's the full moon – you could lead the glamour session."

"Er—"

"Great! That's settled." Amy beamed a smile through her immaculate, white teeth that left no room for compromise, and swiftly turned away from her to talk to her avid followers.

She had tried really hard to like Amy, but no matter which way she looked at it, she couldn't help but think of her as fake. Not a fake witch – no, Amy exuded magic – more like a fake human being. She feigned compassion, Elena was sure of it.

With a slight smile, she reached into her bag as soon as she was outside the meeting room, and pulled out a pen. It was nothing special to look at – a standard fountain pen, with a dark blue, metallic surround. She could have bought it at the local newsagents, but she hadn't – no, she'd found it in the middle of the suspension bridge that hung over the river. She would never even have picked it up were it not for the fact that at that second, she had been on the phone, with notepad in one hand, needing to write down a name her mum was spelling out for her. Her other hand had been rummaging around her rucksack for a pen she didn't have ... and then the sun had bounced off this one...

Knowing she really shouldn't, but itching to let out some real magic, Elena pulled out her notepad and started to write...

Suddenly and completely out of the blue,
Amy Langdon's skirt fell from her hips
and pooled around her ankles.

From behind her, back in the room she'd just walked out of, Amy let out a squeal of horror as a few hushed giggles floated on the air.

"Okay, so I'm officially a bad witch," muttered Elena, "but that was *so* much fun!"

~*~

The smell of roast pork greeted her as she walked into her flat. Karl was cooking roast?

"Hey! I'm home!"

"In the kitchen!"

"You're cooking roast?"

"Yeah, why not?"

"It's Saturday."

"So? Is Saturday roast against the law?"

"No, it's just, you don't cook roast – I cook roast. You cook cheese on toast."

"Well, maybe there are a few things you don't know about me," he teased. "How was your fake witch group?"

She groaned. "Don't. Amy wants me to lead the session next week."

Karl hooted his laughter, which was met with a slap on the arm from Elena.

"Does she know you'll scare away her little band of followers if you're allowed to do such a thing?"

"No. I don't know how to get out of it. It's crazy – I'm twenty-five years old, and yet the woman reduced me to feeling like a clumsy, mute teenager."

"Just magic your way out of it."

"*Not* something I want to resort to. Come on, you know the rules."

"Rules are there to be broken."

"Hmm – spoken like a true non-thirteenth generation witch."

"Well, if you'd do me the honour of making mad, passionate love to me, I'd be a witch just like you."

Elena sighed. Of course this wouldn't be the last time they had this conversation.

Elena had known Karl, "the boy from across the street", since she was five and he was seven. By his declaration, he'd been in love with her ever since he was ten years old and saw her bring a butterfly back from the dead, an act which had shocked her mother into an eerie silence. Elena had never reciprocated his love – at least, she didn't think she loved him. Loved him as a best friend, undoubtedly, but not *in* love with him. It was in fact possible, that by the sheer impossibility of her ever being able to be with anyone at all, she'd simply denied any feelings she may have had – after all, that was better than admitting the truth. The truth would lead only to grief.

"You don't want me, you just want my powers." She knew she shouldn't play this game, but she desperately wanted to make light of the situation. Karl was the least power-hungry person she knew.

"Yep, okay, yes, you win – I want your powers, you're absolutely right ... now give them to me!"

She squealed, half in frustration and half in delight, as he catapulted her over his shoulder and ran for the living room couch.

"Put me *down*!"

"Not until you submit, woman!"

"Never! Never, never, never!"

Regardless, he still dropped her onto the couch. She was not a large wo-man, but she was taller than average, with Karl only half a head taller than her.

"You out of breath?"

"You kidding me? You're a waif." He knelt on the floor and laid his head on her lap. "Elena?"

"Yes?"

"What are your plans for the future?"

A silence filled the air, growing heavier with every heartbeat.

"Aren't you going to burn the pork?"

"It's on a timer. And don't change the subject. I know you don't want to talk about me, or us, but there's still *you*. What are you going to do?"

"Karl..." She really didn't want to talk about this.

"You're a twenty-five year old virgin."

"Hey!"

"Hey yourself – it's true. I know it's not your fault, but ... is that it? You're never going to give yourself to anyone because of a condition?"

"My lineage is not a condition."

"It is if it means you can never have sex ... or never show your love to someone."

"And you're hoping that someone is you, right?" It was a bit of a sneer and she knew she was hitting below the belt, but her irritability levels had shot right up since he'd mentioned the V-word. Yes, she was a virgin. She had no choice in the matter. If she decided to sleep with someone...

"I'm hoping you end up happily married to the man of your dreams and have a hoard of beautiful kids that'll keep you on your toes by turning your neighbours into various types of pond-life." He then shot her his signature grin.

"But if it happens to be me, then I wouldn't say no."

His grin was truly infectious. As a boy, it was the first thing she'd noticed about him – that grin had gotten them both out of trouble on many occasions – and it was framed by a face that had never lost its boyish looks, from the dimples in his cheeks, to his unkempt, sandy blond hair and his sea blue eyes. He was your typical boy next door – the one your mum would want you to marry, unless, of course, you were Elena's mum. Never the social butterfly, Katherine Green, Elena's mother, had never taken to any boy that Elena had found remotely interesting. When she was fifteen, Elena had begun to talk about Karl more – maybe she'd given away something in her eyes, because that was when Katherine had sat her down and told her the awful truth of her magical inheritance...

"I need to talk to you, Elena, about sex."

"Eeew, Mum—"

"No interruptions, please. I've been dreading this day..." Her mother sat down next to her at the breakfast table and took her hand. "Elena ... you're special. Being the thirteenth in our family line makes you special ... with that come certain responsibilities."

Elena rolled her eyes. "Mum, I know about condoms and stuff."

"Well you don't know about this ... you can't ever be *in a relationship."*

"What?"

"Sex is a powerful thing for any witch, just like a first bleed is, but for you, it's ten times more potent."

She remembered her first period. She'd been thirteen and the moment she'd felt that first trickle down her inner-thigh, unearthly storm clouds had drawn in and the sky had been torn apart by thunder – an "April shower of unexpectedly large proportions" is how it was reported on the news, but she had known otherwise. That tingle at the back of her neck always told her when something magical was afoot. The next two weeks had seen her fending off men – all men and any man – apparently she'd become some kind of 'fuck me' beacon, wafting magical pheromones all over the place. The only person who'd seemed completely oblivious to her change was Karl. It had crossed her mind that maybe he was gay.

Thankfully the whole ordeal had lasted for just her first cycle, with no other problems in subsequent months.

"Elena," her mother squeezed her hand, drawing her back to the present. "If

you have sex, you'll be giving away your power – literally. The man you sleep with will take on your magic and you will be left barren of it. You will no longer have any powers and you will never be able to get them back."

"It's sort of like, when Arwen in *Lord Of The Rings* gives up her immortality to be with the man she loves..." She looked down at Karl. His grin was gone.

"You're a beautiful person, Elena, and you deserve a man you love. It may be worth considering giving up your witchcraft for a lifetime of happiness ... for a future family."

"You think I haven't considered it?" she smiled, sadly. "To lead a normal life ... and then I think about someone else having this magic inside them and what a huge responsibility it would be. I grew up with it – I was prepared for it – someone else ... how would they wield all this power? I barely can. There are rules they'd have to follow, entire scripts they'd have to learn ... I'd be changing them forever; Karl, I'd be tearing their lives apart. How can I do that to someone ... how could I do that to you?"

She hadn't meant to cry, but there they were, those tiny, salty rivers carving their way down her face.

Karl kissed her knee. His hands were rubbing her thighs in comfort and not for the first time, she cursed her life – cursed that she couldn't just sit back and give into this, relax into another man's affections.

"You shouldn't do this to yourself," she whispered, tasting her tears on her lips now. "I don't know how you can stand it, being around me all the time, knowing how you feel about me, knowing what you can never have..."

"Ssshhh, baby, it's all right." He got up, shuffled onto the sofa beside her and draped her legs over his lap. "I know you, Elena – better than anyone. I know what you can and can't do, in every area of your life. I know you suck at gardening—"

She snorted.

"But if you ever decide that you've had enough, that you no longer want your magical nature, I'm here. I've seen what your powers can do, hell, I've even helped you with a few spells – you can trust me with them."

She studied him, letting herself drown in the blue of his eyes, something she almost never did, ever since her mother had had the sex talk with her. He really was beautiful. She found herself reaching out and stroking his cheek.

"Are you gay?"

"What? *Gay?*"

His confusion quickly turned to irritation – he actually looked a little pissed off. Elena tried unsuccessfully to stifle a giggle at his expression. It wasn't often that Karl was caught off guard.

Catching her eye again, he raised an eyebrow. "You think I'm *gay?*"

"I wondered just once, a long time ago—"

He grabbed her hips and pulled her down onto her back. His grin turned wicked as he pinned her to the sofa with the weight of his body. Her laughter died in her throat and for a moment, there was only Karl, his eyes dancing like the waves of the sea, his hair the colour of a golden beach. His nose brushed hers, her lips parted, he leaned down—

Beep ... beep ... beeeeeeeeeep.

They froze, then Karl winked – the moment was gone.

"Pork's done."

~*~

Down on the street below, a shadow solidified. It took on the shape of a man, tall and muscular. But he was not a man. His cracked face, grey and hard like stone was turned towards a window two storeys up, his eyes – the clearest green you'll ever see – completely focused on the activities on the other side of the window.

If his solid body could grow harder still, it did. Rage shone in his emerald eyes.

How dare he – how dare he touch what's mine.

Somewhere, a dog barked. He silenced it with his mind, his thoughts strangling the animal until only a pitiful whimper travelled the air. There – he felt better now.

His body began to fade away once more. He could never stay in this world for too long at a time, but before he became one with the shadows again, he breathed out a tiny word, making sure it clung to the air as the breeze carried it to the window that shielded him from the witch – *his* witch...

"Elena..."

Chapter Two

She stared at the pen on her bedside table. Karl was the only other person that knew about it. She'd considered telling her mother, but they really weren't that close, and besides, she hadn't got her head around it yet. She wanted to be sure of what to do with it when others finally knew of its existence.

Letting out a sigh, her mind took her back to dinner. She had to hand it to Karl, that was a truly delicious roast ... and then she was thinking about his lips...

Get over it! It's not something that can ever happen!

Confusion skirted over her thoughts. She really hadn't believed she was in love with him ... could it be that all this time she'd just been kidding herself? She didn't like the way her heart was already beating faster at the thought of their near kiss earlier that night. They should never have bought a place together, but it had seemed so logical. They were best friends, they had always done everything together. So why not live together too? After all, he knew everything about her – she wouldn't have to run around ragged trying to hide everything witchy about her.

She looked again at the pen. Not for the first time, she considered what would happen, what would her life be like, if she had the gall to write a few selfish words...

Elena discovered that all these years,
her curse had been false and she could, in fact,
sleep with anyone she wanted, at any time, with no
magical consequences ... she could fall in love.

God, it was so tempting ... but it still wouldn't solve the fact that he'd be bound to, not just her, but her entire lineage – a responsibility she wasn't prepared to put upon him. But ... what would life be like if he were also a witch?

He finally told her his secret:
he, too, was a great magician

with unmatched super powers.

He would be her equal – it would be so much easier. Not that she didn't consider him her equal in every other way.

With a last sigh at her ridiculous notions, she pulled her T-shirt over her head and stripped her Levi's from her legs. Snuggling down under her duvet she took one last look at the pen that sat atop her open notebook, then she reached out and turned the light off.

"Elena ..."

Her name reached her as a whisper on the cool autumn breeze.

"Elena ..."

Forcing her sleepy eyes open, she looked around for the voice that called to her, expecting to find herself in her bedroom, maybe Karl at the doorway, trying to get her attention. But she was not in her bedroom. Suddenly alarmed, she sat up straight with a gasp. She was still in her bed, but this was nowhere she'd been before. The floor was gritty with sand and dust, an arid red; the room was not a room, but a cave of some kind. Cream coloured, stone walls greeted her, with candles lighting them in various places, flickering orange in the darkness that surrounded her.

Okay ... so I'm still in my bed ... so, this must be a dream ... I hope...

"Elena..."

Her heart hammered in her chest, almost drowning out her thoughts.

If this is a dream, then it's okay to ask who's there, right?

"Who are you?"

Silence greeted her, and an unearthly breeze rippled her bedsheets – not the cool breeze of autumn, but hot and humid, as if a dragon was breathing on her. Beads of sweat began to form behind her neck – this was magic, but not the good kind.

"Elena..." The voice was directly behind her now and her name fluttered against her ear. She spun around, trying to keep her fear reined in and failing when she came face to face with a man, seemingly made out of stone, his face cracked like an old, dry pavement, his eyes the clearest, sharpest green she'd ever seen – inhuman – *a demon.*

She wanted to scream, but her throat couldn't work the sound out. She tried to move, but her body suddenly seemed like stone itself, heavy and cumbersome. And the demon sat at the edge of her bed. With a grey, cracked finger, he stroked her cheek. A shudder vibrated through her still body.

"Sweet Elena, do you like my gift?"

"G-gift?"

"A magic pen – a powerful pen for a powerful witch."

"It's – it's yours?" Her throat felt as dry as the cave floor – her words, barely audible, hurt her every time she spoke.

"No, my beautiful witch, it's yours."

His fingers travelled down her neck. She wanted to smack him, hit him, at the very least swat his hand away, but the back of her neck was burning in warning of the black magic he exuded and she could not move. She could barely shudder, but another one managed to snake its way down her spine.

His fingers stopped at the swell of her breasts and trailed across the edge of her bra. To her horror, her skin began to tingle where he touched her and a warmth spread between her legs.

No!

Her brain suddenly kicked into action and she focused her intent fully on the outcome she desired. She forced her throat to work. *"Saepio, saepio , saepio..."*

The demon laughed. "Your barriers won't work against me, Elena – you have no idea what I am."

"Saepio, saepio, saepio..."

No, the barrier wasn't working, but her body was loosening up, her senses were returning, her throat becoming less dry...

His hand snaked its way around her waist.

"I'm going to show you how to use your new gift." And then she was flush against the length of him, his cheek against hers, his voice a deadly whisper in her ear ... *"I'm going to fill you with my world."*

Her throat felt normal again, and finally, the scream that had been lodged inside her erupted, and shook the walls of the demon's lair, even as everything faded around her.

~*~

Karl had never been a deep sleeper, but never in his life had anything brought him out of slumber so quickly as the ear-splitting scream coming from Elena's room.

His heart leapt right up into his throat as he dove for his door and half ran, half stumbled down the hall. He'd never heard her scream before, not like this, and once again he found himself overwhelmed by the very essence of her – only this time it was her fear he felt – and Elena never got scared.

He bouldered his way into her room to find her sitting up, tangled in her sheets and tearing at air.

"Elena!"

Did she see him? She seemed to be looking at something...

"Elena! Wake up!"

The look on her face almost had him frozen to the spot, but his practical nature always bested him, and he grabbed her shoulders instead, trying to shake her into full alertness. The woman was rigid under his hands, so he tried a different approach. Collecting her into his arms, he planted a tender kiss on her forehead and rubbed her back, speaking softly, "Elena, honey, everything's all right. It's me – it's Karl."

She was burning hot, her skin tacky with sweat, but she blinked.

Yes. We're getting somewhere.

"Elena, it's okay ... everything's okay... "

He rocked her in his arms, back and forth.

"Wake up, baby. Wake up..."

She blinked again and turned her head. "K-Karl?"

"Yes, it's me ... are you all right?"

She looked skittishly at her surroundings, then surrendered into his arms, her breaths coming out sharp and quick.

"What happened?"

"There was ... something was here..."

He frowned at her open window. Did she mean that someone was actually *in* here?

As if reading his mind, she shook her head. "No. It was a like a dream ... but it wasn't a dream."

She paused and seemed unsure of what to say next.

"Do you want to talk about it?"

"I don't know. I..."

She looked at him – looked right into his eyes with her own hazel ones. Up until now it hadn't even occurred to him that they were holding each other wearing not a hell of a lot, and he forced his mind away from the fact.

A slight smile touched her lips. "I like your eyes – I like that they're so blue..." And then her smile disappeared, she looked away and shuddered. His practical self won through yet again, and he used the opportunity to untangle her sheets and draw them up around her – for his sake more than hers. She shot him a grateful glance.

"It was a demon. I think he was in this room, or at least, his shadow was. He seeped into my mind as I was dreaming."

"A demon?"

Nothing about Elena or the life she led should surprise him any more, but he'd never heard her mention demons at all in the past, so here he was, once again taken aback.

"I don't know much about them. There are text books and stuff, but my teachers never concentrated on the demon worlds so much ... guess I'd better get researching."

"A *demon*? I don't know what to say ... how do you know it was a demon?"

"Instinct, I guess ... and he looked kind of ... demonic. Oh, God ..."

"What?"

"The pen ... he said it was his gift to me."

They both looked at the pen that sat atop her nightstand.

"Do you believe him?"

She shrugged. "I have no reason not to, I mean ... the pen just appeared one day out of nowhere."

"So you think he planted it for you to find?"

"I suppose he did, and I'd better find out why fast, because I don't think this was a one-off visit. Karl? Karl – what is it?"

Karl had stopped moving; he'd almost stopped breathing. A feeling of dread had sunk into the pit of his stomach. "Do you always sleep with your notebook open?"

"Yes, it's easier for me to write down dreams and stuff when half asleep."

"Did you write down *that*?"

Elena looked once again at the notebook and spotted what she had obviously missed before. A strangled cry escaped her lips.

The plane's final engine failed, and the passengers screamed as it plummeted.

Chapter Three

"Oh, God, I didn't write that, I didn't..." But it was her handwriting staring back at her, down to the very last detail.

"What does it mean?"

Racing past Karl, she grabbed her clothes and ran downstairs. Throwing on her shirt, she opened her laptop and turned on the TV.

When Karl caught up with her, he had the pen and notebook in his hand.

"A plane's gone down ... a plane full of people."

"You don't know that, Elena."

"Yes, I do! That's what happens when I write with the pen. What I write *happens*."

"Yes, but *you* didn't write this."

"I don't remember writing it, but what if I did? What if I did it while I was dreaming, like sleepwalking – what if he made me do it?"

The laptop was still loading and the TV was blaring at them. Elena skipped through the channels, landing on the News.

"Nothing ... nothing about a plane crash."

"Maybe it hasn't happened yet."

She dropped the control and snatched the pen from him. "Of course! Maybe I can stop it."

"Wait – what if it *has* happened ... and then what you write undoes it. Isn't that detrimental to time, or space, or physics or something...?"

She stopped with the pen in mid-air and chewed her lip in thought. "I don't know. I don't know what happens, but if the plane hasn't crashed yet, the alternative is that all those people die, so I'm willing to take the risk."

At the last minute, by some miracle,
the plane's engines rumbled to–

"Elena, look..." He nodded at the telly.

The footage showed a video, home made and somewhat blurry, of an aeroplane, crashing into a field near some houses. A fireball went up around it.

Residents ran from the disaster, fearing for their own lives, screaming in a language she recognised as Italian – this was happening in Italy. Tears blurred her vision and the pen shook in her trembling hand – she was too late.

"When?" Her knees felt weak.

"Looks recent. Maybe it's just a coincidence."

"There's no such thing ... Karl..." Her legs gave way.

"All right – I've got you." Strong arms helped her to the couch.

"Karl ... I've killed them."

"Now, I knew you were going to say that ... and you know what I'm going to say, right?"

"I did it – this is my writing – I wrote this." The murderous words, scrawled in black ink, danced across her eyes and seemed to laugh at her.

"Elena, listen to me. *If* you wrote this, you didn't do it consciously, and I'll bet you anything your dream demon had everything to do with this. You said, he told you he was going to show you how to use the pen."

"He said he was going to fill me with his world."

His eyebrows knitted together in confusion. "What the hell does that mean?"

Elena felt the blood rush to her cheeks – she wasn't sure she wanted to hazard a guess. "That he's going to turn me into an evil witch? I don't know."

With a sigh, Karl ran his hand through his hair, a mannerism he'd inherited from his father. Elena realised years back, that he did it every time he was trying to gather his thoughts.

"I think you should call your mum."

"What? Why?"

"Self-explanatory, Elena. A whole bunch of people just died, probably because of that pen that you know nothing about, and some demon that you also know nothing about has the power to make you do things you don't want to do."

Again, she felt herself blushing. Thankfully Karl didn't seem to notice.

"Your mum seems the most logical, immediate solution. Either that, or The Council."

She grimaced. The Council? Only as the very last resort. Karl was right, her mother may have answers.

"All right. Pass me the phone."

"Now? It's five o'clock in the morning."

"If I don't do it now, I'll lose my nerve – pass me the phone."

~*~

Elena sat, drumming her fingers on the breakfast table, her lukewarm coffee all but forgotten. The oven clock read 8:30am. Time was going too slow.

Having since learnt that there were no survivors of the plane crash, and having heard some of the passengers' last minute phone calls to their loved ones that were starting to stream into the News, Elena had broken down sobbing. Not even Karl had been able to take away the pain of the reality she had indirectly created. When her silence took over and numbness began to sink in, Karl had sat her down at the table and made her a steaming coffee, leaving her alone to drink it, for which she was grateful. Now the numbness had started to fade away, replaced by the edginess she always felt at seeing her mum.

She had been greeted with the usual stony silence when she'd told her over the phone about the dream ... and about the pen. Every conversation she had with her mum was awkward and cold, ever since that day she'd healed the butterfly. Before that, she had vague recollections of warmth, kindness, laughter ... Okay, so since then, she'd learnt that witches weren't allowed to meddle with life and death, but her mother's reaction had seemed too great for something she hadn't even known she could do at the time. Her eight year old self never really understood what she'd done wrong, her teenage self used to make up scenarios of what the issue might be, and her adult self had given up wanting to know, preferring to keep the peace than open a can of worms that would estrange her even further.

She shuffled in her seat and glanced once more at the clock. She had said that she would be here as soon as she could.

That was three hours ago – she only lives fifteen minutes away, for God's sake!

"Jesus, Elena, chill out. You'll wear a hole through your seat."

"This was *your* idea, remember – I didn't want to call her."

"And was I wrong? What's the alternative?"

Sitting back, she felt a sulk coming on – she couldn't think of an alternative.

"It'll be all right. Do you want me to make you another coffee?"

The doorbell rang. Nervously, Elena jumped up. She really was all over the place.

A warm hand on her shoulder encouraged her back down. "I'll get it – you try and relax a bit."

Picking up the intercom, Karl buzzed her in and walked off through the lounge to open their front door. She heard her mother's heels echoing on the stone stairs outside, getting louder with every step. She heard Karl's warm, friendly hello greeting, and then her mother's voice, curt, crisp – a startling contrast to his – "Good morning, Karl. Still hanging around, are you?"

Elena bit back the anger that surged up her throat. *Just keep your cool. You only have to do this for maybe an hour, two at the most, and then she'll be gone.*

Her footsteps made their way into the kitchen.

Elena rose from the table and turned around. "Hello, Mother."

"Elena. So, where's the pen?"

Straight to business then. No 'how are you?', no peck on the cheek. Typical.

"Right here on the table."

All three of them stared at it, as if waiting for it to announce itself. Of course, it did nothing.

"Goodness, it's so ... unassuming."

"Yes. Mum, do you know anything about it?"

"There's a fable about a 'witching pen' – it was always thought to be a fairy tale."

"Any chance it's not?"

"Apparently so. But first, tell me about your demon."

Elena baulked at the reference to the demon being hers. "I pretty much told you everything on the phone."

"You didn't tell me what he looked like."

"Oh, um ... he ... his eyes were green – a brilliant green, like emeralds shining in the sun. His skin was grey and looked like it was made of stone, and it was cracked, like a dry pavement – and hard, but only like leathered skin, not hard like stone."

"You touched him?" Her mother's voice was tight, her lips drawn in. She looked disturbed.

"No. He – he touched me..."

Unbidden, her mind replayed his fingers trailing down her neck, how they felt on the tops of her breasts ... she knew her face was an obvious shade of red. Out of the corner of her eye, Elena saw Karl fold his arms across his chest.

Shit!

Her mother was eyeing her suspiciously. "Were you attracted to him?"

"What? No!" She answered too quickly, and her face turned a shade darker.

Her mother's eyes narrowed. "I see."

Karl was standing still as a statue and Elena desperately wanted to explain it wasn't what he thought ... or at the very least for the ground to swallow her up.

"You met a Shanka demon."

"You know about demons? What's a Shanka demon? Why have you never told me before? Why don't I know about demons?"

Ignoring most of her questions, as usual, her mother got straight to the point – as usual. "Demons rarely cross dimensions. Shanka demons are one of the few that do. They are a type of incubi, and their women, succubi – they connect with you through your dreams, often to seduce you so they can steal your sexual energy to feed their own strength, sometimes so they can impregnate you to ensure continuation of their bloodline in this dimension, and occasionally for some other, greater purpose that's not always known to us. As a tribe, they have exactly one goal and they are ruthless in attaining it: they want to rule over *our* dimension."

"And ... they're using the pen to help them do this?"

"I would say so – not just the pen, but you too."

Elena's stomach sank. She felt sick. Her throat forced out the word that was eating away at her brain. "Impregnate?"

Her mother ignored her. "The plane crash was a demonstration. It was to show you what they are capable of and that they're serious about it."

"Those words were in my handwriting."

"Yes. Your demon wanted you to understand the power that he has over you."

"Why? And he's not *my* demon."

Her mother sighed. For a fraction of a second, something that looked like tenderness shone through her features and Elena remembered a moment when she was five, both of them laughing together, sitting on the swings in the park ... then the softness was gone and her distant, cold mother stood before her once more.

"You're a thirteenth generation witch, Elena – and a virgin. He's come to claim you, and your magic, as his own."

~*~

Karl's limbs were starting to hurt, because he was stiff as a board. He didn't dare move. If he moved, he may just lash out and hit something. Hearing that Elena was in any way drawn to the demon was enough to churn his blood, but hearing that he – *it* – wanted to claim her, had *violated* her through her dreams, had his blood boiling with an anger very few people had the misfortune to witness. He remembered the scream she'd let loose that had pierced the night. He'd touched her ... he'd *touched* her.

What the hell was 'claiming' her supposed to mean anyway? Elena belonged to no one – she wasn't some kind of possession...

The thought of someone forcing himself upon her sickened him. But this wasn't someone, this was some*thing*. Once again, this was a *magical* incident – once again, he would be rendered useless and unable to do anything to help. Because he was not magical.

He gritted his teeth. If anyone thought he was about to lie down and just let Elena be seduced by some demon, they had another thing coming, magic or no magic.

Elena's pinched tone brought him out of his thoughts. "How do I stop him?"

"I don't know that you can." A crack sounded in Mrs Green's voice. The woman's façade was breaking – twice he'd noticed this since she'd arrived and it was twice more than he'd have expected. Maybe he should be relieved that she wasn't a complete ice queen, but he was more worried about what it meant.

"Then ... how do I stop more planes going down? How do I make sure he can't control what I write?"

"I'm not sure of that either. You'll have to try and fight him, or use a protection spell *before* you sleep; he can only reach you in your dreams – that's the only time he's corporeal. Any other time, he's just a shadow ... maybe have Karl protect you..." She said this reluctantly, her disdain audible. He was used to it by now. He'd always assumed it was because she didn't want her daughter losing her powers to him – he was the ultimate threat to her and her lineage. Until now.

He spoke for the first time since she'd gotten here. "Maybe we should tell The Council."

"Really, Karl ... and what do *you* know of The Council?"

"Mum, stop it – you can't ask Karl to protect me one minute, then treat him like shit the next."

Elena's voice was trembling. She didn't usually speak out against her mother.

I guess feeling responsible for a plane full of people dying will alter your priorities, thought Karl, wryly.

Mrs Green exhaled sharply. "Fine. But we're not involving The Council. They'll turn your lives upside down to solve any problem."

"If people are dying, is that really an issue?" asked Karl.

A smirk turned up the corner of the woman's mouth. "They'll interrogate you, leave no stone unturned and nothing you hold dear will belong to you any more, it will belong to them – you have no idea, boy."

He bristled at the insult, but remained silent, refusing to let her push his button. He didn't know why, but he was sure something wasn't right. All the information Mrs Green had given them had been to the point and concise – too concise...

"Mum, what do you think I should do with the pen? Should I hide it? Maybe then, the demon won't know where it is. You seem to know more about this than me – maybe you should take it and keep it safe."

Her mother looked surprised. "And how would I be able to do that when you're the only one who can touch it?"

Elena looked at Karl in confusion. His super-logic kicked in straight away and he shot her a glance he hoped she'd interpret as 'keep quiet'.

"Yes, of course. In all the chaos we forgot ... Elena, remember what happened when I tried to pick it up?"

"Oh..."

He held his breath, hoping she'd trust him enough to go with the lie.

"Yes, of course..."

Good.

"Well, Elena, I have to go now – I have appointments I can't cancel. But these are for you." She produced two small, leather-bound books from her bag. "This one contains stories of myths and legends; there's one called *The Witching Pen* – maybe you'll find it useful. And this one..." She hesitated before giving it to her daughter. "This is about the Shanka tribe and their history. Consider it your demon bible until we know better what to do. I'll see myself out."

With a curt nod to Karl and not even a goodbye to Elena, Mrs Green made her way out of the flat, leaving them both in silence.

The door clicked shut behind her.

Elena spoke first. "Wow. What a lot of information – and also not a lot, if you know what I mean."

Karl said nothing, lost in thought, staring at the pen on the kitchen table. He walked over to it and picked it up.

"What was all that about? Nothing happens to you when you touch the pen."

"But your mother seems to think it does ... seems to think you're the *only* one who can touch it."

"Why not just tell her the truth?"

"Because I'm afraid we can't trust her, Elena."

"Karl, I know she's cold, but this is big stuff – she wouldn't keep anything from us, surely. Why would she?"

"I don't know why, but she is. You never told her what the demon looked like over the phone, and yet she pulled out a book about that very demon from her bag. She's not telling us everything. I'm sorry, Elena, but we can't trust her."

Chapter Four

Elena's eyes were starting to hurt. All she could see in front of them was black and white print, the word 'demon' and the vision of a plane crashing as people screamed. To make things worse, every now and then she caught an image of her future self, her belly blown out and undulating with demon spawn. *Gross. Gross, gross, gross!*

She and Karl had just read all about 'the witching pen' and the Shanka tribe from the books her mother had given her, and she wasn't sure she was any the wiser. The story of the witching pen was straight forward, the purpose of the pen, a bit clearer – she just had no idea what it had to do with her. The history of the Shanka was interweaved with the myth of the witching pen. From what she could gather it told the tale of the creation of the demon world, sort of like the story of *Genesis,* only for demons. She would therefore assume that some of it would be halve-truths, steeped in age and mystery – clues rather than fact...

At the dawn of time, seven demon tribes walked the earth: the Lagool, the Brujii, the Malattal, the Brokk, the Totilemi, the Dessec and the Shanka.

Lokoli was the queen of all demons, with magical abilities that were unmatched and a bloodthirsty nature that knew no mercy. Similar to any archetypal God or Goddess, how she actually came into being was not known. But Lokoli was responsible for the creation of all demons, able to build and destroy worlds at a whim with her pen – the witching pen. More powerful than her wand and greater than any known magic, it belonged to its master alone, the fires of death coming to all others daring to even touch it.

One day, tired of being alone and of having no one to share her creations with, she decided that she needed a mate – not just any mate, but the strongest, most bloodthirsty demon – one that she would regard as an equal in every way. So, with the witching pen, she wrote six races into being. The Lagool lived in water – oceans, rivers and swamps – and she gave them the gift of sight. The Brujii lived in the forests and woods, and were given the gift of magic. The Malattal lived under the ground, in caves, and held the gift of prophesy. The Brokk inhabited the cold places of the north and were given the gift of immortality. The Totilemi were not limited to a region, but travelled the earth, and were given the gift of knowledge. Finally, she created the Dessec to inhabit the hot deserts, and gave them the ability to bend time.

Observing her work, Lokoli still felt unhappy. She realised that in order for a mate to truly be her equal, they would have to match her in power. So she decided to create one more race: the Shanka. They were given the gift of creation itself – power over life and death would be theirs. But too afraid they would one day use their gift to destroy her, she banished them from the earth, forcing them to live ethereally, only able to enter this dimension through shadows and dreams.

Centuries passed, and the seven demon tribes grew strong and proficient in their separate crafts. The time had come to find her mate. She declared that each tribe must choose a worthy champion to represent them. The champion must show her to what extent he had mastered his gift. The one who had learnt to use it most wisely, to its fullest potential, could claim her as his and share in her power. Together they would rule over all.

One by one, each demon champion showed her the best he could conjure with his gift. She remained unimpressed. They showed her nothing she couldn't do herself – until the champion of the Shanka began to appear in her dreams. He was nameless and faceless, moving within shadows, living only in her dreamworld. She could not grasp him, could not control him, and with every new night, she found herself more and more intrigued by his mystery and powerful magic, until she became obsessed with lust and passion for him. He filled her mind.

She announced him the winner and the new king of demons, to rule beside her. She presented him with the infamous witching pen – now he would wield it too.

That night, as promised, she allowed the Shanka to claim her and her powers. But she did not know the seething anger that the Shanka tribe held towards her – an anger they had kept hidden in the shadows where they lived. Enraged at being outcast from their rightful home, that night, in the throes of Lokoli's passion, the Shanka stole her life as well as her magic...

"I wonder what happened next," said Karl.

Elena flicked through the last few pages. "There's just a bit more about how, even though the Shanka were now rulers of all demons, they couldn't actually rule over them because even with Lokoli's death, they could still not materialise in this world. But they kept the pen, which was now rightfully theirs, and have made it their mission to find a way into our world, which they consider their rightful home ... And that's pretty much all it says."

"Why not just write what they want into existence?"

"Maybe they can't. Maybe the conditions of their creation are too big for them to undo ... or maybe they can't hold the pen because they're not corporeal – who knows."

"So they're using you to do it instead." His voice was as grim as her thoughts. "Why you?"

"Mum said they want my powers. Makes sense. Look what they did to their own queen."

They both fell into silence, yet their thoughts seemed to bounce off the walls: one of these nights, she might be the one to die in her dreams.

"I won't let it happen, Elena."

Glancing up at him, she marvelled at the certainty in his voice. Karl had nothing to protect himself with, nothing to protect her with, and even though she couldn't quite believe his words, they still felt like a warm blanket around her. She smiled her thanks and hid her worry.

"I don't want to leave you, but I've got to go to my group."

"That's okay. It's not even midday – I won't be going to sleep any time soon."

"Yeah, well, call me if you need anything. I'll be back around three."

"You just take care of your group; I'll be fine."

Every Sunday, Karl ran a group called *Fighting Fists.* Ever since he was a boy, he and his mother had been regularly beaten by his alcoholic father, who hosted a lifetime's worth of anger issues. His mother was constantly black and blue, at first in places no one could see; then he got more cocky, and when Karl was around fourteen, she'd started sporting the occasional black eye, or swollen cheek. There were only so many times you could fall down the stairs or walk into a door and eventually, people began to talk. His father was too drunk to notice or care. It wasn't long before the police started to turn up – Karl had even been responsible for a few of those calls. Sometimes, his dad would just get locked up for a night, sometimes they only issued a warning. His mother had been crazy-scared of what he'd do to her if she ever filed a report against him, so she never did.

One day, when Karl was seventeen, he'd come home from school and found his mother dead on the living room floor. Her face had been smashed in with a lava lamp. Who knew those things could be so tough?

Naturally, Karl had grieved, but with an eerie maturity beyond his years, he had also accepted that there was nothing more he could have done when all the help that was offered her, she'd refused.

His father was sentenced to fifteen years in prison with the possibility of early probation after ten years for good behaviour, and providing he remained clean. Since Karl's eighteenth birthday had only been two weeks away, social services had dragged out the initial paperwork so that by the time accommodation could be sorted for him, he'd already become an adult by law. They'd left him alone after that.

Everyone had told Karl he'd been so lucky to avoid his dad's fists; some people had asked him how he'd managed it. None of them realised that he had also, repeatedly, been on the receiving end of his father's tirades, even thrown himself in the firing line to protect his mum. But Karl, was one of those exceptional people that just didn't bruise. She'd seen it herself.

Once, she'd found him at her doorstep, limping because his dad had jumped on his leg after knocking him to the ground. It had been a miracle his bones hadn't cracked. Fully intending to heal him with her powers, he'd pulled down his trousers to reveal unmarked skin where there should have been blue and purple marks. Even though some of the physical pain remained, the limp had all but gone the next day. Eventually, the pain had gone too.

Every Sunday, Karl tried to give a group of strangers, victims of domestic violence, what he couldn't give his mother: the courage to fight back, no matter how impossible it seemed.

Elena looked down at her books, then at the clock. He'd only been gone fifteen minutes. With a sigh she stood and stretched her limbs. She was sick of reading about a problem she couldn't solve. Now would be a good time for the friends she didn't have – catch up on her girly time and get her mind off things.

Maybe I should conjure myself some friends ... she looked at the pen still sitting on the breakfast table and shivered. *Maybe not.*

She wasn't sure she wanted to touch it ever again knowing what she knew now.

The doorbell rang.

She frowned. Had Karl forgotten his keys?

The audio on the intercom hadn't been working for weeks, so she buzzed whoever it was straight in and opened her front door. Footsteps sounded on the stairs, sounding less sharp than her mother's had – no heels.

"Hello?" called out a familiar voice.

Amy? How weird.

"Amy?"

"Yes."

"Up here – just one more flight."

Looking as friendly as ever, Amy's blonde hair seemed to bounce ahead of her as she ascended the stairs. It always looked pristine, as if she'd just stepped out of a shampoo ad.

Elena's hand flew to her own dark brown mane. In contrast, it was thick and unruly. Its only redeeming feature was that, when the sun shone on it, hidden strands of red and gold came to life.

"Elena, I hope you don't mind me turning up. I was passing by."

"Not at all. Come in."

"Thanks." She flashed a smile.

Elena wondered if either of her parents were dentists.

Closing the door behind them, she showed her into the kitchen and pulled out a chair. "Would you like a drink?"

"Do you have any lemons?"

"Yes."

"Great. Can I have a hot water with lemon?"

"Coming right up."

"Wow, what a sweet place. Do you live here on your own?"

"I share with a friend."

"That's nice. I live on on my own and the bills are stupidly high."

"It is nice to share costs, I guess ... So, what brings you to sunny Wimbledon?"

"I'm meeting someone here anyway, and, well, I wanted to call in and say I'm sorry if I upset you yesterday when I asked you to lead the session next week."

For a minute, Elena caught her breath, thinking that Amy had figured out she'd been the one responsible for her flashing the entire group. She sort of re-gretted doing it now.

"I don't want to force you to do it if you're not comfortable with it."

Looking at Amy, Elena realised that she actually looked genuine for a change. Had she been wrong about her?

"Well, I'm not a good social speaker..." To be honest, the whole thing seemed so completely insignificant compared to last night's events. Surely she could lead one session without exposing her magic. "But, no time like the present to learn, right?"

Amy beamed another smile that reached her blue eyes, and Elena found herself smiling back.

"I'm sorry, I've not really made enough of an effort to get to know everyone. Life's just been kind of hectic." She placed Amy's water in front of her.

"Oh, I know what that's about. Thanks."

"Amy, how did you know I lived here?"

Looking sheepish, she wrinkled her nose. "I did a locator spell. Sorry. I know that's kind of rude, but I did try to call you first."

Not seeing her mobile phone anywhere, Elena remembered it was on her bedroom desk, still turned off.

Well, I guess that makes us even – I use a spell on you, you use a spell on me. But part of her was also surprised that Amy had that kind of power. Sure, an air of magic did surround her all the time, just as it did Elena, but it took years to get a locator spell accurate. Amy had obviously been practising since she was young, and Elena was starting to realise she'd gotten the woman all wrong.

"Listen – me and some of my coven members are meeting on Tuesday night for some spellworking. Would you like to come along?"

Would she? She wasn't sure to be honest ... but she had just been thinking it would be nice to hang out with some girlfriends and get away from her thoughts, even from her thoughts about Karl...

"I mean ... you are a Solitary, aren't you? It wouldn't be breaking your own coven's rules?

"No, I am a Solitary." Now was probably not the right time to go into her long and complicated family history. "I think that would be nice."

"Great. Here, let me give you my number."

Before Elena knew what was happening, Amy had reached across the table for the pen and notebook.

"No!"

Something that looked like a small bolt of lightning shot out from the pen into Amy's hand. A scream filled the air and Amy's hand went up like a fireball.

"Oh my God, help me!"

Elena's own magic tingled in response to Amy's cry of pain, immediately dulling her shock as her hands filled with blue light. Trying to zone out the woman's screams of terror, she directed it at the fire and the flames grew smaller, gradually fizzling out. When it had died completely, she took Amy's ruined hand into her own and her light turned green. Amy's hand began to heal straight away. Burnt shreds of skin fell away to reveal new, unmarred skin beneath.

Amy's screams had become whimpers, no longer carrying pain, just disbelief.

When her hand had completely healed, Elena released it.

The air was heavy with shock and the smell of burnt skin, sickeningly sweet, clung to it. She wanted to offer a logical explanation, but none came to mind. The only thing that came to mind, was the certainty that any friendship with Amy had ended before it had begun. So she was surprised when Amy's next words were laced with awe.

"That's some powerful shit you've got going on."

"God, I'm so sorry. Are you okay?"

"Thanks to you. What's with that pen?"

"Er ... it came my way – there's a curse on it. I'm trying to undo it." It was as close to the truth as she could muster. "I should have moved it, Amy, I'm so sorry – I had no idea you would try to pick it up."

Amy let out a weak laugh. "Why would you. Don't worry about it. So ... Tuesday?"

Elena looked at her in surprise. She still wanted her to come over? "Um ... if you're still happy with that, that would be great."

"Okay. Well, I'm going to go now – I have to meet someone." She eyed the pen suspiciously. She clearly couldn't wait to get out of there.

"Yes, you said. I really am sorry."

"It wasn't your fault. It's cool."

With one more of her big smiles, this one more forced than the one before, she headed towards the door.

"Well, thanks for coming over."

"Okay. See you Tuesday. Oh ... I didn't write down my number." She glanced towards the kitchen again, unsure of what to do.

"You know what, I think I still have your number from a few months back when I joined the group."

"Oh, okay then. Well, bye."

And then she was gone.

Elena shut the door.

So that's what happens when someone else touches the pen.

~*~

"Did you see it?"

"Yes."

"Did you touch it?"

"Yes."

"What happened?"

"My hand went up in flames and it hurt like hell. Elena healed it. Powerful."

"Yes, she is."

"I was talking about the pen."

"Don't underestimate her, Amy. She's more than she seems."

"So, what do you want me to do now?"

The Elder sighed with regret. "The pen must be destroyed. I was hoping with your powers, you'd be able to bring it to us. We'll have to think of a new way to get it. While the owner of the pen is alive, no one else can touch it."

Amy fidgeted. "I don't want to hurt Elena. There must be another way."

"You'd better look for it then, because destroying the pen is our priority. If that means killing the witch, so be it."

Chapter Five

Karl and Elena sat at the breakfast table, which also served as their dining table, eating their Indian takeaway. The autumn sun was just beginning to set and Karl was trying very hard not to stare at the way it bounced off Elena's hair, creating a kaleidoscope of the season's colours around her face. If anyone was in doubt she was a magical being, they wouldn't have any trouble believing it now.

She glanced up at him and gave him a quick smile. He wrenched his eyes away and took another mouthful of Biryani.

"Do you think it's a good idea?" she asked.

"Going over to Amy's on Tuesday?" She had filled him in on the day's events. "I don't think it would do any harm – might be good to get your mind off things. We all need a break."

He hadn't meant that last sentence to come out sounding as harsh as it did, but Elena wasn't the only one getting a little frazzled now that night was almost upon them. He'd vowed to look after her while she slept and he wasn't going to go back on his word. Exactly *how* he was going to look after her though, was something he hadn't fully considered. If last night repeated itself, he'd have to pull her out of sleep. Would he have to watch her screaming in terror again? Or, asked the darker half of his mind, would he have to watch her getting hot and bothered while the demon worked his mojo on her? He inwardly groaned at the memory of how her skin felt last night – feverish, sweaty – he should have thought more carefully about how to go about this. Of course, Elena's safety came first, but where she was concerned, he was also a man harbouring unrequited love and unfulfilled needs ... for too many years. When she'd let her guard down and they'd almost kissed yesterday, he'd let himself feel what he never dared to acknowledge: hope. Now, a new fire that was hard to temper kept licking at his heart, refusing to be put out...

"Penny for your thoughts?"

He swallowed the last of his food. "Just trying to plan tonight. Make sure we don't leave anything to chance." His response was purposely ambiguous and he looked at her pointedly to gauge her reaction.

She went a little pale at the mention of tonight and he suddenly felt bad for bringing it up. "I'm sorry—"

"No, don't be. You're right, and I need to think about it. I mean, I have been. I wish I knew how to stop him appearing."

"How about using the pen?"

She shrugged. "I doubt he'd have given me a pen that I could use against him, but it's worth a shot."

It was still there on the table, where it had been since the early hours of the morning. She picked it up along with the notebook and wrote:

The Shanka demon can no longer enter my dreams.

Then she held out the pen to Karl.

"What?"

"You need to write something. You never have. We know you can touch the pen, but we don't know if you can use it."

He nodded, wondering why he'd never tried to use it. He guessed it was because he could never think of anything to write. It was like that with birthday cards too – he never knew what to put in them.

He took the pen and book from her and faltered.

"Just write anything – anything trivial that won't matter if it comes to pass."

"Erm..." God, he was useless at this.

Elena's hair turned blue.

"Hey!"

"What?"

"I don't want blue hair! What the hell did you write that for?"

"It seemed trivial."

"Blue hair – *blue?* That's trivial? What if I can't undo it?"

Karl stared at her blankly. His throat went dry. He felt like a total dickhead, but writing really wasn't his strong point, so he went for humour instead and flashed her a grin.

"I was going to write that all your clothes fall off, but figured you may have a problem with that. This was the second thing that came to mind."

Elena scowled, but a hint of a smile graced the corner of her mouth. "If I wake up with blue hair tomorrow morning, I'm turning you into a toad."

"And if you kiss me, will I turn into a prince?"

She rolled her eyes. "You're impossible."

"No, you're impossible ... and even if your hair was blue, you'd still be the most beautiful woman on the planet."

"Creep."

"Am I off the hook yet?"

She snatched the pen away from him.

He stared at her hair in shock.

Her mouth fell open in horror and her hands flew to her head. "What? No ... oh no!"

"Gottcha."

His fit of laughter was met with her scream of frustration and it wasn't long before they were both running around the flat as she threw inanimate objects at him.

"Conjelo!"

He stopped. He had no choice, his legs were rooted to the spot. "Hey! No fair, you're not supposed to use magic."

"Says who?" she asked innocently.

"You. You and all your rules you like to follow."

"Now, now," she came up behind him, trailing a finger over his shoulder as he struggled to move his limbs. "Who's the one who likes to break them?"

He growled in anger, surprised to find that he actually was angry. Feeling physically helpless was a fear he constantly tried to overcome, ever since the first time his dad ever raised his hand. This wasn't helping.

"Okay, you win. Can you unfreeze me now?"

"Why would I want to do that? It's not often I get you where I want you." Her voice was low and seductive – a warning bell went off in his head.

"Elena?"

She was facing him now, stroking his chest through his shirt. Odd flecks of green shimmered amid the hazel in her eyes and the air filled with a strange kind of heat that felt almost electric. "Have you noticed how you're always so impervious to everything?"

Impervious? She's got to be kidding.

She teased his skin with her fingernails and he quickly became aware of his growing erection pushing against the front of his jeans. When she grazed his nipples, his groan reverberated in his throat – it escaped his lips when she brought a hand down and rubbed it against his crotch.

"Not so impervious now, are we?"

"Elena." He tried to keep the huskiness out of his voice and failed. "I'm not sure this is you."

Those strange green lights were still dancing in her eyes and he had an awful feeling he knew where they'd come from, he just wasn't sure how they'd gotten there.

"Honey, you need to snap out of it." He hoped he sounded more sure than he felt – half of him didn't want her to snap out of it – but he didn't want it to happen like this, under her spell. She rarely used magic on him, and never without his permission.

"Or maybe," she whispered, "I should snap *you* out."

She brought his zipper down.

Shit!

His voice trembled on his breath. "Elena, stop."

The phone rang.

Oh, sweet Jesus, thank you!

~*~

The sound of the phone hit her like a bucket of cold water.

What the hell just happened?

It was as if she'd just landed in her own body, only her body was mashed up against Karl's and touching him in ways it shouldn't be.

When she finally wrenched herself away from him she realised just how aroused she really was. She looked up at Karl in confusion. His eyes held a mixture of desire, anger and ... hurt.

Oh, God, what have I just done?

He pulled his zipper up, then looked at his hands, relief evident in his face. Without another glance at her he ran towards the phone.

Elena's head was in a mess. She remembered them eating, Karl writing something stupid with the pen, them running around the room, then ... then what? That's where her memory seemed to falter. Had she put a spell on him?

Her memory offered up a word: *Conjelo.*

Yes, I put a freezing spell on him.

Her heart weighed heavy in her chest. No wonder he'd looked hurt – she'd practically violated him with magic.

She frowned. What on earth had possessed her to freeze him? There must have been a trigger, but she couldn't recall anything significant before the word came flying out of her mouth. Just ... just that she'd wanted him to stop so she could...

Her cheeks flushed hot.

I wanted to kiss him.

That was it. They were having a laugh and messing around, just like yesterday; she'd remembered their near kiss and had wanted it to happen again. Just like that. So the word had come flying out of her mouth and all sense went flying out of her head. Never in her life had she lost control of her magic like that.

Tears burned in her eyes. *How could I have done that to him?*

Karl reappeared in the doorway and stood there, telephone in one hand. He studied her cautiously.

"Karl—"

"It was your mum. She said she's found some more info – she's going to pop it around tomorrow."

"Karl—"

He held up his hand. "Can we talk about this later? I just need a bit of time, okay?"

"Okay..." she whispered.

He turned and headed up the stairs. A minute later, she heard the shower come on. The tears behind her eyes finally fell, and she sank onto the sofa alone.

She didn't know when she fell asleep, just that she had no idea she was falling.

After Karl had left, she'd turned the telly on to get her mind off the guilt overwhelming her. Some black and white B-horror movie was on. Maybe her mistake was leaning her head on the cushion, but one minute, she was staring at zombies devouring the inhabitants of a village one by one while her mind tortured her with replays of what she'd just done, and the next, she was staring at a pair of green eyes.

No!

With a start, she threw herself backwards, only to realise she was floating in the blackness of space, stark naked, and the eyes were floating after her.

Leave me alone!

A cruel laugh encircled her and took on solid form around her body – a snake – some kind of giant python squeezing the life out of her, and then it shattered into a million little snakes that slithered across her body. She couldn't figure out if her skin was crawling because of the snakes or her repulsion.

Bile rose in her throat and she would have vomited were it not for the fact that she was scared shitless. Snakes found their way to her wrists and ankles, forming shackles around all of them, somehow pinning her to the blackness. She was bound to nothing in outer space and her struggle for freedom only seemed to anger the snakes, which tightened their hold on her.

The green eyes hovered in front of her, about two heads higher than her, then the blackness shimmered around them and form materialised – masculine, muscular, cracked, grey.

"Careful now – my snakes like to bite."

She could feel his laughter on her skin, heating it up. His fingers traced her chest, in the same way hers had Karl's earlier.

"Who's been a very naughty girl?"

"Leave me alone." Her demand was made through clenched teeth that tried to hide her fear and exhaustion.

His fingernails scorched her as he raked them along her skin, again mimicking her own earlier actions. They flitted over her nipples and she gasped in both alarm and disgust as her body began to respond. Desire flitted through her like a mini electric shock. How the hell could such a monster have this affect on her?

"You're just like me – you belong to me."

"No." But her mind wouldn't move away from her own forced seduction upon her best friend, and her protest did not carry the conviction of the previous night.

"Did he beg you to stop or to carry on?"

From somewhere inside, a spark of anger came to life. "What did you do to me?"

"It's not something that's been done to you – it's something you are. Your magic is powerful."

"It's not black magic."

"Oh, but it could be."

His hand travelled down her body. She knew where he was heading.

"I could show you how – you could be my queen."

From very far away, she heard her name and it was enough to ignite her soul into fight mode. She fought for some kind of control. *Elena – she was Elena. She was not evil.* She concentrated on her name, trying to form it on her tongue. Instead she moaned when his fingers trailed beyond her curls and found her virgin opening.

"Elena..."

"Will you beg me to stop, or carry on?"

She bit her tongue, terrified the wrong words would roll off it if she dared to speak. The wrong words would mean he would have her permission to claim her, of this she was sure.

"Elena..."

Karl! It was Karl's voice. She tried to shout out his name, but every time she opened her mouth another moan escaped. A wet heat was building between her legs, fuelled by rough fingers that had no right to know her needs so well.

"Elena!"

His voice was more urgent now, more near.

"Karl?" It was barely a whisper.

"Yes! Again, say my name again."

Dimensions were shifting. The fabric around her was flickering from black to magnolia – outer-space to living room. Green eyes shifted to blue, then back again.

"Karl."

"That's it, come back to me." The desperation colouring his voice strengthened her resolve. But just before she finally wrenched herself free from the demon, his kiss branded her just above her pubic bone.

"You will give yourself to me..."

And then she was in her living room, fully back in her body, baking hot, aching, too aroused...

Karl had pulled her up to sitting and was cradling her, his eyes full of concern, and a hint of guilt, but none of the anger or hurt from earlier.

Relieved, she burrowed herself into him, clung to him, breathed in his scent and ... *No!*

With a choked sob, she threw herself free from his grasp and to the other side of the room.

"What ... Elena it me, it's okay."

"No, I can't..."

Kneeling, he stopped in front of her collapsed form. "You can't, what?"

She buried her head in the knees that she hugged tightly to her chest. She had to force her words out and she hoped he could hear them, because she couldn't speak any louder.

"I want you ... I wanted you ... earlier. And I couldn't stop it, and I couldn't control it. What I did to you, it was all because I want you. I'm just as bad as he is."

Everything around her seemed to still. Snakes and shadows licked at the parameters of her soul, trying to suck her back into their world, trying to change her. Fear grabbed at her – the demon was no longer here, yet there was darkness in her, she could feel it. Where had it come from? Had it always been there?

"It's not something that's been done to you – it's something you are..."

She squeezed her eyes shut against his words and reached within herself, trying to find the light, any source of light that could chase away the shadows.

Hands, as warm as the sun on her skin, gently took her wrists. The shadows grew smaller. The hands trailed its warmth up her arms and pulled them away from her head, letting in a light she didn't know was there. It warmed her. It filled her soul. This was some kind of new magic she wasn't familiar with. The snakes slithered away. A break in her internal cloud let in the light, and black began to fade into colour.

She leaned into Karl's hand, which now held her face, stroking her cheek, with a tenderness that she knew belied his need for her. His thumb stroked her bottom lip. When she opened her eyes, he was just an inch away, his eyes brimming with compassion and love.

I'm in love with him.

The realisation took her breath away. It overwhelmed her, and a stubborn slither of fear wrapped itself around her heart – this was too much. It was a love that was doomed; she'd only end up hurting him.

"Karl—"

"Sshhhh..."

His lips touched hers, and fear, darkness, doubt, even demons, all disappeared into the nothingness they'd come from. All that existed was warmth and light.

~*~

Katherine knew he was in the room before she walked in. It was a type of energy, an essence exclusive to the Shanka that thickened the atmosphere, heated it up, so that all you could think about was how the air felt on your skin. How *they* felt on your skin. The Shanka were the very first incubi. For millenia, they had been seducing humans, stealing their seed, or filling them with theirs, all so they could penetrate this world – the world from which they had been outcast, and the one they must never be a part of, for they would destroy everything in it. So far, their power over life and death was as immaterial as they were, only able to become reality through dreams ... and the mysterious witching pen.

The demon now filtrating her bedroom was a stark and bitter reminder to Katherine, that the person she loved more than anyone else in the world, the one she had so desperately tried to protect all these years, was in imminent danger of losing more than her life. And she didn't know how to stop it.

"Did you really think you could keep her from me, Katherine? Did you think I wouldn't know?"

Her breath caught in her throat as those green eyes glinted from the shadows of her unlit room. It had been a long time since she'd seen him. Not long enough. She had to remind herself he was only a shadow – he couldn't hurt her like this, despite the utter blackness that filled the room.

With a composure that came from years of practise, she wrapped her iciness around herself. Like a familiar friend, it strengthened her resolve and steeled her soul against the fear that had lived in her too long.

"Nathaniel. How has kingship been treating you?"

A laugh, low, rumbling, caressed her skin and she shivered. "So, you have been watching us, making notes. I was supposed to see you dead for killing Darius; the Shanka were up in arms. But you did me a favour."

"You should have killed me."

"I should kill you now, for keeping such a phenomenal secret from me all of these years. Maybe your death will erode her defences; maybe she'll turn to me in the darkest hour of her secret thoughts while she mourns you."

"She hates me. I've seen to it. There is nothing that will make her turn to you, Nathaniel. You have no hold over her."

"And the boy?"

Katherine blanched. *Damn it!*

"Did you know he has the power to pull her from me?"

She held his gaze, saying nothing.

"She loves him, doesn't she? Not even love can keep one from the shadows of their heart, you of all people should know that."

She mentally gave herself a new coat of frosting, refusing to go down that particular road of her past, and kept her gaze steady.

"I would have thought you would have wanted to keep her from that kind of hurt. No matter. He'll be easy to kill."

"That *boy* is stronger than you think."

"I didn't say *I* was going to kill him."

She took in a sharp breath, the implication of his words sinking in.

"You never told her, did you? My, my, Katherine, what will you do? By trying to protect her, you've set her up for a world of pain ... and now you've run out of time. She will have no choice but to turn to me."

She blinked back hot tears, his words ringing with truth. "She will *never* go to you willingly."

"There are very few things, in any world, thicker than blood."

Her lip trembled. "How did you find out?"

His smile was thin, cruel. "I had no idea at first. I only knew she was a powerful witch, the first thirteenth generation witch for centuries. Powerful enough to wield the pen, so I gave her the pen, intending to have her bring down the veil of your dimension with it, so we could finally walk through.

"Then I visited her in her dreams last night and I could *smell* it under her skin – her blood – *our* blood. I held in my arms a thirteenth generation witch with Shanka blood flowing through her veins. I knew instantly who her mother must be. Until that moment, I had no idea what Darius had seen in you. Then all the pieces fell into place. He'd planned it all.

"You've done well to shield her from us, Katherine, but you've failed. She's our salvation – she *belongs* to us, and I *will* claim her."

Chapter Six

The first thing she realised on opening her eyes was that her sleep had been dreamless, the second was that a warm body was firmly wrapped around her, one arm slung around her waist in a protective hug.

The dawn was only just breaking, streaking the duskiness of the bedroom with hues of pink. With a smile, she gently turned. Karl groaned, but didn't wake and his breathing remained slow and steady. The man who never slept deeply seemed to be out cold.

Elena studied his face. She'd always thought he was something of an anomaly. Most people looked young when they slept, their relaxed features bringing out a vulnerability, and a peace and innocence most never got to see. With Karl, it was the exact opposite. When *awake*, he looked young and innocent, even boyish. Most people thought him around twenty-two, not the twenty-seven years he actually was, and if it weren't for the fact that he was generally too broad and well built for a man that young, no one would ever question it. When he slept, however, he looked ancient. His skin was still smooth, he still looked at peace, but his visage seemed to hide a world of knowledge only he could access. She'd noticed it in the past, when they'd stayed up late chatting and he'd fallen asleep on the couch, or even once sitting at the kitchen table, his head just missing a plate of nachos.

He looked that way now – wizened, with a hint of warrior about him – and anything but vulnerable. She put it down to his family troubles and having to overcome such violence, a past that echoed through him as he slept. Yes, she felt safe in his arms – she always had, she'd just never realised it.

He murmured something incoherent and huddled further into her. Her smile widened when she realised exactly what was pressing so firmly against her thigh. God, this was Karl – *Karl!* Her best friend!

She bit back a giggle, not wanting to wake him, but her joy soared silently. How the hell she'd never noticed how she felt was beyond her. Just the feel of him next to her was sending delicious sensations throughout her entire body. She remembered last night, how light and warmth had cascaded through her 'til there was nothing left but total contentment – just with one kiss. How did he do that? Was that what love was? Did everyone in love feel like that when they kissed? And what about ... when they did more?

She heated up at the thought of it. This was an area of her life she felt completely lost in – she may as well still be a teenager. It was as if that emotional part of her had stopped developing when her mum had sat her down and told her all about why she would have to die a virgin. Sure, she'd pleasured herself, she knew how to do *that*. She'd read everything she could about sex in books, online, absorbed all kinds of stories from others at school, she'd looked at pictures in dirty mags, hell, she'd even watched porn a whole bunch of times. But she'd never had the privilege of *feeling* it – growing as a person *with* it. It was always something that she held at arm's length, for obvious reasons. With a sinking feeling, she didn't know how she was going to do that any more, because she wanted Karl in ways she never knew was possible.

Pushing that sinking feeling away, she gave him a quick look. His eyes were closed, his breathing still even. Tentatively, she pulled the covers off them and glanced at his cotton boxers. The material was moulded around his erection, showing off its contours. It looked bigger than she'd expected and judging by the wetness she could feel between her own legs, her body didn't mind.

She held her breath and bit her lip to steady her hand, then hooked one finger around his waistband.

"I will not be held responsible for my actions based on any decision you're about to make."

With a start, she let go of his underwear and the elastic pinged back against his skin.

"Ouch."

"Sorry! I was just—"

"Curious?"

She nodded, her face aflame. "I've never seen one in real life."

His eyebrows shot up. "You're kidding."

"No."

The silence was tinged with her embarrassment, but curiosity still gnawed at her.

"Can I ... can I see it?"

She saw desire colour his eyes. It gave her an illicit feeling of pleasure – something deep and so wonderfully personal.

I make him feel like that.

He nodded.

Tugging at his waistband once more, she pulled down his boxers and released him. Her heart thudded behind her ribcage. It was even bigger now. She'd seen enormous ones in magazines, but those had seemed unreal somehow. *This* however, was very real ... and magnificent. It twitched under her gaze, as if it were alive. With a small moan, she realised that's how it would feel inside her. Alive, moving, hard ... how hard was it?

"Can I touch it?"

"Fuck, Elena, you're going to be the end of me." His voice was hoarse – it drove her on.

"Please?"

With a groan, he nodded again.

She touched it lightly with her fingertips, starting at the top, slowly feeling her way down. It was smooth and warm. She wasn't sure why, but in her mind, she'd always thought it would be cold, like steel or something – maybe because hard things were always associated with coldness.

She wrapped her entire hand around him. It was definitely hard.

Karl let out a noise that had her wanting to throw herself on top of him, and moved his hips up off the sheets. She moved her hand up with him and before she knew it, she was the one lying back on the bed and Karl was devouring her mouth with his own, his tongue sweeping the inside of it.

Last night *all* they'd done was kiss, and this was not like last night's gentle kisses. This was desire and urgency. It was a Karl she wasn't used to and it had her hungry for more of him. It was then that she realised her hand was still gripping him, squeezing harder than before. She moved her fist up and down to match the pace of their kisses. It earned her a guttural mewl of pleasure, and then his hand was on hers, prising her off him.

The weight of her disappointment shocked her. "Did I do it wrong?"

"God, no."

"Then why—"

"I've waited for this for years, I don't want it over in seconds."

"Oh."

She gasped in delight as his mouth found a sweet spot behind her ear.

"So, you liked what I was doing to you?"

He grunted his affirmation.

"What did it feel like?"

He looked at her the way a cat looks at mouse. The morning sun had found its way into the room and it turned Karl's hair golden – he may as well have been wearing a halo, and damn it if he didn't look like some kind of saint. Only the devil was glinting in his eyes...

Her bra was successfully unhooked and whipped off. He latched his mouth onto her left breast, teasing her nipple.

"Oh, God!" This was new.

"It felt like that."

Then he did the same to her other breast.

"And like that."

Fuck!

"But it mostly felt like this." He eased his fingers inside her, stretching her, and began to thrust in and out, heavenly strokes that had her moaning and arching into him. Her wetness engulfed his fingers, which peaked her embarrassment once more, but Karl seemed to think it was a good thing judging by those wonderful noises coming from his throat and chest – he was practically purring. He sunk his fingers in deeper, sending a bolt of fire to her belly. While his thumb worked its magic on the outside, he seemed to find a spot inside her which had her crying out every time he touched it.

A small wave of an orgasm rippled at her core. *Holy shit...*

"Karl—"

"Now, Elena, touch me now."

She didn't hesitate, wrapping her hand around him once more, marvelling at the feel of him. She matched his speed and rhythm, letting herself be guided by the sounds he made – beautiful sounds that played like music to her ears and took her higher.

Opening her eyes to see him, she momentarily lost herself. *What the hell...?*

Light surrounded them. Golden light, and there was no way that was the sun bouncing off his hair. He seemed oblivious to it, his own eyes closed in pleasure.

Am I doing this? I don't know any magic that does this.

And then all thoughts flew out of her head as her climax hit her.

Karl whispered, "beautiful" into her mouth, just before his own release consumed him, and in that shared moment, a warm certainty settled deep in Elena's chest: she wanted a future with this man – the large house, children, the whole damn thing. She wanted to love him freely, without holding back, and if giving him all of herself meant giving him her powers too, so be it. She'd do it.

~*~

Katherine threw the last of her things into her overnight bag. She had hoped to God it would never come to this, but in her heart, she knew Nathaniel was right: she'd run out of time. She had to tell Elena everything, and then she had to disappear without a trace so her life could never be used as a bargaining tool for Elena's own. The Shanka knew of her daughter's existence, knew what she was, and it wouldn't be long before that knowledge rippled out of the demon world and into this one – it wouldn't be long before The Council knew what blood really flowed through her veins. Maybe they knew already.

Hot tears stung her eyes, a stark contrast to the ice that lived around her heart. With a last mental check to make sure she had everything, she zipped up her bag, took one last look at her home and headed for the door ... and froze.

The door was flung open and the Elder stood in its frame, his thick, snow white hair, an aura around his head, his eyes the colour of mud and his expression as unreadable as it always was.

"Katherine," he nodded, stepping into her home and shutting the door firmly behind him.

The anger mounted in her chest and she sucked in a breath through her teeth. "What, you don't knock any more?"

He eyed her overnight bag. "I think it's time we had a little chat, don't you?"

"I have nothing to say to you."

The floor lamp flickered as his voice boomed out, despite it being unplugged at the wall. "Clearly there are many things you *should* have said over the past two and a half decades."

"You lost the right to know anything about me a long time ago."

"This isn't just about you, this is about the whole bloody world. Christ, Katherine, you've always been selfish, but this takes the biscuit."

"*Selfish?* I've spent the last twenty-five years sacrificing everything to make sure my daughter is safe, that she would get to lead some kind of normal life, without risk of ... of..."

"Being kidnapped by demons?"

"And you! You think I don't know what you would have done to her if you'd known? To *me?"*

"The needs of the whole must come first."

"Before even giving Elena's own destiny a chance? You would just read the blurb of her life, assume you know the whole story before it's even played out and to hell with the consequences of your actions?"

"And look where your actions have gotten you."

"Elena's still alive, and up until Nathaniel decided to throw a Freddy Kruger, relatively happy. If it had been down to you, she'd have been imprisoned from birth."

"Measures should have been taken—"

"Nothing's happened – the world is still here!"

"Over two hundred people died in a plane crash yesterday!"

"That is *not* her fault."

"No, it's yours, damn it! She should have been monitored."

"I'd rather die than have her become The Council's personal lab rat."

"That can be arranged!"

The laugh erupted from her throat before she could stop it. Really. Why was she even mildly surprised The Council would dispose of her in a heartbeat?

Oh, I don't know, maybe because my father's a heartless bastard.

Katherine attempted the softest tone of voice she possibly could. "She's your granddaughter – your only grandchild..."

"She doesn't know that."

"Only at your request. She asked about her grandparents growing up. Have you any idea how difficult it was to make up lies about it all, knowing you tutored her, that she *knew* you?"

"And yet you've lied to her about her own lineage – to all of us."

"To keep her *safe.* My lie put my family first; your lie put work and non-sensical tradition before your own blood."

"She is *not* my blood!"

In the stunned pause that followed, Katherine realised that 'heartless bastard' might just be the understatement of the century. "My God, did you really just say that? You're casting her out of the family? She *is* your blood."

"Only half of her, and the demon half will take over – it's inevitable."

"Such faith you have in the strength of your own line," she scoffed. "Jesus, I was right to hide this from you all these years ... and maybe it's a blessing she's never known her relationship to you."

"I was not going to repeat with Elena the same mistake I made with you. It was best for all that she never knew her grandfather headed up The Council; better for teaching her, better for disciplining her, and better for what I have to do now."

Katherine's breath caught at the back of her throat and she felt all the blood drain from her face. "What? What are you going to do?"

"For centuries, *centuries,* we've been working to eliminate demon blood from our kind, to stop our persecution and give us a better name. Her birth should never have come to pass. I have someone conferring with the Dessec."

This time, the ice that ran through Katherine's veins had nothing to do with her shield of protection. Numbly, she shook her head. "No..."

"We will bend time and erase elements over the past thirty years. You will not meet Darius, he will not be killed, meaning Nathaniel will never take his place as Shanka King, and Elena will never be born."

"You can't ... this is *murder.*"

"You can't murder what doesn't exist."

"But—"

"You'll have no memory of events, no knowledge she existed. You'll not be in pain, Katherine."

"You're not God..."

"The Council are the closest thing to God in this dimension, and we will do what is right."

Cold fear erased all words from her mind.

"This is non-negotiable, Katherine. We're cleaning up your mistake. We'll need some of your blood to ensure the erasure is successful. You're to come back to the Round Hall with us where you'll take up permanent residence."

Somewhere amid her numbness, she was talking, thinking and walking, but Katherine was observing it all outside her body, her voice reaching her from very far away. "I'll need to pack more things; give me ten minutes."

Her father nodded.

Her legs carried her body to the bathroom where she unzipped her bag, slid open the wall cabinet and flung the rest of her toiletries into it. Then, making sure her father was watching, she opened the toilet lid, unzipped her skirt and shut the door. Luckily, relieving herself came easily and she used the fact to buy her some privacy, the loud ringing in her ears giving way to the voice of reason.

Get your head together, Katherine. Get yourself together – and get the fuck

OUT of here!

~*~

Teleportation was never easy at the best of times, and Amy found it easier than most. Her natural talent, ever since she could remember, was something akin to shapeshifting – she could make her body weightless, change shape, sometimes solidify, although more often than not, she would remain invisible in her altered form. Dematerialising her body was second nature to her.

Teleporting to the other side of the world, however, was enough to take its toll on even the most powerful of witches and Amy had not been looking forward to this journey to begin with. Such a journey would tire her out, rendering her useless and magically unprotected for at least two hours.

Now as she materialised in Death Valley, USA, she hoped she got the location spell accurate and had landed in the Nevada end, and not the California end ... and it's not like there were any signposts.

Stupidly, in her forced rush to get here – Etienne, that Elder, could be *so* pushy – she'd forgotten to take the time difference into account. She'd dressed light for hot desert weather, not intending to stay for longer than necessary. Unfortunately, it was two in the morning here, pitch black and bloody freezing.

"Shit," she cursed as she took on form. This little trip was wrong on so many levels. Firstly, her bargaining tool with the Dessec was nothing but The Council's word of virtue – *yeah, we all know how well* that's *going to go down* – secondly, she had no idea if she was in the right place, thirdly, and what was bothering her the most, was the very nature of this potential pact: the extermination of Elena Green.

Okay, so supposedly she was here to ensure her erasure from history rather than her extermination, but Amy was damned if she could see the difference. And the truth was, that she kind of liked Elena. The girl was quiet, harbouring your superhero-type powers, but seemingly kind, meek, mild and completely unassuming. She was innocence personified. Fuck it, that girl had been sheltered her entire life, lied to about her very existence, and when the shit hits the fan and the truth comes out, Amy wondered whether she'd curl up and die or make like a bat out of hell.

Innocence personified. And Amy was here to arrange her assassination. Wrong, wrong, wrong. And if she refused? Amy imprisoned by The Council for anything up 'til eternity, because she knew too much. Yeah, the godfather of all the witch covens in the world were a real nice group of people.

With a shiver and a sigh, she looked around and saw nothing but an expanse of black.

There's no way I can stay out here for two hours, I'll freeze to death. She gave herself a little shrug of surrender and chose a direction to go in. *Got to keep moving ... stay warm. No doubt the Dessec now know a foreigner's in their territory – they'll have to come find me.*

She almost hoped they didn't. Although she wasn't sure what would happen if she went back to Etienne with a failed mission. Maybe being eaten by coyotes would be the better deal. The Elder seemed to be taking this whole Elena thing really personally and she had no idea why.

The blast of hot energy hit her from the right, licking at her skin like the heat of a bonfire. Or maybe it was a bonfire, because a spire of flames, reaching up into the night sky, is what she saw when she turned. It grew shorter, filled out and took on the shape of a man, until flesh engulfed flame and a dark God stood in front of her ... well, that was her first thought. Realistically, this was probably a Dessec demon, not a God, but still...

Amy let her eyes roam across his shirtless chest and ... *holy crap – he was wearing nothing but a loin cloth!* Mocha coloured skin wrapped around a warrior's body glistened in the dark. Muscles? Check. Tall? Check. Handsome? Double check.

With a mental scolding, she shook her head – this was so not why she was here.

"You have entered Dessec territory, witch."

Well, duh.

"Yes, I seek the Dessec. I bring a proposition from The Council."

The demon's eyes flickered yellow like a cat's and Amy almost melted on the spot. Jesus Christ, did all Dessec demons look like this? Those eyes were *wild.*

He strode towards her and it was all she could do not to bolt. She was vaguely aware of her legs shaking.

"You're shivering," he stated in that baritone voice of his.

"What? Oh, yeah..." In fact, her legs weren't trembling from lust – she was actually shaking uncontrollably from the cold.

"Are you human?"

"Yes."

"Then you'll become ill out here."

"I forgot my clothes ... I mean, my warm clothes."

Amy, get a grip, you're talking gibberish.

He nodded. "It's hard to teleport with too many material items."

All at once his body started to glow, that fire reigniting on his skin, smaller flames this time, like on a log fire. He took her arm and pulled her towards him.

"Stay close to me. I will keep you warm."

Amy inhaled sharply. If she was going to die out here, it wasn't going to be from the cold.

~*~

Katherine materialised in Elena and Karl's kitchen, the book she had pulled from her overnight bag, clutched tightly in her hand.

"Hello?" she called out, but knew she must have just missed them, even as the word left her mouth. *Damn*.

She'd have to be quick. As soon as her father discovered she'd gone, he'd be here in an instant. She had no idea what a spell to erase history entailed – she'd never had reason to look it up – but she hoped nothing could happen without her blood ... at least not right away.

Hurriedly, she scanned the flat for a place to leave the book. Elena had to find it, but it was imperative her father did not. Running upstairs, she had the sense that time was nipping her heels – ten, nine, eight...

He's knocking on the bathroom door. She rushed into Elena's bedroom...

Seven, six, five...

He's throwing open the door. She looked around, frantically – not the drawers, he'd look in the drawers...

Four, three, two...

He knows I'm gone – he knows where I am! She shoved the book inside Elena's pillowcase, making sure it was sandwiched between the pillow and the bed so the outline could not be seen, hoping to God that if the bed was searched, he'd look under the pillow and not *at* it...

One...

The 'thunk' of materialisation sounded downstairs, and Katherine disappeared.

Chapter Seven

The best thing about working at *Ancient Ways*, was that she owned it and could decide how to run it – it was her baby, and she'd always thought of it as the substitute baby she would never have. Today, however, was different. Today, the best thing about working at *Ancient Ways,* was that Karl worked in *Royal Treasures*, the antique shop just across the road, and their usual lunch date, which was normally casual, would now mean so much more.

Elena failed miserably in hiding the beaming smile that graced her features as she opened her new age shop. Pagan in theme, it was like most other new age shops across the country, with a healing clinic upstairs where various therapies were practised. Elena herself, offered spiritual and crystal healing. Of course, no one knew she could *actually* heal someone in the manner that she could, so on a daily basis, she held back her powers, only letting the tiniest amount of that energy trickle into her clients' auric fields as she worked on them. They went away feeling better and none the wiser, and Elena felt she was making a difference without exposing herself or her lineage.

Like Elena, Karl also owned his shop. In fact, he had taken the leap into retail first instead of attending university, fuelled by a desire to keep busy and start earning money straight away, rather than end up like his ill-fated family. He had always had a love for antiques, and an uncanny ability to know their history; that coupled with his determination had him studying everything he could about the subject, and attending every antiques fair and auction that he could get into. All the while, he worked in the sales department of a mobile phone company, striving for the bonuses that would help him realise his passion. A year later, having scrupulously saved, and gleaned all the knowledge he could, an antiques shop in South Kensington practically fell into his lap. The owners had gone bankrupt, and the shop was all but being given away, complete with stock. With the economy taking a downward turn, and the antiques industry growing too competitive in the current climate, no one would touch it with a barge pole. Karl bought the business for £1 and invested the money he'd saved into pulling it out of debt. He turned the entire shop around by giving it a niche: the British monarchy. Coins, stamps, postcards, letterheads, Tudor furniture ...

if it had anything to do with British royalty, he housed it. A new store name, a re-designed interior, and a busy internet presence complete with an active blog, had tourists flocking to *Royal Treasures* to buy something unique. Five years on, Karl had just started to make a handsome profit.

And it was Karl who had told Elena last year about the gift shop across the road that had just closed down. Bored of her mundane office job reviewing articles for a prestigious and stuffy magazine publication – *not* where she thought she'd end up after her Psychology degree – she was ready for the challenge of something new. She bought the shop, set it up with Karl's help, and never looked back.

God, she thought, still grinning from ear to ear, *we really are like an old married couple!*

The bell above the door tinkled, and her assistant manager walked in.

"Hey, Elena."

"Hi, Mary."

Mary stopped in her tracks and eyed her suspiciously. "Something's different about you ... did you cut your hair?"

"No ... wait – it's not blue is it?" She hurriedly ran her fingers through it.

"Nope – still that gorgeous, rich brown it always was ... blue?"

"Nevermind."

Mary made her way to the staff room at the back, her voice echoing through the corridor. "So, what gives?"

"I don't know what you mean."

"Liar."

"Erm ... less of that, thank you – I am still your boss."

"And if you were anyone else, I would not be saying such things, but you're the best, nicest boss I've ever had, and I know something's up." Mary's head poked around the door, flashing a cheeky grin. "Did you get some last night?"

"What?! Mary!"

"You did, didn't you! I can tell – you look all glowy."

"Glowy?" She looked down at herself to make sure she wasn't actually glowing.

"Yes, you're positively beaming, and it's about fucking time you had a boyfriend."

Elena rolled her eyes, but her smile widened.

"Who is it?" asked Mary, refreshed and bouncing around the corner, her own blue-black hair bobbing up and down with every step. "Do I know him?"

Before she could stop herself, Elena's eyes flitted over to the shop across the road. The reaction did not go unnoticed.

"Oh, my God! Karl – it's Karl!"

"Mary, sshhh..."

"It is, isn't it?"

"Well ... yes..."

Mary squealed like a four year old and wrapped her arms around Elena. "It's about fucking time!"

"You already said that, and stop swearing – people might hear you."

"You two are so perfect for each other; I can't believe it's taken this long for you to *finally* get together – he's been in love with you since, like, *forever*."

"I know, I know, but you don't need to make a big deal out of it, okay?"

"Hey, you're the one with an invisible coat hanger in your mouth."

"Mary!"

"All right! I'll stop..."

But Elena found herself embraced in another bear hug.

Mary pulled back just enough to look at her with those piercing blue eyes that always seemed like they held a millennium of knowledge.

"Elena, I mean it, I'm so happy for you two. I mean, I don't know guys your age that are like you – you both act like you're an old couple most of the time – and if you were anyone else, I'd say, 'get a life, already', but you're both the nicest, most together people I've ever known and you're *supposed* to be together."

With a laugh, Elena disentangled herself from the woman's arms. It never ceased to amaze her how Mary was three years her senior, yet acted as if she was a teenager on a permanent hit of Red Bull. "Thank you, I think. Anyway ... how are you? You sleeping better?"

"Not really," she replied, with a shrug. "It's cool. It's just a phase – it'll pass."

"Normally, I'd agree, but your dreams are ... shall we say, like scenes from a horror movie?"

Mary laughed. "Yep, that about sums it up. But I've had weird dreams before – okay, nothing this bad – but still, they're just dreams. I doubt they're prophetic ... if they are, I pity the poor sods that star in them..."

The door bell rang again as their first customer of the day walked in, and Monday began.

~*~

Amy was walking through Death Valley – only, she wasn't really walking, she was sort of floating ... literally. The Dessec demon, whose name she had learnt was Pueblo, had an arm wrapped around her shoulder in what could only be termed a possessive embrace, as he led her to his ... she wasn't exactly sure where he was leading her. She assumed it was his village, or headquarters, or something. And they were moving at a pace she couldn't walk at. When she looked down at her feet, they were imitating walking, but she couldn't feel the sand beneath her feet.

The flames surrounding his body now also surrounded her own, in a delicious heat that confused the hell out of her. If she was the burying-your-head-in-the-sand type, she would be telling herself that the waves of lust sparking in her body were a side effect of Pueblo's supernatural fire. Unfortunately, Amy was a realist, and could not deny the fact that this demon was eye candy at its best, with or without magic flames. Hell, if she'd known demons could look like this, she'd have been seeking them out a long time ago.

A low laugh rumbled in Pueblo's chest. "We don't all look like this."

"Oh, shit! You can hear my thoughts? You can do that?"

"No ... you spoke aloud."

"I did not!"

"Yes, you did."

I did?

Clearly the flames were getting to her. Half-heartedly, she tried to pull out from under his arm, but he was having none of it.

"Are we nearly there yet?"

He raised an eyebrow at her, looking amused. "You're funny, Amy, I like that."

Her stomach flip-flopped.

How is what I said funny?

"Really, Etienne – that's The Council's Elder – he'll be expecting me back any minute."

"Relax, there's plenty of time."

"All I need is an agreement from the Dessec that I can take back to him."

"What he is proposing is against our morals, and not that easy to achieve. It will take longer than a minute to convince us that his mission is worth our taking part in."

Inwardly, she cursed Etienne. Convince them? She hadn't planned on having to convince them of anything – she barely knew what this whole thing was about. With a sigh of resignation, she realised this little trip may take more than the day she'd put aside. She wasn't sure if Etienne had more than a day to spare – not that there was much she could do about it.

"Why are you here, Amy?"

"I told you, to—"

"No, that's why Etienne sent you – why are *you* here."

"What are you, fucking Jerry Springer? What does it matter?"

"You matter, Amy."

Blood, or magic flames – she wasn't sure which – rose to her cheeks, and she found herself flummoxed. A child's voice, one she recognised as her own when she was little, came forward inside her mind in a hesitant whisper ... *I matter?*

Pueblo came to a sudden stop, causing Amy to stumble against him.

"Hey!"

"We're here." The fire surrounding them faded away into the black of the night.

She looked around, confused. "Here? There's nothing here."

"You can't see what's around you because you're not a demon."

"Oh ... how can I effectively talk to you guys if I can't see anything?"

"Take the essence of a demon into you, and you will see."

A faint ring of a bell, that sounded an awful lot like a warning, went off in her head. "Essence?"

He pulled out a dagger from ... she wasn't sure where. *Did he have that in his loin cloth? What else does he have in there?*

Before she knew it, he'd sliced his wrist. His blood glistened the darkest of reds under the moon.

"Drink, Amy; take me into you."

Her heart thudded in her ears – this was *so* not what she came for. "I can't," she whispered, but she wasn't sure she meant it. When she next looked up at him, his eyes were bright yellow, his pupils slitted like that of a cat's ... only he was more of a panther. *Nothing kitteny about* this *demon.*

That heat rose up within her again, and this time, she couldn't blame the flames, what with them being extinguished and all. "I ... I mean, I..."

"If you do not drink, there will be no negotiations."

"Blackmail?"

"Fact. You will not be able to see us, or communicate with us."

"I can see you."

"I am more accommodating of humans than my peers. I walk freely in your world, like all demons used to, but the others will not leave our protected dimension. You must go to them. And the only way you can do that, is to drink."

He held his wound an inch from her mouth. The scent of his rich blood pierced her sinuses and danced on her tongue. "Consequences," she found herself saying. "There'll be consequences..."

"There are always consequences, for every choice you make." His hand found its way to the back of her neck, and pulled her towards him. Her thoughts were too jumbled to put up a fight.

"Just a taste, Amy; you don't need to drink much." His voice wrapped around her like silk, and all resistance left her. Maybe she was being seduced, but it was only her instinct she could feel, alive and burning within her, telling her this was something she needed to do. She heard Etienne's voice inside her mind, scolding her for her carelessness, but louder still, was the voice of her childhood self – no longer a whisper, it laughed with joy, the sound filling her heart with something she could not name.

Her lips found the demon's wrist and sealed itself around the dripping cut. The strong, metallic liquid hit her tongue, and Amy's soul roared, as it soared out of her body.

~*~

"Open the door, already," Karl mumbled into the back of her neck between kisses, his hot breath tickling her skin.

"I'm trying to, but you're not making it easy."

"You're fumbling."

"Of course I'm fumbling ... mmm ... that's good..."

"You ever had a hickey? I want to give you a hickey."

"Karl, we're not fourteen!"

"Don't bloody care. I was in love with you when I was fourteen – your neck owes me a hickey."

Finally, Elena managed to hold her hand steady enough to get the key in the lock, and they both tumbled inside. With his lips never once losing their focus, Karl kicked the door shut behind them.

"Whoa, Casanova – I'm hungry."

"Mmm ... so am I."

"I'm serious!" Like an obedient child, Elena's stomach growled. "See?"

"Ugh..." With a sigh, he pulled away from her. "Fine, but it's going to be a really big hickey..."

With a triumphant grin, she gave a him a peck and went to the fridge. "We have ... nothing ... because our food delivery's tomorrow ... crap. Wait, we have eggs – you want eggs on toast?"

"Let's see, it's quick to cook, quick to eat, which means I get you on your back more quickly ... yes, I want."

"On my back?"

"Or you could get me on my back, but last time you tried that, it didn't go so well."

She grimaced. "Oh, yeah, the spell ... it won't happen again though ... I don't think..."

"Whatever..." His hands snaked around her waist as she broke the eggs into the frying pan. "I could be persuaded to give that another go."

She turned to face him, returning his hug. "Hey," she said, softly. "I don't ever want to do that to you again – not like that."

"I know. I forgive you, by the way."

"I know you do, but I haven't forgiven me yet, so how about tonight, I leave you in charge of the seducing, okay?"

"I can live with that."

The toast popped up.

"Dinner in two minutes then..."

"I'll lay the table," he said, giving her bum a smack as he went.

Fifteen minutes later, Elena wasn't nearly full enough, but at least her stomach had stopped growling. She sat on Karl's lap as he flicked through television channels, but night had fallen, and neither of them were concentrating on the brash lights and sounds that the box emitted.

"Karl..."

"Oooh, look, it's Buffy."

"Karl, I think we should hide the pen."

"Uh ... all right..."

"Actually, I think you should do it, so I don't know where it is."

"Nothing's happened, has it?"

"No, but I don't want to take any chances. It was horrific what happened Saturday night, but it's kind of more eerie just sitting around waiting for that bloody pen to do something ... and when I fall asleep, I don't want—"

"Hey, nothing's going to happen, not with me around."

"I know you mean that, I really do, but how can you possibly know that?"

"I don't know ... it's a feeling. As long as I'm with you, everything's okay."

She laughed. "This is loved up Karl talking."

"Maybe," he smiled, "but the feeling remains."

"Well, that's good to know ... but I still don't want to take any chances. Please, it'll make me feel so much better."

"All right, darling, I'll squirrel it away somewhere."

"Thank you," she sighed, nestling into his arm. "Do you think it means anything, that he hasn't used that pen against me since Saturday night?"

"I haven't got a clue. But it's only been forty-eight hours ... and he did enter your dreams again only last night..."

"Hey, you're frowning – don't think about that. He's not coming between us. You're the one that pulled me back, remember?"

"I'll always pull you back ... I'll always be there for you, Elena."

"I know ... there's something else I wanted to talk to you about..."

He turned to face her, bringing her up against his chest. "Go on."

She hesitated, not knowing exactly how to say what she wanted to. How did people do this? It must be easier when you're sixteen and ruled by hormones...

"Er ... the thing is ... I-uh ... I love you. Maybe I have for a long time, I don't know. But, really, it's always been you and, I want it to *be* you. What I mean is, that I want you – I want to make love with you."

Chewing nervously on her lip, she peeked at Karl from the corner of her eye. Oh, God, he looked stunned. That was probably not a good sign. "But we don't have to ... I mean, if you don't want to it's fine—"

"Elena," he cupped her face and brought her close, "of course I bloody want to, but you ... you'd be giving up so much."

"I'd be gaining more – a whole life with you. We could have children, we could be together without this constant yearning, or this feeling that we're missing out on something—"

"I'd never feel like I'm missing anything with you."

"Then you're a saint, because I'm pretty sure I would." She rolled the button of his shirt anxiously between her fingers. "So ... do you want to ... with me?"

"Just so I don't make a complete tit of myself, can I assume that by 'want to, with you', you are actually referring to making love with you? In the full-on sex kind of way?"

"Yes. And I know it puts a huge burden on you, what with you becoming a super powerful witch and all, but—"

"You know I don't care about that; I'll deal with it – we'll deal with it together."

She looked at him, guiltily, and they both fell into a silence that was almost uncomfortable.

"I have this horrible feeling I've ruined things..."

"No, never – I'm just ... I've wanted you to say those words to me for most of my life."

"That I want to make love with you?"

"That you love me. A part of me can't believe you're really here – that we're really here, like this."

"Well, I do love you ... more than anything."

"I want you to be sure – I'm not going anywhere, Elena, maybe we should wait a week—"

"No, now," she whispered. "Tonight. I want to be with you tonight. I've spend too many years scared of this. I've never let myself feel anything close to love; I've never even used my magic to its full potential. I've been so terrified of my lineage, of what it would mean to ... everyone, if I did something careless and my powers got lost..." Tears sprang up in her eyes. "I've never lived. Karl, I want to live with you. And I want to start now."

Another silence. She felt her tears trickle down her face, and smiled when she saw Karl's own eyes were shimmering. "God, we're soppy, aren't we?"

He smiled. "It'll be our little secret."

Hesitantly, she leaned in and kissed him. Aware that he hadn't actually said yes to her little proposal, she pulled back, uncertainty ruling her heart. She didn't get very far.

He held her fast against him and crushed his lips to hers. She heard him fumble for the remote and Buffy's voice disappeared as the telly went off. With her mind, she dimmed the lights.

Karl grinned against her. "I thought you weren't supposed to use magic frivolously?"

"I'm starting to think that a lot of things I've been told aren't true. Now are you going to take me upstairs or shall I teleport us?"

Chapter Eight

Amy stirred on the edge of consciousness. She felt groggy. Her head felt like she'd drunk half a bottle of Jack Daniels.

With a groan, she gripped the edge of her duvet and pulled it higher, snuggling down into its warmth. *Wait ... what...?*

A pair of yellow eyes flashed into her mind; a cut on a wrist; blood the colour of ripe cherries...

With a start she sat up, and wished she hadn't. Her room swam around her as her head pounded.

Oh, shit, I'm going to hurl...

The room steadied. She dropped her head between her knees, taking deep breaths, forcing herself past the throbbing in her skull to try and remember what the hell had happened.

"Amy."

She screamed, momentarily forgetting her pain. There were those eyes, beautiful and dangerous all at once, lurching at her from the shadows of her room.

"Pueblo?" she croaked out. If she could just stop her head from stabbing her, and quieten the pounding of her heart, maybe she'd get some kind of clue as to what was going on. "I'm home ... why am I home?"

"I brought you back."

"I don't remember..."

"No, I'm sorry. The meeting with my tribe was not successful. They asked me to make sure your memory was wiped so you would not try to find them again."

"What? You ... erased my memory?"

"I had no choice."

Anger replaced the grogginess she was feeling. "There's always a choice."

"Well, my choice was, wipe your memory, or get us both lynched by my own kind. I chose the first option."

"Why are you here?" she asked, suddenly more irritated than anything else. "And how am I back home?"

"I teleported us."

It was then that she realised, to her horror, she was stark naked and flashing all her assets to the demon.

With a squeal, she grabbed the duvet and pulled it flush against her body. "*Why* am I naked?!"

He raised an eyebrow in amusement. "Do you know how hard it is to teleport two of us at once across such a distance? I needed to get rid of all material items."

"You still have your loin cloth on."

A smirk appeared on his face, so sure of itself, she wanted to slap it off. "If it would make you feel better, I'm more than happy to lose the garment." He hooked his thumbs into its waistband.

"No! God, don't!"

To Amy's relief, he removed his hands from the well-worn leather and leaned back against the wall.

"How did you know where I live?"

"My blood is in you," he said, softly. "It was easy for me to find where you live."

"Oh."

"And you will be able to seek me out also, whenever you need me." He sounded so warm and caring in his tone, she almost forgot she was mad at him.

There was an awkward pause, while she tried to figure out how to put some clothes on with him in the room.

"Okay, you can go now."

Instead he strode towards her and perched himself on her bed.

She tightened her hold on the duvet.

"Not until I know you're all right."

"I'm fine."

"You didn't look so good when you woke up."

"Well, since then, I learned that you've taken my memory, stripped me naked and bonded me to you through your blood, so I'm just peachy now!"

His laughter boomed around the room.

"What's so funny?"

"You. Your anger is beautiful..."

"To a demon, maybe."

"And it'll keep you alive."

"Or it'll give me an aneurysm."

Suddenly, she stiffened, a familiar sensation creeping up her spine.

"Amy, what is it?"

"Etienne. He's on his way here now – you have to go."

"How do you know?"

"We have this connection thing ... he's going to be here any minute, you *have* to go."

He frowned. "Connection? Maybe I should meet him."

"Are you *insane?* He hates demons; he'll probably annihilate you on the spot!"

"I'm not that easy to get rid of."

"No kidding ... please – I'm already in for it when I tell him I've brought him back nothing."

"All right," he nodded. "I'll go, but I'll know if you're in danger, Amy. I'll keep you safe."

"Whatever ... just get the fuck out – he'll be here any second!"

Before Amy saw it coming, Pueblo smacked a kiss on her lips. Sparks of what felt like electricity crackled between them. Logic told her they should have thrown her from him, but instead she found herself pulled further in, a moan escaping her at the strange sensation.

He broke the kiss, flashed her a grin, then dissipated before her eyes.

Etienne knocked on the front door.

Well, at least he knocked, she thought, wryly.

Throwing on the first outfit she could find, she rushed downstairs to open the door, and hoped her still aching head wasn't about to get a whole lot worse.

~*~

Karl was in heaven. Long, dark, lush hair cascaded across his chest, stroking him like feathered wings, as the love of his life swept his mouth with her soft kisses.

Stripping her had been the most beautiful, surreal experience of his life, and the time it took to get her naked had gone far too quickly ... not that having her skin flushed against his own wasn't a luxury in itself.

A single candle lit Elena's room.

He let out a small sound of approval as she made his way down his neck.

"Did you hide the pen?" she asked, into his neck.

Ugh, that bloody pen. "Yes, just fifteen minutes ago before I shut the bedroom door behind us."

"Thank you."

"Have I told you how beautiful you are?" he said, desperate to get that God-awful pen out of her mind. It had done enough damage already – he was damned if he was going to let it ruin tonight.

She laughed. "Lots of times."

"Mind if I keep saying it?"

"You can say it as often as you like, as long as you keep doing whatever you're doing with your fingers."

"What, this?" he asked, lightly running them up and down her backside.

"Mmm, yes – who would have thought my bum could be so sensitive? I sit on it every day."

His own laughter ripped from his lungs. "You're so amazingly innocent."

"Hey..."

"No, it's a good thing. I almost don't want us to do this in case you turn into a wanton harlot."

She slapped him lightly on the arm. "Am I supposed to think that's some kind of compliment?"

"Your innocence is gorgeous, Elena. You should never be ashamed of it."

"To me, it just symbolises everything I've held myself back from. I take it..."

"What?"

"You're not ... innocent? Stop laughing at me!"

"You mean, am I a virgin? No. There have been other women; can't say it was very fair on them."

"What do you mean? And how do I not know about these other women?"

He shrugged. "I never told you – because it was never right that I was with them. It was when you went to university. I missed you like crazy. I, er, overdosed on women for a short while, in a futile attempt to convince myself you weren't the only one for me."

"You became a man-slut?"

He sighed. "Now, see, this is why I didn't tell you."

"I'm kidding."

"No, you're right. I'm not proud of it. I was always safe with them, by the way, in case you're wondering. I always wore a condom."

"Do you ... do you want to..."

"You're crap at finishing sentences."

That earned him another slap. "I've not had much practise at saying stuff like this!" She took in a breath before continuing. "Do you want to wear a condom tonight?"

After knowing her for twenty years, she still had the ability to knock him off his feet – or he would have been had he not already been lying down. "Are you suggesting we don't?"

"I don't know, I just ... with anyone else, that wouldn't even be an option, but ... there's never going to be anyone but you, Karl. We both run our own businesses, have our own place, earn enough money ... I suppose I should be cautious about getting pregnant, what with this being our first time, but I can't say it would bother me. We've already lived together for three years. I know being in a relationship is different, but, well, in some ways, we may as well have been in a relationship all this time, just look at how we are with each other. Maybe it would be different if I was just a regular person, but us making love is such a huge thing anyway, with me losing my powers, you gaining them, then there's the whole thing with the pen, and people dying ... me getting pregnant just seems so ... *small* in the greater scheme of things."

She'd been looking away from him all this time, and now she focused those big, brown eyes on him.

He tried to speak, but the words caught at the back of his throat and all he managed was a stutter.

"Phew," she exhaled. "You really just need to tell me to shut up sometimes – like I said, I'm not very good at this—"

He pulled her down towards him, cutting her off with a kiss. "Yes, you are. I love it that you just say what you're thinking, that you're open enough to – that you trust me enough to.

"I'm lying here trying to think of one good reason to not go into this with you full throttle, so to speak. And I keep expecting to feel some kind of fear, or something, at the thought of starting this future with you now. Well, I can't think of one good reason, and the only thing I feel is elation."

He brushed her bottom lip with his thumb, looking upon the face he knew so well – warm, compassionate, wise despite her innocence. "I've wanted this with you, before I even knew I wanted it. So, yes, let's do this how we want to, and let's see where it goes."

The promise of their unknown future together, was sealed as their lips met again. Their kiss deepened and he drank her in – her scent, the feel of her, everything. If he remembered only one thing from of his entire life, he wanted it to be this. Nothing in his twenty-seven years, compared to this moment. He moved his hands across her body, touching her anywhere that would cause beatific noises to erupt from her throat. Although he knew it couldn't entirely be avoided, he loathed that this would be painful for her, when all he'd feel would be pure bliss.

"Do you want to stay on top?" he murmured against her. "It's sometimes easier the first time."

She nodded, and shifted her body lower, her kisses becoming more urgent, her breath more shallow, as his hands caressed her in all the right places. When he felt her slick sex graze the tip of his cock, his brain almost exploded. "Christ, this feels too good already..."

Then millimetre, by agonizing millimetre, she lowered herself onto him. He sucked his breath in between his teeth and stole a glance at her. Swollen lips sounding out little gasps of pleasure, and glazed eyes staring back at him in total surrender, had him struggling to keep his release under control. He felt her barrier nudge him, and she stopped.

"You all right?" he whispered.

"Mm-hmm," she nodded. "I'm going to do this is one go, okay?"

Before he could answer, she drove herself down the rest of the way.

A little cry of agony left her throat, as a groan of ecstasy escaped his. She didn't slow down, but moved herself up and down his length again, and again. The grimace on her face broke his heart just a little.

"Wait, it's okay; just wait for a minute. Let your body get used to it."

She stopped, letting her full weight fall on him.

Another moan of pleasure escaped him. He moved his hands to her hips, holding her still as he began to rock in her just a little.

She emitted a little sound of surprise, then followed his lead. It wasn't long before they had a rhythm going, slow at first, then becoming more furious in pace. Her little gasps turned into long moans that were music to his ears.

His hands left her hips and made their way up to her breasts. This earned him something close to a growl from her, and he realised, with some chagrin, that he wasn't going to be able to hold out for much longer. He began to change their rhythm, but she slammed a hand against his chest.

"Don't you dare."

"Elena, I'm close..."

"So am I – Don't. Stop."

Her eyes were closed. She threw her head back and rocked faster, harder...

Jesus ... this was so fucking wonderful – no way was he going to last.

"Elena..."

Her insides gripped him.

Oh, shit, I'm gonna come.

"Elena, I'm—"

When she looked down at him, her eyes were radiating bright, green light.

Everything that happened next was a blur in Karl's mind: he saw Elena smile, and tell him he was glowing again – he had no idea what that meant, and anyway, he was trying to tell her about her eyes – the words never made it out of his head. The green disappeared as she squeezed her eyes shut, and he heard her scream out his name as her climax hit her. At the same time, the most powerful orgasm of his life racked through his body, coupled with the most terrible pain he'd ever felt. Ecstasy and torture warred with each other in his body, as he wondered what the fuck was happening. His hands gripped her in anguish. He tried to scream at her to stop; he tried to throw her off – nothing worked.

She rode him to completion, both hers and his.

A sickening tearing sound filled Karl's mind, he finally managed to let out his scream, and then his world went black.

Chapter Nine

Elena fell forwards and slumped onto Karl's chest, completely sated, allowing her face to nestle in the crook of his neck. "Oh. My. God. That was ... is it always like that? That was *amazing.* I've heard it's usually crappy the first time – that was so *not* crappy. I wasn't expecting that bit at the end – you *glowed,* as in, really glowed. Everything was gold all around you – I felt the light *enter* me. I can still feel it – you – inside me. Was it good for you? Was I okay? Karl?"

She glanced up at him.

"Karl?"

He looked ... not quite right. His smooth face seemed smoother than usual, his eyes were open and still, no – wait – his entire body was still. Her mind started to piece together what she was seeing, and a cold dread she'd never experienced before seeped into her.

"Karl?" Her voice shook as she fought against the scene in front of her.

No ... this is a joke. Karl likes to joke.

"Karl, stop it." She reached up and swatted her hand right in front of his eyes. He didn't blink, or flinch – not a single muscle moved in his body.

No, no, no no no no...

"Karl!" She shook him by the shoulder, then poked him in one of his open eyes, a ridiculous action that would have had her laughing at any other time.

Nothing.

"Oh, no! God, no!"

Pulse ... feel for a pulse!

She grabbed his wrist between her unsteady hands, then remembered that it would be easier to feel for the beat in his neck, so she jammed her two forefingers there instead, right against the carotid pulse – or where it should be, anyway.

Tears welled up in her eyes, and she had a vague sense that she was losing it. Nothing. She couldn't feel a damn thing! She pressed harder, moved her fingers around a bit. Thirty seconds passed. *Oh, God! Hold it together, Elena – Karl needs you to hold it together...*

She climbed off him and shuffled beside him on the bed. Tilting his head back, she cleared his airway, then sealed her mouth around his and breathed.

Breathe!

And breathed.

Breathe, for fuck's sake!

She clasped her hands, one on top of the other, and prayed she had the right spot before pushing down hard into the centre of his chest. She continued the compressions ... how many times was she supposed to do this? Fifteen times? Thirty? She went for thirty, then breathed into his mouth again. Then started on his chest again.

"He's dead."

With a startled cry, she whirled around to face the all too familiar voice behind her, and saw nothing but shadows ... of course.

"Show yourself, Shanka!" she demanded.

"My name, is Nathaniel."

"I don't care what your name is. What did you *do* to him?"

"I did nothing."

"You're lying."

"I don't lie – there's little point in it."

"He's not dead."

"I can't sense a life force, can you?"

Life force? An image of the butterfly she'd resurrected sprang to mind and hope flared in her chest. "Life – I can bring him back to life."

"No you can't."

"Shut up! Better still, fuck off."

His laugh rippled around the room, surrounding her in waves of that incubus energy. She ignored it – he was just a shadow. Unless she was dreaming. *God, please let me be dreaming...*

But the starkness of everything around her told her she wasn't. She closed her eyes and thought of the butterfly; thought of herself as a child. She'd never resurrected anything after that day, too frightened her actions would unbalance the world or something. No such fear lived in her now, nor had it when she'd held the butterfly in her hands all those years ago ... with Karl beside her.

Karl.

A terrible anguish washed over her, but she pushed it aside and concentrated harder. *Focus!*

She knelt beside him and lifted his head, cradling it in her arms, stroking his hair. She felt the power of life and death surge inside her, and she willed it to travel into him.

It didn't.

It should have flowed through him, as if they were one, but for some reason the life force she was emitting hit a barrier. She tried again to no avail.

"I can't ... oh, no..."

Reality finally sank in. A deep wail that sounded nothing like her, wrenched itself out of her throat. Grief dominated her, as her tears streaked rivers down her dead lover's face. Dead.

Dead.

"Karl's d-dead..." she uttered between sobs.

"Yes."

"Why c-can't I b-bring him back?"

"Because you were the one that killed him."

The room was filled with her stunned silence.

She shook her head. "No..."

"Haven't you figured it out yet? What you are? What you can do? *Succubus...*"

Dumbly, she continued to shake her head.

"Your father was a Shanka. Your mother never told you. You, Elena, are half-Shanka demon, and half-thirteenth generation witch."

"You're—"

"Lying? I already told you, I don't lie – your mother's the one that does that."

"Mum..." *No.* It was too much – this was too much to take in. She looked up at Nathaniel with a determination that surprised her. "You have to leave now. I want you gone."

"I can bring him back ... for a price."

She paused.

"A Shanka cannot bring back that which was taken by his, or her, own hand, but they can ask another Shanka to do it."

"And the price?" she asked, flatly.

"Come with me. Be my bride. Be mine."

Her laugh came out hard and shallow, sounding alarmingly like the demon's own, now that the truth had taken seed. She tightened her hold on Karl. "Never. Nathaniel, I will never be yours."

The single candle flickered in the room as the demon let out a growl of frustration. "You *are* mine, Elena. I'll come for you when you next sleep, and this time," he spat out, "your lover won't be there to save you."

"Go to hell," she whispered.

"I suggest you flip your pillow over, witch."

She stared him down, hiding her confusion, and then he disappeared.

The silence in the room grew oppressive. Elena stared down at Karl, reached across his face and brought his eyelids down. There. He looked so peaceful now.

She could feel another sob caught at the back of her throat – she wanted to cry, to howl, to pour out all this pain – but she suddenly felt strangely numb. Her mind was overloaded with information, and her body was still overloaded from her earlier orgasm. A brief hope lit her up when she wondered if writing with the pen would bring Karl back ... then she remembered that he'd hidden it. She could try to go find it, but that would mean leaving Karl. No, she didn't want to leave him – what if...

What if, what, Elena? What if something happens to him? He's already dead.

One by one, she felt her internal processes begin to shut down. She had no idea what to do next. So she reached over to her right and flipped her pillow over. A bulge under her pillowcase caught her eye. She reached inside the pillowcase and pulled it out.

She thought Nathaniel must have put it there, but when she opened it, it was her mother's handwriting she saw. *A diary ... this is my mother's diary. What's it doing in my pillowcase?*

With a sense of trepidation, she began to read. Nothing made sense at first, but odd words and phrases jumped out at her: Shanka, seduced, in love, Darius, father, mother, Elena, daughter, demon, powerful, the power of life and death, succubus, kidnap, kill, hide ... and on and on it went, for pages and pages.

Three quarters of the way through the book, some part of her brain started to piece the story together. Not only that, but that same part began to remember her childhood – the butterfly, the moment she began to menstruate, her mother explaining about her sacred virginity...

She looked down at Karl again. Then at her own hands. She flexed them, willing them to produce that healing light she so often used. It did. She still had her magic. Karl was dead.

Glancing down at the book, one final word caught her eye – the word that fit the final piece into the jigsaw: Lie.

Her life, her past, her future, all shattered before her eyes. Rage, like she'd never known, coursed through her being; her hands glowed red. She smelled burning flesh and realised she was burning Karl's face with her hands. With a cry of alarm, she let him go and stood up.

Her fault ... this was her fault.

Karl was dead...

And I killed him!

Her hands itched. It felt like her blood was boiling, and she let it, because her rage was the only thing she had left. Looking down at her fiery hands, she noticed the skin on her arms had started to crack and turn grey, like an old pavement.

She saw black, and the anger erupted from her in a scream that would have put banshees to shame. Her windows cracked, shards of glass sprayed everywhere, her room shook, and the building that she lived in exploded in a gigantic ball of fire.

~*~

Amy was standing outside Elena's flat wondering what on earth she should do. Her conversation with Etienne had been so brief, she knew it wasn't over. But Etienne had received a vision shortly after arriving at her home. Etienne's visions were always abstract, coupled with a 'sense' of what was happening rather than the full-on, 3D version. This vision had been no less strange: he'd seen a butterfly dying. That was it. But his senses told him Elena was involved, so he'd asked Amy to come here. Why he couldn't come himself was beyond her.

Irritable, tired, with her head still aching, albeit less painfully, Amy – still unable to teleport – had jumped on a tram from Croydon and made her way to Wimbledon. It was quarter to midnight, and the residential street she stood in was quiet and empty – almost empty. Out of the corner of her eye, she caught a movement on the other side of Elena's apartment building. She wasted no time in wrapping an invisibility shield around herself.

A woman, who looked around the same age as herself, stepped into the moonlight. Highly attractive, she stood tall and her hair was so black, it glinted blue under the dim rays. She didn't seem to be going anywhere; much like Amy, she sort of just lurked. As she got a little closer, Pueblo's demon blood grew cold inside her.

Interesting.

Wondering whether she should make herself known to her, she was suddenly thrown meters in the air when Elena's building exploded. Heat from the fireball washed over her, but never made it past her shield, for which she was grateful. Her luck ran out when she hit the floor, landing shoulder-first. A scream ripped out of her, and she heard footsteps thudding towards her.

The woman with the amazing hair was leaning over her with concern etched in her face.

Hmmm, my shield must be down. And why is she not on fire?

The woman's eyes, a piercing blue, the colour of tropical oceans, were even more amazing than her hair.

"Are you all right?" she called out.

"I don't know ... my arm..."

"Your shoulder looks wrong. I think you might have dislocated it."

"What the hell happened?"

"The building..."

"Oh, my God ... Elena..."

"You know Elena?"

"We have to go see if she..." She left her words stranded in the air, mid-flow, as Elena walked out of the inferno. Only...

"Oh. My. God."

The woman beside her sucked in her breath and she felt her stiffen.

Amy struggled to her feet, with her help. "Tell me I'm not seeing this."

"If you're seeing a naked woman, who sort of looks like Elena, with grey skin that's ... broken or something ... and glowing green eyes, then you're seeing what I'm seeing."

"Shit. What's she carrying?"

The woman squinted. "I think ... Holy Mother, it's Karl! *It's Karl!*" And without any warning she sprinted towards them.

"Wait!" she called, as she ran after her, trying not to pass out from the burning pain in her shoulder. When she caught up with her, she and Elena were both staring at each other. Elena – if this *was* Elena – had Karl cradled in her arms. Apparently, she was super-strong now, and Amy could only assume it was Elena's own magic that had protected her and Karl from the blast. One of her hands clutched a small book.

Elena turned and looked straight at Amy. "He's dead," she stated in a voice so hollow, it made her shudder. "I killed him."

"No," said the other woman, firmly. "I know you, Elena, and I know Karl. You did *not* kill him."

"I did kill him, Mary. I sucked the life right out of him. I can feel him inside me – his glow." And then she suddenly stared – *really* stared – at Mary. "Did you dream this? Is that why you're here? Did you *know* this was going to happen?" Her voice was low and deadly, crackling like the fire behind her.

"No! Of course not. I dreamt about a fire tonight, and I dreamt about this building, and when the dream woke me up, I was worried about you – I had to come see if you were okay..." Tears danced in Mary's eyes. "God ... Karl..."

Elena ignored them and leaned towards her instead. "What are you?"

Mary shook her head. "What?"

Sirens sounded in the background.

"Elena..." Amy tried to speak as softly as she could. "Can we think about Karl? Fire engines are coming – there'll be an ambulance. Will you let them look after him?"

She tightened her hold on him, her eyes flashing.

"I know you don't want to let him go. But if he's truly dead, he deserves to be at peace, and if there's the tiniest chance he's still alive, a hospital will be the best place for him."

Elena hesitated.

"He's human, Elena."

Those seemed to be the magic words. She lay him down with a gentleness that looked out of place with her new demeanour.

Mary took off her coat and covered his naked form as best she could.

Elena shrank back.

"Wait, where are you going?"

"No one can see me like this," she whispered. "Look at me."

Sure enough, Amy didn't know how any of them would explain Elena's appearance. "Where are you going to go?"

She stepped forwards one last time, and thrust the book she was holding, towards Amy. With her good arm, she reached out and took it.

"What's this?"

"The greatest lie of all," she spat out, bitterly, hatred etched in every word. "The real reason Karl is dead. I'm going to kill them all."

Elena became one with the shadows, and disappeared.

The fire engines and ambulance pulled up.

"You need to get that shoulder fixed," said Mary.

"What are we going to tell them?" asked Amy, staring at all the uniforms.

"Let me do the talking."

"Gladly."

"And then I'm going to need a stiff drink."

"Mind if I join you?"

"Please do."

"I'm Amy, by the way. I'm a witch."

"I'm Mary," she smiled. "And I don't know what I am."

Two and a half hours, and two shots of Tequila later, the two women sat in Mary's living room in silence, having just read Katherine's diary.

It was Mary who spoke first, voicing what they were both thinking. "We have to help her. We have to bring her back from ... whatever she's becoming."

"Do you think we can?"

"I refuse to think we can't. This is Elena. She's the exact opposite of evil – we can't do nothing."

"What do you think she's going to do?"

"Sounded like she was planning a killing spree to me. I think she's gonna find a way into Shanka territory, and try to exterminate them all."

Amy wrinkled her nose in a half-grimace. "I think you're right, apart from the planning bit. Elena may just be the most powerful witch to ever walk the Earth, whether she knows it or not. I don't think there's any planning, I think she's just going to go in there and let all hell break loose."

"Because she's got nothing to lose."

Amy nodded.

"Any result from that location spell?"

Amy glanced at the map on the dining table, looking for that magical red marker that would indicate where Elena was. "Nope. But I don't even know if this spell would work on a Shanka – they're not like other demons – they become shadow."

"Elena's half-human."

Amy sighed. "I hope she's still half-human."

"She *is*," insisted Mary.

Amy stared at her new, accidental ally. Over the last couple of hours, she had discovered next to nothing about Mary – not that she had divulged anything of herself either – but she trusted the woman. It was obvious she cared about Elena ... and Karl. But she couldn't ignore the fact that the demon blood she'd drunk, which now seemed to form part of her DNA, whether she wanted it to or not, didn't like Mary one bit. Her blood grew cold and hummed in her ears whenever she got too close. She had no idea why that was. But her human self, told her Mary was safe, and since she'd known her human self longer than she'd known Pueblo, and all the craziness that came with him, she listened to her human self.

Speaking of Pueblo, her new blood heated up a couple of notches, suddenly roaring inside her, and she found herself turning towards the front door.

"Oh, no," she muttered.

"What?" asked Mary.

There was a heavy, insistent pounding on the door.

Mary jumped up.

"No, Mary, I know who it is. I'll get it." Ignoring Mary's quizzical look, she rushed to the door and flung it open.

Just as expected, Pueblo filled the doorway, a look of fury painting his features.

Irritatingly, she realised she actually felt a little scared, and pushed the feeling away with a huff. "What are you doing here?" she hissed.

"You're hurt."

"My shoulder got dislocated; paramedics fixed it."

His frown deepened.

"Okay, *maybe* they wanted to take me to hospital, and I *may* have mentally persuaded them to fix me as best as they could on the spot, but there are serious things happening here – I don't have time to go to hospital."

"Did they fix it right?"

"It's fiiiiiine, Jeeeez!"

"Here." He placed his hand on her tender shoulder. It instantly warmed under his touch. Energy coursed into it, weaving through every sinew and tendon. A sigh of relief escaped her as she felt every last trace of pain evaporate.

"You can heal people?"

"No. Only you."

"Blood bond?"

He nodded.

She had no reply to that. She was grateful; she just kind of wished she wasn't tied to him.

A cough sounded behind her.

"Oh." Amy stepped to the side. "Pueblo, this is Mary; Mary, meet Pueblo."

"Hi," she smiled.

"What is *that?*" Shock reigned the demon's face, his eyes wide with ... not exactly fear, and not exactly awe...

"Hey," came the contentious reply, "I'm the *human* that lives here."

"Human?"

"Yes, human."

"If you say so."

"I do."

He continued to stare at her ... which irked Amy, somewhat.

She stepped back into his line of vision. "Look, Elena's Hulked out on us, and probably gone on a Shanka killing spree. We need to get her back to her sane self. Think you can help?"

"I will help. The Dessec are the Gatekeepers of chaos; we manage it, trying to make sure it never grows to large proportions. We never want to be in the position where we have to undo time to fix an event that chaos caused."

The women stared at him, wide-eyed.

"Okaaay," said Amy. "Peublo, you're going to need clothes. You can't walk around in this dimension looking like that."

"Can you magic him some clothes?" chipped in Mary.

"Yes, I suppose I can..."

"Okay, great. We have an army of three. Pueblo, come in."

The demon entered, and Amy shut the door behind him. "So, we need a plan."

"Elena is bound by blood to the Shanka tribe," began Pueblo.

She crossed her arms to hide her exasperation. What was it with demons and blood?

"She will be drawn to them. We will follow her."

"I hate to burst your bubble," said Amy, "but we have two problems: one, we can't find her anywhere; two, she's had Shanka blood in her all her life – I don't believe she's ever been drawn to them before."

"That's true," said Mary. "I've known her for almost a year and, as I understand from what I've learned tonight, it's only in the last few days that the

Shanka's been around ... and it was the demon that sought *her* out, wasn't it?"

"That's what Etienne said – speaking of whom, I may need to cloak this flat. He's good at finding me."

"Do what you have to, Amy."

Amy nodded her thanks. Since reading Katherine's diary and discovering Etienne was Elena's *grandfather* of all things, she needed time to figure things out – time *away* from Etienne. Her heart ached at his part in all this. If only he wasn't like a father to her...

"It makes no sense that Elena would not have discovered the Shanka earlier in her life. Her blood would have demanded it. Unless..."

"Unless what, Pueblo?"

"The only thing more powerful than a blood bond, is a soul bond. A blood bond needs physical form to be created; a soul bond, does not. A bond between souls is ancient – older than the planet."

"Are you saying, that Elena would not have been affected by her demon blood, if she was already bonded to a ... soulmate?"

"Yes, soulmate. But there are not many bonded souls left in the world nowadays."

"Karl," said Mary. "Karl's her soulmate, I'd swear my own life on it. Those two ... you should have seen them together..."

"Then we must find this Karl – he will bring her back from the Shanka's shadows."

Mary bit her lip and let her tears fall for the first time that Amy had seen that night. "We can't," she whispered. "Karl's dead."

"How?"

"She said she killed him."

He looked surprised. "One does not kill their soulmate easily."

Amy sighed at the hopelessness of the situation. "You know that Elena's a thirteenth generation witch, and that she's half Shanka. What you don't know – what none of us knew – was that Elena was a virgin. Until tonight."

Pueblo's face turned grim. "So, she did kill him. When he took her virginity, her succubus energy would have become fully accessible to her, and as a newling, she would have been hungry – she sucked his life right out of him."

"But she didn't *mean* to," Mary interjected, angrily, her tears streaking her face. "She had no *idea* what she was until she read this diary just a few hours ago. Her mother always told her that if she gave up her virginity, she would lose all her powers and the right to her lineage – that was her mother's, if I might add, *poor* attempt to protect her from her inner-succubus."

"Mary, she didn't tell her the truth, because Elena simply knowing it would have sent an energetic alert, rippling through dimensions, straight to the Shanka, that she existed."

"But if she'd known ... if she'd just *known* before she slept with Karl, she wouldn't have slept with him, and he wouldn't be dead right now."

Amy placed a hand, softly, on the woman's arm. "I suspect that's why this book was left for Elena to find – she just clearly didn't find it in time."

Mary shook her head. "Her mother should have told her. Instead, Elena was led to believe all she was giving up was her magic, when in actual fact, whoever she lost her virginity to would be giving up his *life!*"

"Mary, calm down."

"I told her to go for it. At the shop, earlier today. She told me they'd started seeing each other, that she had something special planned for tonight. I was so happy for them both, and I teased her and told her it was about fucking time, and I told her to go for it. God, I told her not to come in tomorrow, that I would open up ... I told her..." She broke down.

Amy kept her hand on her arm and squeezed in reassurance. She wondered if she should hug her, but felt what she really needed was space. "You didn't do this Mary. You didn't know, and none of this is your fault."

"I never thought I'd be the reason behind one of my dreams," she whispered.

"What?"

"It doesn't matter..."

Pueblo's voice broke through the dense air. "We're wasting time."

"Have a heart," Amy snapped at him.

"No," Mary sighed, "Amy, he's right. I'm done now. I'm fine. Thanks."

"You sure?"

She nodded. "So ... where were we? Oh yes – the only hope we have of saving Elena, is dead."

They all looked at each other.

"What now?"

~*~

His footsteps made no sound as he made his way down the long corridors towards the morgue. It was five in the morning, and no one was around this section right now. There had been two deaths from that explosion in Wimbledon: one was a sixty-two year old man, that lived alone in the basement flat, and the other had been Karl Warden. They'd been pronounced dead on site, and brought in around 1 a.m. But humans, as wonderful and genuinely caring as they could be, had always struggled to look beyond the end of their noses. They loved the world black and white – it was so much easier to handle that way.

Voices sounded far off down to the right. He stopped and waited, making himself temporarily invisible until the two nurses had passed.

Unlike others of his kind, he loved hospitals. *Loved* them. Nowhere else in the world, could you find such a mix of real emotions. Nothing's hidden, nothing at all. Love, grief, fear, anger – it was all real, bold and in your face. At hospitals, people became their real selves with no masks to hide behind. It was a great shame that it always took such a life changing event for those moments of honesty to become manifest in the human world.

He continued on his way, taking a right turn, then another left, until he finally reached the morgue. The security box on the wall by the steel door flashed its red light in a silent command, a little arrow pointing downwards towards the slot where the identity card should go. He ignored it and walked through the locked door instead.

He knew exactly where to look – the boy's blood sang to him. Draw number 72. He pulled it open, revealing the covered body, then pulled the sheet off him.

Karl Warden looked dead ... to the human eye.

He leaned down and placed his ear to Karl's chest, and waited. One minute passed ... two minutes, then three...

There. There it was, the heartbeat he was waiting for. It would only ever beat about once every five minutes from now on, each beat holding all of human life within it.

"I hope you're ready for this, son, 'cause you don't really have much of a choice," he muttered. He placed his hand on Karl's chest, over his heart. The golden light that came from his hand was strong and sure; the light that came from Karl's chest was weak. "Not for long..."

He allowed the light to glow, surrounding them both in an aura of what could only be termed, holiness. A sense of bliss, peace and powerful ecstasy showered over him. It wasn't often he got to do this – it wasn't often his bloodline sang in someone's DNA so strongly – it didn't suck. Lost in the moment, he gave in to the pressure between his shoulder blades and down his spine, and his wings erupted – great, white feathers reaching out for metres either side of him, almost touching the ceiling. He smiled and stretched like a cat, unfurling them to their full extent, and thanking God that this particular morgue was especially roomy.

A small groan sounded from the metal table.

His smile widened. "Wakey-wakey, rise and shine, my boy – welcome to your new life!"

Chapter Ten

When awareness finally stirred within him, the first thing Karl felt was warmth – beautiful, wonderful warmth, flooding his being. *Maybe I've swallowed the sun,* he thought, then laughed at himself. *Funny how you think strange things when you're on the brink of death...*

Brink of death?

Memories he couldn't quite get at pressed at the corners of his mind. He groaned. A strong, Cockney dialect bounced off his ears, bringing him one step closer to reality.

"Wakey-wakey, rise and shine, my boy – welcome to your new life!"

He slowly opened his eyes – slowly, because he wasn't sure what scene was about to greet him. *What in God's name...?*

His thought ended right there, as he found himself ogling at a pair of enormous, white wings. Tracing them down from the ceiling, he discovered they belonged to a man who looked like an ageing rock star.

"Dead," he muttered, his voice hoarse. "I'm fucking dead."

"Nope, my son, you are not dead."

He glanced gingerly around him. "Am I in a morgue?"

"Yeah, but not dead."

"You sound like Alan Sugar."

"I have been told that, yes." The ... *angel ...?* folded his arms across his chest.

"Are you an—"

"Angel? Yes. You can call me Gwain."

"You look like Roger Daltrey."

"What, all angels need to look like prissy twenty-year olds?"

He had no answer for that, so he tried to get up instead. "Ugh ... I ache."

"Well, your soul was almost ripped from your body by a succubus – so technically, you should be dead. Thank the Lord, you're not entirely human."

"I'm not? *Succubus?*" And every memory of the night's events hit him all at once. "Elena!" He scrambled off the table and stumbled.

The angel caught him by the arm. "Easy. You need to give yourself a minute here."

"What happened to her? Is she all right?"

"Well, that depends on what you mean by all right. She's alive."

"Thank God."

"She's also so consumed by grief, and a blind rage, that it'll turn her into a full-blooded Shanka demon, unless we do something fast."

Karl felt all the blood drain from his face. "How did this even happen?"

"I'll fill you in..." He paused.

"Go on then."

"Yeah ... er ... you may want to put that sheet there around you."

He stared down at his naked body. "Oh, right." He grabbed the sheet Gwain was pointing at, and wrapped himself up as best he could.

"Okay ... I need to give you access to the Akashic Records. Do you know what they are?"

"Elena mentioned them once, I think. Is it like The Bible, or something?"

"Ha! Yeah, if The Bible was actually the size of Mount Everest, and, you know, complete. The Akashic Records is the whole story, my boy. Everything that's ever happened, on Earth and in Heaven, is written in them. Now, this is gonna feel strange – just go with it."

Karl nodded.

The angel – *Gwain* – came up close to him and cupped his face in his hands, a dreamlike expression taking over his face.

Okay, this is *strange.*

"Open your mouth," he said.

Hesitantly, Karl obeyed.

Gwain closed his mouth over Karl's, sealing it completely, and exhaled.

Images flooded his mind, like a movie on fast forward, painful at first – wings, swords, blood, clouds, fields in bloom, men, women and children, animals – all the images told a story, but he couldn't catch what they were. So he closed his eyes and gave into what was happening. As soon as he did, a sensation like nothing he'd ever known caressed his body.

Gwain pressed up against him in a tight hold. The images sped up, and Karl relaxed into the angel's body as bliss took over his being. He moaned into his mouth. Floating, he was floating. And then all the stories began to make sense – he understood it all. Clarity took form in his brain and expanded to embody all of who he was.

My God!

And he meant it. His connection to God was astounding – he *felt* it. He knew his mission, his purpose in life. And he saw himself, as he truly was – he saw his wings. *I have wings!*

The images slowed down, and came to a close, the euphoria fading slightly.

Gwain pulled away. He looked at him, tenderly, compassionately, proudly.

Karl was lost for words, his breathing uneven, still reeling in the rapture that racked his body.

"Take your time," Gwain said softly.

"I-I'm ... there are memories that are ... I'm an angel?"

"You're half-angel. The other half of you is very human. There are many humans with angel DNA in their bloodline, but yours ... the angel within you has always been strong."

"I've always healed quickly; I've never bruised."

Gwain nodded. "You're not quite immortal I'm afraid, but your life expectancy has just increased by about five hundred years."

"No way!"

"Yes way."

He suddenly turned to look behind him. "Do I have wings?"

Gwain laughed. "You young ones always want the dessert before the main meal."

"How old are you?"

"A little over ten thousand years."

Karl whistled.

"Yeah, Roger Daltrey never looked so good ... Right, if you're ready, we have to get going."

"Elena..." As soon as Karl thought of her, everything that had happened made itself known to him. "Oh, no ... I can't believe it..." His heart ached for her.

"Yeah, she's not in a good place."

"How do we save her?"

"With your love for her ... and with this."

Gwain flashed the witching pen in front of his nose.

"How did you—"

"I went back to that rubble of a building right before coming here to get you."

"You can hold the pen?"

"All angels can. That's how you've been able to hold it all this time."

"Why can angels hold the pen?"

"Because, my boy, we're the ones that created it."

~*~

"I've got her!" Amy shouted, almost choking on her second coffee. She ran into the living room, only to see Pueblo and Mary sleeping on the sofa, their heads touching. It caught her unawares, and for a moment her stomach lurched and she felt sick, then she pushed the feeling to the back of her mind and kicked Pueblo in the shin.

"What?!" He jumped up and Mary fell onto the couch.

"I've been working my arse off in the kitchen while you two have been sleeping."

Mary yawned. "And that was the best sleep I've had in months."

Amy scowled. "Well, I've found Elena."

That caught Mary's attention. She was suddenly standing up and striding towards the kitchen, with Amy and her annoying attachment not far behind.

Amy glowered at Pueblo. "Did you sleep well too?"

He gave her a lopsided smile. "Yes, I did, thank you – Mary's got a comfy head."

"Where?" asked Mary, bringing them both back to the reason why they were all here. "Where is she?"

"Here." Amy pointed to the glowing red spot on the map. "Hyde Park – right in the middle, where these three paths make a triangle."

Just then, there was a knock on the door.

They all stopped.

"Amy? Did you do that spell to shield us from Etienne?" whispered Mary.

Amy nodded.

"You guys stay here, I'll go get it."

Mary disappeared. Five seconds later they heard her scream.

Running full speed out of the kitchen, and ready to attack, Amy froze mid-stride and Pueblo ploughed into her from behind.

"I don't believe it," she whispered.

Karl was standing there wearing a white sheet around his waist, with some bloke that looked like he'd had one too many spliffs in his day. From the looks of things, Mary had thrown herself upon him and wasn't about to let go.

"It's you!" she cried out. "It's really you!"

Karl hugged her back. "Yes, it is. Good to see you, Mary."

She finally peeled herself off him, smiling and crying at the same time. "You're so much less dead than the last time we saw you."

"I feel less dead too," he smiled back, then he made his way towards Amy.

"You're Amy, aren't you?"

She nodded. To her surprise, he took her into an embrace. She heard Pueblo let out a small, possessive growl.

"Thank you for helping Elena," said Karl.

Guilt washed over her. Of course she wanted to help Elena, but her part in this had been anything but saintly. She was still warring with her own feelings towards Etienne. She started to shake her head, but Karl interrupted her.

"I know. I know this has been hard for you. Thank you."

Unexpected tears sprang to her eyes. She nodded, and looked at him gratefully.

"Everyone, this is Gwain. He's going to help us get Elena back."

"Wait." said Mary, "How are you even here?"

"I know I owe you all an explanation, but I'm not sure we've got time ... and I'm not sure how ready I am to talk about it, if I'm honest—"

"He's an angel," cut in Pueblo, disdain audible in his voice. "They both are."

Amy and Mary both gawped at Karl in shock.

"Or, we could talk about it *now*," Karl retorted.

"It's all right, Dessec," said Gwain, his coarse, Cockney accent bouncing off the walls. "We've got no war with you – we're here for Elena. We know you are too."

Pueblo nodded, and, thankfully, left it at that, but he didn't look all too happy.

"Angel?" asked Mary.

"Wait," cut in Amy. "Mary, I don't think we do have any time for this. Karl, I've found Elena."

Amy led them all into the kitchen and pointed to the location on the map once more.

Gwain muttered something incoherent under his breath, and looked at them, grimly. "That's a hotspot – a place of convergence. Portals can be opened by using hotspots. She's going to travel to the Shanka's shadow world."

"There are no portals to the Shanka world," said Pueblo. "Lokoli made sure of it – they do not live in a dimension, only in shadows."

"I've got a feeling that may not matter to the most powerful witch in existence."

Karl ran a hand through his hair.

"Yes, my friends," continued Gwain, "Elena is going to create her own portal to the Shanka world, by ripping a hole in reality."

Pueblo looked more than a little alarmed. "She can't do that! That's what they want – they will seep through the rip and fill the Earth with darkness. Even demon tribes will be destroyed, if they have anything to do with it. Why would she do that?"

"Because the only other way to get to their world is through sleep."

Understanding fell across Pueblo's face. "As a young succubus, she will not be able to sleep for weeks, perhaps months now, until she is fully fed."

"And she doesn't want to wait that long."

"Wait..." Amy was trying to take this all in. "So, if she can't travel to their world to kill them, she'll bring them to *our* world to kill them?"

"I don't think that's her intention, Amy. I believe she wants to enter *their* world to kill them, and close the portal behind her."

Karl's face went pale.

"The problem arises if something goes wrong and the portal remains open. If the Shanka go through it, they'll become corporeal on Earth."

Pueblo cursed. "The Shanka are *never* supposed to become corporeal on Earth. They will shower death upon us all."

"We need to get there fast. Amy, is it possible for both you and Pueblo to join your energies and teleport Mary there, as well as yourselves?"

"I think so."

"Good. Karl and I will make our own way."

"You gonna fly?" asked Mary.

Gwain grinned. "Of course."

"Wait," said Amy. She gestured at Pueblo and Karl, then muttered, "*Ornata.*"

Jeans and a T-shirt covered each of them, replacing the loin cloth and the sheet.

"Thanks!" smiled Karl.

"I'm uncomfortable," complained Pueblo.

"Okay, let's go!" Gwain grabbed Karl. "We need to make a detour. We'll meet you guys there."

"Where we going?"

Gwain's face tightened. "A portal to the shadow world has never been created before. I need to find out how to close it, in case she can't."

"Gwain, I can't lose her."

"Let's not think about that, stud. Let's go." And they went out the door.

"Hmmm," said Mary, "I'm kinda disappointed I didn't see them fly."

Amy shrugged. "Your window's too small for them to fit through. Pueblo?"

"I'm ready. Are you feeling strong enough to teleport again?"

"Never better. Will we all need to strip for this?" she asked sarcastically.

He laughed. "No, there should be enough power in both of us to carry our clothes as well as our bodies."

"Well, thank God for that," said Mary. "Guys, what are we actually going to do once we get there?"

"Try and talk Elena out of creating the portal."

"And, what if we're too late and demons are running around everywhere?"

"We fight," said Pueblo. "We'll have no choice. Can you fight?"

"Er, I do kick-boxing – does that count?"

"We'll watch your back."

They all joined hands. Amy felt Pueblo's power seeping into her palm, and she let her own flow into his. With their other hands, they offered their energy to Mary. She took it whether she realised it or not. Her eyes widened. "Holy sh—"

And then they were hurtling through space.

~*~

Elena paced up and down the hotspot, trying to find the exact centre of those currents of energy. All hotspots nestled where three or more ley lines crossed. Today, the magnetic fields in the atmosphere seemed weaker than usual. She needed more of a surge, more power. She wasn't performing a circle-casting, for God's sake, she was about to punch a hole through to another world, and she couldn't wait – couldn't *wait* to see its inhabitants suffer and die. She knew how it would end – oh yes. This wasn't a careless mission. She wasn't being reckless. She didn't want the Earth overrun with Shanka demons. Once she created the portal, she would close it before any demons escaped. The only way to close it was with her own blood. Not much blood, just one drop, falling anywhere within the triangle would do it, coupled with the words from the spell she'd memorised. Through her blood, the portal would also claim her and she would be sucked through it as it closed. And that was the whole idea – she wanted into their world, and this was the quickest way to get there. She was going to annihilate the Shanka on their own turf, and she was going to go down with them. It was the only acceptable redemption, really, for what she did to ... him.

Grief fell on her hard and fast. She called on her anger instead and let it overtake any other emotion. Grief had no place in the heart of a Shanka demon. Especially not one that was going to kill them all.

She looked at the horizon and guessed it was about half past six in the morning – the sun would be rising soon. The park was already open – it opened at five – but was relatively empty. Most who came across her hurried away in the opposite direction. A young couple, obviously very much in love, thought she was pavement entertainment, and tossed her a pound coin. She had to force herself to focus on the reason why she was here, so she wouldn't shred them to pieces.

A familiar sensation crept up her spine.

It's here! I've found it!

She wasted no time. She stood at the centre of the hotspot and power surged through her; she barely had to call on it at all. She raised her right hand.

"Gladium meum."

A dagger materialised in her palm, and she closed her hand around the cool metal.

"Aperite ostium meum sanguinem, ad tenebris umbram saeculi!"

Under her feet, the Earth seemed to tremble just a little.

She brought the blade down to her wrist and slashed it once, a small, clean cut. A second later, red seeped through the slice in her demon skin, looking like a welcome flood on dry, arid plains. She let her arm hang, and waited for the needed drop to hit the ground.

"No!" came a scream from behind her.

She turned and saw Amy, Mary, and a dark-skinned guy she'd never seen before. The cry came from Mary. Amy ran towards her. Elena didn't think, but sent her flying backwards with a wave of her hand. She landed on the guy, who grunted at her weight, but didn't fall – didn't even stumble – which had Elena wondering if he was human.

"Karl's alive!"

She froze.

It wasn't possible! She could feel him inside her – the glow she'd stolen from him – his soul. He couldn't *be* alive. There'd been no pulse.

"Karl's alive!" cried Mary, again. "He's on his way now."

Logic fought instinct within Elena, but the hope had already flared in her heart, confusing all her senses. If he was alive...

Too late, she felt the drop of blood tickle her skin as its small weight left the end of her finger. *"No,"* she whispered, but the little droplet followed gravity's command, not hers. It hit the ground.

A blast of light, so bright it hurt her eyes, threw her on her backside. Amy, Mary and the man, rushed to her side. The four of them stared into the space, a few feet above the ground, where the portal appeared. It did, in fact, look like a huge rip in the sky. The rip itself was a dark purple, like a bruise; the colour of the air surrounding it, a cobalt blue, all of it crackling and rippling, like lightning upon waves. It would have been a morbid beauty had none of them known what it actually meant.

Reality came crashing down upon Elena, and with it the realisation of the only possible outcome. "What have I done? Mary ... is Karl really...?" She couldn't even say the word.

Mary nodded.

"We have to be ready. The Shanka will be coming through any second." That was the man talking. He looked positively furious.

"I can close it. I can close the portal." She tightened her hold on dagger. "Mary, tell Karl I'm sorry."

"Tell him yourself."

Elena merely shook her head, fighting back tears, and brought the blade down—

"Elena!"

Oh, God!

She couldn't help it – not one hundred horses dragging her in the opposite direction would have stopped her from turning towards that voice in that second.

There he was. Alive.

His face was a mask of fear and desperation as he looked up at the gaping hole above them.

He knows ... he knows what happens next...

And then he was there, in front of her, taking her in his arms. She sagged into him. Her world lit up and died at the same time.

An older man stood behind him, a grim look on his face. "What a mess you've made, young lady," he tutted.

"I can fix it."

"No!" said Karl, bringing her closer into him.

She looked up at him, suddenly too aware and ashamed of how she looked. "Karl ... I never thought I'd see you again. And I'm so glad I'm able to. I'm so, so sorry."

"Ssshh. You didn't know – none of us did."

"Let me fix this – I'm the only one who can."

The older man put his hand on Karl's shoulder. "There's no other choice, son. We're too late."

Karl nodded, but the sobs he fought to contain threatened to rack his body.

"They're coming! Hurry!"

She turned to see shadows moving on the other side of the portal. Elena held the knife over her wrist once more, and pressed down. But before it could break skin, it went hurtling from her grasp through the air. "What...?"

They all turned to find Etienne standing a few metres away, now holding the knife.

"Etienne ... why?" called out Amy, confusion in her voice, and something else ... grief. Elena would recognise that emotion anywhere.

He said nothing.

A look passed between Elena and himself, and Elena felt her anger return ... *Grandfather.*

Pueblo gave a shout, or maybe it was a war-cry.

The first Shanka demon fell through the portal, closely followed by two more, and all hell broke loose.

Chapter Eleven

Karl couldn't fly yet, not really. He couldn't even make his wings appear. Gwain had carried him wherever they went, which left him reeling at how strong the angel actually was. He'd had that moment of clarity at the morgue, when everything had been revealed and the world had made sense. It had lasted seconds, and now he was as befuddled as before. In some ways, he felt even more useless. He was an angel, or half an angel, but he still couldn't get his head around that. And he was trying very hard not to blubber like a pansy about Elena having to sacrifice herself to save the world, but he wasn't having much luck with that either.

Still, demons were coming at them from all angles now, and when backed into a corner, his instincts came alive. His only thought was to protect them all, and the thought seemed to surge from his chest, rather than his head – it always had. Only this time, it *literally* surged from his chest, surrounding them all in a golden light. The light acted as a shield, pushing every Shanka it could to the periphery of the light.

"Er ... Karl?" voiced Elena.

"Yeah – Elena, there are a few things we have to talk about."

They all stood within the shield, looking out as more and more of the Shanka fell through the portal. As a unit, they honed in on Elena, and began to pound the shield.

Karl grimaced, each pound sending a blast of pain into his solar plexus.

Pueblo and Mary looked at each other, seemed to make a silent decision, then jumped out of the shield and began fighting demons. Pueblo, unsurprisingly, moved like a pro, but Mary ... he had to hand it to the tall brunette – she was awesome ... and different. Something was definitely different about her, but he couldn't tell if she had changed, or if his new angelic eyes were seeing something he'd never noticed before.

He couldn't tell where Amy was at first, then realised she was having an argument with the white-haired man. His angel-mind understood straight away that this was Elena's grandfather. And it was clear that he meant something important to Amy.

Gwain seemed to have disappeared.

Mary cried out as one of the demons threw her face down onto the ground. He straddled her back, grabbing her head to smash it down. Elena left his side and was upon the Shanka in the time it took to blink, sending them both sprawling away from Mary, who simply got up, dusted herself down and carried on sparring.

With his shield mostly redundant now everyone was outside it fighting, he focused the best he could, pulled it back into himself, then jumped into the foray with everyone else.

~*~

Amy was more upset than she'd like to admit.

"Etienne, *why?* Elena was going to close the portal."

"It will also suck her in through it when she does."

So *that* was her sacrifice for creating the portal – she knew there'd be one. She flinched at the thought of Elena, forever a prisoner in the Shanka's world. Poor Elena ... poor Karl.

As much as Amy didn't want that to happen, she wasn't naïve enough to think that Etienne had Elena's best intentions at heart.

"You're the one that wanted to erase her from history, remember?"

"I want to erase *demons* from history. I did a little research since you told me the Dessec were not cooperative. It turns out, that with Elena's great power as a witch and half-demon harnessed, I can use it to destroy *all* the Shanka. She is of use yet."

She inwardly cringed at how his bigotry overshadowed everything else.

"At the expense of this portal killing us all first!" She looked around at her friends. They all had their hands full, and the number of demons was just increasing. "Etienne, you've not always been like this. Are you really so focused on your prejudice that you'll endanger the entire world, to see your hatred of demons satisfied? We *have* to close the portal."

"Oh, yes, Amy, we do – I completely agree."

"Then let me take the dagger back to Elena."

Instead he gripped her arm, his hold vice-like.

"Ouch! You're hurting me!"

"The direct translation of the instructions to create a portal are as follows:

only a witch by her blood shall open the door; only a witch by her blood shall close the door behind her.

"It doesn't specify which witch."

Horror froze her insides. "No..."

He brought the blade down to her wrist.

"No!"

She sent a blast of power into him, but he was fully expecting it and had already shielded himself. So she kicked him in the shin instead, as hard as she could.

He stumbled and groaned, but tightened his hold on her arm. In his other hand his fingers whitened as he gripped the dagger, and then it was slicing her arm. It went deep and her scream filled the air.

Everything seemed to still for a minute – all sounds of fighting stopped. Pueblo cried out her name and started running towards her, but Etienne sent him flying with nothing more than a thought. And then all chaos resumed, the shouting louder and more urgent than before, from humans and demons alike. She looked for Elena, probably the only person who could fight Etienne, but she was already fighting off about six demons ... my God, they really were out-numbered.

She struggled with everything she had, but was also scared that her struggling would move her arm in such a way that the blood would fall sooner.

Etienne simply laughed and threw her on the ground with himself on top of her, holding her down with his body, as he held her arm up above her head. The blood trickled down her arm at an alarming pace. He did cut deep – there was so much of it. Seconds ... her life as she knew it would be over in seconds.

"Why are you doing this?"

His eyes hardened as he looked at her, disgust colouring his features. "You took him into you," he spat out. "I trusted you and you drank his blood!"

Even with his evident loathing of her, his eyes still shone with tears. "You're nothing but a demon whore!"

Tears fell from her own eyes. She shouldn't have given him the satisfaction, but love was a funny thing. He had been like a father to her her entire life – to hear those words directed at her with such repulsion was more than she could bear.

"I'm so sorry," she whispered.

His eyes softened for a second, then grew harder than before. He began to chant.

~*~

Elena was exhausted, as well as beside herself at what was about to happen. They were also fighting more demons than they could handle, and they kept on coming. She used her magic whenever she could, but more often than not, she got knocked from behind, or from the left, or right, before she could even finish a thought-form. They were all battered and bruised – well, except for Karl, who didn't bruise. But he looked like he was about to collapse.

Pueblo – or at least she assumed that was his name, since she'd heard it being directed at him several times – was desperately trying to reach Amy, but like her, he got knocked back with every step he took.

Then Elena heard Etienne begin to speak the words that would close the portal.

Oh, God! Amy!

And then she heard another, familiar voice, chant with him. She caught Etienne's look of surprise, just before she turned to find the source of the voice herself.

Her mother stood directly on the hotspot, below the portal, a shield of protection surrounding her, keeping everyone away. Unlike the rest of them, she looked refreshed and calm. Clearly none of them had noticed her teleport in. What Elena did notice – what no one could miss – was the knife in her hand, the blade glinting red. Her wound ran straight down her wrist in a long gash.

"Mum..."

The last word of the spell left her lips, and her blood hit the ground half a second before Amy's did.

"No!" she heard Etienne shout.

The Earth began to tremble and the portal expanded and contracted, expanded and contracted...

The Shanka scrambled over each other to get away from it, but the portal was like a giant Shanka magnet, and they all found themselves being pulled upwards, toward it.

At that moment, a man flew – yes, *flew* – from the opening onto the ground, with a very impressive sword in one hand, and ... Nathaniel's head in the other.

"Oh, my God!" she found herself saying, partly because of what he was holding and partly because of his *wings!* He had *wings!*

"Gwain!" exclaimed Karl.

He knows him?

You went into their world?" he asked, in an unbelieving tone.

Gwain simply shrugged and smiled at the head, which he held like a trophy. "We had business, him and me. I've been waiting for this opportunity for a long time – I wasn't going to waste it."

The demons looked at their King's head in horror and fury, but there was nothing they could do about it. They disappeared one by one back into their shadow world. And then Elena felt herself being pulled towards the opening and screamed!

Karl grabbed her hand, and yanked her back down, showering light around them both.

"It wants me."

"Because of your Shanka half. Don't let go of me."

She didn't.

He held her fast, increasing the glow around them, until she couldn't feel the pull anymore.

Elena stared at her mother. There were so many things to say ... none of them could be said in just a few seconds. So she said the only thing that could. "I love you."

Her brown eyes, a shade lighter than Elena's owned, shimmered in tears of gratitude. "It's been so long since you've said that to me."

"I don't want you to go," she said in a small voice, suddenly six years old again.

"I know, baby. I wish I could hold you right now."

Instinctively, Elena stepped forward, but Karl pulled her back.

"You can't," he said, his voice pained. "I'm sorry."

Her mum looked at Karl, and smiled a smile she'd not seen for almost twenty years. "You look after her, boy."

He nodded.

Then her mum looked at Gwain, and at the head he was holding. A silent understanding passed between them.

They know each other.

Elena suddenly realised that she was witnessing something she wasn't privy to. Reading her mother's diary, it had hit her personally. Without even realising it, she had made it all about her – it never once occurred to her, in her traumatised state, that it was *her mother's* diary. It wasn't about Elena at all. It was about her mother – her mother's life. Something she didn't know very much about, and would now never get the chance to.

The last Shanka demon was sucked through the opening.

Her mum looked at her, one final time, and beamed with joy, even as tears fell down her cheeks. "I'm *so* proud of you, Elena."

And then her body was jerked backwards through the eye of the portal, it closed down on itself, and both portal and witch were gone.

Elena turned away, beside herself, and sobbed into Karl's chest.

Everyone grouped together in shock, not knowing what to do or say next ... until Pueblo's strained voice broke through the silence. "Where is Amy?"

All eyes fell to the spot where her and Etienne had been. Her blood stained the ground. Neither of them were anywhere to be seen.

"He's got her," said Pueblo. "He's taken her ... somewhere protected. I can't sense her."

Mary placed a hand on his shoulder. "We'll find her ... but we all need to rest."

He nodded, his face grim. "You all rest. I'm going to start searching now." And he dematerialised.

"Mary, can we all use your flat to regroup?" asked Karl.

She nodded, and the four of them, too tired to travel by any other means, and looking like the cast from a B-horror movie set, walked eastwards towards the now rising sun, and towards the gates that would lead them out of Hyde Park.

Epilogue

The rest of the week went by very slowly. Despite them all having so much to come to terms with, they were also mourning the two souls that they'd lost.

Pueblo had made it his personal mission to search for Amy – he spent every waking hour looking for a clue as to her whereabouts. Unfortunately, every clue he found led to a dead end.

They couldn't all stay at Mary's house, so Karl and Elena had moved into Karl's parents' house, which had been empty for little over a month since the last tenants moved out.

Mary had all but forced Elena to take the week off work, to which she had no choice because her skin was still cracked and her eyes were still bright green. But Elena had another problem. She was now fully awakened to her succubus Shanka half ... and it was hungry. So Karl had phoned John, his second in command at the shop, and arranged to have the week off as well. They both spent most of their days naked, Elena needing satiating at least every four hours.

Needless to say, she was reluctant to even go near Karl again after what she had done to him, but her demon's needs couldn't be ignored, and won out each time. Besides, he was an angel now – something which blew her away, but at the same time seemed to make perfect sense. His angel half could handle her succubus half, for which her very hungry, newling succubus half was grateful. Every time they made love, he glowed gold light – he didn't mean to, it just happened. "Love," Gwain had said, as a way of explanation, and that was all he'd said.

Karl's light kept her shadow back, and her succubus from losing control. It also gave her super-powerful orgasms – something else for which her succubus half was grateful. In fact, Elena was pretty damn sure her succubus was as much in love with Karl's angel, as their two human halves were.

Now lying, curled up in his arms on the living room floor, she took one of those rare moments, where she allowed all thoughts to fly out of her head, so she could solely concentrate on how wonderful it felt to be with him. The moments never lasted long – merely seconds – because guilt always crept in to rule her heart.

"Karl?"

"Mmmm?"

"I need to get her back."

She felt his arms stiffen around her.

"I know you won't want me to go, but I can't leave her there; I just can't."

"I know, darling ... I know. I'll go with you. We'll see if Gwain can, too."

She nodded her thanks.

"It should have been me."

"Sshhh..."

"I don't understand how you can all forgive me, after everything that I've done, everything I put you through..."

"Well, I'm not sure Pueblo *has* forgiven you ... but you'll always have my forgiveness," he said softly.

She squeezed his hand in silent thanks. "I wonder where Amy is ... what Etienne's doing to her."

"I know."

"My father was a demon; my grandfather's crazy ... no wonder I lost it. I think I'm totally fucked up sometimes."

"Look at your skin, Elena."

She looked down.

"See? The cracks are disappearing, and your colour's coming back."

It was true. They had noticed that the more contact she had with Karl's glowing self, the less demon she became.

"Just a few more days, I reckon, before you look like your old self. You're not fucked up – you've just had a lot to take in all at once. What you learned about yourself – how it all happened – it would send anyone around the bend."

"What about you? You're an *angel.*"

He laughed. "Outrageous, isn't it?"

"Actually, I think it makes perfect sense. I've always teased you about being saintly."

"And I teased you about becoming a wanton harlot – guess we were both right."

"Hey!" She elbowed him in the stomach, which earned her a small groan, then she turned to face him.

"What happens to the witching pen now?"

"I'm not sure. Gwain's told me next to nothing – just that the angels created it, which is why I've been able to hold it, and that it was going to help save you. I don't remember seeing him use it, and as far as I know, he still has it – he can keep it as far as I'm concerned."

She nodded. She didn't much care if she never saw it again, but something told her that wouldn't be the case.

She cuddled up closer to him. "So ... what d'you wanna do now?" she asked, coyly.

Amusement crossed his features. "Don't tell me you're ready to go again?"

"Of course I am."

"Well, I'm spent."

"Liar – you're glowing already."

"Damn glow ... hey, wanna see something cool?"

"Always."

He rolled her on her back, and lay on top of her. "I learned how to do it today ... Ready?"

She nodded.

Wings erupted from his back.

She squealed in delight! "Oh, my ... they're beautiful!"

She meant it. They were enormous, the feathers mostly white, but they shimmered a light blue whenever the light caught them.

He stretched them full, and she gasped. They reached from one end of the living room to another.

There was a crash as he knocked something over.

"Oh," he grimaced. "That better not have been the Byzantine vase."

Elena was in awe, still staring.

"You like?"

"Oh yes."

"I can't wait to learn how to fly – I can't wait to take you flying," he smiled.

"In the meantime..." She shifted beneath him, rubbing her body against his.

He leaned down and kissed her, pulling his wings back in.

"No," she whispered. "Leave them out ... please."

"Kinky."

She laughed. "You've seen all of my demon – I want to see all of your angel."

He rubbed her nose with his.

Her mind flashed back to Saturday night, when he'd done the same thing, both of them lying on the couch of their now ruined flat. Had that only been six days ago?

Guilt rode her once again, as she suddenly thought of that poor man who had lived in the basement flat. Another death she was responsible for ... she'd only spoken to him a couple of times...

Then she found herself wrapped up in Karl's glow, it washing away any dark feeling harbouring within her.

"All of me belongs to you Elena – it always has."

Her eyes welled up and he kissed her again.

Elena looked up at his wings, thought of that butterfly once more, and smiled.

~*~

She stood in the middle of the desert, shivering. It was so cold – she couldn't believe how cold it was, and she wondered why it was, because the sun was beating down on her. She should have been sweating and blistering, not trying to fight off hypothermia.

Instinctively, she looked for what she knew would keep her warm. Where was it? Where was it when she needed it? And then she caught sight of the huge, black cat, its coat wondrous, and glossy like silk; its eyes yellow and strong.

"Hey," she called out, softly, extending her hand. If she could just touch it, if she could just hold it, she'd be warm, and she'd be safe ... and she wouldn't be alone anymore.

"Here, kitty."

The panther's tongue lolled out, as if it was pleased to see her, its amber eyes glinting in the sunlight.

It was so close now...

And then the snow leopard attacked. She screamed at the panther to get away, but she was too late, and the leopard landed on its back, claws and teeth ripping. Blood matted both their coats, and she sat frozen to the spot. She'd always be cold now – if the panther died, she'd always be cold.

The leopard turned towards her, leaving the panther writhing on the sand in pain. She wanted to reach it, hold it, but her shivering was uncontrollable and prevented any steady movement. The leopard stood over her now, emitting no warmth, and looking hungry.

Maybe it's going to eat me, she thought.

Instead it sniffed at her neck, rolled its tongue out and licked her face. She would have thought it was an act of care if she hadn't felt so cold; nevertheless, she was surprised. She reached out as slowly as she could. Maybe she could trust it ... maybe—

It slashed her arm with its claw, and she screamed, staring in horror at the bleeding gash on her wrist.

Then the leopard jumped on her with its huge paws, pushing her backwards onto the sand. It towered over her, baring its teeth...

Oh, my God ... it is *going to eat me...*

She awoke from the same nightmare for the third night in a row, her sheets damp and twisted around her waist, a scream lodged in her throat, tears matting her hair to her face.

She struggled for breath, taking a while to realise she wasn't stranded out in some desert, but here, in this room – this room she didn't know. She had no recollection of anything, no memory of who she was, what she did – she hadn't even remembered what she looked like until she'd seen herself in the mirror, for what may as well have been the first time, just three days ago. She winced slightly, as pain made itself known to her, and realised she was clutching at her wounded wrist. It had bled a little again, a bit of red seeping through the bandages. She had been told, she tried to commit suicide. She wished she could remember.

She scrambled off the bed and looked in the mirror again, hoping desperately to jog some kind of memory, anything familiar, anything at all...

There was nothing.

The odd thing was, in the dream, she always seemed to know who she was – she could never get at her name, but she knew who she was within herself. She had a life and a purpose, and she knew, without a shadow of a doubt, that it had to do with the black panther. Somehow, that cat existed in real life, and she had to find it.

There was a knock on the door.

"Come in," she croaked out.

A head of dark brown hair appeared between the door and frame.

"Are you all right? I heard movement."

"Paul ... I'm fine, thank you."

He came in anyway ... which irritated her a little.

"Are you sure? You're still healing..."

"It was just a bad dream."

"The same one as before?"

She sighed, wishing she'd never told him about the nightmare the first time she'd had it. But he was all she knew now. Her first memory of this new life, which may as well be her first memory ever, was Paul. The man who had found her three days ago, and saved her from killing herself.

"I ... I'm sorry, Paul, I just don't really want to talk about it."

"Of course, Elizabeth, I understand."

Elizabeth. Really?

The name sounded so foreign to her. He'd told her that was her name. Paul was, apparently, her husband. But the name sounded wrong, it felt wrong that she was married, and the ring weighing down her finger also felt wrong.

To Paul's credit, he'd given her her own room and left her to her own devices. Thank God. She wasn't ready to get personal with someone she couldn't remember.

"Thanks for checking, though," she smiled.

He smiled back, hesitated, then leaned in and gave her a quick hug.

She didn't flinch, only because she'd practised how not to over the past few days. But every time he touched her, she felt a chill right through to her bone.

He left the room and shut the door behind him.

She made her way to the window, knowing she'd never be able to get back to sleep, and looked out over the scenery. She was greeted by snow-capped mountains, deep green valleys, and misty blue lakes. They spanned all around her. At any other time, or maybe in the lifetime that she couldn't remember, she would have found it all breathtakingly beautiful. Right now, she found it cold and lonely. It made her feel trapped. She longed for the sand and sun from her dreams ... and the panther – she longed for him too.

Him?

Yes – it felt like a 'he'.

"Where are you?" she whispered out the window, wondering if some kind of magic could carry that whisper over the mountains to whatever lay beyond. Maybe he would hear her, if she believed hard enough...

"Where are you?"

About The Author

Dianna Hardy is a UK-based, independent author of occult writings, gothic poetry, adult urban/dark fantasy and paranormal romance. As well as *The Witching Pen Novellas*, she is working on *The Last Angel* spin-off novel, all of which will bring demons and angels together, in an Earth-shattering way.

Dianna resides in Surrey with her husband and daughter.

Official site:
www.diannahardy.com

Wilted
(A Witching Pen Novellas Prequel)

This short story, specifically created for fans of the series, takes place ten years before the events of The Witching Pen Novellas.

Also available in digital format, from Bitten Fruit Books.

~*~

Elena stared at the daffodils in her window box. They were starting to wilt, as if the weight of the grey sky was pushing down on them. She hated it when flowers wilted – they looked so sad that way, as if they were crying and no one could tell.

The energy in her body hummed and coursed towards her palms, lighting them with the subtle green glow she was so familiar with. Instinctively, she walked towards her window.

Surely this isn't the same as bringing an animal back to life, right? This is a plant – plants are different.

Who was she trying to convince? She damn well knew that if her mother found out, she'd be in for it big time. Still...

She leaned across her sill, and hovered over the window box, her hands coming up of their own accord, or so it seemed. Bollocks to it, she just couldn't help it – this is what she did best: heal things. Bringing one, tiny plant back to life could hardly unbalance the world, could it?

Her hands glowed more brightly.

A car sped by in the road below, reflecting its colour in the window as it did so. She ignored it, but was startled out of both her thoughts and her healing trance, when across the street and five doors down, Karl came – half-running and half-limping – out of his house. A tirade of verbal abuse followed him, tingeing the air with its malice.

One glance at her best friend's stricken face was enough to have her hurtling out of her room and down the stairs, already opening the front door with her magic.

Another thing mum would kill me for, she winced. *Mustn't use magic frivolously.*

Her heart hammered in her chest. Karl never looked distressed – not even at the worst of times. She was the panicky one – he was the rock.

She reached the front door, just before he reached the steps leading up to her porch.

"Elena..." he panted.

"God, Karl, what is it?"

"Dad..."

And that was all he needed to say.

Elena ushered him in, closing the door behind him. His legs didn't seem to be holding him up too well, and when he stumbled over his own feet, Elena caught him under the arm, and offered him her shoulder. She might be two years younger than him, but at fifteen, she was tall – almost as tall as Karl – and her wiry body, which she so often hated when looking at her friends' blooming breasts and hips, always surprised her with a physical strength it didn't look like it should be capable of.

Karl's dad had beaten him; she was sure of it, despite her not being able to see any bruises.

"We need to go to my room," she told him.

He groaned as he glanced at the stairs. "I don't know if I can climb..."

"Mum'll be back soon, and you know how she gets when you're around. We'll have more privacy up there. Come on – lean on me."

Although he clearly hated the idea of putting his weight on her, he did it anyway, and allowed her to support him as he dragged his feet up the steps. When they finally made it to her room, he tumbled inside and aimed straight for the bed, where he lay on his back, hands covering his eyes. They were shaking slightly. Elena wondered if he was trying not to cry.

She closed her bedroom door, and stuck her dressing table chair under the handle for good measure – her mum could be a little unpredictable when Karl was around, and without a doubt, she'd be able to sense he was in the house as soon as she got home.

She perched on the edge of her bed, with her hands on her lap, and waited.

Eventually, Karl's trembling ceased. When he looked at her, his blue eyes burned hot, making him look like he had a fever. He was holding back tears.

Her own eyes welled up in response. "I'm so sorry."

He took her right hand in his. His touch was gentle, but when he spoke, his voice broke with anger. "Don't you *ever* apologise for him. Fucking bastard."

She flinched. Karl didn't get angry often. He avoided anger like the plague, because anger was everything his father was, and everything he swore he'd never be.

She squeezed his hand in comfort. "What happened?"

He bit his lip, shook his head, and then took in a deep breath. "Mum knocked over his whisky glass. It broke. He went mental – he hit her, then pushed her onto the shards of glass on the floor." His voice went up a notch as he forced the words out. "I lost it ... I lost it, Elena."

"It's not your fault."

"I grabbed his shirt, pulled him off her, and barrelled him into the kitchen away from her. I got a good punch in, but ... well, look at me..."

Karl wasn't exactly a buff seventeen-year-old, despite all the time he spent on the athletics track – he was only just starting to fill out. Maybe in a few years he'd have a chest as wide as his outstretched arm – his ex-army father certainly did – but not yet.

"He pounded me. When he'd brought me to my knees, he started kicking me in the stomach, then ... *Christ...*" He ran a hand through his sandy blond hair. "He started *jumping* on me – he jumped on my legs."

Elena grimaced at his story, and then realised she was squeezing his hand too tightly – or maybe he was the one squeezing.

"He just kept jumping. He didn't stop until the phone rang. I can't believe I walked out of there."

"Actually, you sort of stumbled," she said, in a vague attempt to lighten his mood. Anyone else would probably think the remark callous, but Karl knew her like the back of his hand.

His lips tilted upwards in a small smile. "I did stumble, didn't I?"

She nodded. "Like your legs were made of dental floss."

He laughed. "What a sight for all our neighbours."

"I don't think anyone else saw."

"I'm sure they heard."

She placed a hand on his thigh.

He winced.

"Can I see your legs? I can heal them."

"I was sort of hoping you'd offer ... but I hate asking you..."

"Don't be daft. Always ask, okay?"

He shot her a grateful look, and then undid his trousers. With a cry of agony, he lifted his hips up and slid them down over his backside.

Elena pulled them the rest of the way down to his ankles, ignoring the building heat in her cheeks. It had not escaped her notice that in the past few weeks, she would occasionally become flustered around her best friend, and she had a sneaky suspicion she knew what that meant. But it was also a little startling, and more than a little frightening, because they'd known each other since she was five and he was seven. They'd shared paddling pools and baths; they'd shared popcorn at the cinema, and pizzas over homework ... it was a friendship she couldn't bear to lose.

Pushing the thoughts out of her head, and hoping her face wasn't noticeably red, she brought her attention back to Karl's legs.

"There's not a mark on them," she stated, and she wasn't surprised. Karl was one of those people that just didn't bruise. In all the time she'd known him, she'd never seen a bruise on him once. A cut, yes – he bled like a normal person – but even his cuts had never welted blue and purple around the edges.

"Well, the bones feel broken," he said, his voice laced with pain.

"Okay ... keep still." She lay both her hands on him, one on each thigh, again ignoring the way her heart sped up a fraction. Closing her eyes, she concentrated on the energy that so naturally flowed from her palms. It was warm – beautifully warm. She worked with it, the energy and her in unison. It travelled out of her and into him, and in a way, so did she. In her mind's eyes, she saw her green, healing glow wrap itself around his legs like bandages, the light seeping into him, connecting with nerve and muscle ... but she needed to go deeper to mend bones. Focusing harder, she pushed further ... strange ... the bones didn't *seem* broken... Nevermind – the healing couldn't hurt, so she sent it into his bones as well. The sensation was actually a little shocking; she was so deep inside him. She worried her bottom lip with her teeth – was that her breathing that had turned ragged?

"Elena..."

She felt a tug on her wrist, and with effort, mentally disengaged herself from Karl.

"Elena, stop now..."

"I am ... give me a minute."

Whoa ... she felt hot. She could do with a drink of water.

When she opened her eyes, they rested on her friend's face. The look on it froze her to the spot, even as his gaze burned into her. His eyes were hooded, his lips parted, his chest rising and falling in rapid succession, his blushing neck the colour of a red sunset.

Her stomach lurched, and her hands gripped his thighs tighter of their own accord.

He also tightened his hold on her wrist. "Elena," he whispered, "please let go."

Confused, she looked down at her own hands, and had to practically will her fingers to uncurl. At the same time, she suddenly noticed that, at some point, he had thrown a corner of the duvet across himself, and he now held it firmly over his boxers as if his life depended on it.

Oh, God!

"Okay," she squeaked, and all but threw herself up to standing. "I'm sorry," she blurted out.

His eyebrows furrowed. "No, don't be sorry ... it's fine – I'm fine. I just need to think of ... er..."

"Horrible things that make you want to puke?"

He looked at her, amused. "Yeah. Margaret Thatcher in a bikini, for example..."

She giggled. "Your dad in a bikini?" she offered.

"It would suit him better than the whisky," he retorted.

He leaned forward for his trousers. "My legs feel better – there's still pain, but it's less – thank you," he smiled at her.

"Good," she nodded.

There was an awkward pause. Her heart sank. They rarely had awkward pauses ... was this the beginning of the end? It was no secret that Karl had 'feelings' for her, although they never talked about it. What *was* very much a secret, was that it seemed she was developing feelings for him too. What did she do with these? If it meant the end of their easy, close friendship, she was ready to bury them forever. God help her, he was the closest thing to ... *anything* ... that she had in this world. When she had started her period two years ago, it hadn't been her cold, unfeeling mother, she'd gone running to first ... it had been Karl. She couldn't lose him – she just couldn't.

His attention-grabbing cough brought her out of her silent distress. He had the waistband of his jeans in one hand, still clutched the duvet with his other, and was looking at her quizzically. "Do you think you could..."

"Oh! Right, of course," she swivelled around to face the door so he could dress himself, the rustling denim and sliding zipper sounding ridiculously loud as he did so.

"So, what's going to happen when you go back home?" she asked, glad to steer her thoughts – both their thoughts – onto a different path.

Karl snorted. "Dad will be slumped in front of the TV ignoring everything but the football, and Mum will be fussing over him, pretending nothing even happened."

"And what will you do?"

"Eat pizza with you. It's Thursday – study night. You're still coming over after dinner, right?"

Relief melted her insides. Their study nights were utterly pointless for him, because he was two years ahead of her and knew everything anyway, but he still insisted they have them, and if he wanted to meet tonight, that meant all wasn't lost.

She whirled around, unable to stop tears from springing to her eyes. "So we're still friends?"

He looked at her, surprised, and then his face softened as he walked towards her and briefly took her in his arms. "Of course we are, idiot."

She guffawed.

"I'm sorry I..." he paused, then met her gaze with nothing but openness and honesty. "I find it hard to control myself around you sometimes. But you don't have to worry."

He flashed her that smile she knew so well, and for the first time she could ever remember, it made her insides go gooey.

"You don't have to control yourself all the time." It was out of her mouth before she could stop it. Sirens went off in her head.

What the hell did you just say?!

His smile faltered, and that same look he gave her on the bed resurfaced for a second before he fought it back. "Erm..." He looked confused.

She was more confused ... especially when the next thing she did was take a step towards him so she was right up against his chest.

Earth to Elena! What are you doing*?*

What *was* she doing? She had no idea. It was as if something inside her was ruling the show, leading her legs, controlling her lips, which had now parted and hovered just centimetres from his.

Karl's hands encircled her waist – maybe he meant to push her away, but instead, he just seemed to become as rooted to the spot as she.

Her heart thudded, pulsing blood through her veins at the speed of a gale. The roar in her ears was deafening. She could feel the air between their lips thicken, become electric...

Karl let out a little moan, and without warning, his hands slid up her back; fingers caressed her long, dark hair, tugging at the strands, tilting her head back... He lowered his mouth, their noses brushed together—

"Elena!" Her mother's shrill voice from the bottom of the stairs shattered the moment, and that 'something' inside Elena screamed in rage. It was momentary, and then the panic set in.

They stared at each other in shock, then leapt apart. Working in synchronicity, Karl straightened the bed, as Elena removed the chair from under the door. She smoothed her hair down; he smoothed his T-shirt down. Her mother's heels sounded outside the door.

"Mum?" Elena called out, trying her best to sound casual. "Come in."

Katherine Green, mother turned stranger, opened the door. She stared at Karl, icily. "I thought you might be here." Her clipped tone cut through the still lingering heat in the air, and Elena hoped to God she couldn't sense what had just taken place.

Her hope died when she saw her mother's eyes narrow, then widen slightly in surprise, before becoming clouded with an expression she couldn't name.

"I bought us Chinese, Elena. It'll be ready in fifteen minutes." She turned back to Karl. "I trust you're just leaving, boy?"

Elena caught the clench of Karl's jaw out of the corner of her eye, and her own anger swelled, although for the moment, it wasn't quite as imminent as her sense of panic. Karl hated being referred to as 'boy' and her mother knew it – which is why she did it. It was a dig at his too young looks, his too smooth chin ... his inadequacy in general. Of course, he wasn't inadequate at all, but what an awful thing to make him feel, when she knew the family issues he struggled with on a daily basis.

Elena steamed. She wondered if her mother wanted her to hate her, because this was the right way to go about it.

"Yes, I was, Mrs Green."

Considering the way he was feeling when he'd first stumbled into her house, Elena thought it a small miracle his voice was as steady as it was right now.

He turned to her. "I'll see you after dinner for study?" he asked, gently.

"I'll be there," she replied with a smile.

Karl held her gaze a second longer, then strode past Elena's mother, and down the stairs. For some inane reason, she felt like crying when she heard the front door shut behind him.

She looked back at her mother, and thought she caught sorrow in her eyes, but then it suddenly wasn't there and she was sure she must have imagined it.

"Fifteen minutes, Elena," came the curt order, as she swivelled and walked out of the room, then, "We have a few things to talk about."

Great.

Just great.

~*~

Nowadays, dinner – which they always ate at the breakfast table, because the dining room was her mother's second office – was the only time she and her mum ever talked. It hadn't always been that way, but Elena had committed a fatal crime when she was eight years old: she had brought a butterfly back from the dead. Of course, it was by accident. She'd seen it wilt in flight; she'd seen it fall. At eight years old, she hadn't been able to bear the sadness of it. She'd held out her hand, and the falling butterfly had landed in her palm. She had surrounded its still form in green light, felt life flow through her and into it; it had fluttered its wings once more and then flown away. It had been the first time her hands had ever glowed – the first time she had ever used her healing magic – and it had been nothing but pure instinct. Her mother had told her she was special – had told her about how she was a witch with a lot of power, but not in a million years would she have dreamed she could do *that*.

Karl had been with her. His ten-year-old self had been struck dumb, as they'd both watched the tiny creature climb the air currents towards the rays of the sun. She had turned towards him, beamed him a joyful smile, and giggled at the look of adoration on his face.

"You gave it wings," he had said, awed. Then he had leaned in, pecked her on the cheek, and said, "I love you," to which her giggle had turned into unrestrained laughter.

Her joy had plummeted as fast as it had soared when she'd caught sight of her mother off to the right, standing under a Willow tree. She knew instantly that she had seen the entire thing.

When she'd finally approached them, her face had been expressionless and for the first time ever, her eyes had been cold ... and without being able to put it into words, Elena had known at that moment, that by giving life to the butterfly, she had killed a part of her mother. If she had known that would be the last time she'd see her laugh, or the last time they'd ever sing songs together as they sat on the swings in the park, she would have let the butterfly die.

"I need to talk to you, Elena, about sex." Her mother's voice brought her out of her reverie, and she was disturbed to find her heart heavy with sorrow at the past memories. Then she realised what her mum had just said.

"Eeew, Mum," she mumbled over her last forkful of noodles.

"No interruptions, please. I've been dreading this day..." In an unusual gesture, her mother reached across the breakfast table and took her hand. "Elena ... you're special. Being the thirteenth in our family line makes you special ... with that come certain responsibilities."

Elena rolled her eyes. "Mum, I know about condoms and stuff."

"Well you don't know about this ... you can't ever be in a relationship."

She laughed, amused that her mum had finally cracked a joke after all these years. It faded as soon as she met her eyes. She was deadly serious.

"What?"

"Sex is a powerful thing for any witch, just like a first bleed is, but for you, it's ten times more potent..."

But Elena couldn't quite take in her mother's words, because all she could hear in her mind was 'can't ever be in a relationship'. Of course, it was Karl's face that instantly appeared in her mind's eye. Was this some kind of sick joke? Was this because her mum thought there was something going on between them? She knew it, *knew* she'd given something away in her eyes earlier when her mum had walked into the bedroom...

What was she saying now? Was she talking about her periods? Yeah, she remembered the first time she'd bled – what a weird experience *that* had been ... but what did that have to do with 'can't ever be in a relationship'?

"Elena," her mother squeezed her hand, drawing her back to the present. "If you have sex, you'll be giving away your power – literally. The man you sleep with will take on your magic and you will be left barren of it. You will no longer have any powers and you will never be able to get them back."

"I don't understand," she said dumbly, annoyed that her voice was shaking.

Her mother sighed. "You can't have sex, Elena – ever."

"Mum, there's *nothing* going on between me and Karl—"

"This isn't about you and Karl, this is about any boy – or man – that you end up with."

Elena sat back in her seat, bewildered. "Are you telling me, that because I'm a witch, I have to be a virgin *forever?*"

"Not just a witch, a *thirteenth generation* witch."

"I didn't ask to be a thirteenth generation witch!"

"And I didn't ask to birth one!"

Elena froze. She wondered if she'd been slapped, because those words stung.

Her mother sagged. "Oh, Elena, I didn't mean it like that ... I just meant that we can't always choose our path."

"And my path is to be alone and die a virgin?" she snapped. "What if I want to give up my powers? What if I *want* someone else to have them?"

"Would you really place all that responsibility on someone else's shoulders? They'd have to learn the ways of the Craft, their entire life would change beyond measure ... they'd have to answer to The Council. They'd never be able to lead a normal life again."

Tears pricked at her eyes. This couldn't be real. "I can't believe this ... I *don't* believe this."

Her mother held out her right hand. "Check if you don't believe me," she said, her voice calm and steady. She was referring to what all the kids at The Council dubbed the Lie Detector Spell. A brief touch with her mother's mind would ascertain the truth of the matter.

She couldn't stop her hand from trembling as she placed it in her mother's. She reached out with her mind, and touched hers briefly. Her eyes welled up, tears spilled over and a sob escaped her before she kicked back her chair, and ran to her room.

~*~

Sex was something she had never really thought about before, not to the extent her friends at school did. They were all into the idea of it, most of them eager to share their snogging stories and whether so and so had groped whoever's tits yet. Elena didn't have a so and so in her life, and she sure as hell didn't have any tits. Of course, none of that mattered now ... and now that it didn't matter, all she could think about was sex. Life was cruel. Very cruel.

She shifted on the floor where she'd been sitting curled up for the past half an hour – her bum was getting numb. She could feel where her tears had dried on the skin of her cheeks. A glance up at her bedside clock told her she had to be at Karl's in fifteen minutes. Fresh tears threatened to brim over her eyes, but she pushed them back with a shake of her head. No more crying – she could do this.

Nothing had even happened between her and Karl earlier – it was a non-kiss, and she could forget about it. She *had* to forget about it...

And Karl would forget about it too, because Karl was Karl. He was easy going and accepting of the things that got thrown his way; besides, he was two years older than her – no doubt she'll be finding him with a girl on his arm before too long. Her throat constricted, and she almost threw up at the mere thought of it.

She pulled herself to standing and glanced at the photo of her and her mother, on her bookcase. It was the only photo of them together that she had, and it had been taken at the park when she was six. They were both beaming happiness – Elena at the camera, and her mother at her.

On the other end of the same shelf, was a picture of her with her friends, Sophie and Laura. Sophie had moved to Lancaster a year ago, and Laura no longer hung out with her, preferring the company of those who were a little more part of the 'in-crowd' than Elena was.

Every other photo she had in her room was of her and Karl, or just Karl. A lot of them consisted of them pulling stupid faces together; most of them held treasured memories for her. Her favourite was the one taken about two years ago. They both sat in a field of Lavender, under an August sun. They had placed the camera on a log and set the timer on it, then rushed back to position before it went off; only a rabbit had darted past them at the last moment, and Elena had squealed with delight. At the exact same time, the sun had burst forth from behind a cloud.

The resulting photo consisted of her, wide-mouthed, jumping up and pointing off to the right, and Karl looking up at her, laughing. The sun's emerging rays had bounced off the lens, causing a reflective spot just above Karl's head.

It made him look like he had a halo, and where the light refractions spread out and ended, gave the illusion he had wings.

With a startling clarity, she all at once understood that she would never get over Karl – she had nothing and no one to get over him with. She had no ammunition. She could never move on. She'd never know if she could have loved him – she would never know love at all.

The air seemed to suffocate her.

This was the end. Love. Ends. Here... Now.

Catatonia rose within her – she couldn't breathe.

Something tapped at the window. A stone?

Somehow, she managed to put foot in front of foot and make her way to her sill. The sky was just fading into twilight, and its grey clouds had finally shed their water – it was spitting with rain.

Karl stood on the road looking up at her. He raised his hands and signed, *Hello.*

A faint smile touched her lips. This was one of their things – they had learnt basic sign language a few years back. It had started late one night, when his parents' arguments had gotten so bad he couldn't stand to stay indoors any longer, so he'd tapped her window with a pebble, and since scaling the front of her house was damn near impossible, they'd spent a rather amusing evening trying to guess what the other was saying, like a really bad game of charades. After that they'd decided they would learn to sign, so that if it ever happened again, at least the night would go by more smoothly.

I still have five minutes, she signed back.

I know, but I was worried about you ... you okay?

He always knew when she didn't feel right. Her smile widened, even as a tear betrayed her and slid down her face. Nevermind, he wouldn't notice it this far away.

Mum just gave me some bad news ... I'll tell you about it in a minute.

Okay... He hesitated, then raised his hands again. *I'm always here for you, you know that, right?*

I know ... thank you.

As he turned and walked away, fresh panic took her over. She'd never get to say it, to anyone, ever, so she said it now to his back, hands and fingers trembling as it made the shapes of the words.

I love you.

Forcing herself away from the window, she gathered her homework and stuffed it in her rucksack.

I can do this, I can do this, I can do this... She could do this for Karl.

She couldn't give of herself – he needed to let her go. She would tell him what her mother had told her, and she would act like it was no big deal. She would spend the next three years not falling in love with her best friend, then she would go to university, and he would be free. She could do this for him.

She slung her rucksack over her shoulder, and glanced around the room to make sure she hadn't forgotten anything. The yellow of the daffodils in her window box caught her eye. The rain was falling harder now, pounding them into submission.

She straightened her back.

Flowers wilted.

She would not.

~*~

Katherine's hands shook as she placed the last of the plates in the dishwasher.

She heard Elena's footfalls on the stairs as she bounded down. Without a word, they continued on down the hall, then out the front door. The door closed with a firm bang.

Not able to hold herself up any longer, Katherine sank to the floor with a keening wail. She clasped the amulet around her neck – the one that had hidden the lie from Elena's mind – and ripped it off her. Self-loathing coursed through her, and what a wretched emotion it was. She wondered if she'd burn in hell for this... Better her than her daughter.

Taking in deep breaths, she tried to gather herself ... and failed. Sod it. Five minutes ... she'd allow herself five minutes...

The foreign sound of her desperate sobs filled the air.

She'd be fine in a moment. In a moment, she would stand up tall, harden her heart and carry on as normal.

"I can do this, I can do this, I can do this..." she whispered, holding onto the words like she'd hold onto a life raft. And she could – she would. She would do this for Elena... She would do anything for Elena.

The Sands Of Time
(Book Two of The Witching Pen Novellas)

Seven days ago, Elizabeth May tried to commit suicide. She was found by Paul, her husband, who took her under his wing and back to their home. But the attempted suicide is not Elizabeth's main problem – Elizabeth can't remember who she is, or a single thing about her life beyond the past week.

Plagued by nightmares about a familiar black panther, and a terrifying snow leopard, she is convinced that the dreams are trying to show her something important, and is determined to regain her memories, one way or another.

Meanwhile, Pueblo – the demon blood-bonded to the witch, Amy – is going insane trying to find her. Amy disappeared one week ago, and it seems not even their bond is strong enough to penetrate whatever magic hides her.

As Pueblo enlists the help of angels and demons alike, Elizabeth begins to piece together parts of her forgotten life. But what she uncovers may just have her wanting to turn away from who she really is ... for good.

There are three books in
The Witching Pen Novellas series.
All details can be found at
www.thewitchingpen.co.uk

Other Titles

A Silver Kiss (Vampire Poetry)

A dark and daring addition to the literary world of vampirism, this is a collection of rhyming and freestyle poetry that explores the often taboo themes of power, possession and seduction.

Emotionally charging, each poem is written from a different perspective, be it the hunter or the hunted and inspires a deeper look into the psychology of the human mind and the darker aspects of human relationships and society.

Age range: suitable for older teenagers to adults.

Published by Bitten Fruit Books

All details can be found at www.vampirepoetry.co.uk

Lightning Source UK Ltd.
Milton Keynes UK
UKOW030000290512

193490UK00002B/139/P

9 780956 719263

FTL

REACH FOR THE STARS - BOOK 1

JOHN WEGENER

FTL

John Wegener

Written by John Wegener.
Published by John Wegener .

Contact: John Wegener

CONTENTS

1

INTRODUCTIONS

Ethan was doing what Ethan always did — concentrating on his work, trying to spot the problem, and fixing it. He couldn't help but fix things that were broken and attempt to understand how everything functioned or didn't. It was in his blood.

It was a shame he wasn't as good at fixing relationships. His ability to be single-minded was science's gain but not always the best thing for Ethan. Despite being handsome and still young, he rarely socialized and never with women. He didn't even see his own siblings anymore, not because he had driven them away but because he never knew what to say to them. Perhaps if they had shared his passion for science, it might have been different. He kept meaning to reconnect with them — after all, he had virtually raised them after their mother died and their father was away so much — but somehow, it never happened, nor did they reach out to him. His shy, introverted nature meant that he led a lonely life. Most of the time, this did not bother him, but there were days when he wished he could be different.

Today was one of those days.

He was sitting in his research laboratory at Caltech's Astro-Chemical Engineering research establishment when a colleague walked it.

"What are you up to, young Einstein?" the colleague teased.

Ethan kept his eyes on the notes on his laptop, annoyed at the interruption.

"I'm trying to work out why this muon wave resonator isn't working as it should. The theory says it should behave, but it's not."

"Theories can be temperamental."

"Yeah. I know. And I usually throw it out and resort to my practical 'if you do this – that happens.' But in this case …" Ethan's voice trailed off, and he glanced up and blinked twice to reinvigorate his eyes. He was working on his second Ph.D. at Caltech, concentrating on warp bubble theory and technology. "I've never worked out why Alcubierre theorized the warp bubble concept in the 90s."

"How does any radical advance in science occur? Consider Einstein. Why did he develop relativity when he did? Most researchers must've considered him nuts."

"Yeah. I remember reading in a history book that most scientists thought they just needed to tidy up the Newtonian laws of physics back then — and then Einstein came along saying 'you ain't seen nothing yet.'"

Ethan's colleague chuckled. "Anyway, can I help?"

"No, not really. I'll just revisit the design and check where it's misbehaving. I might've made a mistake in one of my calculations."

"You? Make a wrong calculation! I'd die to see that … and watch you admit it."

"Shut up! Everyone makes mistakes." A smile appeared on Ethan's face at the tongue-in-cheek accusation.

"Sorry. I couldn't help myself. I'll see you later. Looks like the professor is about to pay you a visit."

Ethan looked out the window and saw the professor headed in his direction accompanied by two strangers. No point in returning to work, he thought, so he sat there after his colleague left contemplating whether he had indeed made a mistake. *I hope I haven't. I don't want to disappoint everyone after all the money I've spent. They've trusted me too much. I don't know. Am I a failure? It wouldn't surprise me.* He continued wrestling with self-doubt until Professor Burton walked in with two people in tow: a large Caucasian man and an exotic Asian woman. "Hello, Professor," he said, waking from his bout of dejection and gulping as his eyes alighted on the woman. Any woman scared Ethan, but a beautiful woman rendered him tongue-tied. And this woman was stunning.

"Hello, Ethan. I have two people I want you to meet. In fact, you'll be working with them."

Ethan stared at the professor in dismay. "Really? Why? Aren't I doing a good enough job?"

The Asian woman raised an eyebrow in surprise at Ethan's blatant insecurity.

"In one of your moods, Ethan? You are, aren't you?" The professor turned to the others and said, "I'm sorry. Ethan sometimes has self-confidence issues."

Ethan hung his head in shame at his outburst and embarrassment at the professor's patronizing manner.

"Anyway," the professor continued, "Ethan Richards — meet Ching Hu from China and Apep Chernakov from Russia. Hu, Apep. Ethan."

Ethan got out of his chair and walked over to the visitors to shake their hands warmly, trying to make up for his outburst. As he took Ching Hu's hand, he glanced nervously at her, hoping she did not notice his discomfort around her, but it soon became clear that he hadn't fooled her.

"This will be interesting," Hu said with a glint of amusement in her eyes as they drilled into Ethan's.

"What do you mean by that?" Ethan felt himself turning red as he struggled to keep eye contact.

"You'll find out," Hu replied, still with that glint.

"Let's stay on topic, shall we?" Professor Burton butted in. "Hu and Apep are working in the same field of research as you. You must have read their papers. Our governments have had a chin wag and decided that you three should put your heads together. Two heads are better than one. Or in this case three."

Ethan's eyes widened. "Of course, the names sounded familiar. I'm not very good at names. I thought Hu was a man, though." His face reddened further at this confession, and he stared at the floor, his embarrassment intensifying.

Hu laughed. "I must correct that right now. I am a hundred percent female — I can assure you of that."

"So I see." Ethan gulped.

Hu laughed again. It seemed to Ethan she understood the impact she was having on him. He would discover later that she recognized her physical assets and used them to full effect when it profited her.

"Well, this relationship interesting," Apep piped up, in slightly broken English, clearly amused at the interchange.

"Yes. Interesting," Hu agreed.

Ethan knew he looked frazzled, and he felt it. What was happening? He had been comfortably sunk in his nice quiet, solitary world, and now his equanimity was being threatened. He had to cooperate with these researchers. But how could he do that? Didn't the professor understand his working habits? Maybe he did, and he considered this the solution. But since he'd be working with these two, he'd better get used to it, Ethan decided.

"Welcome to Caltech."

"Thank you, Ethan," Hu responded.

Apep nodded in acknowledgment of the welcome.

"Well, I'll let you three acquaint yourselves," the professor said and walked out.

Hu and Apep inspected the room, a typical laboratory with mechanical and electrical devices being tested, parts lying around haphazardly, and cables strewn across tables to power supplies.

Ethan watched them, wondering what they were thinking. "If I had known you were coming, I would have cleaned up," he mumbled.

"No need. Untidy lab is busy lab," Apep reassured him.

"There may be more work here than tidying the lab," Hu replied, giving Ethan a playful look.

Ethan reddened again. He was so embarrassed at being so near Hu that he could barely raise his eyes from the floor. He wondered why she was doing what she was doing and not earning big money in an international modeling career or something. The thought was sexist, he knew, but he couldn't help it.

Not knowing what to say, he mumbled, "Well ... anyway ... we'll have time."

Hu laughed. "Yes, we will. So, what are you doing?"

Ethan was unsure how forthright he should be, but he assumed the authorities had not put them together to keep secrets from one another, so he decided to be frank. "I've been working on a muon wave resonator, but it's not behaving itself."

"Can we help?"

"Not at the moment. I need to review my theory. I must have calculated something wrong. What are you two working on?"

"I'm researching wormhole practicalities. We've been studying potential methods of keeping wormholes large enough and open long enough to make them practical," Hu replied.

"Any luck?"

"Not yet. It's annoying me. Everything we think should work doesn't. I'm not getting anywhere in a hurry."

"Know the feeling," Ethan commiserated, feeling slightly more relaxed now that he'd found some common ground. "And you, Apep?"

"We look at warp drive options. We also no luck. Seems they put unlucky eggs in one basket, yes!"

Ethan and Hu laughed at the comment. While Hu's English was fluent, Apep's was charmingly flawed.

"So why aren't you busy in your own countries solving your own problems?"

"What Apep said is true in principle. Our governments have put 'the unlucky eggs in one basket', as he puts it, to determine if together we can develop something useful."

"Let's hope that comes true." Ethan felt himself relaxing more around the newcomers, even with Hu, who seemed to understand his personality shortcomings.

"Yes. Who knows? We might even get to go faster than light in our lifetimes."

"Yeah, that would be amazing ..." Ethan started daydreaming about the implications. Daydreaming was a tendency he had. He jerked back to the present when he realized that his two visitors were staring at him. "Anyway, it would be good. So, what are you doing now?"

"I unpack in new office and make comfortable," Apep said.

"Me too," said Hu. "Then I'm going on a tour of LA to get my bearings. Check out where these stars hang out."

"Good luck with that," Ethan commented.

"Why don't you come with me? You can show me the sights and what to avoid if I want to stay out of trouble," Hu suggested.

"I'd like to, but I have work to do here," Ethan said, turning shy again. He wasn't comfortable at the thought of accompanying such an attractive woman, especially one that he'd only just met.

"Suit yourself. Might be your last chance to be alone with a delight like me," Hu teased, a mocking twinkle in her eyes.

Apep chuckled.

Ethan muttered, "I'm sure there'll be another time." He turned back to his work.

"I will see you later on then," Hu said.

"See later too," Apep agreed.

"Yeah."

Hu and Apep left the room, and Ethan returned to studying his notes on his laptop, trying to find out where the problem lay with the resonator. After scrolling through them for a while, he gave up pretending he was concentrating on them and started contemplating the recent arrivals instead. They would add much-needed brainpower to the research effort, he thought, especially if Hu was as good as her published papers implied. She had fascinating insight into space-time properties and how they interacted with exotic matter. Discussing the topic with her would give him food for thought in the field. If only she were a man ... Ethan's thoughts broke off in confusion. *Why am I like this?* He descended into moping again, as he always did at the mere thought of interacting with attractive women.

2

DISASTER

The days wore on, and Ethan, Hu, and Apep soon developed a working relationship as they progressed their individual avenues of research and discussed their issues. In fact, they became inseparable, as the other researchers at the center noted. They often walked to the cafeteria together, discussing this or that scientific principle, or extolling the virtues of their current favorite topic. People would smile tolerantly as they passed them in the corridor.

Ethan learned a lot about Apep from Apep as he was a friendly person who was open about his life and consistently upbeat. He told Ethan he had grown up in Tosno, a small village near St. Petersburg, raised by poor but loving parents who noticed his academic potential early and gave him the best education they could afford. As a boy, he particularly liked to read textbooks on science and space. Fortunately for Apep, the government prized academic achievement — a reason Russia's scientific progress had kept pace with the rest of the world. The government provided lucrative scholarships at the St. Petersburg State University, and Apep came onto its radar for top-level academic achievers. By studying quantum physics and engineering, he was one of the very few Russian scientists allowed to transfer to Caltech for part of his post-Ph.D. years, where he met and was now getting to know Ethan Richards and Ching Hu. While he missed his wife and children back home in St. Petersburg, he regarded himself as very lucky to have this opportunity.

As for Hu, Ethan's intense discomfort around her had gradually lessened, especially when discussing work, but there was still a noticeable awkwardness around her. Embarrassment sometimes showed in his body language, and his conversation became ragged whenever he tried to hide his predicament. Hu, it seemed to Ethan, found it amusing, but she said nothing to increase his torment.

It was another lunch in the cafeteria, and Ethan was discussing his current dilemma with Hu and Apep. "I can't pinpoint the problem. The theory is sound, and the calculations are correct. You've even looked over them, Hu, but it doesn't work."

"What is your definition of not working?" Hu asked.

"I should get muon wave resonance, but it won't reach the saturation point."

"How do you confirm the correct frequency?"

"The theory predicts a coupled harmonic, dependent on the mass and energy of the muon particles. It targets a specific set of frequencies, but it doesn't resonate at those frequencies. It's not as if I don't have the power for it. I need little, and there's plenty in reserve."

"Conceivable based on other behavior. Particle interacts with objects, yes?" Apep interjected.

"You could be onto something there," Hu continued. "What if the muomagnetic and the electromagnetic radiation waveforms interact with each other? Maybe the electromagnetic waves leaking from the electrical equipment are interfering with the muomagnetic waves."

Ethan thought that over for a while. "Well, I could consider that. If you're right, I'd need shielding to prevent interference. That won't be easy to find."

"Nobody said it would be," Hu replied.

"OK. I'll review the theory and introduce electromagnetic waveforms into the calculations to examine what effect they might have on the resonant frequency of the muomagnetic waves." Ethan took another mouthful of his lunch and chewed absentmindedly. His thoughts were on the changes he would need to make to his calculation strings.

~

ETHAN CAME RUNNING along the corridor to Hu's office, flushed with excitement. The door was open, so he ran straight in. "You're right!" he practically shouted.

"Of course I am! Right about what?" Hu asked, astonished at the unexpected interruption.

"About the interference between the electromagnetic and muomagnetic waveforms."

"Oh! And how do you know?"

"I plugged the electromagnetic wave equations into the calculation string, and I got the behavior of my experiments. That's how."

"That's great!" Hu replied, catching Ethan's excitement. "So, what's next?"

"Don't know yet. But at least I know the problem."

"So, if you avoid the interference, you will achieve your original resonator design, which should then produce the results you want."

"Yeah, in theory. The problem is: what's needed to block it?"

"Doesn't a Faraday Cage shield electromagnetic fields?"

"Yes, but it's not that simple. It would interfere with muomagnetic fields, too. But you're on the right track. I need a material that stops electromagnetic fields but not muomagnetic ones, or vice versa ..."

"Well, good luck. I can't think of any."

"Yeah. Gotta go," Ethan said as he rushed out of Hu's room to return to his laboratory, leaving Hu shaking her head in amusement. *That's the first time he hasn't been nervous around me*, she thought.

~

ETHAN SPENT several weeks working on the shielding problem, both in theory and practice. He tried many promising materials but received no satisfaction in solving the issue. Not until he stumbled by accident on one that he thought might do the trick: osmium tetroxide, known for the plus-eight oxidation state of osmium. He looked at its molecular crystal matrix embedded in a graphene medium, and the shielding effect simulations showed the results he desired. His heart pounded faster when he saw them, and he couldn't wait to try the material. The developed compound was fragile, so he immersed the entire matrix in a polymer substrate to obtain the structural integrity he needed. After lining the resonator chamber with the produced sheets, he prepared for another test.

His excitement was palpable as he set up the experiment and powered up the muon wave resonator. Standing at the control panel, which was several meters from the actual resonator, he could see the instruments relaying their information from the resonator back to the control panel.

He opened the muon source gate. Muons streamed into the resonator, and ...

~

HU HEARD the explosion as she sat at her desk reviewing equation sequences and tensed as she realized it emanated from Ethan's laboratory. Trying to figure out what it meant, she remembered Ethan was testing the new material today and sprang into action. Only seconds elapsed from the explosion to Hu bursting from her doorway into the corridor, where the sight of the dust and smoke fumes billowing from the gaps in the laboratory doors filled her with dread.

Apep emerged from his office. "What was that?" he asked.

"Don't know. But let's find out fast," Hu said as she sprinted toward the lab. She stopped at the doors and pushed one ajar cautiously. Dust and smoke billowed, but at least there was no fire.

Once she confirmed the room was safe to enter, she darted through the doors, Apep at her heels.

Hu soon spotted Ethan lying face up amidst broken tables and equipment. He had several cuts on his face and was motionless. Hu tensed with trepidation over the possibilities.

As she started toward him to find out if he was still alive, she called over her shoulder . "Apep, call Security and request a medic's attendance here yesterday."

"Of course." Apep left immediately to carry out his task.

Standing over Ethan's inert body, Hu leaned down and placed her fingers on his neck where his pulse should have been. After several seconds, she breathed a sigh of relief. "He's alive." She could now sense Ethan's chest rising and falling, though barely. She scanned for the medical first aid kit and, seeing it in place on the wall, rushed over to it, opened it, and grabbed the thermal blanket to keep him warm while waiting for professional medical help.

By then, many sightseers had started congregating at the doorway to view the destruction, craning their necks to gain a better perspective.

Hu glanced up, saw the crowd, and said with disdain, "Either make yourselves useful or leave. We need good access for the medical team."

The mob guiltily broke up and drifted away.

Meanwhile, Hu removed the debris surrounding Ethan, careful not to cause any further injury. She couldn't see any serious injuries, but she feared internal organ damage or bone fractures. She prayed that there was no spinal or neck trauma. After making him as comfortable as she dared, she sat and gazed at his face, concerned for his welfare. *Please don't let it be serious*, she prayed. *He is so young, and he is a genius. We need him.* As she looked at him, Hu realized that her friendship with this shy young man ran deep. Not romantically, she concluded, but a strong affection, and she dreaded losing him under these circumstances. The thought frightened her.

The campus medic burst through the doors, kit in hand. He looked around and, spotting Hu and Ethan, rushed over to where they were. Hu moved to make way for him. The medic kneeled with practiced efficiency and opened his kit to extract his diagnostic device. "What happened?" he asked, looking at Hu for answers.

"I don't know. Ethan was in here on his own. He was conducting a test, and I heard the lab explode from my office up the hallway. I rushed in and found him here."

"Have you moved him?"

"No. I removed the debris and placed the blanket on him — nothing else."

"Good." The medic turned his attention back to Ethan. After several minutes, he looked up again. "He's lucky. I can't find any serious injuries at present. Paramedics are coming. They'll take him to the hospital for further tests, but it just looks like a severe concussion. Let's hope."

"How long till he regains consciousness then?" Hu asked. By this time, a noticeable lump had appeared on Ethan's forehead.

"Don't know. Depends on how hard it was. It's different for everyone, too."

Apep came back into the room. "Ethan good then?"

"Good may not be correct, but he will survive. He's used up one of his nine lives, though," Hu told him with a relieved smile on her face.

"Ah. Wait till we get hold of him," Apep continued, attempting to cover up his concern with humor.

"Yes, he will need to explain himself."

At that moment, Security led the paramedics into the lab. After discussing Ethan's prognosis with the campus medic, they sprang into action.

Professor Burton entered, looking around the room perturbed. He walked over to Hu and Apep. "What's Ethan's condition?"

"According to the medic, Ethan will be alright. He might have a splitting headache when he wakes, but at present, it appears he has escaped serious injury," Hu told him.

The professor showed noticeable relief. "That's good news. I always dread these things happening, despite our safety efforts. We use hazardous substances here, and you can't guarantee mishaps won't occur the first time you conduct an experiment, regardless of the precautions taken."

The paramedics had secured Ethan to a stretcher by then,

preparing to transfer him to the waiting ambulance. Breaking away, the lead paramedic approached the group. "Who took care of him while waiting for medical help?"

"I did," Hu responded.

"You learned your first aid well."

"Thanks."

The paramedics took Ethan out to the ambulance while Hu, Apep, and Professor Burton observed.

Hu stood in silence, contemplating her next move. Once she decided, she turned to the professor and said, "I will attend the hospital and stay with Ethan — if that is acceptable to you, Professor?"

Professor Burton looked surprised. "Is your relationship more than professional?"

Hu laughed. "No, Ethan's just a good friend, although I have only just realized it. I think he would appreciate a friend there when he wakes."

"By all means. It's an excellent idea. Ethan's always been a solitary chap. He doesn't have any family as far as I know, and he doesn't seem to have close friends either. A friend is what he needs now. Keep us informed of any developments."

~

HU SAT in a chair next to Ethan's hospital bed the following day, watching him as he lay, still unconscious. His face looked peaceful despite the blotched blue-purple bruises now covering it. The doctors said he had suffered no long-term harm. He had no broken bones and would wake from the coma when he was ready. His brain had sustained slight bruising and swelling, but nothing that showed any permanent brain damage. "He'll wake up with one hell of a headache," the doctor had quipped. Hu smiled at the thought. He was lucky. That blast could have killed him or maimed him for life.

Ethan stirred as Hu kept vigil, causing her a moment of excitement and relief. Two minutes elapsed before he opened his eyes into slits. His head faced Hu, so he saw her sitting there.

"What are you doing in my bedroom?" Ethan asked, confused.

Hu smiled. "We are not in your bedroom," she replied.

"Wha ... Ahh, ow," Ethan grunted, exasperated as he tried to raise his body only to have shafts of pain radiate through it. He collapsed back onto the bed, sweat breaking out on his face. "Where am I?"

"You are in the hospital."

"Why? What happened?"

"Don't you remember? You had a mishap in your lab and got knocked out. Don't worry if you don't recall it yet. The doctor said you might have amnesia when you woke. How is your head?"

"Mishap? My head is killing me. Did I drink too much? What mishap?"

"Lie still, and I will tell you. OK? Yesterday ..."

"Yesterday?"

"Yes. You have been unconscious. Let me continue. Yesterday, you were testing your muon wave resonator when something went wrong. It blew up and wrecked the lab, you with it. You are lucky to be alive. Apep and I rushed in to investigate and found you lying on the floor, unconscious and half-buried in a pile of junk. You have many superficial cuts and bruises, the reason for your pain when you move. The doctor reassures me you will survive, but you'll be licking your wounds for a while."

"Yesterday? Why are you here then? Have you been here since then?"

"Most of the time. I felt you needed a friend nearby when you woke."

Ethan gave Hu a puzzled look. He wasn't sure how close this friendship was that she had mentioned, but not wanting to appear churlish, he said, "Thanks."

Hu sensed what he was thinking and attempted to lighten the mood. "You're welcome. You will pay, though, you know. I will be sending you a check."

Ethan tried to chuckle at this, but the pain from the bruising stopped him. “I make one plea. Please don’t make me laugh.”

“That depends on you. Don’t give me a reason to,” Hu joked.

Ethan winced again. “Stop, please.”

“OK.” Hu sobered. “How are you otherwise?”

“I’ve got a splitting headache, and everything aches when I move. Other than that, I’m hunky-dory.”

Just then, a nurse poked her head through the doorway. “I thought I heard talking. You’re awake. And how are we feeling, Mr. Richards?”

“I don’t know about you, but I feel like shit.”

She chuckled as she entered the room. “A sense of humor. That’s a good sign.”

“Depends who is on the receiving end,” Hu butted in, smirking.

The nurse smiled. “How’s your head?” she asked the patient.

“Terrible. I’ve got a splitting headache.”

“Concussion will do that. I’ll return with medication for it. Do you suffer any other pain?”

“Only when I move.”

“That’ll go away in time. You’re fortunate, I hear. You’re lucky to have such a dedicated friend here, too.”

Hu blushed in embarrassment.

“Now that you’re awake, the doctor will examine you soon.”

“Thanks, and I’d appreciate something for this headache.”

“I’ll be back in a moment,” the nurse promised and left the room.

“Why are you here?” Ethan asked Hu again, still puzzled.

Hu glanced at her lap and then back at him. “I’ve experienced waking up in a strange place with no friendly face nearby. It is lonely and confusing. I didn’t want you going through that, I suppose.”

Ethan smiled as much as he could manage without incurring too much pain. “Thanks.” This time he meant it.

“Do you require anything?”

“A memory would help.”

“The doctor says it will return with time. What else?”

“How long will I be in here for?”

"I do not know. That is up to the doctor. A few days perhaps."

"Maybe my data tablet."

"You need a new one, I'm afraid. The last one does not exist anymore."

"Oh! Can you get me one? I'll pay you back."

"Sure. I will bring it in tomorrow."

The doctor walked into the room. "Hello, Mr. Richards. The nurse tells me you have a headache."

"Dwarves are hammering my skull."

"Well, I will go since you are awake," Hu interrupted as she stood up. "I will leave you to the doctor and rest. I will return tomorrow. See you soon."

"See you, Hu, and thanks," Ethan replied.

"Now, let's check you over," Hu heard the doctor say as she left to go home for some much-needed rest of her own.

~

HU RETURNED JUST after lunch the next day with a gift for Ethan — his new data tablet.

Ethan was sitting up in bed when she arrived, gazing out the window despondently.

"Hi!" Hu greeted him in a cheerful voice.

"Hi," Ethan replied dully, glancing at Hu before his gaze returned to the window.

He's in one of his infamous bouts of depression, Hu thought, and her smile faded.

"What is wrong?"

"My memory has returned. I'm a failure — the story of my life."

Hu couldn't believe what she'd heard. She wanted to hit him, to wake him from his despondency and self-pity. What had caused it? He had a setback and was lucky to be alive. He looked ready to despair, not only about his current project but with his very existence. Hu considered what was happening and decided on her approach. "So, you are a failure. Why do you think that?"

"Well, isn't it obvious? I blew up my test lab because I was careless, and I can't solve whatever it is that's preventing the resonance from working. I'm a failure."

"Why does that make you a failure?"

Ethan looked at Hu for the first time. Despair was etched on his face as if the devil himself was tormenting him with his most secret failings, thrusting the dagger deeper and twisting it harder. "I have always failed, Hu. I couldn't care for my brother and sister, and they got fed up with me and left."

Frustration rose in her. She couldn't understand why he felt so responsible. "Where were your parents?" she blurted out with too much force.

"My mother died when I was young, and Dad traveled with his work. He returned home from time to time and always left me enough money to survive and care for my brother and sister, but it was no picnic. I wasn't good at it."

"Where are they now?"

"My dad is dead. Drank himself to death. He never recovered from Mum dying. He felt it was his fault. I don't know where my brother and sister are. They left home when they became independent. I lost contact afterward."

Hu's heart melted at the confession. But pity wouldn't make the talented Ethan return. She needed to get him to understand that he wasn't a failure. He was brilliant and should be proud of himself. She realized he required a tough approach. "Listen to me, Ethan, before I shake you. What would your mother say if she could hear this drivel? You are one of the brightest minds on this planet. She would reprimand you for wasting that brilliance in self-pity. She would tell you how proud she is of you. Wake up and examine what happened. Learn the lessons. From where I stand, you almost achieved your goal. You just overdid it, and the reaction became unstable. You need to find the problem and fix it. I hear you're good at that."

Ethan stared at her, blinking. He opened his mouth and closed it again. He looked away and back again. Tears started flowing from his eyes. "My ... mother ... would ... be ... proud ... of ... me," he got out with jagged slowness as emotion overcame him.

"Yes, she would," Hu said firmly. After a moment, she added more gently, "And your father? Did he not see your talent?"

Ethan focused his eyes on her and said, "Yes, he did. He put me in touch with an engineering friend, once he saw where my interests lay. The friend let me tinker in his workshop, building many contraptions. What I learned there helped me excel later in astroengineering and quantum physics. That drew NASA's attention, and they sponsored my tuition through UCLA, majoring in astrochemical engineering." Ethan paused as he reminisced and added softly, "My father did what he could for me, even though he had his demons."

Slowly, Ethan brought his emotions under control again. "You know, my brother and sister always looked up to me, wanting me to succeed," he said. "They even sacrificed small luxuries, so I had enough for the education I needed. They watched me reading and reading and then writing the most amazing equations at home. I think they knew that my destiny was for bigger things. Maybe that was why they left. I miss them so much."

Humbled at him opening up to her, Hu said gently, "They would want you to recover, wouldn't they? And what's preventing you from trying to find them?"

Ethan looked away again, staring out the window at the outside garden. It was spring. Blossoms covered the trees, and the flowers were in full bloom. He smiled at the spectacle and wiped away his tears. "You're right," he said with a placated smile. "I should stop moping and try to put things right with them and work out what went wrong with the experiment."

"Good. I brought you a new data tablet," Hu said as she handed Ethan the package she had on her lap.

"Wow! Where did you buy that?" he chirped, his depression receding.

Hu laughed. "You enjoy gadgets, so I purchased the biggest and best there was. You owe me when you're discharged. That wasn't cheap, although I received a discount."

Ethan had unwrapped the packaging and booted up the tablet before she had finished speaking. He followed the first-use instructions, and the unit was operational within minutes. He looked up. "Thanks. This will keep me occupied now."

"Don't overdo it. You had a nasty bump on the head, remember. How is your head?"

"Still sore, but better than yesterday."

"So, you said that you remember. What do you recall?"

"Well, I had installed the osmium tetroxide lining in the resonator and placed power on it. It was behaving like a dream, and the measured shielding effect was perfect. But when I started introducing the muon beam into the chamber, something happened. It was going to plan. The resonance was starting up as I had expected. Then everything escalated out of control. An unstable positive feedback loop developed, like when one of those electric guitars sits next to its amplifier speaker. That's what I remember until I woke up here."

Hu got excited by the news. "So, you nearly succeeded. But you shielded the chamber too well."

"Yeah, you could say that." Ethan appeared to be thinking. He continued, "There was another substance that I considered. It was inferior to the osmium tetroxide. I wonder if that might make it more stable?"

"What is the material?"

"Iridium tetroxide."

"Worth a try if you think it will accomplish your aims. It's preferable to blowing up the lab. You may not be so lucky next time."

"Yeah. I must find more funds first. Sounds like my lab's a mess, and I'll have to start from scratch."

"I'm sure Professor Barton will offer the funding, especially when you tell him how close you were."

"I suppose." Ethan returned his gaze to the window with a satisfied smile and what Hu took as an edge of determination in his jawline.

She looked outside with him, content to sit and enjoy the medley of flowers swaying in the breeze. They reminded her of her time as a child when she wandered through fields of blooming azaleas. Returning to the present, she asked, "Have they told you when you can leave?"

"Tomorrow or the next day, depending on how my head goes. They don't want me leaving any wackier than when I arrived."

"Fat chance of that," she joked.

"You're lucky I'm incapacitated, or I'd punch you for that."

"Like to see you try."

They both laughed, Hu happy that his depression had lessened.

"Well, I should go. Some of us must work, not laze in bed." Hu rose from her seat.

Ethan lunged toward her in a mock attack but was pulled up short by an upsurge of aches and pain running through his body. "Suppose I'll just stay here. I'm keeping count, though."

They laughed again.

"Do you need supplies?"

"No. This'll keep me occupied for now."

"Good. I will see you then."

"See you, and thanks."

"You're welcome," Hu said as she went out the door.

~

TWO DAYS LATER, Hu entered Ethan's lab. She had heard a noise from it while working in her office and had come to investigate its source. As she opened the doors, the sight of Ethan rummaging through the rubble of the blast, trying to find items to salvage, confronted her. She noted he limped from the injuries he had sustained in the explosion.

"Anything good enough to sell?" she asked.

"Not likely. Most of this stuff is unsalvageable. What a mess. I'll have to start again."

Hu smiled. "Welcome back, but shouldn't you be taking it slow until you recover more?"

"Thanks, but if I take it easy one second longer, I'll do myself another injury just to relieve the boredom."

Apep arrived to investigate the talking. "Ahh! Friend Ethan. You are well. Welcome. We have work to do, I see."

Ethan smiled at Apep's perpetual exuberance. "Yes, we have work. You can help."

"Afraid these hands too delicate for manual labor."

They laughed.

It took several days for Ethan to clean up the mess with two technicians to aid him. Hu and Apep ended up pitching in too.

A month elapsed before his laboratory could be returned to its earlier condition and the experimental equipment rebuilt. Ethan worked long hours once most of his injuries had healed, keeping busy with the physical lab and apparatus setup, and reviewing the theory, predicting the effect of the iridium tetroxide. Another failure wasn't an option, since he wanted to stay in one piece, taking special note of Hu's advice about him being lucky once.

At last, he was ready to trial the iridium tetroxide liner inside the resonator. He had arranged a blast wall construction with a suitable window so he could view proceedings under safer conditions.

Hu and Apep joined him to witness the test and offer any help he might need.

He powered up the resonator as before and waited. Everything was running as predicted, but it frightened him to continue, knowing what happened last time.

"You will not find out by standing there," Hu prompted with a wry smile.

"I know. I'm just nervous." Ethan took a deep breath. "Well, here goes."

He opened the muon beam gate a crack. A stream of muons cascaded into the chamber, and the reverberation frequency increased. The amplitude of the waves rose beyond control at first but then stabilized. He let out a loud breath, as he had been holding it, and checked the monitoring routine on the screen. Everything looked positive. He increased the gap a touch more. The amplitude increased again but at a controllable rate.

"How does it look?" Hu asked.

"Good. We're still here, and I believe I can regulate it now. The frequency is lower than I need, so I must increase it." Ethan adjusted the frequency inverter to the value he wanted. The amplitude jumped, as did Ethan, anticipating a non-existent explosion. Afterward, the resonator hummed with an enigmatic resonance, and a luminescent ball surrounded the resonator as they gazed through the window.

"What is that?" Apep asked.

Ethan turned to Apep and Hu with a sweeping smile of excitement. "That, my friends, is a warp bubble. I believe the first one ever produced."

Apep came over to Ethan and slapped him on the back. "Well done, Comrade, whoops, friend. Old habits."

They laughed.

"Yes, congratulations, Ethan," Hu agreed and hugged him.

Ethan, embarrassed by the hug, but realizing it showed friendship, returned to the screen to check everything was stable, which it was. It was a marvel to view and know it confirmed the forecasted results. He opened the muon gate a crack more. The hum increased in volume, and the space-time bubble enlarged. He checked the bubble size against the rate of muon supply, and it matched his prediction perfectly. He edged open the gate until it was open the most, and the bubble grew to the predicted fifty centimeters. The resonator was small, thirty centimeters, so the largest bubble size was modest too. He left the unit running for ten minutes while taking various other measurements. He then closed the muon gate. The warp bubble disappeared. He turned the resonator power off together with the other equipment. Ethan let out a sigh of satisfaction.

"This cause for celebration, yes?" Apep suggested.

"I think so," Ethan agreed. "What about you, Hu?"

"Would not miss it for the world."

THEY MET at the Sips and Surf, their usual haunt for relaxing, for a few refreshments at 7 pm. Ethan was shouting the drinks to celebrate his success. Apep and Hu didn't complain. They talked and joked together into the night.

A wicked grin appeared on Apep's face during the evening, which they both saw.

"What is it?" Hu asked with disquiet. She knew that smile.

"Well, Hu, you only one with one-syllable name. No good. Must have two-syllable name."

"Oh no. What are you going to suggest? I will not enjoy this."

"I think we call you Hugo. Good, potent name, yes?"

Ethan burst out laughing. "It's great."

Hu sat stunned, unsure of what she thought of it. "Isn't that a man's name in English?" she asked.

"Yes," responded Ethan with a grin, "but you always say no one can mistake you for a man."

She ran the name through her mind and decided she liked it as a nickname. "OK. This is acceptable. You can call me Hugo."

"Hu go here, Hu go there, Hu go everywhere," chanted Apep.

Enlightened, Ethan burst out laughing.

"Do ... not ... dare ... say ... that ... again," Hu said, but she too was laughing.

They continued celebrating, leaving late in the night for home and sleep.

From that time on, Hu became Hugo to Ethan and Apep.

3

SEPARATION

The news of Ethan's breakthrough rocketed throughout the scientific establishment. Momentum increased as scientists and governments realized that faster-than-light space travel was a distinct possibility. Already it was being referred to by the abbreviation FTL.

Governments locked themselves in secret conclaves to discuss the political and military implications. Top of the agenda was figuring out how best to keep this breakthrough from damaging international relations. The chief governments involved were China, Russia, and the United States, none of whom wanted to jeopardize the negotiated accords they had worked so hard to set up over the last decade. Once their militaries advised that the new technology provided no clear military advantage, these governments jointly decided that FTL space travel, when available, would be accessible to any country that wished to develop it.

Ethan was feeling miserable, the publicity distracting him from his work. He wanted to lock his lab doors until the hype died down. But that was not to be. Social media was congested with cries for comment from Ethan. The media companies were crawling over each other for access to him as a guest speaker on their various broadcasts as they tried to get "his side of the story." Caltech management did what it could to protect him, but it, too, was overwhelmed. Ethan's depression deepened by the day.

"I want my normal life back," he complained to Hu and Apep one day at lunch in the Caltech cafeteria.

"Sorry, you celebrity now," Apep advised.

"It will blow over soon," Hu assured him. "Just wait for the next bit of news to attract the media's attention."

When Ethan grumbled to Professor Burton, the professor intimated that American military intelligence might help, perhaps by placing a cordon around Ethan to protect him from the outside world.

Ethan wasn't sure he liked the sound of that either, but he tried to keep busy in his lab and not be distracted by his growing unhappiness. He was not getting enough sleep either, which didn't help.

A few days after his conversation with Apep and Hu, Professor Burton walked into the lab with an army general at his heels. Ethan glanced up and groaned. The general was the epitome of the clichéd army man — straight back, uniform without a crease, shoes polished to a mirror sheen. He looked in his late thirties, was wide-shouldered and clean-shaven, and had a powerful jaw.

The professor chuckled. "It's not that dreadful, Ethan. Besides, I've brought in the cavalry."

Ethan rose to his feet, weary from the emotional seesaw of the past weeks, and faced the pair as they approached.

"Ethan, let me introduce General John O'Conner from the Pentagon."

"Good afternoon, General."

"Good afternoon, Ethan. I'd add I've heard impressive news about you, but who hasn't these days? You can call me John."

"What brings you here?"

"You. Or I should say, your protection, to be more precise."

"I don't need protection. I want to be left alone," Ethan responded, getting even wearier and becoming agitated at the suggestion that he needed personal security.

John cocked an eye at the response. After a slight pause, he turned to the professor. "Would you give us some privacy?"

"Sure," the professor replied, happy to do whatever the general wanted. "Just inform me if you need anything else." He left the lab without further comment.

"Ethan, I can only imagine the emotional turmoil you're going through, changing from an unknown engineer to a celebrity overnight. Honestly, it would frustrate the hell out of me. But it's happened. Extroverts revel in such attention; you aren't one of them. Let's go someplace peaceful and chat. Do you have a garden or secluded park nearby?"

Ethan watched John closely as he spoke, warming to him because he could detect both sincerity and empathy. Could a general be empathic? "Yeah, OK. This building has a small courtyard. I often lunch there, especially these days. The media don't know it's there — yet." Ethan gave a wry smile as he made the last comment.

They walked outdoors and were met by a sunny day and a gentle breeze. The grass was green and mown short, dotted by patches of flower-edged garden beds. Ethan led John to a bench nearby, and they sat. They admired the view until John turned and faced Ethan so he could make eye contact with him as they talked.

"Ethan, security may have been a misnomer for my visit's purpose. You are an enormous asset — to America and the world, and you need protection. But please, this discovery is greater than its monetary value. We still expect big things from you."

Ethan's eyes widened with surprise. John chuckled. "Yes, we want more from you still. We demand every drop of blood from you before we discard you. I'm jesting. But seriously, you've only just begun here. You are young and have your whole life ahead of you. We need to make sure you continue your research. The professor has advised that since your achievement, these distractions have ground your work to a halt."

"Yeah, well, I just wish people would leave me alone without making me answer this call or give that media comment. I can't handle it."

"What should we do about it? You still need a life. Locking you away somewhere wouldn't be pleasant for you, and yet my compatriots have suggested it."

Ethan panicked at the last statement. "You can't do that. I won't agree to it."

"Stay calm. I'm not an advocate of that suggestion, and fortunately for you, my word carries. I want your life returned to normal, as much as it can be under the circumstances, so you can concentrate on your research again. So how do we achieve that?"

Ethan thought things over for a while. "How did the military get involved?"

"Even though we agree faster-than-light space travel has no specific military interest, that doesn't mean that we don't want it developed. We do. We became concerned when rumors of your distraction started filtering through to us and decided that we needed to nullify those distractions for you as best we could. That's why I'm here."

"I want to go back to my dull existence."

John smiled. "That won't happen, not in the short term."

"No. I suppose you are right there."

Ethan considered his predicament for longer. As the general said, the publicity wouldn't vanish, but how should he move forward with his research? He realized that the preferred path from his current dilemma was to start a new project, something that would absorb all his attention and distract him from his unwanted celebrity. He needed a goal to occupy his time. What he had achieved already was but a small milestone toward FTL space travel.

John sat with patient eyes, observing the thought processes flittering across Ethan's expressive face.

Finally, Ethan said, "I need a project."

"Can you expand on what you mean?"

Ethan's eyes lit up as he realized what was missing and what was needed. "To get serious about this, I need a decent project to build an FTL-drive spaceship to travel through space."

John's face brightened as he recognized the reasoning behind

Ethan's suggestion. "That's the most adventurous idea I've heard in ages. I love it."

"Let's face it. What I've achieved is great, but it won't get us traveling faster than light. There's much more to discover. Currently, we conduct ad hoc research worldwide, but there's no concerted effort. Even Apep's and Hu's research projects are just a minor facet of the full expanse of inquiry. No one is considering the immensity of the overall concept and saying, 'OK, how do we do it?' I want to say, 'We will achieve FTL by doing such and such.'" Ethan became animated as he started postulating the possibilities to consider and the problems to solve.

"That's the beginnings of a plan, but you'll need finance," the general said. "That may be where we can contribute, although I'm sure the government will insist on private enterprise contributions. You'll need bigger facilities than your small laboratory, too. I want you to spend a few days or weeks putting together a project definition for me. I must have a document I can discuss with my superiors so that I can lobby for funding. Can you do that?"

"I sure can," Ethan responded with enthusiasm, eager to start.

"Good. Well, I have protected you enough," John said with a wry smile.

They both laughed as they stood.

"I'll let you get started then. I'll find the exit myself ..." John looked at Ethan with a piercing expression. "And I was never here. Got it?"

Ethan stared at him, puzzled. "Why not?"

"I don't need the publicity, and I wish to keep our relationship secret. We may need that secrecy. You never know. If anyone asks, say that I am an old family friend visiting to congratulate you."

"I can keep a secret. How do I contact you?"

"I'll contact you."

"OK. Well, see you then."

They shook hands.

"See you."

John walked off, and Ethan rushed back to his office, eager to get started on his plan for the new phase of the project.

FOUR WEEKS LATER, Ethan, with the aid of Hu, Apep, and others, had developed a project definition, a detailed scope of work, a basic schedule, and preliminary estimated costs. It was a significant sum of money and a five-year project, but he convinced everyone that the long-term benefits would outweigh the cost.

As promised, John took the document and presented it to his superiors, who lobbied the authorities for the funding. Once he submitted the plan, government consultations decided they should assemble an international team to work on the project. The Chinese and Russians were keen to take part, but their tripartite discussions with the Americans concluded that it was worthwhile to continue the three-pronged approach, with the Chinese and the Russians working on their versions of an FTL drive. Ethan's breakthrough had shed new light on where they should concentrate their efforts on their own projects. So, their governments recalled Hu and Apep to their own countries to play major roles in these projects.

The news of Hu and Apep leaving devastated Ethan. It especially upset him that Hu was departing, as they had become so close. She had helped him discover so much about himself and had imbued him with the self-confidence he had lacked.

Hu, he realized, was his closest work associate ever, even closer than Apep. Instead of teasing him, as Apep did, she saw his struggles and tried to help him. Her empathy had encouraged him to confess to her his self-doubt. She counseled him, calmed the storm within, and broadened his focus so he could channel his nervous energy into useful knowledge and problem-solving. He was forever in her debt for that. Her departure would be very hard. He feared he would flounder without her. But like a lioness instructing her young cub, she assured him he had to fend for himself now and would not stumble. Her leaving, she said, would strengthen him, forcing him to make his own decisions with no crutches and to stand by those decisions. Her words proved prophetic.

ON THE NIGHT before their separation, the three friends gathered for a meal at their favorite restaurant. The mood was subdued but celebratory, nonetheless.

"I'll miss you guys," Ethan commented, his voice cracking.

"It is good to miss. You cannot miss what you never had. I, too, will miss you," Apep philosophized, his English showing signs of improvement.

Hu agreed. "Yes, I will miss you both, too. It was a great pleasure to know you these past months."

"Let us toast our friendship," Apep suggested, raising his glass of wine high.

Hu and Ethan copied his pose.

"To we three: Ethan, Hugo, and Apep," Apep toasted in a loud voice that attracted the attention of the other diners.

"To Ethan, Hugo, and Apep," Ethan and Hu repeated as they clinked their glasses together. The three took a sip of their wine amid smiles and cheers from the other patrons.

"How am I ever going to tell my friends back home that you call me Hugo?"

"You'll just have to say that we gave this name to you as a great honor," Ethan said.

They laughed.

"We must keep in touch," Apep said.

"Yes, we must. We will share our findings at conferences, I presume, so we must make sure we dine together when we have an opportunity," Ethan suggested.

"Who knows? They may bring us together again one day," Hu said.

They enjoyed each other's company for the rest of the dinner and said their goodbyes before retiring to go their separate ways.

4

THE PROJECT BEGINS

Caltech moved the international project team to the Jet Propulsion Laboratory, known as JPL, in Pasadena, a more secure location than Caltech and one that had larger and better facilities for their needs. Ethan shifted his office to a recently constructed part of the complex.

A team was assembled for the enterprise. Ethan had nominated himself as the engineering manager, so they needed a project manager. He sifted through a list of applicants for the position that the steering committee had suggested. One applicant stood out: Galena Alvarez. According to her CV, she was Spanish but had good English, having done her major in nuclear physics at Stanford University. After spending some time as a researcher, she had discovered a talent for management and had settled into project management as a career path. She seemed ideal on paper, far ahead of the other applicants, but Ethan met with her before making his final decision to ensure she would be the right fit.

"You have an impressive history in the projects you've managed," he told her when she came in for the interview.

"I've been lucky. A project manager is only as good as her team. I had brilliant teams working for me and, if I hear the rumors correctly, I would again here — if I manage this venture."

Ethan liked the mixture of self-confidence and humility.

"What is a project manager's role?" he asked her.

"Scope, expense, quality, and time — keeping these in balance. Plan well and don't interfere with the workers unless they upset any of the aforementioned."

Ethan grinned. "Good answer. You know you have the job. You just need to convince me we can work together."

Galena's eyes widened in surprise at the news. "No, I didn't know that. Nobody has told me that, just that I was on the shortlist."

"Well, I'm telling you now, but don't let the others know I told you." Ethan smiled at her. "How can you relieve me of this dreaded managing and get me back to engineering work?"

Galena laughed. "You'll never be free of management chores, but after reviewing the project I would be able to put flesh and muscle on the existing skeleton."

"Believe me, there're just bones."

"I think one of my first tasks will be to find the key team members so we can begin working as a unit as soon as possible instead of employing people ad hoc. Hiring people ad hoc can disrupt project performance."

"I can appreciate that." Seeking to unsettle her, he then asked, "And can you tell me anything about yourself that could irritate me or the team?"

Galena was unfazed by the question. She responded calmly but with a twinkle in her eye. "Well, I do have a thing about punctuality — it can drive some people nuts."

Ethan laughed. "Well, as vices go, that's a pretty good one."

The meeting broke up, and they departed after further discussion of minor matters.

The authorities formalized Galena's appointment as Project Manager, and she, true to her word, concentrated on finding specialists for the four project leadership roles. After sifting through a long list of applicants, Galena chose Australian Jade

Powers for the role of quantum physics specialist. Jade, from Adelaide in South Australia, specialized in exotic particles and their behavior.

Next, Galena chose Jezebel Liebmann from Leipzig, Germany, for the role of fusion energy specialist. Jezebel had been operating in private practice rather than academia. She was a foremost authority in her field and in high demand, so Galena saw hiring her as a coup. When asked why she wanted to be part of the team, Jezebel said she was keen to take part in a history-making project.

Rounding out the team was Jake Bodie from Texas, USA. Jake was a flight consultant with a background in spaceship consortiums as an engineer, pilot, and operator. In this project, he would lead spacecraft construction and operations.

Once the core team had assembled in the brand-new meeting room, Ethan acquainted himself with them as a group.

As he entered the room, he saw Galena tap her chronometer with poorly disguised annoyance, indicating he was late. He smiled at her. "Sorry, I got sidetracked for a moment." He scanned the room and saw that the others were studying him in return. He sat in an empty chair to Galena's left.

"Let me introduce you to the team so far," Galena said, "although I don't intend expanding the core beyond what's here unless we must."

"OK." Ethan glanced at Galena for direction.

"Everyone, meet Ethan Richards. He is the Engineering Manager for the project. Ethan, meet Jezebel Liebmann, our fusion energy specialist." Galena pointed to her immediate right.

"Greetings," Jezebel said in a heavy German accent. Her expression was earnest, and her eye contact was direct and steady as she looked at Ethan, who could see she possessed an abundance of no-nonsense German efficiency. She also looked hard to handle — he hoped Galena knew what she was doing.

"Welcome to our little team," Ethan responded with a smile. Jezebel's hard expression softened into a smile, and Ethan felt he had had a small victory.

Galena continued. "Next to Jezebel is Jake Bodie. He will build our spaceship and fly it for us."

"Howdy, y'all. Forgive the strong Texan slang, but I just have ta put it on for the first meet," Jake responded with an exaggerated Texan drawl and a mischievous grin on his handsome face. "I talk like you otherwise," he continued without the drawl.

"Welcome. I'm looking forward to reviewing the ship's design with you," Ethan said, instinctively feeling that he was going to enjoy working with this young man.

"Likewise."

"And last, but not least," continued Galena, pointing to Ethan's left, "is Jade Powers. Jade is our quantum physics specialist."

Ethan turned to look at Jade. His eyes froze on her for an instant when he saw her face, and he lowered his gaze in embarrassment. *She's so beautiful* was all that he could think. He had improved tremendously in his interactions with women since meeting Hu, but now he felt like he was back at the start.

"A pleasure to meet you," he finally managed to say.

Jade smiled warmly, oblivious to the struggle going on in Ethan's head. "Pleased to meet you too, Ethan."

Clearing his throat and keeping his eyes well away from Jade, Ethan continued, "Well, now that we've got acquainted, let's begin the meeting. I take it you've read through the material that I sent you? Good. Let's start ..."

~

THE DAYS ROLLED on for the team as they delved into the details of the project, solving problems as they arose.

Ethan was sitting in his office reviewing engineering specifications when Jade knocked on the doorjamb. "You have a minute, Ethan?"

Ethan gulped his nervousness away. "Sure. Come in and take a seat."

Jade walked in, watching Ethan with interest as he lowered his gaze, pretending to be finishing the reading that he was doing. She sat and waited until Ethan looked up again.

"Sorry. What's on your mind?"

"You know how we've been investigating suitable material for muon production?"

"Yes."

"Well, I believe I've found one."

Ethan gave Jade his full attention, as producing muons in large quantities was proving to be a huge stumbling block to the project. "Really? What is it?"

"It's good news and bad news. The theoretical calculations and earlier experimental results conducted by a researcher five years ago suggest that astatine might do the trick. It has unique properties that concentrate and amplify the muons released in preference to other particles when alpha particles bombard it."

"That's great," Ethan responded enthusiastically. "When can we try a sample?"

"Well, that's the bad news. Astatine is the rarest element on Earth, so it's difficult to come by. It only has an eight-and-a-half-hour half-life on Earth, which is why it's so rare."

"Oh. So, how does that help us?" Ethan looked crestfallen.

"Well, it may be possible to produce astatine by bombarding Bismuth-209 with alpha particles."

The news stimulated Ethan's interest again. "Can we produce a quantity to test it?"

"We may need Jezebel's help there. We should discuss it at the team leaders' meeting tomorrow. But there's more ... I've also talked with a colleague of mine, who's a scientific trivia buff, and he commented that one of Saturn's moons — the third largest, Iapetus — has an odd appearance. Spectral analysts speculate that it may have astatine on it. If that's true, for reasons we don't fully understand yet, astatine doesn't decay there."

"How do we discover if Iapetus has astatine?"

"I've heard there's a team sending a probe there and landing an analyzer on the surface to confirm its composition. I suggest we contact the team leader for the launch and get them to add astatine to the list."

"Great. It'll be good to make significant progress for a change."

"Yeah, it will," Jade said, looking at her chronometer. "It's lunchtime. You want to grab a bite to eat?"

Ethan became uncomfortable again, his mind freezing in mid-response. "Umm. I have to finish reviewing this specification," he blurted, averting his eyes and reddening.

Jade looked disappointed. "Well, next time then," she said as she stood to leave.

"Yeah, maybe next time."

What a jackass. That was a perfect opportunity to spend time with her. What's wrong with you? Have you learnt nothing from Hugo?

Jade disappeared out the door. And Ethan sat staring after her, baffled by his behavior.

5

OPPORTUNITY

Loki Mason sat in his office looking at the person talking to him on his desk comm. His heart was pumping fast. The potential business opportunity he expected from the information was making his adrenaline flow.

"A probe has just sent back results of a chemical analysis of Saturn's moon Iapetus. It confirms that half of the moon's surface is full of astatine. You know what that means," the voice said.

Excitement was written all over Loki's face. "Yes. Yes. And it's the only material available for the warp bubble drive?"

"Well, I wouldn't say one hundred percent that they won't find something else, but it's the only substance they know of at present, and they've trialed many."

"So, you're saying whoever claims the astatine deposit on — what was it? Iapetus — controls the means of faster-than-light travel?"

"Yes, if everything works as it should."

"This is the opportunity of a lifetime. If I get there first, I will control immense wealth, and you will benefit too. In time, I'll transfer jurisdiction over to you, and you can make your name and fortune, too."

Stars lit up the person's eyes on the comm. "Yes, I knew you'd approve."

Loki thought matters over for a moment. He realized he didn't have a spaceship capable of reaching Iapetus in the timeframe required. He did, however, have a sophisticated space yacht under construction. His people could improve it with high performance drives for the journey. He must arrive on Iapetus first. "Listen, I need you to do something for me."

"Anything, Loki, I'll do anything."

"You need to cause minor incidents on the project, delays, until my ship can get to Iapetus. It shouldn't take long for me to change the ship I am building. Can you do that?"

"It won't be easy. I will need to consider it, but I'll find a way for you. How long?"

"I don't know yet. Only a few months. I'll tell you once I find out."

"And the Chinese and Russians? They're getting close, too."

"Don't concern yourself with them. I'll look after them. I just need you to do your part."

"OK."

"And don't call me on this line anymore. It's not secure enough. Use the emergency number. And it will be safer if we use codenames. You can be American Pie. Call me Blackjack."

"OK."

"You've done good. I'm proud of you."

"Thank you, Father."

Loki choked on the word 'father'. He had a rare condition that meant he was infertile, so he never thought he would ever hear himself addressed by that name. "You're welcome, but stick to my codename. See you and good luck."

The connection broke, and Loki sat back, thinking about American Pie, whom he regarded as one of his greatest achievements. He had stumbled on the kid decades ago while looking at a local newscast at one of his many estates around the globe. The kid's parents had died in a vehicle accident, and there was something about that shell-shocked four-year-old orphan that had moved him. On impulse, he had taken the kid under his wing. Now twenty-five years later he was reaping the rewards. The kid had blossomed at a prestigious university and then taken on a stellar career, always showing him unwavering devotion. This was the closest he ever might get to fatherhood, Loki mused, so perhaps he should make their relationship legal. Once this matter was resolved, he vowed, he would make American Pie his heir. After all, they were on the same wavelength about many things.

In his occasional introspective moments, Loki sometimes wondered whether his childlessness was the main reason he threw himself so much into his business empire and the accumulation of wealth and power. His only other obsession over the years had been making sure this kid had a childhood very different from his own.

Loki had been brought up by his natural father, who should have loved him but didn't. He could only remember psychological abuse and humiliation from his father, who always nagged him and appeared disappointed in him. Well, he got back at him. His father had nothing now. He had crushed him. Loki took away everything his father had built and claimed it for himself. He never felt so satisfied as the day he told his father he was no longer chairman of the board and had lost his business interests. Loki emphasized it by telling him he amounted to nothing, just like he had always told Loki. Well, he mounted to something now!

Loki returned to reality. He needed to make plans. He called his personal assistant and asked her to contact Carson — another success story for Loki — and tell him to come see him at once.

Stan Carson was Loki's right-hand man and confidante. He was cunning and ruthless, which made him a perfect fit for Loki. Loki had discovered him many years ago wallowing in the New York slums after his release from yet another prison term. Loki had needed a henchman to do a task for him. He had needed someone expendable. Carson had done such a good job that Loki took him under his wing instead of discarding him as he usually did after a clandestine transaction. Carson had proven his dedication, efficiency, and loyalty time and time again until he was now the person whom Loki trusted above everyone else. Loki trusted nobody, but Carson was the exception.

"You are in luck, sir. Carson is standing with me. I'll send him to you."

"Thank you."

Within moments Carson was entering Loki's office. "What can I do for you, boss?" he said as he strolled to the chair across the desk from Loki and sat down.

"We have an opportunity coming up, but I need my new yacht improved to travel faster and over a longer distance. We need a more powerful EmDrive for it. Can you arrange that?"

Carson eyed his boss with interest. "I'll work out the possibilities. What's the go?"

"We have an enormous business opportunity, but it requires a long trip."

"Where?"

"A fast flight to Saturn. Hence the beefed-up drives."

"Hmm! Interesting."

"Yes, interesting. I need you to make other arrangements, too."

"Such as what?"

"You have heard of the projects to develop faster-than-light spaceship drives?"

"Yes. The Americans have an international team. And the Chinese and Russians are researching it, too."

"Correct. Plant a person in the Chinese and Russian teams to sabotage their work, so we delay their projects. Nothing dire at this stage, but we may need to resort to more drastic measures if we can't get the delays we want. They must understand the consequences of failure, too."

"That shouldn't be difficult to arrange. I can use one of my usual methods."

"Good."

"And the Americans?"

"I have someone there already."

"OK. Anything else?"

"That's it for now."

"I'll get on to it then. See you later," Carson said as he rose from the chair, arrested in mid-movement when Loki suddenly asked, "Was there a reason you were with my PA?"

Carson looked at Loki cautiously. "ESP."

Loki smiled. "Yeah, ESP. Get out of here."

Carson left.

If he weren't so valuable, I'd have him whipped for chatting up my staff. But I've got more important things to think about now. I need information on the moon Iapetus. How much material is on it, and how do I mine it? I'll call one of my scientific contacts to put together a factsheet for me.

6

AMERICAN PIE

The latest team leaders' meeting was in progress. Ethan noted the project's five-year anniversary was approaching, and they were nearing its completion. They were preparing to trial the bubble drive.

"Where are we at with the muon generator equipment, Ethan?" Galena Alvarez enquired.

"We're in the final stages of assembly and should be ready to commission tomorrow," Ethan replied with enthusiasm. He was keen to play with his new toys. He cast a quick eye over to Jade Powers, whom he hoped was impressed by his achievements. She was dithering with her tablet notes, though. He glanced away when she looked up, embarrassed that she might have caught him, catching a smile as he lost view of her. Despite signs that she was interested in him, he was still too shy to ask her on a date. He even found excuses when she suggested something.

"And the muon field concentrator and wave resonator?" continued Galena.

"Powering up now. They should be at full power by Thursday, ready for integration of the generator."

“That looks on schedule. How is the fusion generator assembly going, Jezebel?”

“It should be ready to power up in a week,” Jezebel replied.

“And the astatine production setup?”

“The reactor is being commissioned for the production run to supply the trial. It will be ready when we need to test it,” Jezebel continued. She had expertise in isotope generation. They knew little else about her as she tended to keep her private life private. Ethan’s initial fear about how well she would fit into the team had proved justified, although he had no complaints about her dedication or the quality of her work. He tried, too, to cut her some slack as he suspected she suffered from his malady: shyness.

“Good. And the first warp bubble generator trial design, Jade?”

“I’ll approve the trial procedure and log the safety brief by Thursday. This should be achievable.”

“Jake, how is the ship preparation going?” Ethan asked.

“Things are behind schedule. Expert help is hard to find — I’ve tried to drill efficiency into the technicians, but I may as well be talking to monkeys sometimes!”

“How can we help improve your progress?” Galena asked.

“I have my supervisors reviewing the quality of their mechanics, and I’m considering rearranging the schedule. We’re sourcing a few more technicians to work in parallel, too.”

“OK. Keep me informed. It looks like things are coming together well. I must tell you, though, there’s disturbing news surfacing of sabotage impeding our achievements, so be on your guard for suspicious activities and report them to me.”

“What activities?” Jake asked, cocking an eyebrow. “I’ve heard nothing.” Nor, it seemed, had the others present, who glanced around with inquiring expressions.

“Equipment supply delays because of lost parts, etcetera. But no one can explain why, so stay vigilant.”

“Yeah,” everyone replied in unison.

“OK. That’s it for today. Let’s get on with it.”

With that, everyone exited the conference room. Jade paused outside for Ethan. "That was impressive!" she said with a cheeky grin when Ethan emerged. His thoughts elsewhere, his cheeks flushed with embarrassment at seeing her. He averted his eyes and then glanced at her, catching an unusual expression in hers for a fleeting moment, something that went beyond mere professional admiration. But why would this beautiful woman, who could have anyone, be interested in him?

She turned and walked down the corridor away from him, but not before shooting him what was unmistakably a flirty grin.

Ethan sighed as he watched her disappear around the corner. *I wish I knew what to say.* With that depressing thought glued in his mind, he headed to his office to tackle the next problem.

THE WARP DRIVE POWER-UP TEST, which would verify whether they could develop a warp bubble with the drive, was ready. It had to verify the bubble's size, too. After that they needed to produce a stable bubble environment to enclose the drive and the spaceship that contained it and then fly FTL from Saturn to Mars — once they had traveled to Iapetus to collect the astatine supply.

Jade had discovered that astatine could supply the quantity of muon particles required to incite a stable quantum field bubble around a large object (a spaceship, for example), which could, in theory, speed up to any velocity. Current analysis showed that energy requirements limited the speed to a hundred times the speed of light (100c). Astatine was element eighty-five in the periodic table. Unfortunately, its unstable nature on Earth, having a half-life of only eight and a half hours, made it the rarest element. It was an important contributor to other avenues of FTL inquiry being conducted by others, too.

After painstaking research, it was now understood that the interactions between complex sub-atomic fields unique to Earth catalyzed the element's decay. This had led to the belief that it might be more prevalent elsewhere. Review of data from unmanned space probes had provided promising conclusions that there were significant deposits on Iapetus, a moon of Saturn. This moon displayed a peculiar characteristic, having one hemisphere much darker than the other. The probe had sent back spectroscopic analysis the year before, confirming that the dark hemisphere of the moon possessed pure astatine, existing as a thin coating of the material on the surface. Scientists postulated that the substance had been deposited many millions of years ago when the solar system traveled through a super nova nebulous cloud containing a high astatine concentration. They had planned the trip to Saturn to collect a sample and place it in the muon generator connected to the drive power supply for a full drive test. It was vital to lay claim to the supply to guarantee availability without being held to ransom by an unscrupulous person or country. The international project was just that — international — and the member countries held equal claim to the deposit for future developments, as set out in international law. There was the usual political intrigue between different countries, but relationships had stabilized since the latter years of the twentieth century, especially with Russia and China, although these two states were working on their own versions of the drive.

The days passed quickly, and Ethan wondered how he found any time to sleep, never mind eat, but he managed. He arrived at the test center early the morning of the test to check that everything was ready. The room was in the middle of the International Space Drive Project's center at JPL. They housed the equipment in a large basement two floors underground with only one entrance. There was no fire escape, so it didn't bear thinking about if a fire started with you inside.

Another entry hatch existed in the roof, but that provided access for a lander to load and transport the equipment to the interplanetary ship when they were ready to fly to Saturn. They sealed it closed until ready to transport and install the machinery. Marines with top-level clearance from the American Criminal Intelligence Agency and the National Security Council guarded the entrance. They said nothing to Ethan whenever he passed them, just standing at attention with their MP5Ls at the ready — laser rifles developed to update the 9mm machine gun of the last century. Fingerprint and retinal scanners and facial recognition secured access. In theory, only people with proper clearance could gain access, but Ethan sometimes wondered about that.

The view from the entrance always impressed him. The walls were bright white, and the floor polished to a sheen any cleaner would envy. An array of sheet lighting covered the ceiling that shone with subdued brilliance. Equipment stood on the far side and the control console sat ten meters from the doorway. During construction, they considered placing it in its own cubicle to protect it from any drive mishaps. But they realized not much could save it or anyone present from an explosion, given the power involved, negating the usefulness of a separate room.

Ethan stared at the drive itself sitting in the basement center, together with the primary controls and power source. It resembled an old jet turbine engine with a central teardrop-shaped part and an outer toroid when viewed from the front. The toroid was five meters in diameter outside, four and a half meters on the inside, and ten meters long. The central unit, which was the muon wave resonator, was one and a half meters in diameter midway along the axis, tapering to each end, and ten meters long. A fusion reactor of one-hundred-gigawatt capacity powered it, although the trial would use only a small fraction of this. With a successful trial, they hoped to place the unit into test runs consuming much higher power levels. The power source produced a stream of alpha particles that, when colliding with astatine atoms, generated muons. It then concentrated these muons into a tight beam that entered the resonator, producing the warp bubble. The main control cubicle held the controls for the reactor, the muon generator, the muon field density concentrator, and the muon wave resonator. The local panel where Ethan now stood monitored and regulated the equipment.

As Ethan took in the scenery, he reviewed the basic project plan in his head. They were to test the drive in this basement to prove and sustain a stable warp bubble of the predicted size. The minute supply of astatine made the test short. With a successful experiment, they could transport the drive to the spaceship waiting in orbit and install and integrate it into the ship drive and control circuits. Once they had collected a larger supply of astatine at Iapetus and placed a supply in the drive containment chamber, they would trial light-speed flight, powering up the drive to propel the ship to Mars at 2c. If this went to plan, immense celebrations would erupt when everyone returned to Earth. There was further test work scheduled after this to test the systems and travel faster and further, ironing out any bugs discovered during the return to Mars. Ethan shivered with excitement whenever he contemplated their intended venture.

Ethan proceeded into the room and went to the drive control panel. They had a temporary terminal connected to the main control processor so they could conduct more detailed analyzes on the systems and operating specifications. As he looked at the screen of his portable muon field density meter, he noticed an unusual random glitch in the field stability matrix reading. That was strange and hadn't been present when he checked the equipment three days ago. He delved deeper into the diagnostic routines, which caused an even stronger concern that something was wrong. It would have to happen today of all days. "Murphy's law!" he ruminated as he worked. Further diagnostics pointed to the hardware connections being the source of the problem.

He wandered over to the linkages panel and removed the main cover. A chill ran down his spine as he viewed the cabinet internals. There was significant damage to the primary connection conduit — sliced, deliberate, and just enough to concentrate the muon particle stream current to a high density in that spot, overheating the wiring, vaporizing the connection, and exploding with unknown strength as the wiring separated.

This was sabotage. But who had done it, and when? He had checked the panel only three days ago, and it was in pristine condition then. Few people had basement access, and that unnerved Ethan. Was there a saboteur in their midst? Everyone working on the project had passed through the highest security and background checks. Ethan had to alert Galena, but first he had to fix the conduit. He resolved to watch those present at the test for unusual behavior when nothing failed. Anyone absent would arouse suspicion too, as he suspected that person would prefer to be well away from it when the conduit blew.

~

STANDING at the door of Galena's office, Ethan asked her, "Do you have a minute?" She was conducting a staff meeting and looked surprised at the interruption. "In private," he added.

The staff stared at Ethan, puzzled. Galena raised her eyebrows but immediately dismissed the others and invited him in.

He entered and marveled over the tidiness, as he did every time that he entered her office. Her desk stood away from the door, next to the window, so she could swivel ninety degrees in her chair and gaze out into the nearby foothills while she pondered. Ethan had that same view straight in front of him now. A large inbuilt bookshelf and storage compartment stood to his right. A meeting table and six chairs were on his left.

Galena closed the door and gestured Ethan to the table.

They both sat in chairs next to each other. "You seldom storm in demanding a private conference," Galena remarked. "What's on your mind?"

"I've just come from the testing room where I've been for the last hour and a half, replacing the main energy field transfer conduit. Someone vandalized it."

Galena's eyes widened in shock. Her brows then furrowed in concern. "Are you sure ...? Oh, that's a dumb question."

"Yes, I'm sure. I checked that panel three days ago, and everything was in top condition. I only discovered it this morning because I conducted a final equipment check. The field stability matrix circuit had an anomaly and when I opened the cabinet, I spotted the hacked conduit. The entire project would have exploded when we started the drive power for the test if I hadn't noticed it."

"You said that you checked it three days ago?"

"Yes! What puzzles me is no one's entered the room, not according to the entry log. We conducted the pre-commissioning checks remotely, negating the need. We have a brilliant saboteur."

"Why? Why sabotage the project?"

"Maybe we are getting too far ahead of someone else."

"Maybe." Galena rubbed her chin in thought. "What should we do?"

"Keep a very close watch on those attending the test this afternoon. See if anyone acts surprised when no mishap occurs. We should note any suspicious absentees. The damage done could have caused a massive explosion. The person would know that. I'm sure I wouldn't risk my life by being there."

"Good thinking. I'll tell my superiors and get intelligence involved. In the meantime, we need to keep this to ourselves. That way, we might catch out whoever did this."

As Ethan walked away, an unwelcome thought occurred to him. Should he have kept Galena in the dark a little longer? How did he know he could trust her? Another chill ran down his spine at the thought of the project manager being the saboteur. He gave himself a shake — of course he could trust Galena.

7

CHINESE CHECKERS

Chang Jian Zha was contented with how the research was developing. The scientific team had made significant progress in their search for wormhole generation technology and the factors in maintaining wormhole cohesion. They had help from the Americans, thanks to their exchange of information. Now they could concentrate on constructing a workable wormhole transport technique. They just needed to discover a means of long-term stability so that they, the Chinese, could have their own methods of long-distance space travel without relying on other countries. It would be a contingency against any future deterioration in diplomatic relations.

Jian called his researchers to a meeting in the main conference room of the Chinese moon base. He wanted updates on progress. As he waited, he pondered the achievements of the Chinese in establishing the base. They had placed it in the north lunar pole, in the terminator zone, a hundred meters below the surface. The Americans, Europeans, and Russians had established bases on the moon, too, but the Chinese were more advanced and used the base for their top-secret scientific research, including the wormhole generator.

Development had taken ten years, but the base now generated its own oxygen, water, food, and energy. They had discovered water deep in the moon's crust in large enough quantities of ice to drill and extract. Electrolysis then produced oxygen from the water, regenerated from carbon dioxide scrubbers and dissociaters. The hydrogen released by the electrolysis was used to produce other materials required for the base.

Micro-fusion reactors had made this possible. They provided electricity for the energy supply and were now commonplace. Humans had mastered the means of safely producing large quantities and densities of energy from hydrogen fusion in small reactors established as mainstream technology twenty-seven years ago.

The other technologies that had enabled the economic expansion of humankind with colonies in space, for whatever reason, were the EmDrive and the local gravity field matrix. The EmDrive was a sophisticated propulsion method for spacecraft, and the local gravity field matrix, which fully simulated gravity conditions, had led to safer travel.

Intense microwaves injected into a unique conical-shaped chamber produced the thrust for the EmDrive. The intensity was possible because the micro-fusion reactors produced large quantities of energy over an extended period. Reactor life before requiring recharging was usually five years. While spacecraft speed was limited to 0.2c, the technology allowed convenient transport over short periods to most parts of the solar system, the regions of current interest.

The local gravity field matrix permitted comfortable travel while experiencing Earth-strength gravity within the designated areas of the spacecraft requiring gravity. In theory, they could adjust the field matrices to any desired strength. Multiple matrix grids meant they could produce different gravity fields in different areas of the craft as desired. They used the technology on spaceships and anywhere they needed it, which was why the Chinese establishment on the moon enjoyed half Earth-strength gravity.

The Chinese had adapted a version of this gravity field matrix for spacecraft when descending to or ascending from a planet, the so-called improved generalized force model known as IGFM. It could produce an inverse gravity field, anti-gravity, to brake for landing and speed up the craft for takeoff. They used the EmDrive for this too but, because of the size of the equipment, the spacecraft using these drives were built in space and stayed in orbit around a planet. Landers equipped with an IGFM conducted transfers between the ship and the planet.

Jian watched each research team leader enter the meeting room and sit at the table. A person's instinctive preference for the same seat amused him. Jian often sat in a different chair than his usual head position to observe people's reactions. He chuckled to himself on those occasions when he saw the confusion on people's faces as they wondered where to sit.

Chen Liang entered the room first. He was thirty-four, tall for a Chinese at 190 centimeters, and the most prominent quantum physicist in China. His greatest talent, though, was sifting through the details of an issue and quickly identifying the causes. The state had noticed his intelligence at an early age and taken over his education, moving him from his home in Suzhou to a specialist school in Beijing. As a result, he had no strong family connections and was a total introvert. While his dedication was unquestionable, his aloofness kept people from getting to know him. Jian, however, liked him and saw great promise in him.

Liang moved around the table to sit to Jian's right, as was his habit. "Good morning, Leader Jian, sir," he said before proceeding to sit.

"Good morning, Member Liang. I wish everyone followed your example of punctuality."

"The others are approaching."

Ching Hu entered a few moments later and veered to Jian's left. "Good morning, Leader Jian, sir."

"Good morning, Member Hu."

Hu sat. She was the chief engineer for the project and at thirty-one years had risen in the hierarchy at a meteoric pace, not surprising given her brilliance in engineering. She stood 163 centimeters tall and exuded an inquisitive mien. At that moment, however, she appeared preoccupied, wearing a slightly worried expression.

Wong Bingwen and Jiang Minzhe came into the room together, earnestly discussing an issue they were working through and whispering so the others couldn't overhear them. Bingwen was the project's fusion specialist, and Minzhe was the chemical specialist and the Communist Party representative. In the latter role, it was his duty to report to the party on political conformance of the project to the party's policies. They ended their discussion as they entered, and Bingwen closed the door behind him.

"Good morning, Members Bingwen and Minzhe."

"Good morning, Leader Jian, sir," both responded and sat in their respective seats.

"Shall we get started?"

"Yes, sir," they replied in unison.

"OK. Let's start with the fusion reactor, Bingwen."

"The reactor construction is proceeding to schedule, sir. The coils and superconductors are in position. We have tested the control units, and the fuel delivery equipment is in place. We should be ready for inserting the fusion feed material in two weeks, once we have pre-commissioned the reactor, sir."

"Have the conductors been factory-tested?"

"Yes, and they have issued the Quality Assurance Certificates, sir."

"But did you witness the tests? The certificates are not worth the paper they're written on."

"Yes, sir. I attended the factory tests," Bingwen replied in a wooden tone. Jian was pedantic over personally witnessing equipment hold points.

"How is the reactor feed material purification going then, Minzhe?"

"The tritium concentrators are operating twenty-four hours per day, sir, and at current purification rates, there will be enough supply feed for the first test work and power up to operational status."

"Good. Hu, report on the wormhole generator."

"There we have a problem, sir. They delivered the electromagnetic field flux concentrator damaged."

"What!" Jian shouted once the implications sank in, his face reddening with rage. He bounced to his feet, leaning over the table toward Hu. "How could you let such a thing happen? This is not acceptable. You must rectify this!" He sat again, slower than he rose, regaining his composure from his supposed outburst. He felt pleased with his acting, although was uncertain how much the people on the receiving end believed it.

Hu sat calmly looking at Jian, unruffled by his performance. She knew it was for Minzhe's sake and his report to the Party.

"Sir, you misunderstand my report," she said. "Let me explain the issue in more detail. No one at the base damaged the part. It arrived damaged. Nor do we believe it was damaged during transportation from Earth. The destruction occurred sometime between my inspection three days ago and packing and loading in the transportation container. And, sir, when I say damaged, it's not incidental damage. This concerns me the most. A saboteur has maliciously smashed the concentrator."

Everyone trained their eyes on Hu in disbelief.

No longer acting, a worried Jian said, "How can this be? Who could damage the part without detection? This is unacceptable." Jian realized full well that this meant a delay. He knew his superiors' response to the news, too. They would interpret it as an attack on the Party. "Is there information on the culprit?"

"I have just started investigating and have sent a message to Earth to confiscate video recordings from the security systems and have requested an investigation by the Ministry of State Security. I have advised that you will contact them to confirm the investigation application, sir."

"Good. Let us find the culprit, at least. What is the status, then?"

"With regret, sir, the concentrator is beyond repair. We need another part manufactured. Even with an emergency order, I believe that this will take five weeks."

"This is not good. Not good at all. We must do everything in our power to improve delivery, Hu."

"I'll do my best, sir. I ask permission to return to Earth to help with the investigation and oversee the manufacturing arrangements for the new concentrator so that we receive it in the least time."

"Who will cover your activities while you are absent?"

"They are routine, sir. My deputies can supervise them."

"OK, but I want you back in a week."

"Noted, sir, and thank you."

"Any other reports on the generator?"

"No, sir. Everything else is proceeding according to schedule. This headache is enough."

"Very well. We will meet again in one week when Hu returns."

Everybody stood and prepared to exit the meeting room.

"Hu, can you stay behind for a minute, please?" Jian asked.

"Yes, sir."

The others filed out. Jian stood, walked over to the door, and closed it. "This is disturbing, Hu. You are unaware, but it's the second incident of sabotage plaguing this project. We had reactor parts lost three months ago. I said nothing because we found them and presumed them merely misplaced. But I believe this incident sheds new light on that matter."

"I did not know. Yes, it looks suspicious now that this damage has occurred as well. We are entering a crucial stage in the project where we will start testing the theory for wormholes. It is as if someone wants us to fail — or at least retard our progress, sir."

"That's what I was thinking. Can you investigate the earlier incident and assess any connection between them? Peng Zedung will give you the information."

"Will do, sir."

"And when I talk with State Security, I will inform them you will contact them to help with the inquiry. Don't concern yourself rushing back if it's necessary to stay longer on Earth for the investigation. I am confident your deputies can cope provided there is regular communication between you. Stopping any further mishaps is a higher priority until the new concentrator arrives."

"Noted, sir. I will keep you informed."

"Dismissed. Now to psyche myself up to break the news to my supervisor."

"Yes, sir. I do not envy you that," Hu commented with a sympathetic smile.

Jian sighed melodramatically as they walked out the door.

HU LEFT for Security to get the video file of the concentrator part's delivery at the moon base. She requested the cargo hold footage of the shuttle that delivered the parts, too. Footage on the supply side was only available on Earth. She downloaded the required videos to her secure cache to view later and continued to see Peng Zedung. She chimed his closed office door, and, after a slight delay, the door opened.

Hu entered. "Hi, Zedung. Sorry to interrupt you, but Jian Zha just told me you had reactor parts go missing a few months ago."

"Come in and sit. You are giving me a break from tedious filing. Yes, I did. They turned up again after several weeks, but it was odd because I had supervised their storage. They need special cradles to rest in until we install them, so they don't get damaged."

"How large are they?"

"They are not heavy. Only six hundred grams, including the cradle, so it's possible for someone to just pick them up and move them."

"When did you first notice them missing?"

"Oh, three or four days after I placed them into stores. I went to retrieve them for installation, but they were not there. It put me in a bind, as they were my responsibility. I talked to Jian Zha without delay."

"Did you look at the surveillance footage?"

"Yes, I did, but nothing showed, although a gap of twelve minutes occurred with a blank screen on the store's camera. I suspect that was when someone took the parts. When I asked Security how the blank twelve minutes could occur, it confused them as much as me."

"Could they use them for a different purpose or sell them?"

"No. They were a special design, so unsuitable for normal machinery."

"And when they showed up again?"

"Another gap in the video footage. I was searching for a part and saw them in their correct spot. I had already ordered replacement parts by then. At least now we have spares, I suppose. Spares are always handy."

Hu contemplated the information that Zedung had given her. "There was mysterious damage to a part delivered on the last shuttle. The destruction happened before the part arrived. I am trying to decide if there's a connection between the two cases. What do you think?"

Zedung considered the possibility. "Very possible that they are related. Consider the implications of both events. My parts going missing delayed me for several weeks. It could have delayed the entire schedule, but I rescheduled another part to compensate. Your incident is an escalation, to make postponement an absolute certainty. I take it you can't reschedule your activities to avoid a delay?"

"No, I can't. Not this late in the program. You could be onto something there. It's an increase in the sabotage's severity. Maybe the culprit is getting bolder and more desperate."

"So, where to from here?"

"I need to examine the video footage for my incident to check for a discrepancy here or during the flight. I must return to Earth to review the video file from the supplier and the transporter and negotiate a replacement unit."

"Lucky you, going back to Earth," Zedung said, smiling with envy, as most people seldom returned to Earth from the moon base.

"Somebody has to do it," Hu responded with a grin as she rose from her seat to leave.

"Inform me if you need anything more from me."

"Will do," Hu replied and left Zedung's office, heading for her quarters to pack for the trip back to China.

8

RUSSIAN ROULETTE

Apep Chernakov sat in his office contemplating the future direction of the warp drive project. He worked at the Russian Space Science Research Center near Serov, deep under the Ural Mountains. The project was not progressing well, even with the full dedication of his team of scientists and engineers and despite the known potential punishments for failure. If Apep had believed in such things, he would have said the project was jinxed.

His team had built and assembled a prototype warp drive test center over the last few years. However, elusive, mysterious gremlins kept causing delays and complications with its construction. Parts went missing or arrived damaged. They delivered incorrectly assembled components when detailed procedures were available. Machinery failed basic tests. *This state of affairs must change, or I'll be fronting the firing squad,* Apep thought with a touch of black humor. He sensed deliberate sabotage of the project to keep it in stasis — not failed, just delayed.

Apep's desk comm buzzed, and he leaned over to press the speak button.

"Yes, Olga?"

"Comrade Stenanko wishes to meet with you, sir," Olga Chekov replied in her usual official voice. She had been Apep's personal assistant for a long time, but her formality never wavered. Apep was sure she spoke the same way to her spouse at home. *Is it how she tells her husband she has the urge ... ooh, stop that Apep!*

"OK, Olga. Show Alexi into the office." Apep sighed as his thoughts returned to the present. *I wonder what's happened this time.*

Alexi Stenanko was the chief engineer for the project, and he was an excellent engineer. Unfortunately for him, that meant problems of missing or damaged parts came to him first, and so he was the one who reported them to Apep. It sometimes seemed Alexi was always in his office.

Alexi opened the door and entered, closing it behind him.

"Comrade Chernakov," Alexi said with a nod of the head.

"Alexi," Apep replied informally. "Enough Comrade rubbish between us. Yes, No?"

"OK. Just habit."

"We should get an extra desk in here for you, Alexi. You're in here more than I am," Apep quipped. "What is the issue this time?"

"Another damaged assembly, Com– Apep, I'm afraid," Alexi said. "One of the main booster coils. Someone took to it with an ax. It's deliberate. They knew what part to damage to cause a major delay. We can't progress on the project until we get a replacement."

Apep glanced at Alexi, concerned, and considering his next step here. *Who is behind this and why?* "We can't let things continue like this, can we, Alexi?"

"No, we can't. But what can we do? How do we find out who's masterminding it and stop them?"

"I have an idea. Let me talk to my friends in the Federal Security Service. Can you chase up another coil in the meantime? How long will it take?"

"I need to check. They are custom-made. It might be a month."

"Ouch! That will hurt."

"I will push to get it quicker."

OK. Do it. I'll inform my superiors and discuss ways of stopping this sabotage with the FSB. Who supplied the part?"

"Oligov Electrical Industries. They are in the suburbs of Moscow."

"I can pay them a visit while I'm in Moscow, yes? See if I can motivate them."

"Good idea, but the owner is a slimy salesman."

"I know the type. I can manipulate people like him. Don't inform him I am coming, though. I want to surprise him."

Apep always enjoyed his business trips to Moscow, even when the business was unpalatable, as it was now. The city was such a contrast to the remoteness of their offices and living quarters in Serov. In particular, he enjoyed viewing the grandeur of Red Square with the Kremlin, St Basil's Cathedral, and the other stunning buildings surrounding the open plaza and parkland.

First, he needed to talk with his associate, Kristina Zlanovik, at the FSB about the sabotage issue at the project. Kristina was short and plump, which made her look like a ball, but it was not wise to underestimate her. She had the eyes of a hawk for seeing and analyzing people's behavior. Over the years, she and Apep had developed a strong private and professional relationship.

Her assistant ushered him into Kristina's office.

"Good morning, Comrade Zlanovik. How are you today?" Apep greeted formally for the assistant's benefit.

"Good morning to you, Comrade Chernakov. I am well. I wasn't expecting to see you. Have a seat. Would you like a tea?" Kristina replied.

"Yes, please. Black and no sugar." Apep was conscious of putting on weight and was trying to avoid sugar, at least in his tea.

"Sophia, make my usual and a black tea, no sugar for Comrade Chernakov, please."

"Yes, Comrade Zlanovik," Sophia responded and walked from the office to get the beverages. She closed the door behind her.

"And how have you been, Apep? I was not expecting to see you so soon, not that it isn't always a pleasure to catch up with you."

"Ah well, the pressures of work keep me sleepless, and another gray hair pops out every day." Apep sighed with an air of resignation.

"You must learn to relax more and enjoy your life before you grow old," Kristina said sagely with a friendly smile.

"I would, but I must justify our wonderful country's faith in me."

A knock rapped on the door, and Kristina voiced admittance. Sophia entered with two cups of tea in her hands. Placing them next to the respective recipients, she left, closing the door behind her.

"So, how can I help you?" Kristina asked, sipping her sweet black tea.

Apep cradled his cup, wishing it had sugar in it. Gathering his thoughts, he began, "Disturbing incidents are interrupting my project."

"What do you mean?" Kristina interjected, alarmed.

"Objects going missing, parts damaged, delays. It is putting us long behind schedule, and there is pressure on the team and me to improve. But we can't progress with these constant interruptions. The last incident has us convinced now of deliberate sabotage, not merely incompetence. The saboteur purposely ruined a delivered part, so we need another one to go ahead. It's as if someone is delaying the project for their own reasons, whatever they may be. It has to stop, but I don't know how to make it stop. So, I visit you."

"That sounds very serious, Apep. Yes, you are justified in discussing this with me," Kristina responded, her voice laced with concern. "This will cause pressure from above for things beyond your control. It must be very stressful. Do you think someone on the team is responsible?"

"It could be anyone, I suppose, but I don't think so. I have known them for many years. There is no reason for their betrayal by delaying the project. Their security checks are of the very highest standard. Not that one hasn't slipped through — it has happened."

"Since you mention it, I recently read of similar occurrences in a report. Just wait a minute." Kristina turned her attention to her data screen for a few minutes, viewing several emails and files collected on distributed intelligence briefs to FSB directors. "Yes, as I thought. We have had rumors of similar incidents occurring with the Chinese and Americans on their versions of your project. And now you ... that is no coincidence," Kristina said, pensive, turning again to Apep.

"No, it can't be. But it makes little sense either."

"What is the common thread here?"

"We research faster-than-light travel technology, but who would obstruct that? Aliens?" Apep said with intentional exaggeration, throwing his hands up in exasperation.

Kristina chuckled. "I am sure a more rational explanation exists," she said as she returned to her data screen. She turned her attention to Apep again after a couple more minutes. "I read you are friendly with a Mr. Ethan Richards from the USA, yes?"

"Yes, we became acquaintances when I conducted my research at Caltech. We chat at conferences. I like keeping tabs on people."

Kristina chuckled again. "Yes, we are excellent at that skill. Did you know he is a key member of the American team for its faster-than-light project?"

"Yes, I did, although, as you'd understand, circumstances restrain our discussions. It's an international team, not just composed of Americans. In fact, the Chinese and we would have taken part in the team too, but our governments decided they wanted to develop it themselves, the alternatives suited a three-pronged approach when the respective governments discussed it, I believe. I don't think it was for any security or strategic reasons, though."

"Is that right? No, I was not aware. We will make an excellent spy out of you yet, Apep," Kristina quipped. "I brought Ethan Richard's name up because it might be a good idea for you to see him and compare notes on this issue. You may find a pattern emerging. Normally I would suggest contacting him on his comm, but this communication is too delicate to risk people snooping — the wrong people. From what you tell me, they keep well informed of our progress."

"Maybe you're right. I can't afford the time, but the sooner we resolve this, the better. Very well, I will make the arrangements. You will prepare the security clearances?"

"Yes, I will. In the meantime, I will assign our people to investigate this matter for answers. Anything else?"

"No, that was it."

"How is your family, then?" Kristina continued, sitting back in her chair to catch up on gossip while they finished the last of their tea. Apep's wife had died several years ago, and he was raising his two children, now almost adults, on his own. "Your children must be ..."

AFTER THE MEETING WITH KRISTINA, Apep found himself thinking a lot about Ethan. His airy remark to Kristina about keeping tabs on people did not reflect his real feelings for Ethan. He regarded him as a valued friend and went out of his way to socialize with him whenever they were at the same conference simply because he enjoyed his company. They sometimes shared general intelligence but never any information their respective countries would consider secret or sensitive. Ethan was as patriotic as himself in that respect, and neither he nor Apep would ever risk their friendship. But Apep's achievements were unraveling with this project. Kristina was right — he needed Ethan's help.

9

PROGRESS

Ethan was busy preparing for the warp bubble drive test with his technicians when the others filed in to conduct their own measurements and witness the test. He didn't let technicians in the basement without one of the key project members present, which presumably excluded them from the suspect list of saboteurs. The person couldn't have damaged the connection unnoticed while someone else was there. The condition was an inconvenience, particularly during the drive equipment's construction period, but necessary for security reasons. Ethan had spent many hours in the room doing his normal duties while the technicians worked on the machinery, only providing support when an issue arose with implementing the design.

Jake entered for the test first. "Well, it's getting to the business end of the game."

"You could say that. We'll know after today if our design's workable, or it's back to the drawing board."

"Mister Optimism himself here, I see." Jake and Ethan had become close friends over the preceding five years.

"I am optimistic. I was just stating a fact. After today's test, I expect us to say goodbye to this baby and put her in her proper place in the big world in space."

"That's more like it. How are the preparations going?"

"Good. Just a few more commissioning checks before we can power it up for first-stage field establishment."

"Where's Jade? I thought she'd be here," Jake said, scanning the room as though he expected Jade to pop up from behind the furniture.

"Yes, she's running late," Ethan responded, trying not to sound concerned. "She should be here any minute now."

"Speak of the devil!" said Ethan as the door opened, but Jezebel entered the room.

"Hi! Hope you've all been behaving while I was away."

Jezebel had been on board the ship for a day to get the ship's fusion reactor running.

"Why, where have you been, Jez? Didn't even notice you weren't here," Jake responded dryly.

"On your ship, smart ass, as you very well know. Nobody gets onto your ship without you knowing it," Jezebel retorted with a smile, though Ethan thought she also sounded slightly annoyed.

Ethan's comm chimed. "Hello, Ethan here," he said after disposing of his tools.

"Hi, Ethan, it's Galena. I'm calling to tell you the director's called me to a meeting, so I won't be witnessing the trial, not that you need me."

"OK. No issues, I hope?" Ethan asked.

"Only the one we discussed. Is everyone there yet?"

"Almost. We're just waiting for Jade."

"Good! See you soon and good luck."

"Thanks, but luck doesn't exist. The test will work without a hitch." Ethan only had a slight concern for the test's success, but its failure would be his fault. Ethan hung up and put the comm back in his pocket. "That was Galena. She's got director problems — so she won't be here."

"I hope nothing serious," Jake said.

"No, just the usual stuff. A budget issue," Ethan lied. He knew very well the meeting's agenda.

"Jade's still not here," Jake remarked.

Just then, the door opened again, and Jade entered in a rush.

"Sorry I'm late, Ethan. An issue came up with the muon resonator simulation model. I needed to review it and tweak the settings."

"That's fine," Ethan said, the nervousness in his stomach subsiding. "You're here for the show."

With that, they prepared for the test.

Ethan connected his calibrator and a source generator to the muon field strength meter in the warp drive field concentrator. When he reviewed the readings at various source levels, he detected the meter was reading much less than it should. This worried him because it could generate more muon-field strength than required, overloading the drive. It was puzzling because he had only just checked it with Saul, the technician working with him, two days ago.

"Saul, have you made any adjustments to the muon field strength meter calibration since we looked at it last?" Ethan asked.

"No. What's the problem?" he replied, looking mystified as he stepped toward him.

"It's out of calibration. Help me set the calibration again, please."

"Sure."

Ethan and Saul reset the meter. After further checks that lasted another hour, the drive was ready.

"OK! We start it up now." Ethan told the others. "Where is the astatine, Jezebel?"

"The reactor was producing it overnight, and the purified sample is here ... now!" Jezebel announced with a melodramatic flourish as the door chime rang and a guard carrying the canister appeared. Jezebel accepted the cannister and carried it with care into the room, the door closing behind her. She walked over to the muon generator and inserted the canister into the slot designed for it, twisting it to lock it in place with an audible click.

They had produced a small quantity of astatine in a cyclotron, bombarding bismuth with alpha particles. Even with the cyclotron's enormous size and the concentrated alpha particle bombardment, it took time and effort to produce enough for a successful warp bubble drive test. They needed to make it just before using it because of the material's short half-life.

"Ready when you are, Ethan," Jezebel responded once the canister was in place.

"OK, thanks." Ethan began to test the startup sequence, starting by switching on the muon wave resonator. The resonator powered through its steps, and the green ready light activated. He then proceeded to the next step and powered up the muon field density concentrator. That showed green after a short time, ending its startup sequence. Both units were ready. "Jezebel, is the fusion reactor ready?"

"Ready when you are."

"Good! Let's do it." Ethan placed both the concentrator and the resonator in operating status and started the muon generator. He opened the gate to the astatine canister and cycled through the transfer sequence to place the astatine at the center of the alpha particle bombardment target.

"Open the particle transfer gate five percent, Jezebel."

"Particle transfer gate at five percent."

Alpha particles flowed from the reactor, hitting the astatine, and producing a stream of muons that channeled through to the concentrator. This focused the particles into a high-density ray, creating a muomagnetic beam as one would an electromagnetic beam but with muons instead of electrons. The beam proceeded through the transfer tunnel to the resonator, where the muons deflected between muon mirrors before collapsing into an energy sink. The mirrors allowed the muon beam's frequency to vary until it resonated at a point where it should create a space-time bubble around the resonator. The bubble resulted from a change in the quantum string resonance state on the sphere boundary produced. The bubble size depended on the muon wave frequency, which depended on the power channeled into the muon generator — the higher the frequency, the larger the bubble, but the greater quantity of alpha particles required. As they had a limited supply of astatine, they could generate only so many muons before they depleted the source.

Ethan adjusted the mirror settings until it produced a resonant wave. The team watched with nervous expectation in their expressions as the resonance intensified. The screen showed a space-time bubble, although it was a small one at present. Ethan had deliberately limited the power to make sure the equipment worked as planned. They expected the bubble size to encompass the whole expected volume in one establishment sequence once their confidence increased. Otherwise, interesting space-time problems could occur if part of the spaceship was inside the bubble and part of it outside.

Everything showed stable on the monitors.

"Increase to twenty percent."

Jezebel eased the opening to twenty percent, which released more alpha particles, creating a greater supply of muons. Ethan watched the muon wave frequency control loop adjust as the frequency and the beam density intensified, ensuring that they maintained the resonance. The bubble size increased in volume as the frequency rose. "Gate at twenty percent," Jezebel acknowledged.

"Bubble size one point six meters and stable," Ethan announced. "Increase to forty percent."

Jezebel increased the opening to forty percent. "Bubble size twenty-one meters and stable." The tension in the room mounted as the actual test now started. They had produced the current results before, but nothing beyond this. "OK. Let's increase the opening to seventy-five percent, Jezebel, and be ready to hold or reduce."

"OK. Increasing now." Ethan noted Jezebel's profuse and uncharacteristic perspiration.

As she eased open the orifice, the bubble size grew. At sixty-nine percent opening, a slight disturbance destabilized the resonance. "Hold!" Ethan shouted as he got the resonance control loop-setting screen onto the display. Adjusting the gain and integral settings enabled the resonance to stabilize again. "OK, increase," Ethan said, after allowing time for him to satisfy himself that the resonance was under control. The bubble was now 102 meters in diameter. Ethan paid close attention to the resonance stability screen as Jezebel increased the power again.

"Seventy-five percent," Jezebel announced. The bubble was 191 meters.

"We aren't getting the expected bubble size. The efficiency is below par. Any ideas?" Ethan asked.

Jade responded, after a time, in a tentative voice, "We were never sure how the distance between the resonance mirrors affected the resonance frequency conversion efficiency. So, we designed the resonator with a mirror distance adjustment ability while it ran. Can we try reducing the separation?"

After further discussion, everybody agreed to make the change. Ethan entered the mirror distance setting screen and keyed in an adjusted value. The bubble size jumped, threatening to upset the resonance and collapse the bubble. But the resonance held, and the bubble grew to 273 meters. "That's better," Ethan stated with satisfaction. "Shall we adjust it further to find the optimal point?"

"You'll need to keep your eyes on the time. We only have just over an hour's supply of astatine left," Jezebel warned.

Ethan spent another ten minutes adjusting the mirror distance and arrived at the optimal point with the bubble size at 305 meters.

"OK. Let's do the rest, Jezebel. Increase to one hundred percent open."

"Increasing now!"

Anticipation in the room increased as the power level rose. Ethan concentrated his attention on the frequency stability, making minor adjustments to the control settings along the way. Eighty-five percent power produced a 560-meter bubble. The mirror adjustments made a dramatic improvement to the efficiency. Ninety percent ... ninety-five percent ... ninety-nine percent ... one hundred percent power and a bubble size of 783 meters. Everyone cheered at their success. The theory calculated a bubble size of 775 meters, an educated assumption for the efficiency quotient being used. Everything looked stable to Ethan.

"Twenty minutes' source left, Ethan," Jezebel said.

"Has everyone collected the data they need?" Ethan asked. The others said yes. "OK Jezebel, let's reduce the power and shutdown the unit." Jezebel lowered the energy to the muon generator while Ethan monitored the controls for the bubble field as the bubble collapsed with the reducing energy. As the gate closed, the concentrator and resonator lost power, and everyone relaxed again. "Well, Jake, I think it's time we get to the business end of the project and move this drive upstairs."

Jake beamed. "I'm for that."

The team tidied up and checked everything was in order. Jezebel removed the astatine canister, her expression wooden. Ethan wondered what, if anything, got her excited. He made backups of the test recordings, and once they had completed the tidy-up work, they returned to their offices.

Jake poked his head in the doorway of Ethan's office. "Cause for celebration, don't you think?" he said.

"Sure," responded Ethan, "tell the others." While Jake gathered Jade and Jezebel, Ethan walked over to the drinks cabinet and pulled out some glasses and a bottle of whiskey kept for special occasions.

The others, including Galena, arrived and they toasted a successful day. Jezebel excused herself after downing her whiskey and, after a second whiskey, Jake and Galena said they had to be off too. That just left Jade, who showed no signs of needing to be anywhere else.

She wants to do more than talk shop, Ethan thought. *Oh well, here goes. If you don't ask now, you never will.*

"I know a pleasant bar that I go to in Santa Monica. It's called Sips and Surf, right on the beach. Fancy dinner there tonight?"

"Great!" Jade responded and then added less enthusiastically, "Shall I tell the others?"

"Just us, I think," responded Ethan.

Jade beamed.

ETHAN AND JADE met at Sips and Surf as arranged at 7:30 pm.

Ethan was tense at first, as he always was around attractive women. Despite Hu's efforts to boost his self-confidence, he had still not learned to socialize with a woman, let alone form a close bond. But Jade's warm intelligence with a hint of the imp was getting under his guard.

"This is a lovely restaurant, Ethan. Nice pick," she said, sipping on her cocktail.

"I come here now and then."

"Pickup joint?" Jade teased.

"No, no. It's not," Ethan responded, coloring, hoping Jade didn't notice.

Jade laughed. "Sorry. That was unfair of me. Just can't help trying to embarrass you sometimes. Must mean I'm attracted to you," she probed.

"I like you too, Jade. You work hard, but you have your devilish side, too. I like that."

"You don't socialize around women much, do you?" Jade asked more seriously.

"No, I find conversation difficult. I suppose I'm afraid of being boring. But you're different. I can communicate with you."

"Well, suggesting this spot this afternoon was perfect."

"Thanks."

"The test went well, didn't it?"

"Yes, it did, but I don't want to talk shop. If there's one thing I've learned, it's never to talk shop on your first date." Ethan cringed as he said the last words.

"Date now? You work fast," Jade teased, laughing when Ethan reddened.

The banter continued into the night, in between revelations about each other's backgrounds. Ethan felt contented as he reclined in the taxi on the way home after an enjoyable evening, the like of which he had never experienced before.

10

A SETBACK

Loki Mason sat musing in a typical pose, his hands folded behind his head and leaning back in the massive leather-covered chair in his office as he gazed out the window at the familiar Pacific Island palms. Whenever he had quiet time, he enjoyed recalling his meteoric rise since inheriting an already successful business from his father.

At least that was his version of events. His having manipulated enough board members to vote his father out as chairman, and Loki in, meant nothing to him. It was business, not personal, although it gave him immense satisfaction to see his father destroyed. He removed the board members who voted against him from office, and he reduced the influence the others held on the corporation to puppet status. His business skill was prodigious, and his management style required absolute control. He saw excellent business opportunities long before his rivals did, resulting in his wealth rocketing to astronomical proportions, making him the richest person on the planet. His total value was greater than the gross domestic product of ninety percent of countries around the globe.

The venture he was most proud of — if he had to say so himself — was space mining of the asteroids. His company smelted the ore and brought the refined product to its Earth-orbit-based manufacturing platform for transformation into metals. It then shipped the products to Earth or used them to expand the ever-growing industry base surrounding Earth and its moon. Prospecting of the asteroids was meticulous, so the perfect one could be claimed for mining at a large profit. The right asteroid had grades of ore far greater than equivalent ores on Earth. That made refining easier and less expensive. The company usually found the fuels, oxidants, reductants, and fluxes required to refine the ores on the same asteroid or ones nearby, reducing material transport expenses. The EmDrives developed by the military and now in commercial use made the enterprise practicable. The drive enabled inexpensive travel costs in space, especially compared to the cost and danger of the chemical-based propulsion of yesteryear.

Loki's business was the most prominent presence amongst the asteroids. Because of the *International Solar System Entity Ownership Act*, it was the largest owner of asteroids and other bodies in extraterrestrial space. The first landing on a solar orbital body permitted unequivocal ownership of that body, just like a parcel of land on Earth.

Loki had just returned from an update meeting with his business unit CEOs. The units ran like a Swiss watch. A few issues needed closer attention, but nothing too troublesome, and his underlings weren't hiding problems. They knew what would happen to them if they did. Not a nice way to resign. *Yes, he ran a well-oiled machine*, he thought.

Loki now pondered his latest project, the one that would give him honors in the annals of business history forever. It was the boldest and most ambitious move he had ever attempted, but success would bring unlimited rewards. He had funneled a mammoth allocation of resources into the venture, so it must not fail. It would not fail.

Loki had a worldwide network of spies gathering intelligence on companies and governments of use to him. Occasionally, he directed one or another of his minions to gather or fabricate information on a person of strategic interest who was proving an annoyance to Loki's objectives, removing them from his list of problems.

As soon as Loki had learned about warp drive development and astatine's importance to the technology, the deposit of astatine on the Saturnian moon Iapetus had sent dollar signs before his eyes. Not only would it generate great monetary wealth, but it would also provide significant political prestige and leverage. He must claim the ore before anyone else could. He knew the countries involved had negotiated to share the mineral, and he despised them for it. Surely, the fools must realize the power the material would give anyone able to own it outright.

He must get there first. But it was proving more difficult than expected. He changed the spaceship he planned to build to include more powerful drives and ordered absolute secrecy to avoid awkward questions. The venture was running slower than he wanted it to, and the FTL projects were moving faster than his, resulting in him having to put contingency plans in place.

Loki had infiltrated the projects with saboteurs to delay their completion. These saboteurs were clever people, above suspicion themselves, but able to manipulate workers and constructors in strategic areas, some of whom were responsive to bribes, others to threats. Loki was no murderer, mainly because that would bring too many awkward questions, but he was not above letting people think that he was. That way, he kept everyone on their toes.

The buzzing of his personal comm interrupted his rumination. He pressed the audio button. "Yes?"

"Blackjack, this is American Pie," a low voice issued from the speaker. "Can we talk?"

Loki sat bolt upright in his chair and responded. "You are not to use this number except for an emergency. Why couldn't you use the other channel?"

"My report couldn't wait. I need to inform you they discovered the assigned parcel. They completed a successful drive test, and the next phase is starting."

"Hmm, that is disappointing. Give me the details as usual. Let's see," Loki said as he pondered his next move. "We will use Code Delta. Do you know about Code Delta?"

"Yes."

"In the meantime, go into ghost status."

"Will do."

"Thanks for the update, but I must tell you I am most disappointed. Out," Loki said, ending the call.

Loki swiveled in his chair and gazed out of the window of his complex. The view overlooked a horseshoe-shaped bay with a sandy beach and an expanse of palm trees on either side, morphing into a dense jungle. Waves lapped the shoreline. The occasional seagull squawked overhead and jostled for position on the sand. Several guards were patrolling the shore and a contingent of his harem enjoyed the sparkling water. Usually, the scene lulled him into a sense of serenity. But now, Loki was seething with anger, and no scenic charm could calm his emotions. *How could they have discovered the sabotage?* he fumed. They had planned the delay to the last detail. *Is there a leak? Did American Pie make a mistake? No, there was too much at stake. One of the team members must be meticulous in their preparations. Oh, well, no point in crying over spilled milk. That's why they had contingencies.* He hoped he would not have to use his ultimate strategy — the deterrents he was building into the ship. Chinese Checkers and Russian Roulette were under control, at least.

Loki's emotions calmed, and he warmed to the scenery of the sun-soaked bay outside and the bikini-clad beauties frolicking in the swell. *I think I will go join them and unwind, after all. Maybe get them to entertain me.* Loki rose from his chair and left his office for other, more enjoyable activities.

11

THE ORIENT EXPRESS

The shuttle would be ready for takeoff in ninety minutes. Hu needed to be on it to return to Earth. She had packed her travel bag but was unsure of the length of her absence. So, she packed for a week, telling herself she would have a good excuse to go shopping if she had to stay longer. Not that Hu shopped much. She enjoyed exploring the choices when she needed clothing but didn't bother roaming between shops in search of the best offer. Once she spotted what she wanted, she bought it. After completing her packing, she sealed her bag and placed her carry-on items for the flight into her shoulder pack, including her tablet, laptop, and comm. She surveyed her quarters for any last-minute tidying. The room was modest but practical. A sleeping space had an adjacent ensuite and a small kitchen for preparing meals — although they expected everyone to use the main mess hall, people could make their own snacks in the kitchen — and a living section with a lounge chair, couch, and entertainment equipment, including a holographic projection unit. Everything was in order, so she switched off the lights and locked the door.

The trip to the moon spaceport was uneventful. It was only a fifteen-minute walk. Hu checked her baggage in when she got there and waited for the call to board.

The announcement came twenty minutes later. The well-organized spaceport made it easy to locate your destination since only two passenger shuttle spaces existed. Hu swung her bag over her shoulder and walked to the boarding gate. When she showed her credentials, they logged her into the passenger manifest and advised her to board the shuttle. Two other passengers boarded for the trip. One she knew worked on the project and was eager to embark. She presumed he had family back home that he wanted to see. The other person was someone she hadn't seen before today. Hu assumed he was a casual utility worker keen to get back to Earth to spend his hard-earned cash on parties and women before returning to the base again. Those employees came for the money and were excellent at their jobs, but they were reluctant to lift one iota more than the contract required.

The cabin specialist greeted Hu as she entered the spacecraft. "Greetings, Ms. Ching. Nice to see you again. Your seat is on the right. I hope you have an enjoyable flight."

"So do I," Hu responded as she walked to her designated spot.

The spacecraft resembled the shuttles the Americans used in the twentieth century, with the flight deck upfront, a passenger space next, and the cargo hold in the rear. Thanks to scientific advancement, the key differences were the propulsion and the artificial gravity. The passenger cabin was more extravagant than the original ships. The fittings and the service from the cabin specialists reflected a business class experience on Earth's international flights.

Hu placed her bag in the compartment in front of her as she sat. She looked forward to relaxing for the trip. The other passengers sat across the central aisle, one opposite her and the other further back. There were six passenger seats, but only three traveled today. The flight specialist gave her a refreshment as she settled into her seat. She noticed that the utility worker seemed nervous and assumed he was unused to space flight. Getting her Sensobuds out, she connected to the onboard entertainment and reviewed the options, wondering what she had missed out on since the last time she had flown. She selected a documentary on the ancient Mayan civilization and settled for launch.

Sensobuds were a recent invention. Instead of watching visual entertainment on a screen, or listening to audio through your ears, the buds directed the required brainwave patterns to the sensory centers in the brain, blocking out the actual sights and noises that the eyes and ears sensed, to a significant degree. The visual sensation resembled immersing oneself in the pre-defined screen, while still being able to see authentic scenery in your periphery. You nominated the screen's location, as desired, so you could look away from it into reality whenever you liked. You could switch between actual noises and the relayed noises by thought command. Top-of-the-range models included smell, taste, and touch, but Hu thought that was creepy.

The shuttle left on schedule once the access tube retracted, allowing it to rise from the launch pad in silent splendor. Hu always enjoyed the expected shudder. EmDrives were an amazing advancement in space travel. The spacecraft increased its speed, and Hu undid her seat belt and settled in for the ride.

The flight from the moon to Earth's orbit took twelve hours, with average acceleration and deceleration of 0.1g. The gravity field was set at 0.5g as the shuttle left the moon and would increase to full Earth strength by the time they arrived in Earth's orbit.

The flight specialist started distributing meals to the passengers two hours into the journey. The choice was chicken or beef for the main course with various options to nibble on while waiting for their meals. Refreshments were available, too, and Hu chose a particular chardonnay that she had sampled before and liked.

After eating, Hu didn't return to the Mayan documentary but found her thoughts flitting back to her earlier years at Caltech, which of course brought Ethan to mind. She often thought of him but had seen little of him over the years because she rarely had the time to attend international conferences. She wondered if he had changed, and a smile of affection curled her lips as she thought of this shy and reserved young man, so handsome and yet so sweet and innocent. She wondered if any woman had ever managed to bring him out of his shell. Perhaps the two of them could have formed a romantic relationship, but she doubted it. He was too absorbed in his own world and did not even realize when she was flirting with him. But they had developed a close friendship nonetheless, and she would always treasure that. Hu speculated on whether she would ever see him again. Putting those thoughts to one side, she decided to catch up with some work.

She was reading through reports and other project paperwork when a gentle tap on her shoulder interrupted her. It was the flight specialist offering another meal. Hu glanced at her chronometer, surprised to realize she had been working for six hours. Come to think of it, she was feeling hungry. She sat up straight in her seat, put her tablet aside, and stretched her muscles. While waiting for the food, she glanced around and noted that the utility worker was still fidgeting and looking distracted. That was strange. He should have relaxed by now. With her meal placed in front of her, Hu faced the front again and started eating.

She noticed movement out of the corner of her eye as she started her dessert. The utility worker had risen from his seat and was walking past her, she assumed to go to the toilet. He held his arms close to his body, but as he drew level with her, he drew out something that glinted. Just as she turned her head toward him, her subconscious told her it was a small knife. Reacting on reflex, Hu launched herself from her seat, pirouetting on her right foot and placing her right hand around his right shoulder blade, pinching the nerves in the location that she had learned in her Tae Kwon Do classes while grabbing the wrist of the hand that held the knife. With her hands in these positions, she could force the person to let go of the knife, which in the struggle got stuck in the cloth-covered cushioned seat. She dropped him to his knees by squeezing his shoulder nerves harder. The amateur assassin kept repeating, "Must do, must do. Cannot fail. My family," in an agonized whimper. The action happened so fast that nobody else reacted, although both the flight specialist and the other passenger witnessed the incident in frozen horror. Hu's meal tray had sprayed food and drink over the cabin in her immediate space.

"Why are you doing this?" Hu demanded.

"Must not tell. Family. Please ... must not fail," the worker responded with fear in his eyes. He shook uncontrollably.

Before anyone else could help Hu restrain him, he collapsed into unconsciousness, convulsing, and foaming from his mouth as he did so. Hu let go of him in shock. Her restraining holds should not have caused that reaction. After twenty seconds, the man lay still on the floor. Hu squatted to take his pulse in his neck. She couldn't find one.

She looked up at the flight specialist in disbelief. "He's dead."

The flight specialist stared at Hu, glanced at the lifeless man, and returned her gaze to Hu in confusion. "What should we do?"

Hu took stock. She had not meant to kill the man with her defensive moves. They stressed the restrained defense ad nauseam in the Tae Kwon Do classes. She could have killed him if she intended to, and the foaming puzzled her. This was sinister. The police needed to investigate it. "Tell the pilot what has happened and ask him to inform the spaceport authorities."

The flight specialist went to her workstation and lifted the communication handset, putting her in contact with the cockpit. She talked for several minutes and returned.

"We don't usually allow this, but these are unusual circumstances. Would you go into the cockpit and talk to the police, Ms. Ching? You need to tell your version of events because it involved you."

"OK. But move nothing yet. We must get saliva samples before it soaks into the floor and dries."

Hu followed the flight specialist to the front of the cabin, where the flight attendant buzzed on the cockpit door security pad for the occupants to open it. A security code was required to open the cabin door, which they only used in desperate circumstances. The door opened, and Hu entered the cockpit. She stood still and stared at the magnificent scene that greeted her through the shuttle window. The orb of Earth shone in front of her in all its chaotic glory. Despite what she had been just through, she had to pause to take in the vibrancy of the speckled and swirling masses of clouds, dancing to the music of the invisible wind currents circling Earth, interrupting the blue oceans and the browns, greens, and whites of the landmasses. It filled most of the visual angle of the cockpit view from this distance. She had never seen it from this perspective before.

"Incredible, isn't it?" the pilot said, smiling at her reaction. "Everyone has your expression when they see her from here for the first time."

"Amazing. So wonderful," Hu responded. After saturating her senses with the view, she returned to the present and her reason for being there. "I'm Ching Hu, the person the crazy man attacked." Both the pilot and co-pilot nodded. "I understand the authorities want to talk to me."

"Yes," the pilot said. "I will contact them on the comm again."

"Hello, moon shuttle, Ming here. We have the attack victim with us now. Over," the pilot spoke into the microphone.

Several seconds passed before a response came from the other end, despite it taking less than half a second for the transmission to travel the distance.

"Hello, Detective Inspector Chow of the Shanghai Police here. Can I speak with her, please?" The detective had a deep, gravelly voice.

The pilot handed the microphone to Hu, who responded, "Hello. My name is Ching Hu."

"Pleased to meet you, Ms. Ching, if under not so pleasant circumstances. Can you tell us what happened?"

Hu recapped the events to the policeman as she remembered them. He asked several clarifying questions before she heard him turn away from the microphone to talk to someone present with him.

"I have been discussing the symptoms you describe with my Medical Examiner, who is with me, and they are consistent with poisoning. We can't be sure until we get the body and examine it."

This information shocked Hu. "But how? He was eating the same food as the rest of us."

"Maybe when he lunged at you, it was to poison you with something he had placed on the knife. The toxin may have gotten on his skin and that was what killed him. It's conjecture at this stage. If that is the case, you're lucky to be alive."

"That's hard to absorb, Inspector Chow. Who'd want me dead? And how did he expect to get away with such a desperate act in a confined space?"

"Both good questions! We will discuss everything when you arrive. But perhaps he didn't expect to get away with it. Perhaps it was a suicide mission."

The revelation staggered Hu. She had assumed the poor man suffered a mental illness that had made him want to harm someone — anyone — with no thought to the consequences. She had not considered till now that she was his intended target and that he was ready to die in the attempt. She started shaking. Since she had been standing, the pilot invited her to sit down to collect herself.

"In the meantime," Inspector Chow continued, "we understand the body needs secure storage for landing, so you must remove it. Be very careful when you touch him. But, before you move him, we ask you to take photographs of him from various angles without touching him. Photograph where he sat and the knife too. Can you do that?"

"Yes, I believe so," Hu said, her voice shaky, still not believing this was happening to her.

"After that, place the blade in a plastic bag, but please don't touch it. Poison will still coat it if we are correct."

"Will do."

"Place everything that needs moving in plastic bags. We hope you will have enough. That includes leftovers from his meal." The inspector turned to talk to the person with him, his words garbled over the cockpit speaker. He returned to the microphone. "We believe that's everything we will need of you before you land and we can secure the scene. Consider a shot of whiskey to calm your nerves after your ordeal, if you have any on board," the Inspector concluded in a sympathetic tone.

"I may just do that."

"OK. That's it for the moment. We'll talk more when you arrive. Hope the rest of the flight is uneventful. Over and out." The speaker went dead.

Hu sat in the cockpit for several more minutes to compose herself. Afterward, she said she was fine to return and complete the needed tasks. The pilot opened the door, and Hu walked back into the cabin.

She retrieved her tablet from her bag and took photographs. She asked the flight specialist to get plastic bags and rubber gloves. The flight specialist returned with the items and plastic aprons, which came in useful when moving the body. Hu put on the gloves and gingerly removed the knife from the seat, placing it in a bag. She included the gloves, which she turned inside out when she discarded them. The fight specialist helped her bag the items from the place where the assailant had been sitting and get the area ready for landing. They asked the other passenger to don gloves, and they dressed in aprons and moved the cadaver to a vacant seat where they secured it with the restraint. With the tasks completed, they deposited the aprons and gloves in a bag. They washed their hands thoroughly afterward.

Hu gave out a gigantic sigh. "That's enough excitement for one day."

"Sure is!" the other passenger responded, returning to his seat.

"Could you make me a large, strong whiskey if you don't mind?" Hu asked the flight specialist, who nodded and said, "Everyone needs one. Even though it's against regulations for flight specialists, I think this might be an exception." She walked to the galley to pour the drinks.

Hu sat in another vacant seat. She received the whiskey from the flight specialist, sat back, and sipped the fiery liquor with pleasure and relief. Her nerves calmed as the alcohol started to take effect. She spent the rest of the trip pondering the preceding events and their meaning.

12

INTERRUPTION

Apep left Kristina's office in the Kremlin district and booked into a nearby hotel, the Kitay Gorod Hotel on Lubyanskiy pr-d. Basic in functionality, the hotel had upgraded since its establishment but was still low-quality accommodation by international standards. It suited Apep. It was quiet and discrete, and the service was excellent. He could order a drink any time he wanted. He considered what he should do next.

The coil's vandalism disturbed him, the replacement time having a crucial impact on project delivery. He reminded himself that worrying over it wouldn't change the outcome. Alexi was chasing up its reinstatement, and he trusted Alexi to get it in the quickest time possible. He excelled in that — screwing the supplier for everything they had but still getting top quality — and Apep needed to follow up on how the sabotage had happened. He had time before he received the paperwork to travel to America. Apep decided that a trip to Oligov Electrical Industries, the coil's manufacturer, was in order as they might be able to enlighten him on what had damaged it. The FSB would question them, but a personal visit couldn't hurt.

Apep found the phone number on his contact list and dialed the company.

"Hello, Oligov Electrical Industries. How may I help you?" the receptionist said.

"Can I speak to Zalenko Larkonovik, please?"

"Whom may I say is calling?"

"It is Apep Chernakov. Zalenko will know me. Tell him I wish to discuss an unfortunate delivery yesterday to one of his most important customers."

"Thank you. I will forward the information." The woman placed Apep on hold while she contacted her superior. After what felt like ages listening to detestable Mazak, she re-connected with him. "Mr. Larkonovik has time to talk to you. I am connecting you now."

That's courteous of him, Apep thought sarcastically.

"Hello, Apep. It is so nice to hear from you. Hope you are well. How can I help you, my friend?" Zalenko's oily car salesman's voice resounded over the comm.

Apep rolled his eyes. "I am calling for an appointment to meet with you. It is most urgent. I need to discuss an issue with your last shipment."

"Of course. You are a very valued customer. We should review it at once if you have a problem with it."

"4 pm today!"

"Well, I must consult my busy schedule. Let me see."

"It was not a suggestion, Zalenko. I will visit you at four this afternoon."

"My appointments will need re-arranging, but I can squeeze you into my schedule. I will be pleased to see you at four."

"Good! See you at four." *Obnoxious dog*, Apep thought as he hung up the comm and started unpacking his clothing and toiletries for the stay.

Being lunchtime, Apep descended the stairs and out of the hotel to a boutique café he had discovered years ago. He entered it and sat by the window fronting the road. After browsing the menu, he beckoned the waiter and ordered an olivye salad for the first course, a borsch next, followed by the café's signature dish: Beef Vtoroye Bludo. He requested a tea and a shot of vodka, too.

With his lunch ordered, Apep gazed outside at the view of speeding cars and hurrying pedestrians. Everyone seemed to be anxious to get to their destinations. His thoughts returned to the chain of incidents that had occurred at work. Kristina had suggested that similar "mishaps" had been happening with the Chinese and American versions of the project. *That cannot be a coincidence*, Apep thought. The occurrences were not fatal, just causing delays to the project's completion. Another party seemed involved, one that perhaps wanted to get ahead. If so, they possessed an excellent organizational network to coordinate the events in the three projects. *I should discuss this more with Kristina when I return.*

A pleasant young woman, in Apep's eyes — slim, with an ample bust and charming face — served his first course and drinks. She saw him looking at her as she placed the plate in front of him and smiled. Apep smiled in return and thanked her.

Apep looked around at the others in the café as he started eating his salad. Several couples ate and talked at the other tables, while singles like himself just dined and pondered. Some used their tablets, skimming the news or social media sites to occupy their time. Apep continued with his meal, the second and third courses appearing as he completed the first one. He liked the café because it was always very efficient. He poured his tea, his hand then hovering for a moment over the sugar bowl before, with a shrug of defeat, he scooped in three last spoonfuls. Once he finished his delicious tea, he sculled the shot of vodka.

His lunch complete, Apep went to the counter and paid, commenting on the familiar high quality of the food while he did so.

He then returned to his room to freshen up and left for his car, his usual attaché case in hand. It was time to drive to the factory for his appointment. From the hotel, he drove around the outskirts of the central part of Moscow, traveling west until he turned onto Leninsky Avenue. He continued southwest along that road until he reached the Third Ring Road and branched onto it. He traveled southeast along the ring road and exited it when he came to the M4, driving a short distance south along the M4 to the Oligov factory on the right.

Apep parked in a visitors' car-parking space and walked in the reception front door of the factory offices.

"Comrade Chernakov to see Comrade Larkonovik," he announced to the receptionist. "I have a four o'clock appointment."

"Just one moment, please," she responded as she dialed Zalenko's office comm. Zalenko answered after a few seconds, and the receptionist relayed the information. After a brief exchange, she disconnected. "Comrade Larkonovik will be out soon. In the meantime, could you please sign our visitors' register? A cup of tea or coffee?"

"No, thank you. I will be fine," Apep said as he signed the log. He then seated himself in the foyer to wait for Zalenko to arrive.

Zalenko walked into the reception after a few minutes, dressed in an expensive gray pinstripe suit with white shirt, blue tie flecked with white dots, and highly polished black shoes. His black hair was greased back. *He looks like he could get a job in any car sales yard*, Apep thought sourly.

Apep rose to his feet as Zalenko gushed, "Ahh, Comrade Chernakov, so pleased to see you again. It is always a pleasure to meet with you. Did the receptionist not give you a drink?" Zalenko shot her an annoyed glance.

"She offered, but I did not want one, Comrade Larkonovik. I wish I were visiting under better circumstances."

"You must call me Zalenko. Please follow me to my office where we can discuss our business," Zalenko said as he retraced his steps.

They walked through the reception door leading into the offices, an open plan arrangement. Many people were busy about their duties in the company. Equipment littered the space, as one would expect in a manufacturing business. Zalenko had a private office attached to that expanse. They walked into it, and he closed the door behind them, pointing Apep to a seat at a small round meeting table in the right corner of the office. A window across the entire front wall allowed Zalenko sight of his staff going about their activities. This, again, was a typical layout. They sat at the table opposite each other.

"And how can I help you today, Apep? I may call you Apep in private, yes?" Zalenko asked.

"Yes, that is fine. I take it that Alexi has been in contact? I was wondering what arrangement you have come to with him."

"Yes, yes. We have talked, and I am sorry you have this dilemma. I don't understand how this could happen. We keep equipment for clients like you under the strictest security as per our contract. We can insert your new coil at the front of the production schedule. This will upset another customer, so we must offer compensation to placate him. He is very important to our business."

Apep looked away so Zalenko would not see him rolling his eyes. *Yeah! And I bet he will get every ruble.* "Well, that's very good, Zalenko. And what payment have you discussed?"

"We have agreed on ten percent extra for fast delivery of another coil. That is very generous, Apep. We will lose money with the concessions to our other customer."

Bull! You'll make a profit from both of us, Apep thought as he plastered a fake smile of gratitude on his face. "We appreciate your efforts, and I stand by whatever arrangements Alexi has made with you. When will you deliver our coil then — if you don't mind my asking?"

"With the schedule priority stretching our production capacity, I've started an extra shift to the manufacturing effort. It will take two weeks, I'm afraid, but that is the best I can offer, Apep. Yes?"

Apep looked impressed. *Well, at least he has tried in that regard. I wonder how much Alexi had to lean on him to get that timing?* "That is very good of you, Zalenko. Yes, that is acceptable, and we appreciate your effort."

"Ah, you are too kind. Can I help you with anything else?" Zalenko responded with probably genuine gratitude.

"There was one other matter I must discuss. I wish to understand your security arrangements for the components you make for us."

"Well, we follow the protocols detailed in the contract. We have a sealed bonded store where we place the parts once manufacture and quality control are complete and while they are waiting for dispatch to you."

"What surveillance do you conduct on the compound?"

"It is of the utmost quality, I can assure you, Apep. There is continuous video-recorded data both inside and outside the bonded enclosure. An installed alarm activates if infrared or motion detectors sense any movement. Only our security chief and I know the passcode to turn off the signal."

"And you got no activations while you stored the coil?"

"None. I checked the records myself after your Alexi informed me of the mishap."

"Hmm. Strange. Have you viewed the video recording yet?"

"No, I have not had time. I will have my security team review it."

"I appreciate that. Can you download a copy for me? I might spot an anomaly beyond what you might expect. Besides, you will need to give a copy to the FSB when they pay you a visit."

Zalenko became alarmed at the mention of the FSB. "Yes, yes, of course. Is the FSB necessary?" he said with increased concern on his face.

That got your attention, didn't it? Apep thought with a mental snicker. "We have to report these things, I'm afraid. I am sure that you have nothing to hide."

"Of course. I run a legitimate business here. I will arrange the video download, and you can be on your way."

Zalenko hurried out of the room, leaving Apep alone for several minutes. He returned with the data and handed it to Apep as he asked, "Is there something else that I can help you with today, my friend?"

"No. That was it. Since I was in Moscow, it was opportune to ask you for the information in person, instead of by comm," Apep replied, rising from his seat.

"Yes, it's always best to discuss these matters face to face. It's more personal, and we can sort disagreements out faster. Do you care for dinner together tonight? We could consider other opportunities," Zalenko said, probing for an excuse to grease his pocket more.

Apep rose from his chair. "That is kind. Unfortunately, I have other issues that need my attention. Time is precious for a project manager." Apep sighed with fake disappointment.

Zalenko chuckled. "Yes, always something that needs doing. Well, until next time. You are most welcome at our factory anytime, Apep." Zalenko extended his hand.

"Yes, till next time." Apep shook Zalenko's hand.

Zalenko opened the office door and escorted Apep back to reception.

"Have a happy stay in Moscow, Comrade Chernakov," Zalenko said, reverting to formal naming for public appearances as they shook hands again.

"Thank you, Comrade Larkonovik."

With the discussions completed, Apep logged out and walked to his car. Zalenko watched with a false smile as Apep left the building.

Apep traveled to his hotel, wondering how they had ever signed a contract with such a person. It wasn't his place to give his opinion, apparently.

BACK IN HIS HOTEL ROOM, Apep reviewed his messages to check if his security clearance to travel to America had come through. It had not. And it wouldn't get approved tonight since it was already after 6 pm, and office workers would have left for the night, which meant he was stuck here for longer. He placed a call through to Alexi, who answered on video after a brief delay.

"Hello, Apep. How are things?"

"OK, I guess. And you? Aren't you home with your family yet?" Apep asked, seeing the office behind him.

"I have matters to complete here first. I talked with Oligov—"

"Yes, I know," Apep interrupted. "I gave our charming Zalenko a visit this afternoon. You agreed on a reasonable settlement. But I can't understand how you can do business with a straight face. His game is so obvious."

Alexi chuckled. “Yes, he is a snake-oil salesman, and thanks. Sorry about the extra ten percent, though.”

“Don’t be. If it gets us the coil two weeks earlier, it will be worth it. Anyway, I wanted to tell you that I’ll be away for several more days. A matter arose during my discussions with my contact in the FSB, and we both agree that I must attend to it. So, I need you to keep the project running until I return. Is that alright with you?”

“No problem. I am not going anywhere. I can handle my wife complaining that I never see the kids for a while longer,” Alexi responded with a tired smile.

“Sorry to put more stress on you. It’ll only be a few days, I hope. I suggest you go home now and relax for the rest of the night.” Apep had a pained look on his face as he liked Alexi and knew he was committed to the project.

“I might. Was that it?”

“Yes, I just wanted to inform you I had visited our friend Zalenko and of my absence. By the way, I got video footage of the coil storage at the factory before they shipped it. I will send it through to you so you can review it, too. Have a good night.”

“You too,” Alexi said and disconnected.

Apep retrieved his tablet and checked his time zone clip — naming conventions had changed from programs to applications, then apps, then clips — to find the American west coast time. It was 7 pm in Moscow, which made it 5 am in Los Angeles, too early for a call. He decided to compose and send a message over dinner instead.

Apep gazed from his window at the blustery weather. It looked like it might snow, so he decided to dine at the hotel’s restaurant. He hoped he could get a table, given the weather. The hotel was popular, and people preferred dining in-house to stay warm. He would have to take his chances.

Apep arrived at the restaurant reception and waited to be seated. The maître d’, seeing a waiting customer, started walking toward him, checking the service was up to expectations with patrons along the way. When the maître d’ arrived, Apep said, “I haven’t reserved a table, but is one available?”

"You are Comrade Chernakov, yes?" Apep nodded. "You are a regular here. I remember. I am sure that we can accommodate you. We are not as busy as I was expecting tonight. Let me check." The maître d' consulted the reservation book and exclaimed in delight. "Yes, Comrade, I have an excellent table for you. Please follow me." He gathered a menu and wine list and escorted Apep to the designated spot.

Apep followed, and when he got to the table, he agreed it was excellent: a table for two by the window and overlooking a park. Apep assumed they reserved it for romantic couples. He sat in the seat next to the window and allowed the maître d' to give him the menu and wine list.

"A drink while you consider your choice, Comrade?" the maître d' asked.

"Yes, could you get me a Baltika number eight?" Apep thirsted for a beer.

"I hope you have an enjoyable meal," the maître d' commented as he wrote down the item and walked away.

Apep perused the menu and selected what to order. The ale came while he was considering his choices, and he thanked the waiter as he placed it before him. After deciding on his meal, Apep pondered the wine list while he sipped on his beer. Once he chose lamb for his main course, he decided on a Cabernet Sauvignon.

Placing the wine list on the table, he beckoned the waiter to order his dinner. "A borsch followed by Piroshki Kapustoy and a Baranina na Kostochke for the main." Apep loved Cabernet Sauvignon, so he ordered a bottle of Balverne 2063, which he knew was an excellent year, even though it came from America. The waiter noted the choices and left.

Apep relaxed with his beer and considered what to write to Ethan Richards. He got his tablet out, opened the messaging clip, and started typing.

< My friend Ethan. I hope you are well. It has been a long time since we last met. I am flying from Russia soon to visit Los Angeles on business and was hoping we could meet informally. I believe we have

had some similar recent experiences, which we could discuss over a drink and a meal. Please recommend the soonest occasion for you. Regards from your friend still (I hope), Apep Chernakov >

Apep re-read the message and satisfied with the wording, pressed send. *Let us see what eventuates*, he thought as the waiter arrived with the wine. The waiter pulled out the cork and poured a sample into the wine glass for Apep to taste. He sipped and nodded, so the waiter filled the glass, set the bottle to the side, and cleared away the empty beer bottle. Another waiter delivered the borsch and placed it in front of Apep.

He sipped his soup while he gazed out of the first-floor restaurant window. The view from his seat displayed a park across the road illuminated with LED lighting to protect pedestrians from the darkness. Colored lights oscillated at regular intervals to display an interesting pattern throughout the park. The top of the Kremlin buildings jutted above the foliage, lit with various floodlights. Apep thought it looked wonderful and enjoyed gazing at it as he ate.

Apep could also see the maître d's counter from his position. He noticed the same two people enter the restaurant several times, puzzling him. *Maybe they're searching for someone.*

He finished his meal in peace and felt contented as he signed the check and left. He strolled back to his room, feeling relaxed and mellow. *Maybe I had too much wine. Oh, well. I can sleep it off now*, Apep thought. As he reached his room, the door opened, and a man rushed out, almost knocking Apep over as he sped to the emergency stairwell. The incident was over before Apep grasped what had happened. He stood stock-still for a moment, confused. He considered whether to alert Hotel Security but then realized there was no point. The trespasser was long gone. He entered his room and switched on the light to check if any items were missing. The intruder must have had a torch. There were signs of disturbance, but nothing appeared to be missing. His belongings, laptop, and other valuables were still there. It was a conundrum for Apep. He didn't know what the thief was searching for — unless he had interrupted him before he could start. Apep didn't think so. The burglar had disturbed his possessions enough to show he had searched for a significant time. Apep knew he could do nothing about it, although he reported it to Hotel Security so they could review the matter further if they considered it worthwhile to do so.

He retired for the night with thoughts of the lovely cafe waitress at lunchtime as he drifted off to sleep.

13

INVESTIGATIONS

The police met Hu as she disembarked from the moon shuttle when it landed at the spaceport near Shanghai. One of them escorted her to an interview room. Other travelers glanced inquisitively in their direction but returned to their activities once they saw little excitement. Officers cordoned off the shuttle door, securing the scene and preventing any further contamination of the evidence as detectives and specialists entered the ship to investigate.

The remainder of the flight had been uneventful, and Hu rested as best she could after her ordeal. She settled herself in the interview room, sitting in a chair at a table. The policeman asked if she wished for refreshments or desired anything else. She declined.

Detective Inspector Chow entered after half an hour and sat across the table from Hu. "Sorry to detain you so long. I had a quick inspection of the scene to familiarize myself with the layout and whatnot. It's the first attempted murder investigation on a moon shuttle for me."

"I can appreciate its unusual nature."

"How are you feeling? Do you need to see a doctor?"

"No. I am fine, thank you."

"You have done a good job bagging the evidence, so to speak. Much appreciated. I understand that you have the photographs."

"Yes, I have them on my tablet. Where would you like them downloaded?"

"I can have one of our constables do that for you."

"I don't wish to be awkward, but I prefer to do it myself. My tablet stores commercial-in-confidence material, and I'd sooner keep it there, considering what has happened."

"I understand. I will get someone to help you with it after we have finished the interview."

"Thank you."

"Then, can you please repeat what occurred during the incident as far as you remember?"

Hu recounted the sequence of events as she remembered them, with the inspector interrupting now and then to clarify a point as he wrote notes on his tablet.

"The man was very nervous," Hu told the police. "And before he died, he started ranting about his family ... I've been thinking that perhaps he had no personal reason to attack me. Perhaps he was being blackmailed."

After the interview, she went with a constable to a download station that the police used and downloaded the photographs she had taken. She was then free to go. The meeting took three hours, and she was exhausted at the end of it — she needed to get to her hotel and unwind.

The policeman ushered her straight through immigration control, as they had already verified her identity chip, so she went to the luggage carousel at the spaceport and collected her baggage. She cleared customs and caught a taxi to the Mandarin Orient Pudong Hotel, right on the Huangpu River near the center of Shanghai. It was 7:23 pm and turning dark when she arrived at the hotel, the city lights reflecting off the river as it flowed past her. She paid the driver and headed for the hotel lobby. The doorman opened the lobby door as she approached and gave her a cheerful greeting.

As she strolled through the entry, she absorbed the lobby's

scenery. The polished, white-streaked jade-colored marble floor gleamed in the light. A brightly illuminated imitation mosaic wall displayed unique designs every ten seconds. Its current scene showed a complex arrangement of fall colors over the entire surface. The lights in the lobby glowed a warm white-yellow color. The reception lay on her right, past and beyond the display, invisible from the entrance. Lounges were scattered throughout the lobby, and varieties of Chamaedorea palms stood potted in different arrangements next to them.

The lobby was quiet, with one customer being served by a receptionist and another receptionist busy with paperwork. Hu stepped to the check-in counter in front of this person, who stopped what she was doing to serve her.

"Hello and welcome to the Mandarin Oriental Pudong Hotel. How may I help you?" the receptionist recited from memory, but with a hint of warmth.

"Hello, my name is Ching Hu. I believe I have a room reservation."

"One minute, please. Yes, you have one reserved for one week. Is that correct?"

"Yes."

"Just one moment while I complete your check-in. I see you are a regular visitor to our hotel."

"Yes. I like it," Hu said as she looked around the lobby approvingly. The other person being served was a man in his mid-fifties. He was of normal height and wore a creased and rumpled business suit. His hair was messy as if he'd had a rough day. He noticed Hu looking at him and gave a nod. She returned the greeting with friendliness and a slight smile. *Careful, don't want to give him the wrong idea*, she thought.

"OK, you are in room 1505 on the fifteenth floor. Here is your security key," the receptionist told Hu as she handed it to her. A bellboy was at her side with her bags in a luggage trolley, waiting. *How do they always know when to arrive?* Hu wondered.

"This way, please," the bellboy said as he headed for the elevators.

Hu followed and entered the elevator with the bellboy and the trolley.

"Fifteenth floor?" The bellboy gave a questioning look to confirm the detail.

"Yes."

He pressed the button. The doors closed, and they stood in silence as the elevator rose. "Level 15," the automated voice said from the speaker as the doors opened.

They went to room 1505 and walked inside. The bellboy brought her bag in and placed it on the luggage rest. "Will that be everything?" he asked.

"Yes, thank you."

"Have a pleasant stay," he replied and left.

Hu flopped onto the bed, exhausted, the day's events catching up with her. She could sleep for a month, she thought. Her whole body buzzed with tiredness. However, she knew from experience that insomnia was her worst enemy when she was in this state. She had to unwind first. What should she do? The bathroom had a bathtub, so she decided a hot soaking bath was just fine for starters.

After resting on the bed for a short while, Hu stood and secured the door. She ran the bathwater. Steam rose from the surface, inviting her to immerse herself in a sample of paradise. A small bottle of complimentary bath salts sat beside the tub, which Hu emptied into the bathwater, mixing the salts through the water. She undressed and lowered herself into the welcoming liquid, the heat conducting through her skin as it soaked into her. She rested her head on the edge of the bath and relaxed. *Ecstasy*, she thought as her body absorbed the warmth, and the water flushed the day's stress away. She didn't know how long she lay there, but she started feeling hungry and could use a drink, so she dunked her head under the surface and washed her hair. Fresh again, she dried herself and styled her hair. Since Hu kept her hair short, which helped when wearing spacesuits, it dried quickly. She donned a white tee shirt with a red moon on the front, blue jeans, and black and white sneakers. She then left and headed for one of the hotel's casual twenty-four-seven bars.

It was almost 9 pm when Hu entered the Qi Bar on the roof. Being winter, the space was enclosed to keep in the warmth. The lighting was dim. Hu strolled to a tall table with stools near the bar counter and beckoned a waitress over to order a drink.

"A glass of brut champagne, please," Hu ordered. "And the dining menu?"

"Certainly." The waitress noted the order and left, returning with the menu moments later. They provided the menu as a clip on a tablet, so you ordered the food yourself once you had decided on your choice. Hu looked over the cuisine and selected pork spring rolls and Kim Chi — it was a favorite of hers, even though it was Korean. The waitress delivered her champagne, and Hu sipped it while she considered her plans for the next day. She needed to call on the manufacturer of the electromagnetic field flux concentrator but, given what had happened over the last twenty-four hours, she resolved she would take a day off to recuperate. She had to contact Ethan and plan her flight to Los Angeles, then visit the factory on the following day.

Sensing herself being watched, she noticed the man at reception earlier staring at her. He hadn't changed from his crumpled, shabby suit. Hu could read his thoughts and the reason for his presence, like knowing that the sun would rise tomorrow. She despised how he leered at her, but she could handle him if needs be. She looked in a different direction. The food came, so she started eating after ordering a beer. She was halfway through chewing a spring roll when she saw him standing by her table with his drink and her beer in his hands.

"You ordered a beer?" he asked with a pretentious air.

Hu glared at him for a few seconds, then said, "Piss off."

"That is no way to answer a person doing you a kindness."

"The only kindness you want is between your bedsheets, so piss off."

"Let us not jump to conclusions here. If you need recompense, we can arrange payment."

Hu looked at him, fuming, wanting to kill him then and there. Instead, she said in a freezing and menacing tone, "I've already killed one man today. I suppose another won't matter. If you want to walk from here in one piece and your bones intact, leave this bar now."

The man froze, and his face drained to total whiteness. "I am sorry. I did not mean to offend you. Here is your beer and good evening," he stammered, leaving the glass on the table. He returned to the bar, finished his drink, settled his bill, and left. Hu continued staring at him in disgust, and she knew he could sense it, despite avoiding eye contact with her. He rushed from the premises.

Hu still fumed, but her effort satisfied her. She was not technically correct about killing anybody, but he needn't know that. It had had the desired effect. A few minutes later, a second beer appeared in front of her.

"Compliments of the house," the waitress said with a grateful smile. "He is a constant pain in here, and we'll laugh about how you sent him packing, disgraced, for a long time. Thank you."

"You're welcome," Hu replied with a growing grin, her tension leaving her as a jest developed in her mind. "That one was for a beer. The next will be much more expensive." They both laughed, and the waitress left, with Hu finally shedding her gloom. She enjoyed the rest of her stay that night, listening to the live entertainment and getting merrier, but careful not to become intoxicated.

She left the bar at 11 pm and headed for the elevator. The man who had propositioned her stood waiting.

"You humiliated me, you bitch. I will make you pay now," he said with a drunken drawl and staggered toward Hu.

"Oh, go away and sleep it off," she said, unconcerned but alert.

He lunged at her, and she sidestepped, caught his arm and shoulder, and threw him to the floor with the ease of someone who had practiced the move a thousand times. Even so, she was amazed that she had had to do it twice in one day.

The drunk lay on the ground, stunned. He vomited. Hu glared at him in disgust and returned to the bar to tell them to call Security. She then retraced her steps to the elevator, avoiding the inert body on the floor. When an elevator arrived, she entered it, the doors closed, and she put the second unpleasant experience of the day out of her mind.

HU WOKE up late the next morning. She felt refreshed from the extra sleep and the room's comfortable temperature, which tempted her to stay in bed, luxuriating in the snuggly warmth. Pity I'm alone, she thought. After ten minutes, and concluding she needed to start the day, she rose, had a quick shower, and headed for breakfast.

She arrived at the restaurant and served herself porridge and orange juice. She had got a taste for the Western style of breakfast from her days at Caltech. Spotting an empty table, she walked to it, placed her items on it, and sat facing the dining room entrance. She noticed the hotel manager arrive and talk to the waiter, who surveyed the room and pointed in her direction. The manager strode to her.

"I understand you had an uncomfortable confrontation in our hotel last night, Ms. Ching. Please accept our apologies. We strive to give our patrons a pleasurable experience when they stay here."

"No apology required. These things sometimes happen despite the best of procedures. You can't count on spotting every idiot," Hu said.

"You are most kind. We ordered the rogue to leave the hotel and never return."

"Thank you."

"I hope the rest of your visit is pleasant."

"I intend it to be, and again, thank you."

With that exchange concluded, Hu started her breakfast. After the porridge, she ate scrambled eggs and toast with plenty of hot black coffee, freshly expressed from the beans. Afterward, she grabbed an apple and banana from the fruit bowl and returned to her room.

She called the Xian Electronics Corporation to schedule a time to meet their Chief Engineer and Dispatch Manager the next day, hoping they could illuminate her on the vandalism and arrange the manufacturing of another part. She arranged the meeting for 11 am since the flight took two hours. *It'll be an exhausting time, but worth it if we understand the sabotage*, she thought.

Hu then opened her tablet and composed a message to Ethan.

< Ethan, buddy. Guess who's coming to town? We have matters to discuss, so please let me know a suitable time for an informal catch-up. Looking forward to sharing a beer with you and having a laugh over old times. See you soon. Hu (go) >

Once she sent the message, she organized a flight to Los Angeles for three days' time to give her a day's buffer in case something came up to delay her. She booked her accommodation in LA and then composed a note to Jian Zha to keep him informed of the arrangements. The day was now hers to use as she wished. As it was just before lunch, she headed for the main retail shopping district, had lunch, and for the want of anything better to do, window-shopped to check on the latest fashions.

14

FOREARMED

Ethan assisted Jake with the equipment transfer to the ship. They disassembled it and packed it into specially produced containers to ensure the parts remained undamaged during transportation. They connected the hatch in the test room's ceiling to a large hydraulic opening mechanism, and the machinery was loaded into a lander, which transferred it to the spaceship. Two or three trips were necessary to move it. Ethan had intended riding with the first load of equipment to help supervise the re-assembly. But before taking off, Jake and he had to meet General John O'Conner in Los Angeles. They were on their way to the hotel, the Hilton, where he had arranged a meeting for 4:30 pm, when Ethan's message service buzzer sounded. Ethan took his comm from his pocket and opened his message bank. To his surprise, the message was from Ching Hu. Good old Hugo. Not that she's old, Ethan remembered with a reminiscent smile. A second message waited for him from Apep Chernakov, sent earlier in the day. It surprised Ethan that he had not noticed it until now. "That's interesting," he said aloud as he read Hu's message and then Apep's.

"What is?" asked Jake.

"I've received separate messages from two old mates from Caltech days both wanting informal catch-ups."

"So?"

"They're from China and Russia."

"Ah, that *is* interesting. You don't come halfway around the world for a chat unless you're a multi-billionaire brat playboy son who's bored."

"No, you don't," Ethan responded, pondering the coincidence.

"What are you going to do?"

"Not sure yet. Let's have this meeting first, and then I'll decide. I may even mention it, depending on what we discuss."

Ethan had no time to consider it further as they had arrived at the hotel. He paid the taxi and walked into the lobby with Jake. They strolled to the reception. It was late afternoon, and the lobby was busy. After a slight delay while the receptionist served other people in front of them, they stepped forward.

"Welcome to Hilton Los Angeles. How may I help you?" the receptionist rattled off as if from a script.

"We are here to meet a General John O'Conner. He's staying here," Ethan said. "Could you inform him that Jake Bodie and Ethan Richards are in the lobby for our four-thirty meeting?"

"Please wait a moment," the receptionist said as she searched for the general's room number and dialed the comm. After a brief discussion with the occupant, she returned her attention to them. "General O'Conner will meet you soon. Take a seat while you wait."

Jake and Ethan moved to a location where they could view the elevator doors. They discussed aspects of the forthcoming transfer of the equipment to the spaceship, bouncing potential issues off each other while they waited. After five minutes, the doors opened on one elevator. A man in full military uniform exited, came a few steps into the lobby, and surveyed the space. Five years had passed since Ethan had last seen General O'Connor. He looked quite middle-aged now, but Ethan recognized him instantly and got his attention. He responded and walked toward them.

"It's good to see you again, Ethan," he said as he neared them and shook Ethan's hand, adding as he turned toward Jake, "And you must be Jake Brodie?"

"Guilty," Jake said and extended his hand.

John reacted with a warm handshake. "Pleased to meet you, Jake." He switched his attention back to Ethan. "You've scarcely changed in five years."

"Likewise," Ethan said politely as he shook John's hand.

John smiled at this. "Ah, ever the diplomat, Ethan. I'm afraid I have more gray hairs than last we met.' Gesturing toward the elevators, he added, "If you don't mind, I've organized a private room for our discussion, including refreshments."

Ethan and Jake followed John, who led them to the elevators. They stood in silence as the elevator rose to the first floor. The doors opened, and the general strode to the meeting room, ushering them inside and closing the door behind them.

It was a small room. A table in the center accommodated six people, and a side table held various refreshments and light snacks, together with plates and serviettes. A floor-to-ceiling window showed a magnificent panorama of the coastline from the front of the hotel across the boulevard toward the beach. The sun was just beginning to set.

"Please grab any snacks you want and take a seat," John invited.

Ethan and Jake surveyed the food, took a plate and serviette each. Ethan selected sandwiches and Jake spring rolls. They both grabbed a soft drink and sat facing the window with a view of the shore and the setting sun. John took sandwiches and poured a cup of coffee from the percolator before he sat opposite Ethan and Jake. Ethan guessed he must be in his forties now, judging by the gray-speckled hair and extra facial lines, but he was still a tall, muscular man who looked like he missed nothing and was ready for anything.

"You know my rank," the general began, "but please call me John here and skip the formalities." He smiled. "If you're wondering, a scrambler surrounds this room so no one can eavesdrop on our conversation. I swept it just now and found no hidden microphones or cameras. The scrambler will alert us if any appear — so you can speak freely."

"You take privacy seriously," Jake said.

"What we discuss today must stay between us three for the duration of your mission unless a reason to do otherwise arises."

Ethan and Jake glanced at each other with puzzled expressions. "Sure," they both responded.

"I am in charge of Strategic Operations at the Pentagon, and we have great interest in your development, as Ethan knows, and in your mission's success. You can, I hope, appreciate the implications of this project for America and internationally."

Ethan and Jake both nodded.

"The recent incidents occurring on your project have come to our attention, and the next phase's progress concerns us. We have supplied 'protection', shall we say, for your ship in case any life-threatening events occur during your voyage."

"What 'protection'?" Ethan asked.

"What life-threatening events?" Jake added.

"Laser cannons. You can place them in several locations around the hull."

"What?" both Jake and Ethan exclaimed in unison.

"Stay calm. You two should enjoy playing with toys, being engineers," John half joked. "You're only to activate them if both of you agree on the need. The ship design includes the mounts and fittings to install the cannons, as we foresaw the potential necessity for them."

"*That's* why those spaces are there. I was scratching my head over them since I had nothing to put there," Jake said, enlightened.

"Yes, that's where they go. Landers have transported the equipment to the ship for you to mount and commission. You have the time available before you leave. Now, you're wondering why you two. There are three reasons we selected you. Fitting and testing the cannons is a two-person job. Two people need to know in case one of you gets hurt. And we only trust the two of you one hundred percent because we know you both from reputation. Hold on ... hold on ..."

John cautioned with his hands raised as both Jake and Ethan started protesting. "It's not that we distrust the others. It's that we cannot be certain that someone has not, or won't, extract information from them before you set off for Iapetus. OK?"

"You're still placing us in an uncomfortable position, but I suppose we'll have to live with it," Ethan said after several seconds.

"We can't help that. Perhaps we're being alarmist, but better that than sorry."

"You have a point," Jake replied. "I'd sooner return in one piece than become a new fragment of Saturn's rings."

"That's right," John said. "I've transferred encrypted folders to your tablets. These folders contain everything you need to install, commission, and use the cannons. Read the files thoroughly. This is the key string that will open them." He pulled two chips from his pocket and gave one to each of them. "Guard these with your life, as your lives may well depend on it. We became more concerned and decided on this course of action when we started hearing rumors that similar 'incidents' had been occurring with the sister projects being instigated by the Chinese and the Russians ..."

Ethan and Jake looked at each other.

"What?" John queried.

"Well, it just so happens that two close colleagues from my Caltech days — a Chinese and a Russian, who are both key members of those projects — separately sent me messages today saying that they are flying to LA and want 'to catch-up'. That can't be a coincidence. I was discussing what I should do with Jake in the taxi coming here as I'm scheduled to board the spaceship tomorrow morning."

John sat in silence for several seconds, pondering the new information before he responded. "You should meet your friends. Think of a reason for your change of plans and transfer on the next lander ascent. That's in a week, yes?"

"That's right," Jake said.

"You might get useful intelligence from them."

"It'd be worthwhile having them on our mission, to be honest," Ethan said.

"We could consider that." John sat in thought. "If they are experiencing similar time delays with their projects, I'll investigate the possibility of them accompanying you."

"They are the best in their countries, and Hu's the world's best."

"OK, leave it with me. That's everything I need to discuss for now. I know it's a significant quantity of information to absorb, but you have my full confidence," John said with a smile, "Any questions?"

Jake shook his head, but Ethan hesitated. Both Jake and John stared at him for a response. "I've been wondering what excuse I can give for staying on Earth and can't think of a convincing one. But it'd be different if you forced me to stay — say the military posted a quarantine on me while they investigated the sabotage. If I'm the culprit, nobody wants to send me to the spaceship, right?"

"That sounds reasonable," John said as he considered Ethan's suggestion. "We'll do that. It's easy for me to invent a trumped-up charge to slap on you to keep you here, and this meeting is the perfect cover for it. I'll deliver your quarantine order to Galena within the hour. Hope you're a talented actor, though. Your frustration needs to look genuine."

"I played Peter Pan once," Ethan joked.

The others laughed. "You may need to act better than that," John said.

"Yes, I will. I think I can play the part. OK. That's settled. That's it from me too."

"In that case, let's eat and chat before we leave for our duties. By the way, I almost forgot. My contact information is in the file transfer if any urgent matters arise. And again, discuss it with no one."

They stayed for another fifteen minutes before Ethan and Jake left to return to their workplace. They went downstairs, hailed a taxi, and piled into it, directing it back to JPL.

"That was an eye-opener," Ethan said to Jake in the taxi.

"You got that right."

"This sabotage issue has them concerned if they're giving us those toys."

"Yeah. We'll need a secret code between us, so we know when to use them."

"Let's not talk here," Ethan said. Taxis were now driverless, automated vehicles, but it was still wise to be cautious.

Jake nodded. "Interested in a drink?"

"Good idea. Let's pack up when we return and head to the Sips and Surf once the shit of my impending quarantine hits the fan."

"Perfect."

"Don't forget the launch."

"No problem. Launch time is 8 am tomorrow. That's plenty of time for me to prepare. We have things to discuss."

"Yeah, we do. I might ask someone else to join us."

"Anyone I know?" Jake queried, raising his eyebrows in surprise. "Unusual for you to invite someone."

Ethan felt his face grow hot and hoped it didn't show. "You know her. It's Jade." He gave a sheepish grin.

"Wow. She's a terrific catch. The boldness is unlike you, though," Jake ribbed. "I thought something was brewing."

"Not sure I had any choice. But I enjoy her company. She's great fun. We've only dated once. It was to the Sips and Surf. Had an excellent outing."

"Good for you. Hope something comes of it."

"Let's not rush things too much."

"Always the cautious one."

"I suppose I am."

They reclined in silence for the rest of the trip to JPL.

~

ETHAN'S personal comm was buzzing him as he walked into his office. He noticed that it was Galena Alvarez, composed himself, and answered the call.

"Ethan here."

"Where have you been?" Galena asked, sounding perturbed

"A general from the Pentagon summoned Jake and me to a meeting. Why?"

"What did you discuss?"

"The project. They know of the sabotage I discovered, and they're concerned," Ethan said. "Why? What's wrong?"

"Whatever you told him, he's not happy. He's slapped a quarantine on you till further notice. You can't leave Earth."

"What?" Ethan exploded in mock astonishment. "They can't do that. I have to board the ship tomorrow morning."

"You're not going anywhere. I suppose it's not the end of the world. It should only take a few days to sort, I hope."

"Yeah, OK," Ethan responded in a despondent voice. "It's just annoying. I thought I was doing them a favor."

"Yeah, well, go home for the rest of today. I'll investigate what I can do to settle this."

"OK, see you tomorrow," Ethan said, still glum-voiced, and broke the connection. He placed his comm in his pocket and smiled to himself. *I think I pulled that off rather well.*

Ethan packed up his belongings and left. As he walked past Jake's office, he stopped. "See you there," he said with a wink.

"See you soon," Jake responded with a smile.

Ethan walked past Jade's office, but she wasn't there. Just as well, he thought. It would give Jake and him time to talk. He strolled to his vehicle and drove away.

~

ETHAN ARRIVED at the Sips and Surf at 7:15 pm, after detouring home to freshen up. He scanned the area for Jake but couldn't find him. Seating himself at his favorite table by the window facing the beach, he ordered a Budweiser lager and decided to call Jade. He reckoned by the time she got here that they would have finished their discussion. Ethan got his comm out, found Jade's number in his contacts, and called.

"Hi, Ethan, what's happening to you? I just heard the news," Jade said.

"Don't worry — it's just a misunderstanding. Still, it's depressing. You want to help me wash the blues away? I'll explain then," Ethan replied.

"You don't sound too unhappy."

"Shit happens. You'll make me depressed if you say no, though."

Jade laughed. "OK. I'm not doing much. Where are you?"

"I'm at the Sips and Surf."

"Give me forty-five minutes. See you then."

"See you."

Jade disconnected. *That's done*, Ethan thought. *Just need to finish our secret discussion. Where's Jake?*

Jake came through the entrance, and Ethan waved at him. He sat opposite Ethan and ordered a Budweiser, too.

"So, I contacted Jade. She'll be here in forty-five minutes. We have till then to sort out business," Ethan said.

"That gives us plenty of time. I've been thinking it over on the way," Jake said as his beer arrived. "I'll start installing the hardware on my own, but I'll wait for you to connect and test the systems. Is that a plan?"

"That sounds good." Ethan sipped on his drink. "Two issues to sort, especially when we leave. We need a safe place to talk in private. And a code word or phrase if we must activate the weapons."

Jake stayed silent for a while, savoring his beer. "Got it. There's a compartment with windows in the engineering section in a position to spot anyone lurking long before they see us."

"Sounds good. Any thoughts on the phrase?"

"How does 'D-Day has come' sound?"

"That's great. I just thought of something else. We're vulnerable if the wrong people notice this. We have no weapons on board to protect ourselves."

Jake raised his hand to show that it wasn't a problem. "Before I came here tonight, I opened the folder we received from the general. I wanted to discover what he sent. An item on the list is two pulse pistols — one for each of us, I presume. Have you ever fired one?"

"Yes, when I did marines training. I thought of becoming a marine but changed my mind. They're easy to use and a great deterrent, or a great way to inflict pain without using excessive force."

"Yeah, an excellent piece of gear."

"Well, that covers it."

They both sat in silence, sipping their beers, feeling satisfied with the arrangements.

"You guys are a barrel of laughs," Jade announced behind them, startling them from their reverie.

"How did you get here?" Ethan asked, beaming a smile.

"I came in the other entrance."

"What other entrance?"

Jade laughed. "This is your hangout, and I know it better than you do. Hi, Jake."

"Hi, Jade," Jake said, watching Ethan's reaction to Jade with amusement. "Go easy on that smile, Ethan, before your face cracks."

Ethan rapped Jake on the shoulder, joining in the laughter.

"Is anyone going to offer me a drink, or do I buy my own, as usual?" Jade taunted, gazing at Ethan with sparkling eyes.

Ethan gaped at how brilliant green and stunning her eyes were. After too long spent studying them, he realized where he was and recovered from the spell. "Oh, sorry, of course. What's your drink?"

Even though Jade relished having Ethan gaze at her, she blushed. "Umm. Bourbon on the rocks, please," she said.

"I'll leave you two lovebirds alone and check out the bar," Jake teased.

"Ooh, stop it," Ethan protested, exchanging a sheepish glance with Jade before getting a waiter's attention and ordering Jade's drink and two more beers.

"We've been out having drinks together before," Ethan said.

"True," Jake retorted, "But it's the first time I've seen those looks from you two. But I'm pleased for you both. I hope something more develops for both of you. You're good people."

"Thanks," Ethan and Jade both responded.

"So, what's with this house arrest, Ethan?" Jade asked, looking worried.

"Nothing. It's a misunderstanding. And I'm not confined to my house. I just can't leave the planet," Ethan said. *She looks gorgeous even when she's worried,* he thought.

"That's disastrous enough. Not good for your résumé for starters. What caused it?"

"Jake and I met with a Pentagon general this afternoon to discuss the sabotage I discovered before the last test. He wants to investigate it further and needs me here."

"What sabotage?" Jade asked, surprised.

"I'm not supposed to tell. I found that the main connection conduit between the muon generator and the density concentrator was almost severed. It could have destroyed the basement, and us with it, if we had conducted the test."

"That's terrible. Do you know who did it?"

"Not a clue."

"Why didn't Jake get grounded?"

"The general interviewed us both because he didn't know who knew of it. When he realized Jake was off the hook, he just quarantined me." Ethan resented having to lie, but John had sworn them to secrecy. The knowledge could endanger her, too.

"How long will they ground you?"

"Not long, I presume. I hope to go up on the next launch in a week."

"Well, I suppose that gives us more time, and without interference from you know who," Jade whispered, pointing her eyes at Jake with a sly grin.

"Oh my God!" Jake shook his head. "I don't need this. I hope you won't keep this up on the voyage." Everyone laughed at that.

They bantered with each other until 9:30 pm, when Jake announced, "I'll catch you two later. Someone's got a lander to board in the morning. Don't you do anything I wouldn't do."

"Doesn't leave us much," Ethan responded. "See you soon." He stood and gave Jake a hug.

"Safe trip," Jade said.

Ethan and Jade ordered another drink and talked more until they were ready to leave.

"Share a taxi?" Ethan suggested.

"Sure, why not?"

Ethan hailed one, and they both got into the back. After Jade gave her residential number to the taxi, she moved closer to Ethan and placed her arm inside his. Ethan felt her warmth soak through his clothing and smiled contentedly at her. "I noticed tonight what amazing eyes you have."

"Thank you."

They embraced each other with a tentative kiss before enjoying a more passionate one.

"I wondered when," Jade said, her voice husky and her face radiant.

They both settled, Jade placing her head on Ethan's shoulder for the rest of the drive to her place. They said their goodbyes and gave another parting kiss before Jade exited the taxi and closed the door. Ethan waited until Jade had entered the apartment complex where she lived before providing the taxi with his house location and left.

THE NEXT MORNING, Ethan responded to both Apep and Hu in the one message.

< Good to hear from you, and I'm eager to see you again. Today is Tuesday, January 15th. If you can arrive by the weekend, I'll arrange a restaurant for dinner on Saturday evening (19th). Please confirm with me and I will go ahead with the booking arrangements. Regards, Ethan >

Ethan then proceeded with his usual duties for the rest of the day.

15

RESUPPLY

Hu awoke at six in the morning and eased out of bed, sitting until she woke fully. She stood up after a while and performed stretching exercises to limber her muscles. She then got ready to leave for the airport.

Packing her belongings for the trip, she spotted a message from Ethan. A satisfied smile spread across her face as she read it. *Working out perfectly*, she thought. She then noticed that Apep Chernakov's name was included in the reply. *Interesting*, she thought. *A coincidence that both of us want to meet Ethan, or is it?* Grabbing her tablet and comm, she left for the lobby to catch a taxi to the airport, arriving just after seven. Checking into her flight and going through security checks, she entered the concourse and looked for the airline's lounge and breakfast.

After showing her boarding chip, the lounge foyer attendant registered Hu in their database and welcomed her. She placed her belongings on a seat and dashed to the food bar comprising Chinese and Western sections. She selected a chicken chow mien and a guava juice and returned to her seat. Given the early hour, few people dotted the lounge as she ate her meal and drank her juice. After getting a coffee, she opened her tablet and continued reading a book she had started on the adventures of Marco Polo. The history of West meets East in times past fascinated her. Then the call to board sounded. She boarded the plane and departed, arriving at Qingdao at ten thirty-five on schedule, which was unusual, but Hu wasn't complaining.

She walked through the exit of the terminal and arrived in a taxi at the Xian Electronics Corporation factory soon afterward. Hu entered the factory office reception. White and black marble tiling covered the reception floor, and dark-brown walnut paneling lined the walls and the reception desk. Several holographic photos showed scenes of the factory's history throughout its 150-year life.

Hu walked to the reception desk to introduce herself.

"Good morning and welcome to the Xian Electronics Corporation. How may I help you?" the receptionist greeted her.

"Good morning. My name is Ching Hu. I'm here for an 11 am appointment with Mr. Chan Ling."

"I see, Ms. Ching. Just a moment while I tell him you have arrived. In the meantime, could you please sign the visitors' register?"

"Certainly," Hu said and grabbed the stylus from its holder to record the information.

"Mr. Chan will see you soon," the receptionist said after a brief conversation on the office comm. Hu nodded and walked around the reception, looking at the holographs and the inscriptions underneath them.

Mr. Chan stepped toward her a few minutes later. "Impressive history there, don't you think?" he commented.

"Yes. Inspiring how you developed the firm from such a modest beginning."

"My great-great-grandfather started the business back in 1921 and handed it to the next generation. Each generation since then has grown the business and changed the organization's activities, taking the developing technologies of the time into account and exploiting them as best we could. But I prattle. Welcome, Ms. Ching. I am Chan Ling."

"It's fascinating. You must be proud of your achievements. I wish this visit were just for pleasure, but we must discuss serious matters."

"Yes, you bear disturbing news. We have tried to give you complete satisfaction with our contract with you. The business is vital to my plans. Please let us find a conference room to talk in private. Coffee?"

"Yes, please. I've been up since early this morning, and the coffee on the plane is not exactly renowned for its excellence."

"Come with me. I think you will find that the coffee we serve here is indeed excellent."

Ling waved her to a conference room a few meters away, where his PA was already delivering the coffee.

Hu took a seat next to Ling and started the conversation. "I wish the visit was under less serious circumstances. I came here for two reasons. We received a damaged electromagnetic field flux concentrator."

"That is terrible," Ling said with a concerned expression. "What happened?"

"From the damage, we conclude sabotage. The part is beyond repair. We are not blaming your company. I was here to supervise the packing myself. I am retracing my steps to find who might have done this."

"This is most unsatisfactory, Ms. Ching. How could someone do this? How can I assist you?" Ling looked disturbed and eager to help.

"I need your video from when you packed the part to when it left your factory. I will also need the transport company recording that you used to convey it to the lander terminal."

"Let me arrange that straightaway," Ling said and pulled his comm out. He contacted his security manager and organized the uploading of the footage to his cache. "And the second thing on your mind, Ms. Ching?"

"You must dispatch the replacement part in the shortest possible time."

"Let's see," Ling said, considering the predicament. "Do you have any visual data on the damage?"

"Yes, I do," Hu said, reaching for her bag to retrieve her tablet. She located the file in her cache and ran the video, showing Ling. He requested her to run it again, which she did.

"Stop there," Ling prompted Hu at a specific point in the recording. Hu stopped the video and reversed the footage to the spot of interest. Ling took the tablet and zoomed in on the damaged region of the part. "Can you transfer this file to my cache? I have a clip that produces a 3D hologram from a video." He gave her his cache ID. The required file was transferred after a few moments.

Ling extended the computer screen from the conference table in front of him and logged into his cache to retrieve the file. He then switched on the 3D hologram-producing clip and ran the video into it. After several minutes, a 3D image appeared. He reviewed the hologram to make sure it showed the needed clarity, which it did. He then activated the room's holographic display tab. A form of the part materialized in the middle of the table.

"Wow, that's fantastic!" Hu gazed with wonder. She liked any new gadgets. "I must get one of those."

Ling chuckled. "Yes, it's amazing. It is very useful to us in sorting out design issues. We can reconstruct the parts as a holographic image and view the image from every angle. This spot interested me," he said, pointing at the damaged location.

"Aha. What am I supposed to be seeing?" Hu asked, puzzled.

"The saboteur was not very experienced. Let me explain," Ling said. "This part has several sub-parts in its assembly. We connect these three parts to the mainframe with fastening bolts." Ling pointed at the specific spots he described.

Hu nodded and then a light bulb came on in her brain. "We don't have to replace the entire unit," she said, excited.

"Exactly," Ling said. "And it's fortunate the damaged part is simple to make. We can deliver it in two weeks. You will need to fit it at your base. You need a day for assembly, and we'll supply the assembly and disassembly instructions for you."

"That is good news." Hu sighed with relief. "If we settle on a price, I can sign off the order now."

"Let me see," Ling said and returned to the computer terminal. He reviewed his files and retrieved the invoice for that part. "Look at this, Ms. Ching. This is the manufacturing cost. I'll charge you that plus twenty percent for overheads and profit. Will that be acceptable to you?"

Hu looked at the document he had on the screen. "Yes, we can accept that. I wish every acquisition were as open and straightforward as this."

Ling grinned. "We prefer to be forthright with our clients instead of haggling over every yuan, especially with valued customers like yourselves. We push a hard bargain when trying to win a contract, but once you have won the job, the best approach for everyone is to work together."

"I agree. Not with the tough negotiations but with everything else." Hu chuckled.

"So, let me organize the offer documentation, and we can begin once you sign it, understanding that the acquisition order will be forthcoming."

"Perfect."

Ling's comm chimed. He answered it, talked for a time, and disconnected. "The video footage that you requested is in my cache. If you give me your cache details, I can transfer it to you."

"Good," Hu replied, and she gave Ling the desired information.

"Can I help you with anything else?"

"That's it for now, thank you."

"Would you care to join me for lunch, then?"

Hu looked at her watch. It was just after twelve. "I have a return flight to Shanghai for a three-thirty departure. I have the time. Yes, I will."

"I know an excellent restaurant nearby, and I can drop you at the airport afterward."

"That is most generous."

Ling packed up, retrieved his personal items, and led Hu back to the reception. Hu signed out, and they left for the restaurant.

~

Hu arrived at her hotel just after seven that evening. It had been a long, tiring day. She had contacted a person at the Ministry of State Security and arranged for him to visit her at the hotel the following morning at nine. Her flight to America took off late in the afternoon, giving her plenty of time for the meeting. She had nothing else to do that night but contact Jian Zha to update him, which pleased her. She had had a successful day and was looking forward to relaxing.

Hu went to her room, set up the communication link to the moon base, and requested a connection to Jian Zha's identity. After a few moments, Jian appeared on the screen. "You look tired," he said.

"I'll survive. I had a busy day. But I have the required video footage from my last seeing the part to when I discovered the sabotage. I'll review that for clues."

"Good. Make sure you give a copy to the Ministry."

"I will. I am meeting the contact tomorrow morning. Good news on the replacement part, too. After viewing the damage, Mr. Chan worked out that only a sub-assembly needed replacing, and he could manufacture that in two weeks."

"Excellent."

"We need a day to replace the part when we have it."

"Much better than the scenario we expected. Good work."

"I have approved the price and the part's production. I'll send the paperwork through to you to confirm the order."

"Not a problem. I have good news for my superior for a change."

Hu smiled. "Yes, you do. I am leaving for America tomorrow afternoon."

"Have a safe trip, and let's see what you discover from the Americans."

"Thanks." Hu disconnected the link and packed away her tablet. She was getting hungry, but first, she needed a quick shower.

~

HU WOKE from a deep sleep the next morning to the sound of her alarm. It was seven-thirty. She showered and freshened up before eating her breakfast. After returning to her room, she prepared for her meeting with the person from the Ministry, arranging a special folder to transfer to his cache. The folder contained the security footage, the video of the damage, a copy of the police report into the shuttle altercation, and employee records of the offender. With that done, she left to meet her contact.

Hu arrived in the lobby five minutes before nine, so she sat on a lounge chair and gazed out the window, absorbing a view of the vehicles passing the hotel in both directions like trails of ants negotiating routes to their different destinations. Green parkland covered the bank of the river, the flowing water sparkling in the light from the rising sun. It was too chilly for anyone to enjoy the garden, although a few eager joggers ran along its paths. Hu daydreamed, enjoying the scene ...

"Ms. Ching, I presume?" a black-suited man asked Hu's back.

She jumped in her seat and spun around, ready to pounce until she saw the insignia of the Ministry of State Security on his suit jacket. "You startled me," Hu said. She took a deep breath. "Yes, I am Ms. Ching."

"You should be more observant if you want to live." The man produced a wicked grin, noting the irony.

Understanding his intent, Hu smiled and said, "Yes, I must. And you are ...?"

"I am from the Ministry of State Security. But my name is Undersecretary Xiung. You may call me Feng."

"Good morning, Feng," Hu said, standing up and shaking his hand. "I have a small conference room arranged for us."

"Good ... good."

Hu led him to the stairs leading to the mezzanine-level room. They entered, Hu closing the door behind them. It was a simply furnished room with a table and four chairs. Two nondescript holographs hung on the wall. Feng and Hu sat next to each other at the central table.

"I believe you had an exciting journey back from the moon three days ago."

"Yes, I did. Not one that I recommend. It was very traumatic for me, as you may appreciate. Has anyone investigated the attacker's history? As I told the police, the man seemed frightened and, before he died, spoke of his family as though he feared for them. Perhaps he had no personal reason to attack me. Perhaps he was being blackmailed."

"Someone is checking that out. It's true he had no prior record of violence."

"OK. Someone must know why he did it. I suspect a connection between the attack and the sabotage."

"I assume so too."

"I have put together a folder for you. It comprises video from my last inspection through to transport to the lander, the transfer, and its movements on the moon up to when I discovered the sabotage. There is a file showing the details of the damage for completeness."

"Good, good."

"There's footage of the attack, although you may already have that."

"Yes, we do. I'll compare your file with what we have. There may be differences."

"If you give me a cache ID, I will transfer the data."

"Of course." Feng removed his tablet from his case, activated it, typed words into an eMessage, and sent it to Hu's account. "There. If you open that link, you can copy the folder across to me."

Hu opened her tablet and the eMessage and tapped the link. She then copied the information she had created to the destination cache. "Done."

"What are your thoughts?" Feng asked.

"I'm baffled, Feng. It makes no sense to me. The incidents achieve little as far as the success of the project is concerned. The only thing that it has done is delay it."

"Maybe that is the aim."

"Maybe."

"Who could benefit from this?"

"I find it hard to believe that it is anyone in the primary team."

"We shall see in due course. We shall see. In my experience, the culprit always makes a mistake, no matter how experienced they are. We'll find that blunder. I understand you are going to America."

"Yes, this afternoon. They may have had similar incidents. Jian thought it worthwhile to compare notes in person if we find any connection — to reduce the risk of discovery before we catch the culprits."

"That's excellent advice. I hear the Russians have comparable issues."

"Ahh!" Hu said, enlightened. "The message outlining the arrangements from my American colleague included the Russian project manager in the recipient field. Now I understand why."

"That is good. You can compare notes three ways, yes?"

"Yes."

"Well, I need not detain you any longer. Here is my chip if you wish to contact me. I will inform you if we have any breakthroughs in the investigation."

"Thank you."

Feng packed his tablet away and stood. Hu stood too.

"I hope that you have a pleasant flight. Good morning, Ms. Ching."

"Thank you and good morning too, Undersecretary Xiung."

They shook hands and left. Feng headed out of the hotel and Hu walked to the elevators and her room to prepare for her trip. She had plenty of time to catch her flight. First, she replied to Ethan's eMessage.

< Saturday dinner sounds magnificent. Make sure it's not like our Caltech binges! I want to wake the next day with a functioning brain. Send the details through to me. See you then. Hugo >

She then ate lunch in the hotel cafe and checked out, heading for the airport. She settled into her seat on the airplane, placed her Sensobuds on her temples, and closed her eyes as she reviewed the audio-visual selections available. She made her choice and nestled back to enjoy the entertainment — a documentary on computer development throughout history.

The plane took off from Shanghai. The trip to Los Angeles was three hours with the IGFM drive.

She fell asleep soon after takeoff, the Sensobuds switching off when her brain wave patterns changed.

16

FRUSTRATION

Apep woke the next morning with a thumping headache. Had he had too much to drink? He opened his eyes and closed them again. Even with the shades drawn, the light was too bright for him. He kept his eyes shut for a while longer as he lay on the bed, then cracked his eyelids open to let light sneak in between his eyelashes. Even that was painful. Slowly, he opened his eyelids until he could see, if still with bleary vision. Apep rested there until he worked up the willpower to rise. He staggered to the bathroom and straight into the shower. The water turned on as soon as he stepped into the cubicle, and Apep sighed as the warm droplets ran over his body. He stood with the stream flowing from his face, like water cascading from one level to the next. The shower refreshed him and eased his hangover.

He was annoyed with himself for drinking too much, but it puzzled him, too. He had had his usual quantity of alcohol, and yet his thumping head argued with that assessment. Food would help him recover, he told himself as he left for breakfast.

As his security clearance still hadn't arrived, he was unsure what to do with the day. It was Tuesday morning, and he had left the project responsibilities in Alexi's hands. The purpose of the break-in still puzzled him. Perhaps they placed a bug on him, but how could he figure that? He needed advice from Kristina about how one searches for a surveillance device. That would occupy him, at least. He reached for his comm and selected Kristina's contact number at the FSB.

Kristina answered after a few seconds. Once she saw Apep's face, she said, "Good morning, Apep, although it doesn't look like a very good morning for you. Did you not sleep well?"

"You might say that. Good morning, Kristina. I hope I have not disturbed your important work."

"What's more important than my friend? What I was doing can wait. What's up?"

"Well, I have two puzzles you may help me solve."

"And what puzzles are these, Apep?"

"First, someone broke into my room yesterday evening while I was having dinner, but they stole nothing. So, did they secrete a bug on me? But how do I confirm this?"

"That is disturbing. Given our prior discussion, that is a distinct possibility. Most devices are obvious, but I presume you searched for these."

"Yes, I did, and nothing stands out."

"Did you leave a computer or tablet in your room while you were dining?"

"I left my laptop there. Why?"

"An excellent way to keep track of someone is to install a bugging clip onto electronic equipment, typically a computer. Nobody is aware of this until an incident happens."

"So, how can I tell?"

"You can't. Are you doing anything today?"

"No. Why?"

"I'll send our electronics surveillance expert over to check out your belongings and laptop. And, just in case, I'll send you a photo of him. His name is Agent Sarsky."

"Thanks."

"And the second puzzle?"

"It's embarrassing," Apep said with a chuckle. "I woke up with such a hangover this morning, but I swear I did not drink anywhere near enough to cause its severity. I don't understand — unless they spiked my wine during dinner."

"Did you leave your table?"

"Well, yes. I visited the toilet at one stage, but surely the staff keep watch on the tables."

"Not necessarily. Someone may have wanted to incapacitate you so that they could have undisturbed access to your room but misjudged the dose. There is little we can do. You have metabolized any evidence. Just be more careful with your drinks."

"Thanks. I will."

"How are your travel arrangements going?"

"I am still waiting for the security clearance."

"That's strange. They are usually quicker than that. I'll chase it up with them."

"Thanks."

"Anything else?"

"No. That was it. Thanks again."

"In that case, I'll return to my boring office work. Keep in touch."

Kristina hung up, as did Apep. A few minutes later, Apep received an eMessage with a photo of Agent Sarsky.

~

APEP HEARD a chime at his hotel door at eleven that morning. He viewed the in-door screen to see a man standing there that matched the photograph Kristina had sent.

Agent Sarsky stood 1.8 meters tall with collar-length black hair and piercing brown eyes; the sort of eyes one would expect on an agent. His athletic build implied that he worked out. Apep made a mental note to avoid challenging him to a fight. He wore a white polo neck tee shirt and blue jeans, with a thick black coat draped over his arm. A bag carrying his equipment hung over his shoulder.

Reassured that this was indeed Agent Sarsky, Apep let him in, greeting him with a cheery, "I do not know if I have nasty pests. I call the pest exterminator for that."

"Let us find out. Where is your laptop?"

"Over here on the writing desk."

"And may I interrogate it and search your belongings?" Sarsky asked, scanning the room.

"Yes. I want to be clean, and I know Director Zlanovik would only send someone she trusts."

"We earn this director's trust with difficulty."

"She is very good at her job."

Agent Sarsky walked around the room, studying the furniture and fittings. He disturbed the odd item but found nothing unusual. He then looked through Apep's belongings and suitcase, paying the latter particular attention. Once satisfied, he placed his bag on the bed and removed a gadget from it. Turning on the instrument, he scoured the room with the sensor pointed at different objects. He returned to the suitcase, turned the dial to a fresh setting, and re-scanned it.

"There are no physical bugs detected, Comrade."

"Good."

"Please log into your laptop so I can interrogate it."

"Sure," Apep said, moving to the writing desk and turning his computer on.

Agent Sarsky returned the instrument to his bag and removed a laptop. He switched it on and logged into it. He then accessed Apep's laptop and opened the network menu to adjust the settings. "I am pairing your machine to mine on a private network. I can then run your software through a unique clip I developed for these interrogations. Bear with me a minute," Sarsky said.

Apep nodded his head. "Of course."

Sarsky sat at the desk and ran his routine with the laptops. There were many alert beeps as he interrogated Apep's laptop, making Apep nervous. "Ahh! There you are. Brilliant," Sarsky said as his computer emitted a loud alarm. He turned around to face Apep. "You have various troublesome viruses on your laptop, Comrade. You must be more attentive to what you install on it."

"I am sorry. I will try to be more careful," Apep said, embarrassed.

"But here. Come and look at what I discovered."

Apep moved in closer so he could view the agent's laptop screen. "What am I looking at?" he inquired.

"See this?" Sarsky pointed at a list of codes on the display. "They placed that on your computer last night. It is brilliant and nasty as it turns on the camera and microphone and tracks whatever you do on it. It records it and uploads it to a special site when requested via the net. Have you synchronized your tablet to your laptop?"

"No, I haven't."

"Good. It would have duplicated and transferred there."

"Can you remove it?"

"I'll do better than rid you of it. I am forwarding a particular exterminating code to their site. When they access it, two things will happen — it will destroy their site, and it will send me a notification to tell me who and where they are." Agent Sarsky returned to his laptop and typed on its keyboard so fast Apep couldn't decipher what he wrote. They looked at the screens for a few moments, and the offending code disappeared. "Your pests are now gone," he announced, removing the connection and his computer.

"Thank you very much and thank the director if you see her."

"No problem — and she will check up on me. She is good at that." Sarsky smiled as he packed his items into his bag and stood.

"How do I prevent that from recurring?"

"You need to do nothing. If someone tries that again, they'll get a nasty shock. I have installed a special clip on your machine. They cannot install it, and they cannot hide from me," he replied with a sinister grin. "Give me access to your tablet and comm, and I will place a clip to destroy any inquisitive people there."

"I am glad that you're on my side," Apep said, giving him use as requested, and Sarsky installed the nominated code.

Shortly afterward, Sarsky checked his chronometer and wished Apep a good afternoon, as it was now after midday.

"Good afternoon," Apep replied as he opened the door.

Sarsky left, leaving Apep relieved and pleased that he had been cautious and chased his suspicion up with the FSB. He scanned his eMessages, but the security clearance was still absent, frustrating him. Getting one had never been so difficult. He could make comm calls, but he returned to the café for lunch instead, hoping the same waitress would be serving there again. She wasn't.

Apep left for a walk after lunch. The weather was brisk but pleasant. He crossed to the park and wandered the pathways, studying the various statues interspersed throughout. The afternoon passed as he mulled over his predicament. He couldn't reply to Ethan until he had firm plans, but Ethan's need for an answer played on his mind. He could not help that. The security authorization had to arrive first. It started getting dark, so he returned to the hotel. He viewed his eMessages again and grunted again in frustration — still no clearance. With that, he trounced off to the restaurant, in disgust, to have his dinner, deciding to abstain from the wine and drink beer instead. After finishing his meal and fussing over last-minute chores, he retired for the night.

He woke late and immediately checked his eMessages, seeing with relief that his security clearance had finally materialized. At last, he thought. He organized a flight to Los Angeles. The best he could do was the following day (Thursday), in the midmorning, but he booked the trip, thinking at least it fitted in with Ethan's schedule. It just meant he would spend another day in Moscow. Afterward, Apep sent Ethan his itinerary.

Everything was now set. Having done all that he could do, he decided to be a tourist and sight-see for the day to understand what interested foreigners.

Apep left his hotel room and strolled to Red Square, wandering amongst the churches and museums, looking at the history displayed there. Afterward, he walked along the Kremlin walls and towers, taking in details he had never noticed before.

When darkness approached, he returned to his hotel. To pass the time, he read a novel on his tablet that he'd started long ago but left because of his busy project schedule. He got hungry, so he dined at the restaurant again. During dinner, he contemplated what was in store for him in America. Interesting things always seemed to occur when he visited America. He wondered what would happen this time.

Apep retired afterward and slept soundly. He woke up, more refreshed than he had been for ages, had breakfast, and packed for the flight ahead.

He presented his security pass at the airport, with no resistance from immigration control, and headed to the designated gate, ready to board. When they called his flight, he boarded the plane and prepared to enjoy the experience.

17

REPERCUSSIONS

Loki was not happy, and when Loki was not happy, everyone was unhappy if they valued their existence.

He needed to build a spaceship in secret to fulfill his scheme of owning the known astatine deposits — which meant getting possession of Iapetus. His ships were registered, and their movements monitored, so he had to build a new unregistered ship. There would be serious repercussions if they were discovered before he achieved his goal.

Fortunately, he was already building an unregistered liner, so he could change its design for his purposes. He had to build the ship at his maintenance facilities in the asteroid belt to avoid suspicions over material flows for the equipment supply. That had resulted in a sub-optimal construction timeframe. Now his contractor told him construction was behind schedule because of the late arrival of parts, ironic given his skullduggery to sabotage progress on the Chinese, Russian, and American projects.

Now, to compound his woes, American Pie had informed him that the American project was in the final stages before launch of their spacecraft for Iapetus. It was uncertain he could arrive at Iapetus first, and Loki didn't like uncertainty. His father had instilled non-tolerance of failure into him from a young age. He recalled returning home from school once with poor marks and, well, let's just say his father wasn't happy. He did everything he could to succeed after that to please his father.

Loki assembled his team to read them the riot act for not achieving his required timetable. "What's the holdup with the components?" he bellowed at his procurement officer, drilling his eyes into him until he cringed.

"Well, sir, we can't make these assemblies in our shop. We need to buy them and ship them from Earth without people questioning our movements. That takes time."

"And what parts are these?"

"They are the kinetic cannon assemblies. They are very specific, and we must dismantle them and hide them amongst other imports to disguise their nature."

Loki calmed his temper once they explained the holdup to him and why. He desired a means of persuasion accessible to him if someone else arrived at Iapetus first, and he needed threats more persuasive than words. Any other party seeking the same goal would likely be unarmed, being a non-military ship. He wanted ammunition to convince any resistance that their lives were more important than the prize. Any arms were illegal in private spaceships. Laser-based armaments were unavailable because they were so tightly regulated that even he couldn't get hold of them without arousing suspicion. Kinetic weapons were a different question, though. They were not that difficult to produce and hide. Missiles with a compression launch and chemical propulsion integrated into his ship's design more easily. The chemicals he required were available from his mining operations, and the parts were easy to buy, provided they hid their ultimate purpose.

"When will they arrive?"

"The last shipment lands at the end of next week."

"How does that affect the construction schedule?" Loki asked the construction manager.

"We'll have assembly complete in one month — if procurement comes in on time."

"And commissioning?" Loki shot a stare at the man.

"Commissioning will be complete three weeks afterward."

Loki passed the numbers through his head. The schedule would be strained if the Americans departed when he expected. He wanted to avoid such tight timing. "OK. I want no further slippage. Inform me straightaway of any difficulties. Meeting finished. Carson, please stay behind for further instructions."

The other meeting participants filed out, eager to leave. The door closed behind them.

"You know, boss, you drive them too hard," Carson said dispassionately.

"Give them any slack, and they'll take it and more; hold their 'delicates' firmly enough, and they will soon realize that any deviation from my objectives is not advisable." Loki smirked evilly like a James Bond villain as he finished his sentence.

"I'll keep mine in a safe place, then. What did you want to discuss?"

"We need to devise a means of slowing the Americans. We won't be able to stop them altogether. They are too far advanced."

"And the Chinese and Russians?"

"They are no longer a problem. Chinese Checkers notified me they have implemented the delay tactic, although the bonus exercise was unsuccessful. That idiot was only meant to rattle the woman — put her off going to her meeting in Shanghai, not kill her in front of witnesses. A pity, but at least he had the good sense to eliminate himself. Russian Roulette has informed me of the success of that action, too. Unfortunately, they interrupted our acquisition of the data we wanted, so any further information has dried up there. I am still hopeful. But the Americans are still giving me a headache. I can't use American Pie. Unveiling that identity isn't a choice. We may still need a more drastic solution. We just need to detain them for two weeks. Any suggestions?"

"Hmm. I take it you don't want a permanent solution at this stage?"

"No. That's too risky. We can't afford any more direct assaults. We've already attracted too much attention. We need to delay them without uncovering our purpose."

"Kidnapping? Don't harm them, but just detain them for a week," Carson suggested.

"How will that impede the voyage?"

"It needs to be one of the key members of the team. Someone they need for the later phase of the project. What is the next stage?"

"They are to travel to Iapetus, collect a supply of astatine, and try a faster-than-light flight to Mars."

"Sounds like they need a chief engineer for that, don't you think?"

Loki rose out of his seat and considered Carson's proposal, pacing back and forth, assessing risks as he did so. "No violence," Loki stressed, directing his eyes toward Carson.

"No violence. Just take him to a secure location and release him once we achieve the needed delay. If we use experienced henchmen through my obscure channels, the threat's origin will be untraceable. We could even make the operatives disappear afterward if you consider it necessary. That'd be a pity if I use the team I have in mind. They are useful. I'd prefer not to recruit again if it's not essential."

"It shouldn't come to that if you're successful. Yes, I like it. What do you suggest?"

"We need to start surveillance at once and find his routines. Once we've established that, we can kidnap our target. Can American Pie outline his movements for the next week?"

"I'll find out. Get the surveillance under way."

They ended the discussion. Carson left to organize his plan, and Loki keyed the number into his comm to contact American Pie over the black comm.

"American Pie?"

"Yes, Blackjack."

"I need information."

"What information?"

"What are the planned movements of your chief engineer?"

There was hesitation. "Why?"

"Yours is not to ask why."

"They've grounded him for a week until further notice."

"Perfect. Exactly what I wanted to hear. Oh, and don't forget your directive if our goal isn't looking promising."

"I won't."

"Goodbye." Loki hung up and contacted Carson.

"Good news, Carson. We have a week to carry out our strategy."

"That's excellent. I'll keep you informed. How much information do you want?"

"Just that the plan is successful. I trust you to take care of the rest."

"Will do."

"I've also set up a contingency plan with American Pie if the kidnap doesn't work."

"What contingency plan?" Carson asked, not liking the sound of this.

"Never you mind. You just focus on the kidnap."

Loki reclined in his office chair once he had returned to it from the meeting room, a contented feeling passing through him. If only there were more like Carson. The world would be a better place.

Loki mentally checked through his plans for issues to chase up on his project and found none. Everything was in order now. He needed to make travel arrangements to transfer to the rendezvous point for the next phase. But before then ... Loki swiveled in his chair to inspect the young women frolicking on the beach. *Just what I need*, he thought as he rose from his chair and left his office.

18

CONVERGENCE

The quarantine restriction on Ethan soon started to irk him as there was very little for him to do — and if there was one thing Ethan hated it was idleness. Since childhood, he had always needed to keep himself busy. Reading usually helped fill in the downtimes, but right now he was too anxious about the immediate future to settle into reading.

Ethan pondered the prospect of meeting Hu again, which set him off reminiscing about those fun days at Caltech and how well Hu, Apep, and he had worked as a team. It saddened him that their nations had split them up to work on three differing alternatives for the drive. He had considered the decision crazy, convinced at the time that they would have had a far greater chance of success if they kept together — but that was before Galena had assembled the skilled members of the international team here in America.

He and Hu had met occasionally at conferences in the intervening years but only for brief periods before going their separate ways and not for some time. Ethan hoped she could stay longer this time but wondered how Hu and Jade would relate to each other.

That thought set him off thinking about Jade. He wanted to introduce her to Hu because Hu was a significant person in his life. But he hoped she wouldn't become jealous and think there had been something romantic between them. Or maybe he wanted her to feel jealous. It would give him an insight into the depth of her feelings for him and would be an ego boost. He smiled to himself at the thought. This might ...

"Ethan ... Ethan! Your comm is buzzing," someone was calling, bringing Ethan out of his daydream.

"What?" Ethan said to no one, searching for the voice's owner.

"Your comm is buzzing," Jezebel repeated.

"Oh, Ahh ... thanks," Ethan said apologetically, picking up his comm without checking who was calling. "Hello, Ethan here."

"Hi, Ethan. Guess who?"

"Hugo!" Ethan shouted in delight.

"Yes. I'm in LA. If you had used the video, you'd have seen it was me."

"Sorry, I was way off somewhere and didn't hear the chime until someone brought me back to the present."

Hu laughed. "You always were a dreamer."

"When did you arrive, and where are you staying?" Ethan blurted.

"I arrived this morning, and I'm at the Hilton."

"We have to get together. What are you doing tonight?"

"Stay calm, Ethan. Anyone would think you were getting a new toy," Hu said, struggling to contain her laughter. "I am free tonight. I have little planned while I'm here, but aren't we meeting on Saturday night?"

"We are, but we must catch up on old times. There's someone I want to introduce to you."

"That sounds ominous. Have you ditched me so soon?"

"No ... no. You just have to meet her."

"Well, I'll have to *now*. You've intrigued me. So, what's the plan, then?"

"Um ... what about the usual haunt, say seven-thirty tonight?"

"The Sips and Surf?"

"Yes."

"Done. I'll meet you there, and I'm looking forward to seeing you and this friend of yours."

"Me too."

"Zai jian," Hu said and disconnected.

Ethan excitedly placed a call to Jade, waiting impatiently for her to answer.

"Hi, Ethan. What's happening?"

"Are you free tonight?"

"Well ... yes, but what's the occasion?"

"A friend from Caltech is in town, and I want you to meet her," Ethan said.

"Oh ... O... K. Yes, I can come. Why are you so excited? Why is this friend so special? Is she an old flame?" Jade probed with a hint of wariness in her voice.

"Don't be silly. You'll find out tonight. Both of you will have fun. I just know it. I'll pick you up at seven in a taxi. We're going to the usual."

"OK. I can't wait to meet this friend of yours."

"She's a great person. You'll love her, you'll see."

"See you then," Jade said, bemused.

~

ETHAN ARRIVED outside Jade's apartment on the dot of seven, and Jade came out a few minutes later.

Ethan gulped when he saw her. She wore tight blue jeans with a red body-hugging top, a thick black woolen coat, and black leather boots. Her hairstyle consisted of tresses of curls on both sides, accentuating her high cheekbones, which were further highlighted with rouge. She wore subtle green/black eyeliner to emphasize her green eyes and deep red lipstick. Ethan looked at her and gulped. "You look ..." He couldn't get the next words out.

"Stop drooling," Jade said and laughed.

"You just look fantastic." Ethan turned red with embarrassment and averted his eyes. He drew close and gave her a gentle kiss on her cheek that brought a smile of affection from her. "Shall we go?"

"Lead the way."

Ethan took her forearm and led her to the taxi, opening the door for her. She threaded herself along the back seat. Ethan sat next to her. He provided directions to their destination, and they sat back to enjoy the ride together.

Ethan couldn't stay calm. He was too excited about the evening ahead.

"What's wrong, Ethan? You're wound up like a spring ready to uncoil."

"Nothing," Ethan said, embarrassed. "It's hard to explain. I just can't wait to see Hu again."

"You're seeing me now," she said, wondering if he was losing his mind.

"That's her name. Hu. Although we used to call her Hugo. I still do."

Jade raised her eyebrows.

"I'll let Hugo explain it to you."

"OK, but please keep that jackrabbit in check. You're making me nervous just looking at you."

"Sorry." Ethan tried to relax, and they sat in companionable silence for the rest of the drive.

They arrived at the Sips and Surf just before 7:30 pm. Ethan paid the taxi with his chip, and they both entered. He found a table by the window. Hu wasn't there yet, so they ordered drinks and relaxed, sipping them, whispering small talk, and listening to the din of the bar patrons.

The entire room suddenly quietened. Jade and Ethan looked around, searching for the reason. A most exquisite model had just arrived. She was clad in svelte, figure-hugging white jeans matched with a bright azure top that displayed her shapely bust line. She wore black high-heeled shoes. Her shoulder-length black hair was straight, and the makeup she wore emphasized her exotic Asian features to perfection. The men at the bar drooled. Jade's expression became fixed. Ethan burst out laughing. It was Hugo. She deserved such a response to her entrance, he thought.

"Over here," he shouted, louder than he needed to in the suddenly silent bar.

Once she spotted the voice's source, Hu sashayed to their table like a model on a catwalk. The men couldn't take their eyes off her as she stepped past them.

"You know how to make an entrance," Ethan said, still laughing as he stood to greet her. He wrapped his arms around her and gave her a big hug. Jade glanced away, uncomfortable.

Hu and Ethan separated, and Hu noticed Jade's discomfort. "Aren't you going to introduce me to this friend you can't stop talking about?"

Jade looked up, surprised, relieved, and embarrassed. She spotted a sparkle of mischief in Hu's eyes.

"Sorry. Hugo, meet my girlfriend, Jade. Jade ... Hugo. Hu really."

Jade glanced at Ethan, shocked at being called his girlfriend, then stood and went to shake hands. Hu gave Jade a friendly hug instead, which Jade reciprocated.

"Hello, Jade. It's a pleasure to meet you. By your reaction, would it be too much to guess that's the first time he's called you his girlfriend?" Hu asked with a mischievous expression.

Jade blushed. "Hello, Hu. I didn't know that Ethan kept such glamorous company. Yes, he hasn't said it before today." Jade looked adoringly at Ethan, who placed his arm around her waist and returned the adoration.

"Well, thanks for the compliment, but my friendship with Ethan is not like you might be thinking, as I'll explain later. Call me Hugo." Hu swept her eyes around the room and added, to change the topic, "A person could die of thirst in here."

Jade giggled.

"Sorry, Hugo," said Ethan. "The usual? A Budweiser?"

"You bet."

Jade raised her eyebrows at the choice, prompting Hu to explain, "You can't get beer on the moon very often."

Jade laughed. "I suppose not."

Ethan walked off to get Hu's drink.

The bar returned to its familiar noise after the disruption of Hu's arrival.

Left alone with Hu, Jade asked, "Do you always receive such a response when you enter a room, Hugo?"

Hu laughed. "Not at all. But tonight, I must admit that I wanted to embarrass Ethan with a dramatic entrance — not that it worked. He didn't look embarrassed at all. Just pleased to see an old friend and pleased to show you off to me. I can see that he is crazy about you, and I can see why."

Jade reddened. "Thanks. Where does the name Hugo originate? It doesn't sound very Chinese."

"I was the only female member of our research group at Caltech. One day, the third member of our team, Apep, said I should have a two-syllable name so that I sounded more like them. It stuck. I didn't mind. It made me feel like I was part of the gang. I think it helped bind us as a team."

"And how did Ethan and you become such close friends?" Jade continued her questioning.

Hu gathered her thoughts before responding to the question. "The Ethan that's here differs from the Ethan that I met," she started.

Jade listened with intense interest.

"He was shy to the extreme and unsure of himself, especially around women. Very indecisive."

"He still is," Jade interjected. "It took me ages to get him to ask me on a date."

"I'm not surprised," Hu continued. "Ethan has always been afraid of disappointing the important people in his life by making an embarrassing mistake. He had no female role model to learn from when he was growing up, you see. Imagine how messed up he was when he first met me! Before you ask, we were never romantically involved, and we never discussed it. Our relationship was platonic.

We became closer in our friendship, and I encouraged him to risk approaching people with his feelings. I got him to believe in himself. Ethan developed a trust in me and started discussing things with me. We bounced ideas off each other, so to speak. It was a great pleasure to watch him grow as a person. It gave me satisfaction but humbled me to think I'd had a role in molding his personality. Did I do OK?"

Jade nodded, impressed and respectful of Hu. "Yes, you did, Hugo." Jade's voice cracked with emotion.

"And how did you two get together?" Hu asked just as Ethan returned to the table with her drink.

"Well, as I just said, despite your hard work, it wasn't easy," Jade started. "It took a mountain of hints over five years." Jade and Hu laughed, and Ethan blushed. "Jokes aside, it's fair to say we both felt an attraction toward each other. Then we had a successful test in the project, and we gathered to celebrate. The others left us to ourselves, and we just felt comfortable together. The relationship has grown since then. We haven't been 'dating' long, but who knows?" Jade looked at Ethan affectionately.

"Jade's been great for me," Ethan said.

"I can see that. You look like the perfect couple," Hu said.

They sat in quiet contemplation until Jade developed a wicked gleam in her eyes. "So, Hugo, give me the dirt on Ethan."

"No..." Ethan protested.

Hu and Jade laughed. "With pleasure." They huddled while exchanging Ethan stories. Ethan could only sit back in embarrassed annoyance and sip on his drink. He noticed a few men give Hu a lustful ogle now and then while he reclined in his seat. It didn't surprise him. Nor did it surprise him that none of them had the courage to approach her. Ethan knew she was intimidating. She could protect herself with ease, too. He had seen her show that talent often.

After getting the 'dirt' on Ethan, the women allowed him to rejoin the conversation. They talked, laughed, and drank until late. It was eleven-thirty when they called it a night. They hailed two taxis. Hu said goodnight and got into one, which drove off to her hotel. Jade and Ethan jumped in the other and traveled to Jade's unit.

"Hugo is an interesting woman. I like her," Jade announced.

"I'm glad you like her. She is unique. I knew you'd warm to her," Ethan said. "You were jealous at the start, though." He gave a mischievous smirk.

"No, I wasn't."

"It doesn't matter," Ethan said, and gently kissed her. Jade responded, and they separated.

"I hope she can stay for a while. I predict you and Hugo will become good friends," Ethan said.

"You could be right there. She has set my mind at ease on the relationship front. Did you see the ogles she got?" Jade said, lightening the conversation.

"She has that effect on guys. Notice none of them approached her, though. She's somewhat intimidating. Heaven help any man who crosses her! I've seen her in action when they won't take no for an answer. They don't ask again."

"Really? She looks fit, but she appears to lack the strength to win a fight with a powerful man."

"Looks can be deceptive. She has top dan black belts in several martial arts. I've watched her floor someone twice her size, three times, with one maneuver."

"That's a good friend to have."

They concluded their conversation and leaned against each other, content for the rest of the journey to Jade's unit. When they arrived, Ethan escorted Jade to her entrance.

"See you tomorrow?" Ethan asked after they kissed.

"Yes, tomorrow," Jade said huskily.

They had another quick, tender kiss before Ethan returned to the taxi.

As he opened the door, he noticed a vehicle parked nearby. It was not unusual for cars to park on the street overnight, but there was something about this vehicle that disturbed him. He had a sense that there was someone sitting inside behind the tinted windows looking at him. Giving himself a shake for being fanciful, he got into the taxi and let it drive him back to his home and bed.

~

APEP LANDED at LA Airport in the midafternoon on Thursday. Turbulence had made it a rough flight, even at high altitude, which surprised him. After being waved through the 'Nothing to Declare' lane of Customs, he strolled outside to catch a taxi to his hotel. But as he left, he noticed a man with his name displayed on a tablet, so Apep approached him.

"Hello, I'm Apep Chernakov. Why do you display my name?"

"Welcome, Mr. Chernakov. I am a valet from your hotel, and we have arranged transport for you."

"The Hilton?"

"Yes, the Hilton Hotel, Los Angeles."

"Well, what a pleasant surprise," Apep said, impressed by the service.

"Come," the valet said. "Follow me and let me help you with your bags."

Apep handed over his baggage cart and followed the valet from the airport to the waiting vehicle. The ride to the hotel was uneventful. He checked in, and a porter ushered him to his room, arranging Apep's bags on the stand provided and checking the room. Apep almost forgot that you tipped in America. Realizing the porter was waiting for a tip, he pulled his credit chip from his pocket, nominated a quantity, and tapped the porter's terminal on his jacket. The chip gave a soft beep, transferring credit, and the porter left.

The flight made Apep tired, and he wanted to relax, sip a beer, and nap. He retrieved a bottle of beer from the bar fridge and lounged in a chair, thinking. He had two days to kill before the dinner on Saturday night. What should he do? Before he had time to contemplate his choices, the doorbell chimed.

"Room service," a voice announced. The voice sounded familiar, but he couldn't place it.

He rose, strolled over, and pressed the button to display the visitor. A beaming smile came to his face. He opened the door. "Hugo, how are you?"

"Apep! I am well. And you? You have put on weight since I saw you last," Hu said, tapping his expanding waistline.

Apep smiled. "Come in and let me give you a hug."

Hu entered the room and Apep wrapped her in his arms in a tight bear hug. He broke the hug and kissed her on both cheeks. They held each other's shoulders and gazed at each other, comparing the apparition before them with what they remembered.

"Ahh. You are as charming as ever," Apep commented, beaming. "But what brings you here?"

"You always know what to say to a woman, Apep. Must be that Russian charm. I suspect we are here for the same reason. Minor accidents here and there, maybe?" Hu hinted with a querying eye.

"Yes, yes. Accidents. So, you will dine with Ethan on Saturday as well?"

"Yes. I dined with him last night, too. We had a ball."

"Ethan and you always could create trouble, yes!"

"We have matured since those days, Apep. The big news is that Ethan has a girlfriend. I met her last night," Hu said.

"Really? I never believed I'd see it. What's she like?"

"They seem perfect for each other. I hope it works out for them. I don't know if she's coming on Saturday, but you must meet her, too."

"Yes, I must."

"So, what are you doing now?"

"I just started a beer. I was thinking of having a nap."

"That will not do, Apep. We must be tourists for a change. You can be a rich and famous Russian billionaire, and I can be your trophy wife. Do you like that?" Hu said with mischief written on her face.

"You are too wicked, Hugo. Not that I mind walking around with you on my arm. That's an excellent idea, but not today. Let us retire to the bar instead and catch up on gossip. I suppose my little nap can wait."

"Perfect."

Apep checked his things, collected his personal items, and left with Hu, leaving the half-finished beer still standing on the table. He confirmed the door closed behind him. They went to the hotel's main bar and enjoyed the rest of the afternoon and evening, catching up on everything since they last talked.

19

AND THEN THERE WERE FOUR

Saturday evening came. Ethan had booked the Stars Seafood Selection restaurant on the beach in Santa Monica for seven-thirty. It specialized in spectacular seafood dishes, which he knew both Apep and Hu would enjoy.

He thought hard about whether to invite Jade, as he expected they would be discussing sensitive project issues. Could he trust her? On the one hand, she had given him no reason to distrust her or doubt her integrity and loyalty. Her sense of humor was a trifle warped at times, he thought with affection, but her interest in him appeared genuine and not something that was recent. He knew she had been interested in him for years, long before these troubles. On the other hand, a saboteur would probably be gifted at subterfuge and deceit and might adopt a long-range plan. He had been alone and lonely for so long, could his need for affection be blinding him? Yet, if he couldn't trust her, he shouldn't be in a relationship with her, should he? Back and forth his reasoning went until, in the end, he decided that he would trust her.

They arrived at the restaurant together, looking very much like a couple. Without consulting each other about what they would wear, they appeared in matching colors. Ethan wore black trousers teamed with a mint-colored, long-sleeved shirt and black shoes. He added a black woolen coat that extended to his knees, which he removed when they entered the heated restaurant. Jade wore mint too — a dazzling full colored mint dress with a plunging neckline. The color matched the brilliance of her eyes to perfection. She complemented the dress with black high-heeled shoes, a black clutch purse, and a black coat that she removed when she entered the restaurant.

The maître d' ushered them to the pre-booked table by the window and assisted them into their seats. The restaurant gave a serene view of the cloudless sky that night: a waxing moon with moonlight shining on the rippling waters of the Pacific Ocean. Beach sand shimmered like a dimpled silver platter as though ready to serve the most exquisite cuisine in the reflected light. The stars shone brilliantly overhead in the clear night sky.

Jade and Ethan ordered drinks and made small talk while waiting for Hu and Apep to arrive. It didn't surprise Ethan when the two staged an entrance, and a huge grin appeared on his face as he saw them. The maître d' escorted the glamourous couple to the table and stood ready to settle them into their seats.

"Good evening," Apep greeted them. "Let me introduce myself and my charming companion. I am a famous and important Russian billionaire, and this is my trophy wife, Ching Hu, but please call her Hugo. She is funny about these things." Apep spoke just loud enough for the closest tables to overhear. The effect was electric, with people staring in their direction. Jade and Ethan couldn't contain themselves any longer, breaking into fits of laughter, drawing greater attention from the other diners. Both Hu and Apep joined in the laughter while the maître d' continued to wait patiently to help the new arrivals into their seats. His slightly bemused expression increased Jade's laughter.

"Please, no more. My sides are splitting, and you are ruining my eye makeup," Jade pleaded with tears threatening to escape from her eyes.

"And who is this exquisite gem I see before me?" Apep said, gazing in open admiration at Jade.

"Apep and Hugo! Forever the practical jokers," Ethan said once he got himself under control again. He rose from his seat to greet them, as did Jade.

"Apep!" Ethan opened his arms for a hug. "It's great to see you again."

"It is excellent for me too, Ethan." Apep released Ethan from their hug. "But I was not joking about this gem of elegance before me. You must present us, Ethan." Apep turned to Jade.

"You keep your Slavic charm away from her! But I agree — she is a precious jewel. Let me introduce Jade Powers. She has entered my life and changed it for the better."

Jade blushed as she accepted the compliments. "I take it from your entrance that you are Apep Chernakov. I am pleased to meet a Russian billionaire, though I have already met your trophy wife."

Apep beamed. "Yes, yes, I am he. And the pleasure is mine. You are the friend of my friend, so I hope you do not mind a Russian hug of greeting," he said, opening his arms.

"Not at all." Jade stood and responded with a hug. "Hugo, good to see you again, too." Jade gave Hu a kiss on the cheek.

"I'm happy you are here. We can keep these boring gentlemen in check as the night wears on," Hu replied, reciprocating the kiss.

Ethan greeted Hu with a kiss.

"Are you ready to be seated now?" the maître d' interrupted, having waited the entire time they had joked and exchanged greetings. They laughed and agreed that they were ready, at which the maître d' seated Hu and Apep.

The four ordered their meals, and Ethan selected a white and a red wine to enjoy with them. As they ate their way through an entrée and main course, the three friends caught up on each other's doings, careful not to exclude Jade.

Once they finished the courses, Apep gave Jade an assessing glance, then turned to Ethan. "It is time to interrupt this pleasant meal and raise the business for which I traveled to America. I believe it will be of mutual help for us to discuss this. But first — please forgive me, Jade — Ethan, is it acceptable to confer on serious matters in front of Jade?"

Ethan gave Jade an apologetic look. "Yes, Apep. Anything you wish to discuss with me you can say in Jade's presence — except any dirt on me." Ethan cast Apep a mock threatening look as he made the last comment.

"Ah good. I am sorry, Jade, but I had to check first."

"That's fine, Apep. It's better to confirm the arrangements than to blunder into misunderstanding and embarrassment," Jade responded.

"Yes, of course," Apep said. He spent a short time gathering his thoughts. "As you know, our three countries have agreed to, let us say, 'compete' in developing a workable FTL drive — the reason for Ethan, Hugo, and me parting company. There were other reasons too, I believe. And we have been busy doing that these past years. Now, my next words must not leave this table unless we agree to do so. Over recent months, several unexplained events and disappearances have occurred with the equipment for my project. It has been very disconcerting for me, keeping me awake on many nights, as these occurrences have meant slippages to our schedule. I was wondering if you have experienced such incidents, too."

Ethan and Hu exchanged a glance, concerned at Apep's revelation but unsurprised to learn they were not the only targets of sabotage. Jade looked on, puzzled.

Hu responded first. "We have encountered episodes of damage to equipment, leading to delays in our program. It cannot be an accident. And you, Ethan?"

Ethan nodded. "A damaged part could have destroyed the entire project. It was just by chance and thorough checking that I discovered it before we conducted our last tests on Earth."

Jade gaped. "That's terrible!"

If she's simulating shock and horror, she's very good at it, Ethan thought.

"This is too much for coincidence, don't you agree?" Apep asked.

"It looks that way," Ethan said.

Hu stared at the table, upset at the memory. "My latest incident happened on the shuttle as I returned to China. Another passenger attempted to murder me for no reason that I can understand ... Something connects these incidents."

The others gawked at her, alarmed.

"Murder you!" Jade exclaimed. "Are you OK now?"

"Yes. I was fortunate, but I cannot fathom who is behind this and why, especially since they seem to be threatening all three projects."

As Hu's comment sank in, Jade's expression changed from sympathy to suspicion. She asked, "What do these projects have in common?"

They glanced at each other. Hu said, "To develop a workable FTL drive, of course."

"What else?" Jade prompted.

The others studied her before Ethan said, "Astatine. They need astatine to make their technology work. Is that correct?" He checked with Hu and Apep. They both nodded.

"And where's an ample supply of astatine?" Jade persisted.

"Iapetus," Hu said.

"What rights can the first humans to land on a solar body declare?"

"They can claim ownership of that body and its mineral deposits," Apep said.

"Exactly!" Jade concluded, sitting back in her seat and staring at the others. "I suspect that's why the three projects are being sabotaged. Someone else has connected these projects to astatine and realized the great wealth and power they could gain if they controlled the astatine. They are not ready to fly to Iapetus, so they need to delay us to stop one of us from getting there before them."

"You could be right," Hu said, considering the implications of Jade's theory.

Ethan looked worried.

"What is wrong, Ethan?" Apep asked.

"Well, unless I am mistaken, they have delayed your projects for at least two weeks. Is that correct?"

Both nodded.

"That means the American project is the only one ready to fly to Iapetus. So, our project is in imminent danger of escalating attacks. And if they attempted to murder Hugo, this time they might be successful. That's what's worrying me. Do you think it's one of our governments?" Ethan speculated.

"I can't see why they'd want to sabotage their own project," Jade responded decisively. "If they wanted to seize the astatine, our governments could have landed on Iapetus long ago. Instead, they agreed this would be an international project and FTL travel would go beyond political boundaries. Whoever touches down on Iapetus first has promised to share the minerals with the others. It must be an individual operator needing to build a capable ship. A private enterprise landing on Iapetus could claim the moon and its deposits, monopolizing the supply of astatine."

"That makes sense," Ethan said and the last vestiges of doubt about Jade slipped away. She would be hardly likely to volunteer that information if she were the saboteur.

"So, we could have a cowboy desperate to gain possession of the astatine. Cowboys sometimes shoot before they think."

"We must be diligent," Jade said.

"You may have an unpleasant set of circumstances on your hands. I'm not sure how we can support you," Apep pondered, tapping his lip with his finger while clutching his chin with his thumb.

"The best help might be to forward the details of your incidents to us," Ethan suggested. "Meanwhile, I'll talk to a friend of mine to see what he thinks."

"Well, at least we understand what's happening with our projects, and why," Hu said. "We can't do much more tonight. I'm hungry. Maybe we should order dessert." Hu enviably kept her slim figure despite her prodigious appetite.

The others laughed and agreed. Ethan signaled to a waiter.

They spent the rest of the night happily discussing various topics over dessert, coffee, and after-dinner drinks.

Before going their separate ways, Apep said he wanted to make a toast. Raising his glass high, he said, "There used to be three of us ... now there are four."

They all raised their glasses and said, "To the four of us."

Apep then turned to Ethan and Jade and thanked them for a marvelous outing. "Always a pleasure to dine with a beautiful woman," he added, winking at Jade. "Not that you are not alluring, too, my dear wife."

Hu chuckled. "A nice save ... I must agree with my husband that it was a marvelous outing — even for billionaires like us. The seafood was delicious, and the company unparalleled."

"It's been great seeing you both," Ethan said. "I wish you a pleasant stay in my country. I hope we can catch up again before you go."

"Nice to meet you, Apep, and good evening to you both," Jade said.

Their taxis arrived. Hu and Apep jumped into one, and Jade and Ethan took the other. The taxis drove off to their separate destinations.

Jade snuggled up next to Ethan. They sat in silence, immersed in their own thoughts. There was much to consider.

"What might happen if our theory is true? It places us in a dangerous position," Jade said.

"Yes, it does," Ethan said, reaching out for Jade's hand, then deciding against that idea and lifting his arm to wrap it around her shoulders instead, squeezing her against his side. "We don't know yet, so we shouldn't worry too much. Just be watchful, and I'll contact a friend to discuss it."

"Can you depend on your friend? Who is he?"

"Let's just say that he lives in high places, and I trust him implicitly."

Satisfied, Jade smiled and snuggled even closer, closing her eyes for the rest of the journey to her unit.

They arrived, and Ethan turned to kiss her goodnight.

"Want to come upstairs?" Jade asked, a nervous twinkle in her eyes.

Ethan stared at her, nonplussed by the suggestion and unable to answer. His face then softened, his eyes shone, and he reached for her hand. “Yes, why not?” He paid the taxi, and they both alighted from it, holding hands as they walked to the entrance and took the elevator to Jade’s apartment on the seventh floor. Jade opened the door, switching on the lights. They both entered, and she closed the door behind them.

Jade pulled Ethan to her and gave him a long and passionate kiss. She then grabbed his hand and led him into her bedroom.

~

ETHAN WOKE to the sun shining through the window. Jade was next to him, naked under the covers, snuggled up close. He felt her warmth and smiled with contentment.

“Welcome to a new day,” Jade whispered with a flirty huskiness in his ear. “I was wondering when you’d wake. I thought I might have to help you.” She ran her finger along his torso.

“You exhausted me last night,” Ethan said, kissing her on the forehead. Jade raised her face, and they both kissed.

“Want breakfast?”

20

COOPERATION

The President of the United States of America sat in the Oval Office in holo-conference with the President of Russia and the Chairperson of China. They had reviewed several issues, but the issue that they were discussing at present was the individual FTL projects and their progress.

"You both have had unfortunate delays," the US President remarked.

"Not unfortunate but deliberate treachery. But yes, resulting in postponements," the Russian President responded.

"Indeed," the Chinese Chairperson agreed.

"We had an attempted sabotage, too," the US President revealed. "We were fortunate enough to catch it in time, and we could easily replace the part the saboteur damaged."

"Someone does not want us to succeed," the Chinese Chairperson said. "At least not soon. It may involve laying claim to the astatine deposit on Iapetus."

"That notion had crossed my mind too," the US President said.

"And me," said the Russian President.

They sat pondering their predicament until the US President put forward a proposal. "Look, we agreed that the best chance of developing a workable FTL drive was to undertake our own projects and collaborate the results at a proper time. Our team is now ready to make the trip to Iapetus. The astatine deposit is the legal property of those claiming it first, although we'll share that claim, regardless. Agreed?"

The Russian President and the Chinese Chairperson nodded.

"To prevent embarrassment or disagreement, I forward this proposition. It is my understanding that a member of both of your countries' project teams is in America. Would it please you if these team members joined ours for the voyage to Iapetus? In that way, there will be no confusion over claims to the astatine deposit on Iapetus." The US President paused to gauge the response to his proposal.

"That is an excellent idea. I find the recommendation acceptable," the Russian President responded.

"I see the merit of that approach. We can continue our projects in the meantime and bring back the required astatine for our trials. Yes, a splendid solution. I concur," the Chinese Chairperson said.

"Let's make it happen. I presume you will inform your own parties through your chain of command?" the US President asked.

The others nodded their agreement.

The US President concluded the holo-conference.

21

FINAL PREPARATIONS

Ethan arranged another meeting with General John O'Conner on Monday morning to discuss the dinner party conclusions. He drove to the same hotel just before ten-thirty. While he waited for John to arrive, he perused the lobby and noted nothing abnormal. Guests were busy either checking in or out, while staff were moving luggage and communicating in other ways with the clientele. He detected a slight movement out of the corner of his eye outside the window. He wouldn't have given it any attention, except the person was restless and failing to hide inconspicuously. The person's clothes stood out in a cliché spying fashion. It was strange. It gave him the same uncomfortable feeling that the vehicle parked in Jade's street had given him the other night.

John strode from the elevator, dressed this time in civilian clothing, and saw Ethan straightaway.

"Mufti day?" Ethan asked as John stopped before him.

"No. I'm less conspicuous if I dress in civvies. How are you?"

"Good," Ethan said, shaking hands. "Talking about conspicuous, check out the man outside in a very spy-looking outfit."

John glanced casually around the lobby, nodding with a smile on his face. "Yes, I do."

"One of yours?"

"Not likely. We gave away those sorts of outfits long ago. I'd say he's an amateur investigator. Seen him before today?"

"No, but lately I've had a sense that I'm being watched."

"Well, let's retire to somewhere private so we can discuss our concerns," John suggested and led Ethan to the elevators.

They entered the same conference room as before. John closed the door, and they both sat.

John pondered the predicament before commenting. "They might be monitoring you. I don't know why. You need to exercise more diligence and awareness of your surroundings. Don't enter any blind alleys, so to speak."

"You're not serious?"

"Unfortunately, I am. People stalk others for a short list of reasons, one being to get rid of them."

Ethan felt alarmed and started perspiring. "You're making me uncomfortable, but that fits in with our conclusions at my little 'informal' get-together with my Chinese and Russian friends."

"Yes?" John settled in to listen to Ethan's summary of the dinner party's conversation.

"We all have had time-delaying sabotage perpetrated on our projects," he concluded. "Our theory is that another party is aware of our objectives — and let's face it, it's easy to find out — and has realized the monetary implications of the astatine deposit on Iapetus. They want to claim the mineral rights but can't travel there yet. When they can, they'd then monopolize it, charging us exorbitant amounts to use it."

"Hmm. That is an interesting theory," John said. "And because they failed in delaying your project, they might resort to more drastic measures to delay it. For example — kidnap. The voyage would be pointless without you. We'd claim the deposit, but we could do nothing with it."

"Well ... I suppose so. Someone else could do my role, but it'd take time for them to familiarize themselves with it."

"In the meantime, the perpetrator prepares his means of transport and heads for Iapetus," John completed the line of thought.

"So, what do we do?"

"For starters, don't enter blind alleys. We need to get you on the spaceship as quickly as possible. When is the next lander flight?"

"On Thursday. So, you will lift my quarantine?" Ethan said, with a conspiratorial smirk on his face, and relief that his period of idleness was finishing.

"Yes, we can remove it now." John didn't see the funny side of Ethan's question. He was thinking too deeply. "Is anybody else vital to the mission?"

Ethan considered John's query. "Every team member is necessary. Jake's the only other essential person, but he's already on the spaceship."

"Good. In the meantime, I need to protect you until Thursday."

"How will I tell if I spot a bad guy or one of yours?"

"You won't see ours."

"They're that good?"

"Yes, they're that experienced. They may discover who the other contender is. I'll set the wheels in motion."

"Well, that's it then?" Ethan asked.

"Not yet. You remember that other suggestion about your friends?"

"Them joining the mission?"

"It has been approved at the highest level."

"Really!" Ethan said with amazement.

"Yes, they will join you. Keep this quiet until it comes through official channels."

"Of course."

"That's it for now. Unless you have something else?"

"No, I am finished."

John rose from his seat. "It's early, but do you care for a good luck drink with me?"

Ethan stood. "That'd be most welcome."

They left the conference room and retired to a bar on the hotel's top floor.

THE DAYS PASSED QUICKLY as Thursday and the transfer to the spaceship approached. Ethan realized they hadn't named the ship yet. He decided it needed one and christened it *Destiny* because it would transform the destiny of humanity forever.

News that the authorities had lifted his quarantine and Hu and Apep were to join them on the mission came through from Galena on Tuesday. He was unaware of their schedule to board the vessel, but the prospect of working with them again excited him.

Late Wednesday afternoon, as Ethan packed the few personal possessions that he considered essential for the voyage, his comm signaled an incoming call. It was Jade, so he turned on the visual.

"Hello, Ethan, how is your packing going?"

Ethan's heart leaped into his throat as Jade's beaming face sparkled on the screen. "Almost done. What's happening?"

"Nothing. Just thought I'd see if I could tempt you into spending your last night on Mother Earth with me."

"Oh, ahh, yes, that'd be great. What were you thinking of?" Ethan blushed bright red when he realized what he had said. He hoped Jade hadn't noticed.

She gave a shy glance at him and shrugged her shoulders.

Oh! She wants my lead on this. What should I do? "Um, want a bite to eat at Rubicon?"

"That's perfect. Can you collect me?"

"Sure! It's six-thirty now — seven-thirty? Hope they aren't too busy."

"Not on a Wednesday."

"OK. See you soon."

"Bye. Can't wait!"

Before the comm disconnected, Ethan sensed something strange, as though somebody was eavesdropping. *No! I'm dreaming. Enough with this conspiracy nonsense. I must prepare for my date.*

~

Ethan drove his car to Jade's apartment with anticipation of the dinner ahead. He visualized her face in his mind. That cute smile and the sparkling eyes made his heart race whenever he thought of her. Her presence on the mission amplified his delight.

He alighted from the vehicle on arrival at Jade's residence and buzzed her.

"Oh! Hi, I'll be there in a jiffy."

He turned and took in the view. It was a comfortable winter evening; the temperature was moderate, the sky was cloudless, and the streetlamp illumination cast shadows as a breeze disturbed the foliage on the trees. Vehicles were busy going their individual ways like ants scenting the trail to the food supply. Only three people walked on the sidewalks. Not unusual for that time of night. As he absorbed the scene, he sensed a movement in the corner of his eye, as if someone staring at him had darted into the brush.

The apartment building door opened, and the incident slipped his mind as Jade greeted him with a warm smile and a kiss. She stepped out and closed the door behind her.

"Sorry to keep you waiting."

"No problem, just taking in the view," he said as he gave her an impish grin and ogled her, causing her to blush.

Jade laughed. "You can make those compliments any time. Let's go have something to eat. I'm starved."

They strolled to Ethan's vehicle, a two-seater sports convertible, and Ethan opened the door for her as a chivalrous gesture. They drove to Rubicon, a twenty-minute trip.

Rubicon was a traditional Italian restaurant with original recipes for the menu choices. The waiter escorted them to their seats, handed them the food and drinks menus and provided them with water. They sipped the water while they perused what was on offer.

"This place is good, isn't it?" Jade said. "I'm glad that you introduced it to me. I'll never forget it."

"Yeah. I found it by accident one day when I was wandering around searching for a spot to eat dinner. Wine tonight, or should we pass?"

"We won't taste delicious food and drink together for ages, so let's enjoy ourselves tonight. But you still need your strength for later." Jade giggled with a cheeky grin.

"I can live with that. White or red?"

"I want a big juicy steak, so red."

"Sounds good to me. I'll check what they have on offer."

After ten minutes, the waiter came back to their table, and Ethan selected the wine, after which they both ordered their meals. Ethan looked around the room. Wednesday was a quiet night with only a few other customers busily eating. He enjoyed patronizing the restaurant as it had a good ambiance, with a rustic decor that reminded him of twentieth-century Italy. Photos of Florence hung on the wall (or, as they say, Firenze). One pictured the floods of 1966, with a majestic panorama of the Ponte Vecchio. He could still visualize the scenes from his visit there a few years ago.

"What are you thinking?" Jade asked.

"I was just reminiscing about my trip to Florence. It was a fantastic holiday. But coming to other matters," Ethan said, changing the topic, "what are your thoughts on the mission?"

"It's daunting, don't you think? I mean, no one's ever achieved such a goal. We have much at stake. This might be the future of humanity," Jade responded.

"I agree. Many things could go wrong. And I want nothing to happen to any of us. I want to return in one piece ... and I want you in one piece, too." Ethan blushed as he said the last phrase. Jade reddened too and gazed out the window to cover it.

"Who's that?" she asked, pointing outside the restaurant.

"Where?"

"A person staring right at us!"

"That's strange. I've felt someone following me tonight. It's nothing." Ethan did not want to disturb Jade by telling her about the general's warning.

The waiter served the entrée and poured the wine, and they concentrated on enjoying each other's company.

Afterward, Ethan took Jade back to her apartment, and they gazed into each other's eyes. They kissed with abandon, but both realized they couldn't take things further tonight. They separated reluctantly. Jade sighed with disappointment but understanding.

"I'll see you in prep for the voyage tomorrow?" Ethan said.

"Yes, you will. Have a good sleep and sweet dreams," she said, giving him another kiss.

"Sweet dreams too." With that, Ethan walked to his vehicle and drove back to his villa.

As he arrived at his residence, he noticed two strange vehicles parked nearby. They looked suspicious because they were unfamiliar. They didn't belong to anyone in the neighborhood. Ethan broke out in a sweat, sensing danger. He pulled his comm from his pocket and searched for the contact for the protection shift supervisor that John had given him. He dialed the number.

"Hello. Counter-surveillance, Shift Supervisor Casson."

"Hello, it's Ethan Richards. I understand that you have people protecting me."

"Affirmative. Is there a problem?"

"I just pulled up at my home, and there're two strange vehicles parked nearby. They look suspicious."

"Please stand by," Casson said, followed by silence for a period. Casson came back to the comm. "My agents inform me they arrived ten minutes ago. Where are you now?"

"I am still in my car. I'm not sure if it's safe to leave it at present."

"Just wait in your vehicle until it's safe. My agents will go check."

Four people emerged from nowhere, two heading for each vehicle. The agents reached the closer vehicle and knocked on the window. Two people sat inside it. The window lowered, and a discussion ensued. A scuffle erupted as one agent grabbed the passenger in the car, pulling him halfway through the window. The driver opened his door, got out, and started running. The other agent retrieved a stun gun from his jacket, aimed, and stopped the assailant five meters from the vehicle.

Watching this pan out, the other vehicle's driver revved the engine and sped away. The agents heading toward that vehicle couldn't stop it from escaping.

They stunned the remaining man. The agents placed the felons back in the car, cuffed them, and one agent drove them away.

After several moments, Casson returned to Ethan's comm. "You're safe now. We'll keep a perimeter around your home tonight. My agents will escort you to the door and check inside to make sure it's secure."

"Thanks."

"You're welcome." The comm went dead.

Two agents came over to Ethan. He alighted from his vehicle, and they escorted him to his front door. Ethan let them into the villa. One entered while the other stayed with Ethan. After ten minutes, the first agent returned. "Clean," he said. The agents gestured for Ethan to enter. He did so and closed the door. He stared out of the window searching for them, but the agents had disappeared. Although he knew they were nearby, he saw no trace of them. *The general was right — they are exceptional*, Ethan thought.

Ethan finished packing and retired for the last sleep at home until his return. It took him a while to relax and fall asleep.

22

TRANSFER

Ethan woke as a spectacular sunrise exploded above the horizon. *I won't experience one of those for a while*, he thought. His schedule had him departing at eleven-thirty that morning. It was now seven, giving him plenty of time to get to JPL and the specially constructed spaceport with the lander standing ready for takeoff. A vehicle was being sent to pick him up at nine. He hoped the protection detail continued to tail him back to JPL.

While he waited for his transport to arrive, he contemplated everything they had achieved to reach this phase in the project, starting five years ago when research, theoretical general relativity, and quantum mechanics had reached a stage where they could engineer and test practical FTL systems. The political realm had changed to the degree that the superpowers no longer saw the need to compete or protect their confidentiality in the field of space exploration, FTL in particular. That old distrustful behavior had only led to the draining of their ever-decreasing financial resources. Indeed, they realized there was no reason to protect their ability to fly FTL. It provided no extra security to the state. Why travel faster than light, only to return from another star to attack America, or Russia, or China? The more they talked, the greater the nonsense of the argument for secrecy and isolated technology development appeared. Instead, the superpowers agreed that the real purpose was to develop a drive that worked for everyone. With advice from the world's eminent scientists and engineers, they recognized that no single approach stood above other contending technologies in accomplishing this ambition. They then proposed that the best chance of achieving FTL capabilities was to have three 'competing' projects progressing in parallel. 'Competing' in the sense of developing a workable and economic drive first. But they agreed to distribute information on progress, issues, discoveries, and so forth, to learn from each other, thus reducing project costs. They undertook this approach so they wouldn't waste time on areas detouring to dead ends and wastage of resources. A three-pronged attack, so to speak. They decided at the beginning that whoever 'won' would share the technology with any country desiring FTL vehicles. It was a breakthrough for the superpower countries. They continued being as competitive and suspicious as ever in their other political encounters.

And so, they had assembled the three project teams. Ethan recalled his initial disappointment at the three-pronged approach, which meant losing Apep and Hu as colleagues, but he had come to appreciate leading the American-cum-international team with Galena as the project manager, Jade as the quantum physicist, Jezebel as the fusion specialist, and Jake as the mission manager for transportation. Many more contributed to the project, but they were the core members.

They had strived and struggled through long days, with problem after problem, often frustrated and sometimes shedding tears along the way. Test after test failed when the theory said it should at least show some sign of success. It was only when Jade and Jezebel started looking at the fundamental aspects of using alpha particles to generate muons and the various quantum fields required that Jade stumbled on what astatine could do for muon stability. It was as if God had created astatine to offer humankind FTL technology when they were intelligent enough to develop it. The hard work of research and testing lasted five years. It was with a sense of triumph they had finally produced the first usable warp bubble just a few weeks ago. The tenacity and determination of humanity had yet again blazed its shining light in the universe.

The other teams had their successes, too, and were in similar positions to the Americans, until they succumbed to the despicable sabotage perpetrated by unknown identities.

And so, to exchange knowledge and experience and avoid legal misunderstandings, the politicians had decided to place key personnel from the two lagging teams on the voyage to Iapetus. The decision pleased Ethan. It made sense. They were still to progress their respective projects, but they hoped that the learning from the trip would speed up the completion of their drives. One wondered if there would be a warp drive spaceship race once they perfected the three systems.

As he continued to wait for the transport to arrive, Ethan marveled at humanity's ability to strive forward as if on the brink of the next evolutionary stage in its genome.

Nine arrived, and the transport came coasting up the road toward his villa. Ethan prepared his home for its long vacancy and secured it, locking the entry door behind him after taking his baggage to the waiting car.

It took forty-five minutes to make the journey from his residence to JPL with no drama, much to his relief. He dreaded a repeat of the previous night's event.

Another vehicle transferred him to the spaceport preparation lounge while his luggage was sent to the cargo packing bay of the spaceport. Ethan looked around as he left the car. It was a brisk, wintry day but cloudless. The sky was blue. He wondered if he could see *Spaceship Destiny* but didn't know its location. JPL was nestled high in the foothills above sea level, so, on a good day, you could sometimes see the Pacific Ocean. He just spied the sparkling water on the horizon, giving him a sense of peace. He turned and entered the preparation lounge.

Ethan's flight was the only scheduled movement, so only the pilot, crew, and now he sat in the lounge. He was the only passenger. They greeted him and continued their offboard pre-flight checks before they boarded the lander to continue with the onboard checks.

Preparations were nothing compared to the old days. They needed no spacesuits, health checks, or other precautions. It largely matched with boarding an airplane, although more pressure was put on the passengers to review the strict safety procedure checklist, with a test to gauge understanding of the vital safety requirements, the primary one being the passenger's response to equipment failure, including loss of cabin pressure. Ethan went through the safety checklist as he had done dozens of times before. He then waited for the call to board the lander. He fidgeted, eager to see Jade again before leaving, but she hadn't arrived yet.

Jade walked into the lounge at ten forty-five. She smiled. "How are you?"

"Good. I think I've lost the adrenalin rush of flying into space. Have a pleasant sleep?" Ethan returned her smile as a wave of deep affection flowed through him. He decided not to tell her about last night's event. Why worry her?

"In time. I couldn't stop thinking of how much I'll miss you," Jade said with a bashful lowering of her gaze.

"Well, at least someone will miss me." Ethan pulled Jade to him and hugged her. "I'll miss you, too. It won't be for long, though." They stood in each other's arms, content with the warmth of their closeness. He gazed at her. "God, those eyes are gorgeous," he said. He gave her a tender, protracted kiss. As they pulled apart, he could see that those gorgeous eyes were misted with tears. They sat and chatted.

At eleven, they requested Ethan to board the lander. He hugged and kissed Jade again and walked through the entrance chute, which ramped up to its hatch. Four passenger seats stood in front of him as he entered, two spots on each side of a central aisle. He sat in the rear left seat because it offered more legroom to stretch. Windows on the lander's sides provided a view of the external vista. He strapped himself in with the safety harness. It was mostly unnecessary these days, with the gravity grid and the anti-gravity drive adjusting for any turbulence. However, occasions occurred when the instability outpaced the anti-gravity change, causing the lander to convulse enough to cause an injury, so standard procedure demanded using the harness during takeoff and in the lower atmosphere. It was superfluous once the lander was above the jet stream altitude, which was fifteen kilometers.

With five minutes to go, they sealed the lander hatch, and the chute retracted. As eleven-thirty passed, he felt a slight judder as the lander left the ground in a vertical liftoff. He detected no acceleration pressure pressing him against his seat during takeoff. The lander rose two hundred meters from the surface before moving horizontally, the craft aligning itself to travel in a front-to-back orientation. Ethan felt nothing and would not have noticed without windows. Down was always toward the floor, regardless of the lander's orientation.

The lander ascended at an increasing speed as it traveled through the air. Ethan gazed out of the window, watching the ground below recede. The lander rose higher until it was difficult to discern the defined boundaries between objects. He glanced toward the horizon as the lander broke above ten kilometers and he could start seeing Earth's curvature westward, where the Pacific Ocean merged with the sky. The blue sky faded into a darker color until everything turned into the blackness of space at eighteen kilometers. The distinct layer of the atmosphere came into view once they reached the mesosphere at fifty kilometers. As he gazed northward, he could just discern the cosmic rays hitting the upper atmosphere, the auroras writhing across the surface. They now entered the thermosphere at eighty-five kilometers, and the outside temperature started rising. Not that Ethan noticed. They kept ascending and gaining velocity. Ethan could see the entire North American continent, with cotton-ball patches of mottled clouds and angry eddies swirling in the southern regions. He would've seen a brilliant light show if it was nighttime, with great random arcs of lightning seeking Earth to discharge their fury. The view from space always filled Ethan with awe. It made him marvel that humanity could survive on such a thin layer of life-giving air, the constant vacuous tendrils of space attacking the outer reaches, trying to penetrate to devour the life beyond its reach.

They exited the thermosphere and entered the exosphere.

Destiny was parked one thousand kilometers above Earth, traveling in orbit at 7.4 meters per second, so the lander had to speed up to this velocity to dock with the ship. It achieved this with the help of the EmDrive, which started building power once the ship passed out of the mesosphere. The only reason for not using the EmDrive for takeoff was economic.

It took two hours to travel from Earth, achieve the right velocity, and approach the ship. He hadn't seen it close-up before, and he marveled at its design and sleek shape. The ship's main body was an ovoid with a flattened bottom. A trident of stanchions radiated out from two-thirds toward the rear, at a 120-degree angle to each other, housing a huge, truncated cone-shaped EmDrive attached to the end of each of them; each drive compared in size to the actual body of the ship. A massive torus with the vessel at its center was before the drives, one-third from the front. It was part of the warp bubble thrust mechanism. The inclusion of the torus reduced the power needed, increasing the efficiency of the drive. The outer rim of the torus was just larger than the imaginary circle enclosing the three EmDrives. This enclosed the entire ship in the bubble as it propelled it forward. There was no physical attachment of the torus to the ship, magnetic clamps securing it instead. This allowed a quick detachment, if desired, but required a secure magnetic power supply. No one wanted a power failure, which would lose the ring mid-flight. Fins arose from the rear of the ship's main body, dispelling excess heat out into space.

The lander approached the ship from the bottom. Two massive hatch-docking doors swung open as it came closer, allowing the lander to enter the docking bay and land in the designated spot inside the hull. Ethan felt a strange sensation as he entered the vessel, which gave him a nauseous sensitivity for a few seconds. The interaction of the lander and ship gravity fields as it came in caused a slight instability before the lander's grid switched off and the ship's field took control. The lander hovered over its position before settling on the floor, and the doors closed. A force field across the entrance kept the air inside the ship, negating the need for pressurization and depressurization procedures or the need to replace lost air.

The atmosphere and pressurization lights turned green above the entry hatch. The hatch opened, allowing Ethan to disembark. Stairs had extended from the bottom of the hatch to the spaceship floor, and Ethan descended them to Jake, standing at the base, who stretched his hand out as Ethan approached.

"Welcome aboard at last," Jake said.

"Thanks. I see *Spaceship Destiny* in the flesh at last."

"*Spaceship Destiny*?"

"Yes, that's what I call her."

"As good a name as any. It's fitting since that's the reason we built it. Beats USSS 421."

"Exactly. Any chance we can paint it on the hull?"

"I'll arrange it."

They walked to the docking bay elevators and waited for one to descend. "Hope you're ready to do genuine work now," Jake said.

"Sure am. Sure am," Ethan said, gazing in wonder and not concentrating on Jake's words.

23

DESPERATE MEASURES

Loki was sitting at his desk reviewing a report when the comm started flashing. He pressed the reply button. “Yes?”

“Carson’s here for you,” his PA said.

“I’ll see him now.”

The door opened, and Carson walked into Loki’s office. He acknowledged Loki with a nod. “I have bad news, I’m afraid.”

“What news?”

“The target has slipped through the net. It seems he had twenty-four-hour protection. A couple of the guys even got caught, I’m told. Don’t worry,” Carson added when he saw Loki starting to look agitated, “they can’t reveal anything that would be traced back to me — or you.”

“I thought you said they were the best on the market.”

“They are, but a few services aren’t for sale.”

“Rubbish. You just need to find their weak points and their price.”

“Whatever. The target is safely on his spaceship now. They won’t get a bonus, and I’ll consider whether I use them again.”

“Very disappointing. The first time you’ve failed me.”

“There’s a first time for everything,” Carson replied with characteristic composure. "I'm disappointed too. I'll let them know just how dissatisfied I am."

Loki gave a grim smile. "I'd appreciate that." He stood and paced the floor. His circumstances were getting precarious. Delaying the parties to achieve his goal should have been easy, but the pendulum wasn't swinging his way. It was as if the Americans were always one step ahead of him. Or they knew his plan, but that was impossible. Only an elite group of his most trusted inner circle was aware of his plan, and the minions he used had vested interests in staying loyal. They wanted their families to stay alive and healthy. Well, the dice had rolled against him, and he had to consider his options. He might have to become more ruthless in his approach. He preferred not to resort to murder — it had not been his idea to kill that Chinese woman or send that worker on a suicide mission. But ruthlessness might be his only choice. The end game was fast approaching, and the stakes were too high for squeamishness. Too many loose ends could implicate him if he wasn't careful. He still had American Pie in play. That was his last recourse. He didn't want to compromise American Pie's position, though, and would do his best to avoid it.

"What else?"

"The ship's prepared for the next phase. Are you ready to go?"

"Good. I have a few things to finish. Get my essentials packed, and I'll meet you at the lander in an hour."

"Fine. Do you need entertainment along the way?"

"Of course. Have five accompany us. That should be enough."

"Done."

Loki wondered when he would return to Earth again and relax on the beach outside his office. If everything went according to plan, he'd return an even wealthier man with the power to rule the world. He made a few comm calls and messages to keep the business running while he was absent. He wouldn't be incommunicado, but he would need to concentrate more on his primary goal, so he delegated most of the routine decisions of his empire to his trusted underlings. He had siblings but, in his experience, family was more prone to malefic behavior than trusted employees, so he kept family out of his most important work activities.

There was one last task to complete. He dialed the number for American Pie on his comm.

"Hello," a voice answered. Loki thought he detected a tone of dread and hoped American Pie was not getting cold feet.

"It's Blackjack," Loki said, using his code name. "I have a potential job for you. If you approach Saturn and you haven't heard from me, I need you to delay the ship by whatever means at your disposal. Understood?"

"But how can I do that?"

"You're smart. You will think of something."

"It'll be difficult," the voice said.

"You'll think of something."

"Okay, then?" There was no mistaking the dread in the voice now.

Loki disconnected. He had faith that American Pie would not let him down, but he did not want to issue a direct order. Easier to lie later if needs be.

With his chores done, Loki packed his tablet and other essentials into his case and left the office. He said goodbye to his PA and strode to his waiting limousine, which was to take him to his spaceport and his luxury lander. The vehicle would fly him to his new ship, positioned in his maintenance yards beyond lunar orbit, which would transport him to Saturn and his goal. They had built the ship in the asteroid belt and transferred it to an orbit around Earth 10,000 kilometers from its moon, hiding amongst his other facilities at that location. The trip lasted fifteen hours, so he had plenty of time to relax and consider the next phase, checking he'd left nothing to chance. It would take the ship twenty days to travel to Saturn. He hoped he hadn't wasted the money he'd spent to build it.

Loki boarded the lander with the rest of his entourage following in his wake. Three of his staff were coming along: Carson, his personal PA — his office PA would stay on Earth to coordinate issues that arose — and a technical specialist for the ship's installed kinetic weapons. In addition, five members of his harem accompanied him to help him while away the boredom of the trip.

They located their seats and secured themselves for departure. Loki surveyed the passenger compartment. It was the epitome of luxury. Plush, red-piled carpet of Kashmir wool covered the floor. The finest black leather covered the seats and inlaid expensive jade and other gems encrusted various trays and other gadgets. A giant holo-screen hung on the wall separating the pilot's cabin from the main one. Closed-off areas were in the rear for confidential meetings, private calls, and other more intimate activities. They could adjust the strength of the gravity field in the private space, which permitted Loki to enact interesting maneuvers.

A cabin officer walked along the aisle with an assortment of drinks. Loki chose French champagne. The others took refreshments to their taste. As he sipped, Loki felt a familiar jolt as the lander left the ground. He settled back and selected the latest business holo-cast to watch on his personal screen attached to his seat as the lander rose through the atmosphere.

24

TARGET PRACTICE

On *Destiny*, Jake and Ethan spent long hours preparing the warp bubble drive for departure. They checked the other ship's systems to confirm they were ready for *Destiny's* maiden commissioning voyage, too. And they conducted a last check of the EmDrive power supply before pushing energy through it.

"Fusion containment field generator looks good," Ethan reported to Jake from the engineering room.

"I have green on the screen," Jake responded from the Command Center.

"Fusion feed ready."

"Green here."

"Powering up containment field." Ethan closed the switch that allowed energy to surge into the containment field coils. He could hear a hum as the field strength increased, changing frequency from a low throb to a mid-pitched hum.

"Field strength forty percent and rising," Jake called through the ship's communication circuit. "Seventy percent."

"Field equipment looks good. Thermal shedding within limits."

"Strength one hundred percent."

"Good, let's hold for two hours to let it cure. I'll record thermal emissions."

"Confirmed."

Ethan sat at a temporary table near the generator shutdown switch in case he needed to cut the power quickly. He recorded data and caught up on other commissioning reports while he waited. The generator's thermal loss rose as the equipment temperature increased but then tapered, settling to a value well below the design specification. The efficiency was one of the highest he had commissioned. It impressed him.

Jake's voice came over the speaker after two hours. "Generator containment field circuit checked and green."

Ethan roused himself from the report he was writing and turned to the comm. "Confirmed. Will start feed to the containment field for power-up of the reactor." He rose from his seat and walked over to the reactor control panel, where he pressed a sequence of buttons. The containment field's hum changed pitch slightly as the feed of tritium and deuterium trickled into the container from separate ports. The field started a cyclic drone as it rotated the material together, forcing it toward the center at ever-increasing speed and pressure until the temperature rose to the fusion ignition point. It transferred the resulting heat to the electrical generator via thermal fluid, circulating between the reactor and the huge electrical alternators elsewhere in the room. The volume of fuel supplied to the reactor was minimal at present, so the alternators only idled, and it diverted the surplus energy to the main electrical circuits instead of the EmDrives. "Power generation established and at one percent," Ethan said to Jake.

"Green here as well."

"Placing generator into automatic load regulation," Ethan continued. He switched the control setpoint from manual to automatic.

"Check."

They intended to take the ship for a brief test flight to commission and tune the EmDrives. This was the best part of the project, in Ethan's opinion, and Jake and he worked cohesively as a team. They cooperated and knew each other's thoughts, anticipating the next step.

"Shall we go on a joy ride?" Ethan suggested.

"Why not? I'll enjoy a spin to the moon and back. Let me tell Traffic Control and the others on board." Jake placed a general announcement over the ship announcing the impending separation from the construction dock for a round trip to the moon. He gained approval from Traffic Control for a flight lane away from the complex and any traffic around them. They received a departure lane reservation and a mapped path to and from the moon. Traffic to the moon was insubstantial, but regular flights required coordination to prevent collisions even with the minuscule odds of one happening. "OK, Ethan, we're ready. You can direct the power to the drives at your leisure."

"Confirmed and switching now," Ethan said. He pulled the switch on the control panel, diverting power to the main ship circuit and the EmDrives. They felt a strain as the energy flowed into the drives, *Destiny* protesting being restrained by the docking lock.

"Disengaging magnetic lock," Jake said. The ship floated forward and away from the construction dock. It was like seeing a maritime ship leaving its dock and gathering pace to sail to a distant shore. *Destiny* turned and entered the designated departure lane. Once in the lane, Jake increased power to the drives, and *Destiny* gathered momentum as it taxied away from the main traffic areas and out into open space, where they could speed up to a respectable cruise velocity.

Ethan was watching the screens on the control panel in the engineering room. Everything behaved as intended, although the power level was only five percent, still only idling. Ethan changed a screen to an external viewing camera. He saw other spaceships of many sizes float by, like lazy balloons in a wafting breeze on a warm summer's day. Ships stood in various stages of construction, tethered to the construction city orbiting Earth in a slow recession as Earth's landscape passed underneath them. Construction workers jetted to their work destinations like bees going back and forth from the hive to the food source to collect nectar. He watched this in between keeping a check on the generator and drive performance.

The last of the construction city slipped behind them, the openness of space lying ahead and brilliant starlight shining on them. The sun and Earth were beyond their field of view behind the ship. Another ship zoomed past like a shooting star as he watched. *Where is that ship going?*

The moon, on the night side of Earth, shone near full. Jake nudged *Destiny* to a trajectory that angled toward it but intending an elliptical course, so Ethan saw the moon shining in its glory in the middle of the screen. *What magnificence,* he thought. *This is humanity's purpose in the universe. To strive to overcome the prison of Earth, escape the perpetual pull of its gravity, and take its rightful place as rulers of space, basking in the freedom of their achievement.* He noticed the drives' power increasing. It stood at twenty percent now, the generator hum rising in pitch as the energy surged through to the drives.

They steered the ship by differentially directing power to the three drives, changing the ship's axial orientation.

The ship's drives could achieve 5g at full power, but Jake and Ethan had decided beforehand to limit the acceleration to 2g for the maiden voyage. They needed four hours to test the systems, and a round trip to the moon provided this opportunity. The personnel on board felt no acceleration because of the generated gravity field. The ship sped up at 1.2g as Jake increased the power flow to the drives. At thirty percent, the acceleration had risen to 1.8g. *Destiny* settled at 2g at thirty-six percent power, which was better than they had hoped. "Power levels look good," Ethan said over the comm.

"Feel this baby hum!" Jake said from the Command Center with a discernible note of exuberance, which always brought forth a Texan twang. "Astrogation is perfect and direction control's a joy to behold."

Ethan noted that the thermal load dumping through the rear fins was well within design limits. This was one great ship. "I haven't experienced a ship like this. Everything works like clockwork."

"Yeah, hope they build more like this baby," Jake said.

They settled for the rest of the journey. Jake stopped acceleration at one and a half hours into the flight except for any steering necessary to change direction. They passed around the moon at the two-hour mark. Ethan saw the landscape on the lit side from 5000 kilometers away, the radiance reflecting off the many craters and plains on the moon's surface, Mare Tranquillitatis, Mare Fecunditatis, Langrenus, and many other features. They then sped around to the dark side only for the sun-facing surface to re-appear moments later, the moon waxing as they started their trip back to Earth.

Ethan saw industrial complexes on the camera as they traveled beyond the moon's dark side. He knew ore-harvesting companies used facilities there. They processed ore in the asteroid belt and transported the semi-refined material back to Earth. They had set these facilities up as maintenance docks for the ore carriers. A ship departed one dock as he watched. It caught Ethan's eye because it wasn't an ore carrier. Ore carriers had huge central bodies to maximize the volume of material they could carry back to Earth. This ship appeared to be sleek. Ethan zoomed the magnification and centered the ship on the screen. It looked like *Destiny* without the warp drive ring. The ship increased in speed away from Earth as Ethan looked. Such a ship, and that unique design, exiting Earth's domain of space, puzzled Ethan, and he made a mental note to discuss it with Jake.

Two and a half hours into the trip, the ship turned 180 degrees so that the front was now facing the moon, and the drives started exerting thrust to start the required deceleration needed to slow *Destiny* back into Earth's orbit.

Ethan tweaked the settings in the drives that were suboptimal, but the drives' performance overall pleased him.

The ship slowed to maneuvering speeds as it returned to the dock it had left just over four hours before. Jake communicated with the port authorities for a safe docking lane to return to their berth. Space was always busy with Earth traffic and other near-Earth destinations. He received a lane allocation and inched to the vacant dock. The magnetic docking clamps grabbed the ship as it floated sideways closer to the transfer orifice, securing the ship with a dampened restraining force as the clamps brought *Destiny* to a stationary position. They then drew the ship closer to the docking station. Lights turned green as the maneuver ended. A tube extended from the complex like an umbilical cord connecting *Destiny* to the docking station for easy access to it again. Connection lights flashed and hatches opened.

"Hope you had an enjoyable flight," Jake said over the ship's PA.

Ethan laughed out loud as he stood and headed for the Command Center. He wanted to discuss the ship's performance with Jake. He felt great satisfaction with the maiden flight.

"That worked well," Ethan said as he entered the Command Center.

"Yeah. Everything looked good up here. What about your end?"

"I had to tweak a few settings but nothing of any consequence. The drive performance was better than the specifications, and the thermal dumping was exceptional."

"Do you think we're ready?"

"As ready as we'll ever be. We have the warp drive equipment installed and tested for the startup. We just have one thing that we should test before we go."

"What's that?"

"Our insurance policy."

"Oh, that! We can't do that here. Any ideas?"

Ethan thought for a moment. "What about calling tomorrow a recreation day? We can run the ship on our own for a brief trip, can't we?"

"I'm sure we can now that we've removed most of the bugs."

"OK. We'll take the ship out somewhere nearby and have target practice."

"That sounds good, but what can we use for targets?"

"How precise is the targeting control?"

"It's supposed to lock onto a dime from a kilometer away."

"OK. We'll take an automatic drum launcher with us, and catapult used drums from the forward docking bay doors. Then, when they're a respectable distance from us, we'll target them and try blasting them into oblivion."

Jake looked at Ethan, astounded. "Your mind thinks like a demolition expert."

Ethan chuckled. "I can't help my upbringing. I blew up my family shed once."

"That must have impressed your father."

"He wasn't around, but I can still feel the punishment he gave me when he came home. Sound like a good idea?"

"Sounds good. Let's have a drink to celebrate."

"Deal."

~

ETHAN AND JAKE boarded the ship just after nine-thirty the next morning, having slept in the construction complex accommodation that night, and headed for the Command Center. They conducted a quick systems-check. Ethan then left for engineering to double-check the drive and power systems, while Jake got Traffic Control clearance.

"Systems OK in engineering," Ethan said as he entered the Command Center half an hour later.

"Good. I have approval to leave, and we have a lane allocated. You want to take the controls?" Jake asked.

"OK. I'll have you as backup if I stuff up the astrogation."

"You fix your own problems."

Ethan sat in the command chair and pulled the main console around so he could control the ship on his own. He tapped the keys and released the ship from the magnetic clamps while channeling thrust into the drives to maneuver *Destiny* away from the docking station. He checked the lane allocation and transferred the map to astrogation, locking it into the drive controls so that the ship automatically corrected its course while traversing the departure route. With increased power to the drive, the ship accumulated speed. Ethan liked the controls' responsiveness and the ease with which he could maneuver the ship. "This is great," he said to Jake as he viewed the control displays and the external camera screens that showed the view from the ship in the forward 180-degree direction. The ship taxied through the departure lane with ease.

"Thought you'd enjoy it. Don't need a crew."

"Yeah. Where should we go?"

"Let's get 100,000 kilometers away from Earth and outside the ecliptic plane. That'll keep curious eyes away."

"Won't people be surprised about us going outside the ecliptic?"

"If they ask, we'll just tell them we want to keep out of everyone's way."

"OK. Sounds good."

Destiny reached the end of the departure lane. Ethan increased the power to the drives, and they sped up at a decent rate. He steered the ship to thirty degrees from the ecliptic, punched the destination coordinates into the astrogation, and sat back for the ride.

Ethan remembered what he had observed beyond the moon yesterday. "Jake, I had an external camera on in engineering yesterday and noticed something odd."

"I spotted nothing. What was it?"

"You know those ore carrier maintenance facilities out there?"

"Yeah."

"Yesterday, as we passed behind the moon, I saw a ship leaving from there for the outer planets. I suspect that's normal, but the vessel wasn't an ore carrier."

"No. What was it?"

"It looked like our ship — sleek main body with large drives."

"That's odd. I can't imagine someone wanting to use this ship's design to build a luxury yacht. They stay near Earth or, at the most, travel to the moon resorts."

"Exactly. You wouldn't waste the expense even if you were a rev head."

Jake pondered the conundrum for a moment. "You wouldn't even do it to travel to Mars. Mars is nearby, relatively speaking."

"Any ideas on its destination?"

"No, but they must intend it for a long and fast voyage somewhere."

They both sat in silence, pondering the odd sight that Ethan had seen.

An hour after leaving the dock in Earth's orbit, the ship decelerated to a stationary position at its designated location, awaiting further astrogation instructions.

"How do we play this?" Jake asked.

"I'll go set up the drum launcher. It shouldn't take long. Then I'll come back so we can both have practice blowing things to smithereens," Ethan said, flashing a school-boy grin at Jake as he finished his statement.

"Is that the technical term?"

"Yep. Learned it in school."

"Where did you get the launcher?"

"It's not that difficult to snatch one. They use them in war games and sporting activities, so a couple were sitting in the station. I just borrowed one for the day."

"OK. Let's start blowing things to smithereens, as you say."

"I'll be back soon," Ethan said as he left the Command Center, heading for the forward docking bay. The construction crew had loaded the drum launcher the previous evening.

Ethan set up the launcher, making sure that it faced the right direction, and filled it with ten drums to fire out of the docking bay door when triggered from the Command Center. He opened the door and returned to the Command Center.

"Set," Ethan said as he walked into the center.

"OK. Let's have target practice then," Jake said with a glint of enthusiasm in his eye.

They both sat in the Command Center, Ethan in the main command chair and Jake in an auxiliary seat reserved for the communications officer. Ethan dialed up the drum launcher on the command screen and located the launch button he had programmed into the controls earlier. He pressed the button, and one drum shot out of the launcher and the front of the ship at three hundred kilometers an hour. The astrogation screen tracked the drum as it increased its distance from them. Both Ethan and Jake then keyed a code in the secure section of their respective command screens, and the weapons activated, ready for either of them to use. Jake adjusted the targeting and locked onto the drum for tracking only. He zoomed the magnification to get a larger image.

After twenty minutes, the drum was a hundred kilometers away. "Shall we try now and see how it works?" Jake asked, looking like a boy on Christmas Day raring to try out his new toy.

"Why not? We'll see how it performs from here. You can do the honors." Ethan noted the eagerness in Jake's voice as if he were using his entire willpower not to reach out and put his finger on the fire button.

Jake acknowledged the courtesy and went into motion on the screen. He first adjusted the targeting until the hairline indicator changed from red to green and pressed the lock button to lock onto the drum. He pressed the button to release the laser for firing and pressed the fire button. A deep red beam of laser light shot from the ruby-crystal laser cannon. At the same instant, the image of the drum disappeared, vaporized by the intense energy of the laser hitting it.

"Woo-hoo!" Jake shouted. "Bull's eye!"

"Well done. Don't get too excited." Ethan smiled at Jake's exuberance.

"Got any more?"

"There are nine left in the magazine. Let's fire the entire batch off and let them fly further away. We will target one every one hundred kilometers to see how far away we can still hit it," Ethan suggested, grinning with amusement at Jake's enthusiasm.

"Sounds good to me," Jake said as he victory-danced around the Command Center floor, shooting out rabbit punches now and then. He soon exhausted himself and sat again. Ethan just smiled.

Ethan returned to the launcher control screen and punched in information to sequence the launch of the remaining drums at intervals of one minute. He allocated an ID code for each drum, too, so they could track them. He pressed the release button to start the launch sequence. The first drum sped out of the docking bay, and the tracking showed its icon with the respective ID code displayed next to it on the screen. The display provided the distance from the ship underneath the code. Launching them as coded, the drums flashed with their respective data. The batch displayed on the screen eight minutes later, moving in unison like a flock of sheep following each other across the sky.

"Don't suppose that it's worth reloading the launcher. We should get back once we finish this test," Ethan said.

"Yeah, we don't want them worrying that we have hit trouble."

"The laser had a powerful punch. I wonder what the military thinks they can use that for, instead of the more traditional weapons at their disposal?" Ethan pondered, looking at Jake for inspiration.

"Don't know," Jake answered, shrugging his shoulders. "Maybe it's better for space-based combat and cheaper than kinetic missiles. It's quicker, and the target has no time to dodge the bullet."

Ethan and Jake spent the next three hours shooting drums at the designated distance, taking turns in targeting and firing the laser and chatting between shots. They vaporized the nine drums with ease.

"So, it can hit a target the size of a drum at 1000 kilometers. Impressive," Ethan said after the last drum disappeared from the screen.

"Yeah. Hope we don't have to use it, though," Jake added, his expression suddenly pensive.

"Is there a power setting?"

"Yeah. There's an intensity setting on the screen's left. You can change that from zero to a hundred percent."

"OK. Good to know in case we want to send a warning shot or damage a part instead of blowing up the entire thing. Let's reload the launcher and experiment with the range setting," Ethan said.

"Good idea. It won't take that much longer. We'll try it at one hundred kilometers. We have the full power result, so we can see the effects of reducing the intensity."

Ethan returned to the docking bay and reloaded the drum launcher. After launching the ten drums from the bay, Ethan closed the docking bay doors. He then replaced the drum launcher in the storage location, ready for the trip home. He returned to the Command Center and Jake, who was ready to fire.

Jake reduced the power settings by ten percent and fired at each drum in sequence until the drum stayed intact. They took a visual record of each drum position after firing to detect visual residual material and the state of damage if the drum remained intact. Visual images showed that the damage inflicted by the laser was superficial at a thirty percent setting.

"Well, that's it. Thirty percent is the burn-the-paint-coating-off point," Jake said.

"Looks like it. Destroy the rest of the drums, and let's return home for a beer."

"Yes, sir," Jake said with military correctness and destroyed the residual drums displayed on the screen.

Ethan sat in the command chair and steered *Destiny* to the base. After a tiring day, they both looked forward to that well-deserved ale.

25

FORWARD TO WEALTH

Loki's luxury yacht had an uneventful trip from Earth to the maintenance base beyond the moon. The spaceship that was to transport them to Saturn and offer Loki his hoped-for immense wealth was there, hovering in the nothingness of space. He gazed out of the yacht windows as they approached the ship to see the cause of the gaping hole in his income stream. Pride welled up in him on seeing the vessel as he took in the magnificence of its elegant lines and the physical size of the components, showing the latent power hidden in the ship like a gargantuan leviathan sleeping in its den. He had named the spaceship *Loki's Lion*. It was the prototype of a new interplanetary ship that he envisaged would revolutionize space transportation. He intended to make interplanetary travel and tourism available to a whole fresh class of travelers, people who had only dreamed of visiting another planet. The upcoming voyage would be the ship's pilot run to test the potential turnaround times and costs.

As Loki gazed out the window, he reflected on his life. He had achieved so much, through fair means or foul. The only achievement he hadn't attained was to father a successor to his empire. With no child to inherit his corporation, he'd set up an organization people would remember for eternity. *Maybe this ship can be one of my many children*, he thought.

Loki watched the vessel increase in size as the yacht approached it from the stern, edging to the front where the docking bay was, the gleam of the gunmetal skin reflecting the glare of the sun as they floated around the hull. The elegance of its trident drives, ready to thrust the ship to its destination, filled Loki with pride and determination. The income from astatine sales would build the tourist market. He reflected on the triad of drives and pondered how he could use their symbolic design as the logo for the business he was to grow from this embryo.

The yacht moved toward the docking bay, turned, and entered it, hovering above the floor before the landing legs extended, and the ship lowered itself gently to the solid surface. The cabin hatch opened, and Loki emerged from the yacht to the sight of the ship's captain standing to the side.

Loki descended the steps, his entourage following him, and walked over to the captain.

"Welcome aboard, sir," the captain said, extending his hand.

Loki shook hands. "Good to be here, Captain. When can we leave?"

"We're loading the last of the cargo now and expect to be sailing within three hours, sir."

"Very good. Show me to my quarters so I can freshen up. Then you may give me a tour of the ship."

"Sir," the captain said as he gestured toward the elevators and started walking toward them. He pressed the up button, and a few moments later, the doors opened. He allowed Loki to enter first before he entered, with Carson and Loki's PA behind him. Other crew members escorted the rest of the arriving company to their quarters. They gave the harem a cautious, leering look as they corralled them to the elevator. The doors closed behind Loki and his party, and it rose to the residential deck.

The captain led his entourage to the executive suites near the elevator. He pointed to Loki's suite. "This will be your accommodation, sir," he said as he pressed the door-opening button on the wall. "I hope it meets with your expectations. A console in your room gives you communications throughout the ship, and a butler and valet are available. Your personal assistant's room is next to yours," the captain said, pointing, "and Mr. Carson has his room across the hall," again gesturing.

"It looks good, and the room allocation meets my purposes," Loki said. "Does my suite include a private study and a meeting room?"

"Yes, it does, sir, just as you ordered. The meeting room can accommodate six with comfort. Any larger and you may need to use one of the various conference rooms available on the next level."

"That suits me fine."

"Shall I return in half an hour to escort you around the ship and show off its features?"

Loki looked at his chronometer. "Make it forty-five minutes. I have matters to attend to first."

"Sir. Forty-five minutes," the captain confirmed, and he walked back to the elevators.

"Carson, can you come to my suite in thirty? Eleanor, please prepare my business schedule for the next twenty-four hours and have it ready for me before departure," Loki instructed.

"Will do," Carson replied.

"I will," Loki's PA said.

Loki entered his suite, the entrance door closing after him. It was huge. On a luxury liner, it would be called a penthouse. In front of him was an immense living space with assorted tables, couches, and chairs scattered throughout. There was a cabinet on one wall containing various refreshments behind transparent doors. Wooden-paneled doors below enclosed a refrigerator for chilled drinks. The room extended the full half of the ship to the hull, a hundred meters at least. A wide viewing port penetrated the hull. Various holo-paintings hung on the walls, including a large holo-screen for entertainment and other communication activities. A plush smoky-gray piled carpet cushioned the floor as one walked over it. To his right was a partitioned-off room for meetings that held a conference table, chairs, holo-viewer, drinks cabinet, and another table to one side. The captain had given a conservative description when he said it could accommodate six, Loki thought. He reckoned it could fit ten with space to spare. A door at the far end led to Loki's private office. He noted a second exit from the office, allowing him access from the living room. This was what he envisaged for the exclusive luxury cabins of the tourist business, although he had not inspected the other suites.

Loki walked over to the services console and pressed the button for the valet. He turned around and received a fright. The valet was right behind him. "That was quick."

"People like yourself dislike being kept waiting, sir," the valet said. "How may I help you?"

"I wish to have a shower and change my clothes into something casual but not sloppy," Loki requested.

"Sir, the master bedroom is this way, and we have stocked the ensuite with your toiletry needs, including towels. I will arrange your clothing and have it ready for you when you emerge. Shall I offer a choice between alternatives for you?"

The service impressed Loki. "That'll be perfect. Keep up the excellent performance. This is impressive."

"Thank you, sir."

The valet led Loki to the master bedroom doorway, which was next to the office, and Loki entered. The ensuite entrance was opposite him. He walked there and was impressed to see that the shower was large enough for three. Refreshed, he returned to the bedroom clad in a luxuriant bathrobe and drying his hair with a towel. A choice of clothing hung on a rack to his left. He selected a pair of faded blue jeans, a black polo neck shirt with matching black socks, and black sneakers.

Loki felt relaxed and refreshed after his shower. The bell chimed on the entrance door. He walked over and saw Carson on the security screen, waiting. Loki pressed the button to let him enter.

Carson ambled in and inspected the cabin. "More upmarket than mine," he joked.

"Some of us are lucky," Loki said. "Come and sit while we talk. Drink?"

They both went to lounge chairs by the window.

"Is there a beer?" Carson asked as he relaxed.

"I'm sure one exists somewhere." Loki detoured to the console and pressed the button to beckon the butler, who appeared as if from thin air.

"Yes, sir."

"Two beers, please," Loki ordered as he strolled to his seat and sat.

"Certainly," the butler said. He withdrew two small bottles of beer from the refrigerator, placed them on a tray, and opened them. Retrieving two glasses from the cabinet, he filled them, put them on a tray with the bottles and placed the tray on the table between Loki and Carson. "Do you require anything else, sir?" the butler asked.

"No, thank you," Loki said.

The butler then disappeared as mysteriously as he had come.

"Those guys must teleport in or something. No sooner do you press the button than they are with you. Creepy," Loki said, picking up his glass. "Cheers!"

Carson picked up his beer. "Cheers. To a successful mission."

They both sipped a mouthful of ale and gazed silently out the window at the spectacular sight of Earth in the middle of a sparkling star map. The moon shone to the left, in pseudo-eclipsed darkness. A sliver of light highlighted the terminator on one side of it. Loki thought it was stunning.

"What did you want to discuss?" Carson asked.

"I've been considering the potential of a fleet of ships like this one. There's an opportunity for opening tourist transportation and maybe a luxury resort. It could do business throughout the solar system. I know operators offer moon trips, and even trips to Mars, but these cater to the affluent and are unavailable to the general population. We could open space for the masses. What do you think?" Loki asked, Carson leaning toward him, listening.

Carson paused before he responded. "If we can bring the cost per passenger down to a reasonable level, with a good margin, I don't see why we couldn't investigate it more seriously. I'm sure plenty of patrons would jump at the chance, given the right price. Would you manage the resorts as well?"

"That's a possibility, or we could partner with a developer to build and run them."

"It wouldn't be unreasonable for trips to Jupiter and Saturn, even if we take twenty days to travel to Saturn. I'm sure we could develop more powerful drives for the ships traveling those routes to lessen the time further."

"Exactly. I want you to look at the possibilities, generate options. Let's see if we have a business case that our team can detail. I may as well make this ship useful after this trip. We could reduce the size of the suites, though. We need to maximize our passenger numbers."

"OK. I'll start working on it. When do you want a progress briefing?"

"How about an outline of possibilities within ten days?"

"It's tight, especially since I am here, but let's see what I can put together."

"Good." Loki completed the conversation by picking up his beer and taking a long draft. Carson reciprocated. They both gazed out the window, once again absorbing the spectacular scenery.

At that moment, the door chime rang. Loki rose from his chair and strolled across the room. Seeing that it was the ship's captain, he pressed the button to open it.

The door opened. "Hello, sir. Are you ready for your tour of the ship?" the captain inquired.

"Yes. We just completed our discussion here. Let me finish my beer, and we'll be on our way. Do you want to join us, Carson?"

"Yes, I will, given our conversation," Carson said.

"Sir, I'm afraid I neglected to point out several features of the suite. A voice-activated command control exists for you to manage the door and action other commands."

"Is there? How does it work? Can I see the person before I open the door?" Loki asked with surprise.

"Sir, if you will come here, please, and speak on my signal," the captain advised as he walked over to the suite console. He pressed the Voice Command Initiation button and gestured Loki to say something.

"Hello, I am Loki Mason," he said in a wooden tone. He felt stupid saying it in front of the others.

"Hello, Mr. Mason. It is good to meet you. We've set up the voice command console, and it's ready for use. Just give me a name," a female voice said from nowhere and yet everywhere.

Loki considered his choices and settled on one. "I'll call you Dianne."

"Very well, Mr. Mason. You can call me Dianne. Just include my name before or after the command, and I will respond. Have a pleasant day."

"Now, sir. If I go outside again, you can watch how it works," the captain said as he walked toward the door. He opened it and entered the corridor. The door closed.

The door chime rang. "Dianne, show me who's at the door," Loki said, looking at Carson sheepishly. A holographic image appeared in front of Loki, displaying the waiting captain. Loki nodded, impressed. "Open the door, Dianne." The door opened, and the captain re-entered. "Very impressive. It will save time."

"Thank you, sir."

Loki returned to his seat and drank the rest of his beer. "Shall we go, Carson?"

"Ready when you are," Carson replied, rising from his chair and following Loki and the captain out of the suite.

The captain led Loki and Carson through the entire ship, explaining the functions of the equipment and the various compartments, answering questions along the way. The tour ended on the ship's bridge, where the captain explained the many controls and displays.

"Where is the deterrent device if we need to use it?" Loki asked.

"We can access it from the command chair and this auxiliary chair only, sir. But I prefer not to show you until we have undocked," the captain said.

"Yes. We must exercise caution."

The commander on duty entered the bridge and strode to the captain, saluting him. The captain saluted back.

"What is it, Commander?" the captain asked.

"Sir, we are ready for departure on your orders."

The captain looked surprised that they were ready so soon but gathered himself in front of Loki and Carson. Turning to Loki, he asked, "Do you need any delay, sir?"

"No, let's get this show on the road," Loki advised.

"Very well, sir." The captain turned back to the commander. "Let us leave, Commander."

Saluting again, the commander announced to the bridge crew, "Start departure procedures." The crew responded by bursting into a hive of activity.

The captain turned again to Loki. "Would you care to stay on the bridge as we disembark, sir? It's a wonderful sight."

"I'd appreciate that. Where can we sit so that we're out of your way?"

"Those seats are vacant, sir, and they give an excellent view through the window," the captain said as he pointed to the spots. The window in the bridge was large and provided a 180-degree panorama of space.

Loki and Carson walked to the seats and parked themselves. Meanwhile, the captain sat in the command chair where he displayed the command screen and watched the access hatches close. Green lights lit up the display to show the hatch entrances.

"Ready for departure," the commander said.

"Go ahead," the captain said.

"Disengage."

Loki rested in his seat, fascinated with the proceedings. He felt a slight jar as the magnetic clamps holding the ship released and the vessel moved forward. The spaceship increased in momentum as more power was directed to the drives. He watched the maintenance yards drift behind them and other ships in their moorings with robotic machinery crawling over the shells, their extended arms possessing various mechanical appendages at their extremities. They looked like crabs marching across rocks on a beach. As he glanced sideways, Earth drifted to the stern, and the moon's crescent expanded as a more sun-exposed surface appeared. An image then disturbed him — a ship traversing the moon's dark side at speed. He brought the screen in front of him closer and selected a view from one of the external cameras. Once he had adjusted the camera position to point toward the moon and zoomed in, he froze. The screen before him displayed a ship much like his own, except it had a ring around its hull, the purpose of which he could not fathom.

"Is everything alright?" Carson asked. "You look pale."

Loki stared at him. "We haven't left a minute too soon. Look!" He rotated the screen for Carson to see the image on it.

"Oh!"

26

ALL ABOARD

The days after the laser test were busy days onboard the *Destiny*, with preparations for departure now in full swing. Several landers arrived to ferry the supplies and other equipment they would need on the voyage to the ship. The lander that Ethan was watching on his screen now was causing him particular excitement. Hu, Apep, and, most important, Jade were on board. His heart fluttered as he imagined meeting her again. It seemed like an eternity since they had last seen each other. It had only been two weeks, and they had talked via holographic link in that period almost daily — something that would embarrass Ethan if others knew. However, seeing her on a holograph was no match for seeing her in person. As he waited, he got increasingly fidgety, which was an external sign he was getting nervous. He hoped no one noticed.

"She'll be here soon," Jake said, with a teasing smirk on his face as he watched Ethan drumming his fingers on his desk to calm himself.

Ethan blushed with embarrassment. "Shows that much?" he asked sheepishly.

"A blind bull could see your red flag at the moment." Jake chuckled. "Go to the docking bay. She'll be here soon. You won't get any brownie points if you aren't there to greet her."

"You sure you don't need me?"

"Positive."

Grateful, Ethan left the Command Center and started striding to the docking bay to greet the arriving lander.

~

JADE WATCHED the ship grow larger as they approached. She had never seen such a view in her life. It was beautiful. The ship's existence and her living in it for the next month were hard for her to imagine.

The ship rested at one of the many docking stations around the construction facility, an enormous space station called *Ulysses*. A variety of spacecraft hovered like bees around a hive, and other insect-looking machines crawled over spaceships parked at their docking stations. Their spaceship was free of these because it was ready to fly. She had heard that it had already completed its maiden flight, circumnavigating the moon.

Jade was in the lander with Apep Chernakov and Ching Hu, who, for strategic reasons, had joined as visiting members of the project team. Galena Alvarez and Jezebel Liebmann were on board, too. Jade glanced at Hu. They had become good friends in the days that Hu and Apep had joined the group to prepare for departure. The three had compared notes on their respective projects over social meals and drinks together in the evenings after work, too. But Jade still found Hu hard to fathom. Why was someone so stunningly beautiful and so fond of Ethan not with him? Jade told herself that she trusted Ethan and had no need to worry. Besides, she genuinely liked Hu. Still, the nagging jealousy lingered.

Jade stared at the ship and thought of Ethan. Her heart pounded faster, excited by the prospect of seeing him again. She hoped he would be there to meet her when they landed.

They intended to land directly on the spaceship instead of at a station-landing dock, as the ship was ready and going through the station's immigration and emigration procedures would waste time. Technically, it no longer came under the station's jurisdiction.

The lander floated around the ship as it decelerated to match orbital velocity. It felt like the lander was a mote of dust floating in the air, pushed along by a Zephyr past a gigantic zeppelin. Jade could see lights shining from various windows in the ship's hull. The gape of the docking bay doorway came into view as the lander stopped and maneuvered to enter with the correct orientation. Jade lost sight of the bay as the lander rotated to approach the opening, but the interior appeared again as it moved forward. The seat she sat on faced away from the disembarkation hatch, so she only saw the sidewall, roof, and floor of the huge docking bay. She saw little through the lander's far windows. It came to a stationary hovering position twenty meters above the floor. Jade felt a slight jolt when the landing struts disengaged from their flight locations and locked into the landing positions. The lander then descended until it made a cushioned landing on the deck.

"Welcome to our new home for a while," Galena said. She sounded tense, Jade thought. She had been so the whole trip. The others in the cabin made comments of various descriptions, but most showed excitement.

A few minutes passed until the light above the cabin hatch changed from a glowing red to green, and the cabin hatch opened. A stair extended from the foot of the hatch to the docking bay floor two meters below them. Jade sat at the cabin's rear. Being last off increased the tension building in her. *Will he or won't he be waiting?* Jade rebuked herself for worrying about it. She reminded herself that he had a hundred things to do. She stood at the back of the line, impatient to disembark. At last, she reached the hatch — only a few seconds had elapsed, but it felt like hours — and exited the lander into the docking bay. She paused at the top of the steps to search the bay and soon spotted him waving at her. She couldn't help but burst into the biggest smile that she possessed.

An eternity seemed to elapse before the lander touched the docking bay deck and the cabin hatch opened. Ethan stood in a pedestrian section of the bay, away from any craft-landing positions. He was the only one waiting, and he fidgeted as he waited, moving from one foot to the other. A few maintenance personnel were elsewhere in the bay, performing tasks, and a couple waited for the lander to land to check it. This lander and another, an ore carrier, were staying on *Destiny* during the mission. They intended to transport a quantity of astatine back to a near-Earth location — or a Mars location if Mars lacked the catalytic properties that induced astatine to decay rapidly, as it did on Earth.

The lander hatch opened, and the stairs extended. After a few moments, Galena emerged and descended the steps, followed by Apep and then Hu. *Where is she? Is she even on it?* Ethan asked himself, worry creeping into his mind. Jezebel appeared next and then Jade, looking as beautiful as ever. He waved to her as she looked around, and she broke into a huge smile, melting his heart. He smiled back and waited impatiently while the pack of passengers followed the pathway toward him. Hu and Apep had knowing smirks on their faces as they approached, lugging their cabin bags over their shoulders.

"Please calm her," Hu said in an amused whisper as she gave Ethan a hug of welcome. "She's been a bundle of nerves the entire trip."

Apep, Jezebel, and Galena greeted Ethan with handshakes, and then Jade stood before him, all smiles.

She patted him on the shoulder, then opened her arms for a hug, which he readily gave. They held each other for a moment of closeness again, parting only to gaze into each other's eyes, oblivious of everyone else.

"Hem-hmm," Hu softly coughed to get their attention. "Where to from here?"

"Oh ... sorry. Follow me." Ethan started walking toward the elevators, with Jade next to him.

Galena gave them both a look of inquiry. She hadn't been aware of any romantic connection between them. "Should I know something?"

Both Jade and Ethan reddened. "No. We're dating, and we're pleased to meet again. That's it," Ethan said in defiance.

"So long as it doesn't interfere with the mission," Galena said, her tone reproving.

"It won't," they both said in unison and then glanced at each other sheepishly.

Ethan continued walking and pressed the elevator up button. The doors parted, and they piled in. It was a tight fit, but Ethan and Jade didn't mind. Ethan pressed the button for the accommodation level. The doors opened at their destination, and they filed out.

Ethan looked at his tablet with the floor layout displayed and the room allocations listed. "Let's see. Galena, you are in room 1721; Jezebel 1722; Apep 1714; and Hugo 1707."

They nodded in acknowledgment.

"What about me?" Jade asked.

"You don't seem to be on the list. Are you sure you're supposed to be here?"

Jade adopted a threatening stance, hands on hips.

"I'll recheck it. Oh, my apologies. You are in room 1704."

Galena glared at Ethan. "And which room are you in, Ethan?"

"I'm in room 1702, Galena. Is that a problem?"

"No. I suppose not."

Ethan winked at Jade when nobody was looking, and Jade giggled. Galena turned again, glanced at Jade, and fixed Ethan with another glare before she started toward her allocated cabin.

"So, what's the go?" Hu asked.

Galena stopped glaring and waited for a reply as well.

"If it suits you, get settled into your home for the next few weeks. Freshen up, and I will show you around in, say, an hour," Ethan said, searching for agreement.

"That's generous of you," Galena said. "I accept." Everyone nodded and left to find their rooms.

Ethan walked Jade to her room, which was around the corner from the others.

"I take it the cabin choice was intentional?" Jade asked.

"We don't need prying eyes every time we say hello. In saying that, we should try to preserve a professional relationship for appearance's sake — and to keep Galena happy. And yes, the room choice was deliberate. I need you near Jake and me so we can talk undisturbed."

Jade pouted at Ethan's suggestion of keeping their distance for the time being. "I suppose you're right. Jezebel didn't look too impressed with us, either. Sometimes I think that girl doesn't know how to think about anything except work. But I will try to keep my distance from you — for now."

"Here we are." Ethan gestured. "Your room, my room, and Jake's." Ethan pointed to each. Ethan's room was next to Jade's, and Jake's was 1703 across the corridor from Jade. "I missed you, Jade." Ethan became overwhelmed with passion and affection as they faced each other.

"I missed you too. Our separation was harder than I expected," Jade said, embracing him around his waist and searching his eyes. "Those two weeks were the longest of my life." Their mouths met in a passionate kiss that neither wanted to end.

"We haven't started too well with that 'professional relationship', have we?" Ethan jested with a loving smile.

Jade gave Ethan another hug before releasing him. "I had better get ready."

"Yeah, OK. I'll see you in an hour." Ethan reluctantly headed for the elevators again. He felt a glow ignite in his heart, knowing Jade was close by, a completeness he had never experienced before.

Ethan returned to the Command Center to update Jake and check on preparations. "How are things going for departure?" he asked Jake as he entered.

"Good. We should be underway within three hours. The landers are both here." Jake checked the displayed information on his screen. He turned to Ethan with a grin. "And how was the reunion?"

"Remove that grin. Galena was frosty when she found out we were an item. And Jezebel seemed unimpressed."

"They'll get over it. Trouble is, they're both workaholics."

"I'm going to give them an orientation tour if you have everything under control here."

"Fine. Everything's running smoothly here."

While Jake returned his attention to the screen and changed the display to review more data, Ethan parked himself in a nearby chair and daydreamed as he gazed out the window. The view displayed the construction facility to the left and a multitude of stars straight ahead. To the right, Earth shone in its majestic blurred, blue-edged curvature, as if your eyes couldn't gain a sharp focus. A brilliant aurora played out over the North Pole like a laser show orchestrated to synchronize with an imagined musical performance that you could feel with your emotions if you closed your eyes.

"... Hello-o-o-o, Ethan, Ethan, anybody home?" Jake was saying with a raised voice to get Ethan's attention.

Ethan returned to reality with a jolt. "What's wrong?" he asked, alarmed.

"You have a visitor," Jake announced.

"Where?" Ethan swiveled in his chair and burst into a smile when he spotted Jade standing silently behind him. Jade broke her silence with a laugh.

"Stop sneaking up on people. They might have a heart attack," Ethan said with pretended annoyance. "Hope you didn't lose your way."

"I just followed the crumbs you left," Jade quipped. "It's easy to find with the ship layout map in the room. Hi, Jake. How are you? Thanks for not giving me away."

"You're welcome. At least someone can grab his attention. I'm glad you're here at last. Ethan's been a mess ever since he arrived," Jake said with mock concern.

"That's not fair. I was just gazing at the view, and I haven't been moping."

Jade pouted. "So, you haven't been thinking about me ..."

"That's not what I said. You're twisting my words," Ethan defended, becoming flustered.

Both Jake and Jade laughed.

"You'd better stop before you dig a deeper hole for yourself," Jake said.

Ethan calmed. "I think the view of Earth is inspiring."

"Yes, it's spectacular." Jade gazed out the window, too.

"You were quick. Does the room not meet with your satisfaction?"

"The room's fine. It didn't take long to change, and I wanted to talk to you before the tour. You haven't seen her yet, Jake, but Ethan, do you think Galena has changed? She hardly talked in the lander, and she looks worried all the time as if something's on her mind."

"Now that you mention it, she reacted more than usual when she discovered our relationship. She's under a lot of pressure at this stage of the project. Every man and his dog are likely at her, asking for updates. I suspect having Apep and Hu breathing down her neck isn't helping either," Ethan said soothingly.

"Maybe. It's probably nothing. But we should watch her in case there's something amiss."

"Will do," Jake said. "If I can't get a smile out of her, something is definitely wrong."

"Good. So, what's happening?" Jade asked.

"We're just in the final stages of loading and checking for departure. We'll be leaving in two and a half hours," Jake said.

Ethan rose from his seat. "Let's rejoin the others and start this inspection." He nodded his farewell to Jake and walked with Jade to the elevator door to begin the tour with the rest of the project team.

But Jade's words continued to resound in his mind. If there was a change in Galena, it could be overwork, a personal matter — or something more sinister. As for Jezebel, well, she was always a bit cranky.

27

RACE TO IAPETUS

"Ready to leave," Jake announced over the ship's communication network. He was sitting in the command chair. Ethan and Jade were with him. The others were in the observation lounge on the deck above them, which provided a panoramic view of the exterior with a window and televisual screen combination resulting in a 360-degree perspective of space — a dramatic effect. People sat in nervous anticipation of their departure for Iapetus. The project had taken a long time in planning, research, engineering, construction, and testing to reach this point. They were on the home stretch, and nothing would stop them now.

Ethan was at one of the auxiliary stations, reviewing the main ship screens and assisting Jake. Jade seated herself next to Ethan because he was there, and the others in the Command Center ignored her. Jade scanned the room. She noted the layout was horseshoe-shaped, with various stations built in the arc. There was a station for astrogation, one for communications, one for engineering, where Ethan sat, one for drive control (this stood deserted and was for the warp drive when they used it), one for onboard systems, and two spare positions. Jade sat in one of these. Jake perched in the center and had a co-pilot's position beside him, which stood vacant.

Jake's and the co-pilots' stations were the only ones facing the front with a window view, although the other seats could swivel the full 360 degrees.

Ethan said, "Departure clearance green."

"Retracting boarding tunnel," Jake said.

"Check."

"Closing hatch."

"Disengaging magnetic clamps."

"Check."

Destiny drifted away from the construction facility dock. Ethan had mentioned the name to the others during the tour, and they liked it, so he'd made it official, at least in their circle of influence, although Jake had already organized to have it painted on the hull.

"Engaging EmDrives."

"Check."

Jake engaged the drives and increased the energy flow. *Destiny* eked its distance from the station, accelerating and positioning into the allocated departure lane. He increased the power to 1g acceleration until he reached the near station speed limit, at which stage he reduced power to zero, only providing enough for effective maneuvering.

Ethan was reviewing the drive settings on his screen. "Looks good for full power when you're ready, Jake."

"Roger, we'll be out of the departure lane in ten minutes," Jake said.

"I didn't even notice we were moving," Jade said.

"Yeah, she's a beauty, isn't she?" Jake replied.

"Why are ships female? Why can't they be male — or neither?" Jade quizzed.

"It's just a very old naval tradition going back to when most sailors were men. And most ships have a feminine-sounding name. You can't call a ship *Destiny* and refer to it as he!" Jake explained.

"I suppose," Jade answered grudgingly. "Although you could refer to it as *it*." But she let it pass, not wanting to get into a discussion about sexism.

Time passed until Jake said, "OK, we are out of the departure lane. Let's check this baby out." He increased the power to the drives to fifty percent, the acceleration ramping up to 3.1g. "How does it look, Ethan?"

"Perfect. Power transfer is good. Efficiency is the same as last time. Excess thermal removal is good," Ethan said.

They ran at that setting for thirty minutes before Jake increased the power again. He set the drives at eighty percent and increased the power to 4.6g.

Jake asked, "Shall we find her limits?"

"Might as well," Ethan encouraged.

Jade gave a worried look. Ethan glanced at her and saw it. "Don't worry, we know what we're doing. I hope." Jade gave another concerned glance at the last comment.

"One hundred percent and 5.6g," Jake said to everyone's delight. "How's it looking, Ethan?"

"Good. Everything is holding. Temperature's increasing but stabilizing."

Jake held it at full power for a few minutes, and then he reduced it so that they could maintain 5g acceleration. "Now we know what she can do. I can't believe how easy this thing is to fly and so smooth," he said, locking the controls on his screen and relaxing in his seat.

"They didn't skimp on any expense for this one. It's got all the bells and whistles." Ethan rose from his chair to stretch his legs. "How do you like it, Jade?"

"It's unbelievable. It's my first experience on a spacecraft other than a lander. Traveling so far from Earth is frightening. What if a meteor strikes us?"

"We have sensing equipment that detects objects larger than a pebble, so we can maneuver around them or raise our force field strength to deflect them. Smaller bodies just bounce off the force field surrounding the ship."

"How fast are we going to go?"

"We'll increase speed until we reach one thousand kilometers per second. That'll take six hours, and then we'll cruise until we need to decelerate at Saturn."

"Is that the fastest it can travel?"

"No. We could travel much faster. In theory, we could arrive in three days, but there's no hurry. It's our first trip, so we want to err on the side of caution. We will detour above the solar plane to avoid traveling through the asteroid belt. We don't know that environment, so we must be alert to surprises. What do you think, Jake?"

"You've captured the main points. If we don't see any issues, I might push it faster, which means we'll get to Saturn sooner."

"We might need a quicker arrival," Ethan muttered.

Jake glanced at Ethan, raising his eyebrows. Ethan gave him a non-committal shrug. They sat in silence again as they gazed out of the forward window.

Jade rose from her chair. "I might work out in the gym. Want to join me, Ethan?"

"I'd love to, but I have matters to attend to here. I'll join you later for dinner," Ethan said apologetically.

"OK. See you then." Jade strolled to the elevator and left for the gym.

Ethan walked over to the co-pilot's chair and sat down. "So, you haven't heard from our friend either," he spoke at a subdued volume.

"No, I haven't. We might just be paranoid."

"I don't think so. You know what I saw on our test flight to the moon. I sent that information to him, too. I just don't want to raise any suspicions by deviating from our schedule unless we have a good reason. As I told you, that was no moon-tripper I saw. They were going somewhere far away and I'm nervous. And now Galena's freaking out, although that could be coincidental. She's always been a worrier."

"We can only keep alert, I suppose. We have our backup plan."

Ethan rose from the chair again. "I think I'll go to engineering and check out the drives and power supplies. Get the technicians' records on their performance."

"OK. See you at dinner."

Ethan exited the Command Center and headed to the engineering level. He examined the operating reports and reviewed any problems. Everything was running well within their design envelopes, which pleased him. He yawned. It had been an exhausting and emotional day, what with their departure and reuniting with Jade. He pondered his strengthening attachment to Jade. Their separation had been short, but it had seemed like an eternity. He wondered where they were going in their relationship, but a technician distracted him with a question, which he answered. Dinnertime approached, so he left to prepare, as matters seemed in order.

~

ETHAN PRESSED the chime to Jade's room. He hoped she was back from the gym. He had showered and changed out of his standard uniform into casual clothes for dinner. The door opened.

"Hello, handsome, come in," Jade said on seeing him standing there.

Ethan checked the corridor for anyone, but it was empty. He entered her room, and the door closed.

"You don't have to sneak around the ship. We are adults," Jade said, amused.

"I know. It's just ... well ... you know ..."

"Yeah, I understand. But you are off duty now, so what you do in your time shouldn't concern anybody else unless it interferes with our performance, and I'll tell you if that's happening."

"OK. Come here, gorgeous."

Jade raised her eyebrows and obeyed him. They embraced and kissed. "I missed you," Ethan said after their mouths disengaged.

"I missed you too," Jade said in a husky voice and held Ethan tight.

They enjoyed being in each other's arms before Ethan broke their intimacy. "Are you hungry?"

"Starved," Jade said. "Can we get room service?"

Ethan laughed. "No room service onboard, I'm afraid."

Jade pouted in disappointment. "Well, let's go eat then."

Ethan grabbed Jade's hand, and they left her cabin for dinner.

The canteen was up one level, so they rode an elevator up and walked the short distance to it. Hu and Apep were already there, eating their meals in silence.

Jade and Ethan greeted them and headed for the servery to select their meals. Afterward, they approached Hu and Apep.

"Can we join you, or are you two planning to overthrow the world?" Ethan asked in a mock surreptitious manner.

Hu and Apep laughed. "Sit with us if you dare," Hu replied.

Jade and Ethan perched themselves at the table. Hu was sitting opposite Apep, so Jade sat next to Hu, and Ethan sat beside Apep.

"We are just discussing learning from being onboard and seeing equipment for the warp bubble," Apep said.

"What's of interest?" Jade asked.

"We were debating how the muon wave resonator worked," Apep said. "I'm not as adept as Hugo at understanding these matters."

Jade looked at Ethan to check that it was alright for her to reply. Ethan nodded his approval. "Well, muons and electrons are very similar particles. You can manipulate the muomagnetic wave properties, like an electromagnetic wave, by changing the frequency. Get me so far?" Jade started with the explanation.

"Yes, I understand," Apep said, listening.

"When you change the frequency, the resonant frequency of the underlying strings associated with the particles changes. It forms a standing wave in the string vibration when we adjust these frequencies to the right modulation, which provides the conditions to form the bubble in space-time."

"Ahh ... yes. It is easy to understand when you explain it that way."

"That's what *I* said," Hu interjected in protest.

"But Jade says it with such music." Apep waved his arms in the aim as though conducting an orchestra.

Hu huffed in disgust and went back to her meal, while Ethan and

Jade chuckled at Hu's expense, then started to eat their meals. The food was far from Rubicon's standards, but it was edible.

"How are you settling into the team?" Ethan asked to break the silence, the occasional crunch of chewing the only noise.

Hu glanced at Apep and then said, "For me, Jezebel has been helpful and Jake's a hunk, yes?"

Apep rolled his eyes, and the others grinned.

"As far as I'm aware, he's available, but I warn you, he enjoys playing the field." Ethan smiled.

"I agree with Hugo. Jezebel and Jake are most friendly, but your leader she's aloof, or upset by our presence."

Jade nodded. "Something's troubling her. It may just be the extra pressure of you two being onboard. She is a worrier, though."

"I am sure you are right. We'll try avoiding her as much as we can." Apep nodded.

They then kept eating, discussing various interests and concerns, until sated of both food and conversation. Once they had finished their meal, they wandered back to the elevator and the accommodation level. They said their goodnights and left Ethan and Jade alone together.

Jade coaxed Ethan into her room and closed the door. She grabbed his hand and dragged him to the bed. Ethan only gave minimal resistance. They embraced and enjoyed each other with abandon. Ethan sneaked back to his cabin two hours later, careful that no one saw him.

~

THE DOOR CHIME and his personal comm woke Ethan. Nothing unusual had transpired for the last four days, so he was wondering what could have happened as he rose, groggy, from his slumbering unconsciousness. He staggered to the door as he became alert and aware of his surroundings and opened it to the form of Jake. "What do you want? What's happened?"

"Don't know," Jake said with a sleep-affected voice. "John is on the ship's comm, and he wants to speak to both of us. I have directed the call to my room comm on our secure channel. Can you come to my cabin?"

"Sure." Ethan rubbed his eyes. "Just let me put something on first."

"OK. I'll wait."

Ethan returned to his bedroom and donned pants and a sweater before heading out to follow Jake across the corridor. They entered, and Ethan saw John on the comm screen next to a table with two chairs. Ethan and Jake grabbed the chairs and repositioned them to face him.

"OK. We're both here now," Jake said to John, who was attending to other matters offscreen while he waited.

"Good. Sorry to wake you so late." John looked at his chronometer. "Or early may be a better statement." It was three twenty-six in the morning. "I'd have delayed, but we need to discuss my findings as a matter of urgency."

"That's OK," Jake said.

"I'll survive," Ethan said.

"We've followed up on the video footage you sent us, with the extra-lunar activities you saw. It took us longer than expected to receive the intel on it and the implications are not good. The installation belongs to an industrial conglomerate called Mason Intersolar Corporation."

"I've heard of that. It's a big outfit, from my knowledge," Ethan said, "owned by Loki Mason."

"Yes. The money it generates makes your eyes water. It's a maintenance base for their ore carriers from the asteroids. Nothing exciting there. What interests us is the ship you spotted has no known registration and has a similar design to plans stolen two years ago. We recovered the material, so we forgot about it, but it now seems that this corporation copied the plans and constructed the ship. It must have moved there recently since we keep these installations under surveillance, and it wasn't there a month ago."

"Do you know where it was going?" Jake asked with concentrated interest.

"Unfortunately, yes. You'll relish the knowledge as little as I do. It's why I've lost no time in contacting you. It's bound for Iapetus."

"Shit!" Ethan said.

"Damn it!" Jake said.

"Exactly. And you realize what that means?"

"Yeah. They'll arrive first, and we won't get the astatine without groveling to Loki Mason," Ethan said. "Unless ..."

Both Jake and John stared at Ethan.

"How fast does their ship go?" Ethan asked.

John turned away and talked to someone off-screen. "Just wait. I have someone finding out," he said to Jake and Ethan. After two minutes, they could hear the muffled sounds of someone talking to John off-screen.

"Did you hear that?" John asked.

"We couldn't discern the words," Ethan said.

"If they followed the stolen design, the fastest acceleration is 2g."

"Good! Maybe we can fix this. We can achieve 5+g, so if we increase our speed again, we might pass them and still arrive first. I'll have to do the calculations."

"That'd be a welcome outcome. Can you work through your idea and tell me your plan? One more thing. The person who runs that corporation is ruthless in his business dealings. So be careful if you confront his ship. Our intel suggests he is on it. He may have a surprise for you if you threaten his goal."

"We may have a shock or two for him if it comes to that. Lucky we took precautions," Jake said.

"Give me an hour," Ethan said, "and I'll tell you then what we can do."

"Good. I'll leave you to it. And again, sorry for the disruption."

"No problem."

"See you," Jake said.

The screen blanked as John disconnected.

"Well, that's a curveball," Jake said.

"Sure is."

"What can I do?"

"Nothing for now. I need time to do the calculations, and then we'll discuss my findings. You can get me a good, strong coffee."

"Coffee coming up, sir."

Ethan left for his cabin and returned moments later with his tablet. He started calculating speeds, arrival times, and accelerations with the flight calculator clip he had on it. Jake prepared coffee for them both and brought Ethan his cup. He accepted it with gratitude and sipped a mouthful now and then in between data manipulations. After an hour, Ethan had the substance of a schedule.

"I think we can do it," Ethan said.

"We can get there first?" Jake asked.

"Yes. We can arrive at Iapetus and get to the surface before they appear. But we must use full power and do it now."

"How confident are you?"

"Very. If we start now."

"OK. Let's do it."

"I'll reply to John and tell him of our plans."

"In the meantime, I'll begin the acceleration and, Ethan ... at this stage, tell no one you can't trust."

Ethan froze at Jake's implication. "Yes, you're right. We can assume this will generate a confrontation if there's a saboteur on board."

Jake left his quarters for the Command Center. Ethan opened communication with John again, using the protocols he gave them. He came online after several minutes.

"Hello. General O'Conner here."

"Hello, John. Ethan back."

"What do you have for me?"

"I've run the calculations, and we can reach the rendezvous before the opposition and claim the prize, so to speak. Jake has gone to make the changes."

"Confidence level?"

"One hundred percent if we start now."

"It's worth trying, then."

"I agree — if nothing else goes wrong, but I'm worried we might have unpleasant company onboard."

"So do I. How will you manage that?"

"I'm not sure right now. My great concern is, what happens when we get to Iapetus? Is there any chance for backup from your end?"

"No. We have nobody near you. There was no reason to before this. We may need to review our strategic position."

"Well, I suppose just wish us luck then. We may need it."

"I have confidence in you and Jake. But a word of advice — don't forget your Chinese and Russian friends. You might need them."

"I won't forget them. Apep and Hu are two of my most trusted people. They mean that much to me."

"Remember that and keep me informed when you can."

"OK. Talk soon, I hope." Ethan disconnected the communication. He sat and pondered their predicament. This was not in his job description — he should ask for a raise. He started contemplating whether a saboteur or worse was on board and his options if there were. There was little he could do unless the person showed their hand. And that concerned him the most. His chief worry was less for the project than Jade's safety, which puzzled him. Work had always come first for him. He realized that their relationship meant more to him than anything else. *What's happening? Is this love?* It confused him. He shook himself. He had more pressing matters to manage at present. Her safety, and everyone's security, depended on him remaining alert and watchful. That needed his focus, he thought. Even beyond his love for Jade, a fire flared within him as he made his resolve. Ethan rose from his seat and followed Jake to the Command Center.

Ethan entered the center as Jake was completing the acceleration sequence for the drives. They were now at 5g. "I talked with John. He's happy at the moment, but we're on our own. We can't expect help from anyone," Ethan said.

"I didn't think we'd have any. Would have been nice, though," Jake said.

"I'll inform engineering, so they can watch for any systems problems, but I don't foresee any. I'll tell them a story about why we are increasing speed again. When will we reverse thrust direction?"

"Twenty-four hours' time."

"Wow. That's flying."

"Yep, and we'll arrive in just over two days."

~

BEFORE RETURNING to his bed in the hope of snatching a few minutes' rest, Ethan knocked on Hugo's and Apep's doors and invited them to his cabin. With the general's words still ringing in his ears, he thought he should inform them, without delay, of this latest development.

As he spoke, they exchanged a look, which seemed to indicate that this news was no surprise. "What is it?"

Apep spoke first. "We were coming to you in the morning. Both of us received communications from our people during the night about the sabotage to our projects."

"And?" Ethan nodded impatiently.

"It seems one of my suppliers, a slimy guy called Zalenko Larkonovik, was having his palm greased."

Hu added, "And Peng Zedung, the procurement officer in our project, was the source of our trouble. It was he who recruited the guy who attacked me."

"Ethan," concluded Apep, "they've traced all of it back to Mason Intersolar Corporation. Loki Mason."

28

MURDER

"Why are we speeding up so much?" Galena asked Jake as she reviewed the day's log mid-morning.

"I'm getting bored, and they've directed me to check for any problems with long-term top acceleration rates," Jake explained, hoping that the reply sounded plausible.

"Who did?" Galena asked, sounding peeved and concerned.

"The military called me last night. They want me to test it for their planning purposes."

"Well ... OK." Galena looked annoyed and nervous for an unknown reason. She left the Command Center to return to her room. Distracted, she almost bumped into Ethan as he exited the elevator.

"What's up with her?" Ethan raised his eyebrows, glancing back at the closed elevator doors.

"Don't know. She asked why we were increasing our speed. She's preoccupied with something," Jake responded.

"We'd better watch her," Ethan said. "She might be worried about us getting there first."

"Galena. No ... I don't think so. She's too easy to read."

"Not that easy. We can't figure out what her problem is."

"Worry and guilt are two different responses. You can detect guilt a mile away."

"If you say so. We still need to watch her. I just came to check on progress."

"Everything's fine. Running like a Swiss chronometer."

"Good. Engineering is reporting the same. We have one great ship."

"Yeah."

"I'll see you at dinner later."

"Yeah. I'm turning in soon for a nap. I want to be present for the turnaround tonight. By the way, have you seen Jez?"

"No, but that's normal. She keeps to herself at the best of times. She misses her family."

"Just wondering."

"I'll get someone to call in on her."

Ethan returned to the elevator and left the Command Center.

~

JAKE WAS DOZING in his quarters when his comm buzzed. It was late afternoon by ship time. Instantly alert, he rose from his bed to learn who was calling. The comm display showed Galena outside his door. That's strange. He pressed the visual button, and Galena's face came onto the screen. She looked tired and distracted.

"How are you, Galena?" Jake asked. "You look like you have the world on your shoulders. Even more than usual. You want to talk?"

"No. I'm just worried something will go wrong after our other problems. It's a project manager's prerogative to worry. It's in the job description," Galena responded with a weary smile. "Thanks for asking, though."

"So, what's on your mind?"

"I received a call from a lander pilot saying there's trouble with one of the landers. He wanted you to examine it but didn't want to disturb you. I visited the docking bay to get him to show me, but he wasn't there. I tried calling him back but got no answer either, so I wondered if you could go check it."

"Did he say what the problem was?"

"An unbalanced fusion reactor. Beyond my field of expertise."

"That's strange. They're as robust as an asteroid miner. They never need maintenance. Jezebel should inspect it."

"He said he tried to get hold of her first, but she didn't reply."

"OK. I'll go look at it. Who was the pilot?"

"He didn't say. It was the passenger lander, though."

"Thanks for letting me know. And Galena ... everything will be OK. Chill out."

Galena chuckled. "You might be right. I'll join you for a drink tonight for a change."

"That's the spirit. Have one for me too."

"You're incorrigible."

"I know."

Galena cut the link, and Jake sat by his comm, thinking. *That's strange. The whole thing sounds fishy. I wonder where Jez is? She must have her comm off.* He knew she did that sometimes. She once mentioned she meditated. Oh well, no rest for the wicked, he concluded as he rose from his chair. He got dressed and made his way to the docking bay.

As soon as the elevator doors opened, something smelled off to him. It wasn't feeling right, but he dismissed it as his imagination. Galena said the problem existed in the passenger lander, which stood furthest away. He searched for anyone else, but no one was in sight. He walked to the lander and to the engineering compartment containing the reactor. The hatch was open. It was dark inside the space. That was strange. If the reactor was the issue and someone was fixing it, they'd have a light. He called out. "Anybody here?"

Jezebel appeared at the engineering compartment hatch. "Hi! The pilot told me that the reactor was misbehaving. I came, but there's no one here. There's a problem, but I can't figure it out. How come you're here?"

"Galena contacted me. Said the pilot wanted to contact me but didn't want to disturb me. She said that she couldn't get hold of you."

"I was meditating and had my comm in privacy mode. I spotted the message when I turned it on again, so I came to try fixing the problem. The hatch was open, but no one was inside the compartment."

"This is weird. I've never heard of a lander reactor being unstable. It's not supposed to happen. The reactor should shutdown with any instability."

"I know. I've been running diagnostics, but I still can't figure out what the problem is. A second pair of eyes would help."

"Why is it so dark in there?" Jake asked.

"I cut the lander's power until I could figure out what's wrong and satisfy myself that using power won't destabilize it further. Here's a flashlight," Jezebel said as she handed Jake one of the ship's standard flashlights.

"Thanks," Jake said as he accepted the flashlight from her. He turned it on and went inside the engineering compartment. Jezebel followed him.

Jake shone the light around to get his bearings. The reactor and generator stood in the rear. Cooling systems were on his right, and the control panels on his left. He moved to the main control panel and opened the door to examine the primary processor, sensing Jezebel moving closer behind him. He placed his tablet on the fold-down shelf inside the panel and connected it to the processing unit, opening a special clip that he had written himself to interrogate lander controls. The diagnostic screen activated, and he keyed in code to search the parameter history. He was concentrating, so he was unaware of other movement.

"See anything?" Jezebel spoke over his shoulder.

"Not yet," Jake said, half-aware of her presence. He scrolled to more data on the display. "That looks interesting."

"What does?"

"It's hard to explain. A connection's misplaced. It's as if ..." Jake's voice broke off as he slumped to the floor.

~

WHEN HE REGAINED CONSCIOUSNESS, Jake noticed Jezebel entering the lander cabin, where he sat with no understanding of what had transpired. Nor did he have any idea how much time had elapsed.

The last he remembered was examining his diagnostic clip and then a sharp pain. Why couldn't he move? His head was thumping with the world's worst hangover, only one hundred times worse. He felt a warm, viscous fluid sliding down his face. His head leaned back and to one side when he opened his eyes. The roof of the lander cabin and the upper wall were visible. Something was cutting into his wrists. "What happened? How did I get in here? Why can't I move?" Jake asked no one in particular.

"You're smarter than you look. The other two pilots were stupid. They paid for their ignorance. You got what you deserve is what happened," Jezebel said.

"Jez?" Jake tried to turn his head, but it sent jabs of pain through his skull. He turned it slowly until he spotted Jezebel. It confused him. He now saw that a cable tie restrained his feet. He presumed his hands were tied too. Why was she glaring at him in disgust? "What's happening?"

"You couldn't leave things be, could you? You had to speed up again. If you had kept running as you were, our journey would have ended peacefully. My father would have arrived at Iapetus first and claimed it and the minerals on it. But you had to race him to the moon."

"Your father? You are Loki Mason's daughter? You work for Mason Intersolar!" Jake was incredulous.

"Loki Mason will own the galaxy one day, and I intend sharing his glory and power."

"Did you hit your head too? You're talking shit," Jake said, dismayed as he realized Jezebel was the project's saboteur, and that he was in a very dangerous situation.

"Shut up!" Jezebel shouted. "The only reason you're not dead yet is because I can't decide whether I need you to pilot the ship back to Earth orbit or not. Those two were useless."

Jake moved his head more, and his gut wrenched as he spotted the pilots' bodies on the floor. They looked dead. "Why?"

"I can't allow anyone to land on Iapetus before my father gets there. I must make sure Loki lands on it first to claim the astatine deposit, so I had to eradicate the lander pilots, just leaving you."

Jake realized she didn't know Ethan could fly a lander, or the ship, and he wasn't about to tell her. Now his life depended on him convincing her to keep him alive at least until he devised an escape plan. "So, you have us. What are you going to do?"

"I'll have to dump these two out of the docking bay, I suppose, before someone comes looking. You, I'm not sure about yet."

"You realize I'm the only one that can fly this ship, don't you? If we don't reverse and decelerate soon, we'll just keep going faster and faster until no one will ever catch us. You made a mistake. You should have waited until after I started decelerating."

"Shut up and let me think," Jezebel commanded and walked away to ponder her predicament. After a few moments, she returned with her mind made up. "This is what will happen. After I dispose of this garbage," she said, pointing to the corpses, "I'll take you to a safe place where you will teach me how to turn the ship to decelerate. It can't be that hard. If you do that for me, you can live, although I will have to keep you hidden. If you refuse, I will kill you and take my chances flying this beast."

"You're a psychopath."

"No. Just loyal to my father."

"What was wrong with the reactor?" Jake asked, out of interest.

"What do you think?"

"Nothing. You placed a jumper across the terminals in the panel."

"That's right."

As Jake started to reply, a searing pain flashed through his skull. He shouted in agony as his brows knitted together and perspiration beaded on his forehead.

"What's wrong?" Jezebel asked, panicking. She couldn't afford for

Jake to die on her now. Despite her bravado, she knew she didn't have a hope of flying the ship without him.

Jake continued groaning his misery, shaking his head as if to shake off remnants of water. He had his eyes closed tight, and saliva started drooling from his mouth as he concentrated on his torment. His face flushed red with shades of blue as he attempted to last through the wave of flashing pain. His body stiffened, and his eyes opened wide, as if a revelation had surprised him. After a few seconds, he slumped over, motionless.

29

INVESTIGATION

The buzzer of Ethan's comm was blaring away, bringing him reluctantly to consciousness from a deep sleep. He glanced at the chronometer and noted that it was four-thirty in the morning. Not again, he thought as he rubbed his eyes, removing the sleep from them. When he looked at the display, he saw the Command Center was calling him. *That's odd. I wonder what they want.* Ethan pressed the audio button. "Ethan here. What's happening?"

"Sorry to wake you, sir, but the turnaround time is approaching, and we can't locate Jake. He wanted to be here an hour before, but he won't respond to our calls."

"That's strange. Normally, he'd call you to see how things were going," Ethan said. "Has anyone checked his quarters?"

"No, sir. We weren't sure whether we should intrude. That's why we called you."

"Alright, I'll check. When are we scheduled for the turnaround?"

"Five-twelve, sir."

"I'll come up and do it if I can't find him."

"OK, sir."

That was puzzling, and very unlike Jake. *What could have*

happened? Ethan dressed, washed his face, combed his hair, and strode across the corridor to Jake's cabin. He pressed the entrance buzzer several times but heard no movement inside. Ethan returned to his room and retrieved his pulse pistol from the security safe. He adjusted the firing setting to stun and put it in his pants at the small of his back, covering it up with his shirt. With reluctance, he punched the emergency open code into the door-opening panel. The door opened.

Ethan peered inside, searching for Jake or anything amiss. Nothing appeared out-of-place, so he entered, turning on the lights. The door closed behind him, which made him uncomfortable, but he soldiered on regardless. Ethan called out Jake's name to no reply. He crept into Jake's bedroom. It was unoccupied. The crumpled bed covers showed Jake had slept there that night. *Where the hell could he be? Surely, he's not sleeping with a woman tonight and forgot to wake.* Ethan was becoming concerned. It was unheard of for Jake to disappear when a crucial procedure was imminent. Looking at his chronometer, he saw it was now almost five. He needed to go to the Command Center. He left Jake's quarters and headed there.

As Ethan exited the elevator, the Command Center personnel turned in expectation. Ethan shrugged his shoulders. "It's a mystery. He wasn't in his cabin."

"It's time, sir," the officer on duty said.

"Yes," Ethan acknowledged as he walked to the command chair. "Let's get ready."

Ethan seated himself and raised the control display. He selected the menu choice for the turnaround, which displayed the drive controls screen. He conducted preliminary procedures before saying, "Ready for turnaround."

"Turnaround in one minute," the officer said.

"Start turnaround on one," the officer announced. "Three ... Two ... One."

Ethan punched the last button in the turnaround sequence procedure, which adjusted the thrust from the EmDrives to give a differential that turned the ship 180 degrees, as commanded in the settings, after which the drives returned to balance, adjusting to keep the correct direction but decelerating the ship now instead of accelerating it. "Turnaround complete," Ethan advised.

"Turnaround complete," the officer confirmed.

Ethan checked the controls and saw that everything was normal, so he packed the display away and rose from the command chair. "Until further notice, report to me until we can locate Jake," he said.

"Will do," the duty officer said. "It's strange. Jake's always diligent in these matters."

"Yes. I won't let him forget this when I find him," Ethan said, half-jokingly but his voice was laced with worry and concern. "Call me if there's any change. I'll continue looking for Jake." Ethan headed for the elevator to leave.

"Will do," the officer said as the elevator doors opened for Ethan.

Ethan returned to the accommodation level and his quarters to think. Hu had joked about having an amorous interest in Jake, but he was sure she would not have acted on such an impulse last night. Even if she had, she would have made sure he still performed his duties. Still, it was a start, and she could help find him. He headed for Hu's cabin and pressed the entrance buzzer once and then again after a few seconds.

"You know the time?" Hu's half-woken voice moaned from the speaker.

"Yes, I do. I need to talk to you."

Two minutes later, the door opened, and Ethan entered. "Jake isn't here, is he?"

"Jake? Why would he be?"

"Just had to ask. He's missing, and he isn't in his quarters. He missed a ship maneuver, and it's uncharacteristic of him to miss anything important. I'm getting worried."

"I agree. That's odd."

"I'm searching the ship for him, and I need support. I thought of you."

"Thanks for the compliment," Hu said, giving him a wary look. "What are you thinking?"

Ethan paused. "I'm going to have to let Galena know."

"I'll come with you."

They both walked to Galena's quarters, only a few meters away, and Ethan buzzed her. After a significant time, Galena responded. "What now, Ethan ... oh, and Hu?" Galena was trying to focus her eyes.

"Sorry to disturb you, but can we talk with you, please?" Ethan asked.

"Sure. Give me a moment to get decent."

The door opened a minute later. "Enter."

Ethan and Hu entered Galena's quarters, and the door closed. "So, what's on your mind at five-thirty in the morning?" Galena asked, unhappy at being woken.

"Jake's missing," Ethan said with a worried voice and creased brow. "We were wondering if he had contacted you or whether you knew his whereabouts."

Galena said, surprised and concerned, "Yesterday, a lander pilot called me about a problem with one of them. He couldn't figure out what was wrong. The pilot couldn't raise Jezebel and was reluctant to disturb Jake. I told Jake, and he said he'd have a look."

"When was that?" Ethan asked.

"Around five yesterday afternoon."

"Hmm. He needed to complete the ship turnaround this morning, but the crew couldn't contact him. Something's happened to him between your talk at five yesterday and now."

Galena slumped into a chair, her hands holding her forehead as she shook it from side to side in despair. She groaned. "Why is everything going wrong? This project is jinxed."

"Don't be hard on yourself, Galena," Hu comforted, her hand soothing her shoulder. "We don't know what's happened to Jake yet, and you can't prevent sabotage. Believe me, we have tried as much as you, and we failed more than you. You are at least in space. We are still on the drawing board, so to speak."

Galena raised her head in weariness. "I suppose you're right. I'm an obsessive worrier, and it's getting to me. Thanks for the pep talk."

Galena smiled in appreciation, and Hu and Ethan smiled back. "What should we do?" Galena asked once she gathered herself together.

"Hugo and I will go to the docking bay and check for him there. It's strange, though. He's not in his quarters, and he's not answering his comm."

"OK. It's a plan. Conduct a search and inform me of your findings," Galena said as she rose from the chair and shuffled to the entrance to open it.

Ethan and Hu left and started walking to the elevator. Ethan stopped, thinking.

"What?" Hu asked.

Ethan decided. "Follow me," he ordered and strode to Jake's cabin. Using the emergency-open code, they gained entry, and Ethan headed for the cupboard with Hu at his heels. He opened it and the security safe with his combination code. Jake and he had agreed to use the same code when they had discussed the potential risks, so they could access each other's safe if needed. He withdrew the pulse pistol.

Hu raised her eyebrows in surprise. "Wow! You have interesting toys," she said.

"Ever shoot one?"

Hu took the pistol as Ethan handed it to her and studied it. "Basic infantry training in China. Design's different, but the functionality looks the same."

"I should have guessed. It's for your protection if you need to use it. Change the setting to stun. I don't want to kill anyone."

Hu adjusted the firing mechanism and placed the pistol in her belt. "Where's yours?"

Ethan patted his back where he had concealed his pistol. He closed the safe and cupboard, and they left, heading for the elevator and the docking bay level.

On arrival, they scanned the space.

"Well, he's not visible here," Hu said.

Ethan noticed a group of service technicians over in the far corner. “Let’s ask them if they’ve seen him.” He walked over to them. Hu followed.

Ethan approached a technician, who looked around with a questioning expression. “Have any of you seen Jake Bodie?” he asked.

“No, I haven’t. We’ve been here for several hours.” The others shook their heads to confirm the technician’s response.

“What about the lander pilots?”

“No, we haven’t seen them either. You could ask the last shift.”

“OK. Thanks,” Ethan said, disappointed. He glanced at Hu. “I suppose we have to search the bay. Let’s look at the landers first. Galena mentioned a pilot told her one of them had a problem.”

Hu nodded, and they both walked over to the closest lander. She entered the cabin and cockpit while Ethan inspected the engineering and storage compartments. After several minutes, they both reappeared.

“Nothing,” Ethan said.

“Nothing,” Hu confirmed as well.

“Let’s check the other one, then.”

They headed for the other lander, which was further away. Ethan started for the engineering compartment. After a moment, he heard Hu say, “Ethan, this door’s locked. Do you know how to open it?”

Ethan delayed his search and headed to the cabin hatch. He scratched his head, puzzled. “They don’t normally lock them. I wonder who locked this one.” He gazed at the panel. “I can unlock it.” He keyed in an access code, and the hatch light shone green for two seconds to show that it was unlocked.

Hu swung the door open, poked her head in, and screamed with fright. Her face went ghostly pale, and she started shaking. Ethan, about to return to the engineering compartment, turned back, reaching for his pistol. He dashed into the cabin, only to come to an immediate halt himself. His stomach clenched with nausea, and he felt light-headed. He couldn’t believe what he saw. Jake slouched on a seat and the two pilots sprawled on the deck, all eerily still.

Ethan inched toward Jake and touched his neck with his fingers where Jake’s pulse should have been, but there was none. Ethan lowered his head in despair and sorrow. His legs shook and he collapsed to the floor on his knees, buckling under a surge of grief. His breath was rapid and hyperventilating, and he had a knot in his throat as he tried to control rising nausea.

Hu, overcoming her shock, entered the cabin and whispered, "What happened here?" She came closer to Ethan and grasped his shoulder to give him support.

After an eternity of anguish, Ethan recovered enough to speak. In between labored breaths, he said, "I don't know, but I'm sure as hell going to find out, and heaven help whoever did this." His anger swelled as he progressed out of his shock and into a sense of determination. He turned his head and stared at Hu, his eyes red with pained emotion and tears. "It's the least we can do for him ... for them."

"Yes, that's the least we can do," Hu said, returning his gaze, concerned. "Meanwhile, this cabin is a crime scene. We should leave it undisturbed before we gather evidence. I have experience."

Ethan smiled wanly. "Yes, you do." He rose and made a cursory search of the space but found nothing amiss. "Where do we start?" He released a dejected sigh.

"We must re-lock this cabin and get a tablet to take photos and bags to collect evidence. I'll find talc to check for any unusual fingerprints to photograph, although I doubt we'll have much luck in that department since so much traffic has passed through here."

"Sounds good," Ethan replied, reasoning and sanity returning to him after the shock of what had happened.

They both exited, and Ethan closed the hatch, locking it with a different security code. He told Hu the code so she could enter without him. Hu whistled at the technicians, who were still working in the bay. She gestured two to her. After a few moments, they approached.

"What's up?" one said.

"We have a mess here, and we need you to guard this hatch until we return. Don't let anyone in except for one of us. Got it?" Hu commanded. They both nodded their understanding of her instruction but were confused and waited for the reason. They glanced at Ethan for confirmation. He reinforced her order.

"I don't care if God comes and wants to get in there. Deny everyone entry." The technicians nodded again and stood on either side of the hatch.

"We will return soon," Hu said as she motioned for Ethan to follow her to the elevator. They both walked there and entered.

"Shall I start while you have time to recover from the shock?" Hu asked with compassion as the elevator rose to the accommodation level.

"Thanks. We had better tell Galena first."

The doors opened. Hu and Ethan got out and walked to Galena's cabin door. Hu buzzed. A few moments later, Galena opened the door and stared at them. "What's happened?"

Hu glanced at Ethan and took the lead. "Jake and the two lander pilots are dead. We have a murderer on board."

Galena's face changed from concern to shock to despair in seconds. "Why? Why?" she wailed. She shook. Hu sped forward and grabbed her before she collapsed. She helped her into the room and to a couch, noting a medicine bottle on the table. She checked its contents. It was Valium, and it was open.

"How many have you taken?"

"It doesn't matter anymore. This disaster has ruined everything," Galena said in despair.

Ethan looked at Galena in dismay. She was usually a rock.

Hu stared at Galena, too, poised in thought, and then she slapped her face. "Get a hold of yourself, Galena. A murderer is on board, and you're the senior project leader. Self-pity can come later." Hu displayed a hint of contempt, but compassion filtered through, too.

Hu's slap shocked Galena. But it worked. She came to her senses, red with embarrassment as she felt the slap's welt. "You're right, Hu. I'm sorry." She sat still for a moment to bring her emotions under control. "So. What do we do?"

"I'll collect my tablet, bags, and talc powder and return to the lander and record the scene as best I can. Ethan will take a break to calm himself. Once he has come to terms with this, he will join me. You'll make sure the rest of the team stays put. Got it?" Hu ordered.

Galena thought through the instructions. "How do I know you aren't the murderer?"

"It's obvious the perpetrator is the saboteur. He's getting desperate because we are approaching Iapetus. Since I wasn't present at the earlier attempts, it's a good bet I'm not the person, and neither is Apep."

"That's logical." Galena's mental capabilities were improving.

"With your and Ethan's approval, I'll start."

Galena looked to Ethan for advice. Ethan gave a confident nod. "OK. Do it," Galena said. "Let's get to it then."

Hu smiled, approving. Galena was taking command again. She walked out of Galena's quarters with Ethan close behind her.

"I'll be with you as soon as I can," Ethan advised Hu.

"Take your time. We're not going anywhere, so to speak."

Ethan left to go to his cabin, leaving Galena alone in hers. He trudged in misery, but before he entered, he decided to inform Jade. He plodded to her door and buzzed. Two minutes passed before it opened.

"Ethan," Jade said, alarmed. "You look a mess."

"Can I come in?"

"What's happened?"

Ethan entered, and the door closed. He staggered to the couch, collapsed onto it, and started crying as he let his emotions spill out, stunning Jade, who didn't know what to do. She stood in confusion, then indecision, until she worked through what was happening. A flood of love and compassion covered her perplexity. She sat beside Ethan and put her arms around him. He nuzzled up to her shoulders and kept weeping. Eventually, the storm subsided to sobs and then calm.

"Sorry."

"Don't be sorry, just explain," Jade said, stroking his head.

"Jake's dead."

Jade stopped stroking. "What! How?" She stared at Ethan with simultaneous shock, alarm, and compassion.

"Someone murdered him, along with two pilots."

"I don't understand. Why do that?"

"I don't know. Maybe the murderer thought that, without them, we couldn't land on Iapetus and claim the astatine deposit."

"That sounds logical but desperate. So, what now?"

"Hugo is gathering whatever evidence there may be. I'll join her as soon as I can."

"You're not going anywhere yet. You've had an enormous shock and lost your best friend."

"He was my second-best friend. You are my first," Ethan murmured to Jade as his mouth moved toward her ear.

Jade tightened her grip on him at the compliment and suppressed her own tears. "You idiot. You can't get intimate now."

"When then?" Ethan asked, pushing away to gaze into her eyes.

Jade's eyes misted. Ethan wiped away his tears. The link of love between them was electric. Ethan snuggled up to her again. "You're right, but thanks for the support. I'll never forget this. And I am just stating a fact."

Jade responded by stroking Ethan's shoulder, struggling to contain her emotions.

"So. What now?" Jade asked.

"I'll join Hugo and help with the investigation. I'm going to catch this bastard."

"Are you up to it?"

"I am now, and thanks."

"You're welcome. But what can I do?"

Ethan thought, then said, "Just mix with the project team and note any unusual behavior. Galena is freaked out of her skin. She's taken Valium."

"I can do that. When will I see you again?"

"Soon, I hope."

"Take care."

"I will," Ethan said as he reluctantly inched away from Jade's embrace and rose from the couch to return to the docking bay. It was becoming an endless day, and it hadn't even started yet. Before he departed, he returned to give Jade a long, loving kiss.

Ethan walked to the door, pressed the open button, and left.

Minutes later, he arrived at the docking bay and headed for the lander where the dead bodies and Hu were. He looked through the hatch. He saw Hu methodically collecting forensic information before the bodies could be moved into cool storage somewhere as it would be several days until the ship returned to anywhere that could handle them.

Ethan felt devastated by the business but knew it was necessary. As he entered the cabin, Hu glanced up at him. "Hi! How're things?" she asked with compassion.

"Better, but healing will take time. How can I help?"

Hu straightened. She wiped sweat from her brow and thought. "You haven't examined the engineering compartment yet, have you?"

"No. I haven't."

"Can you check that out? Let me know if you find evidence to photograph before we move or bag it."

Ethan acknowledged the suggestion and walked out. He stopped and turned to Hu again. "If you bomb out of engineering, you have experience for a second career path," he jested.

"Get out of here," Hu admonished him, threatening to throw a brush at him.

Ethan feigned a sidestep and left. He headed to the engineering compartment, opened it, stepped inside, and looked around, spotting a horseshoe-bent piece of electrical wire on the floor and a bar with blood on it. The murder weapon, he thought. As he started calling Hu, he noticed something else on the deck further in and strode to it, careful not to disturb the other evidence, for a closer look. He squatted. It was a button. It must have come off someone's clothing, possibly one of the victims — or perhaps the murderer. This could be a breakthrough. He might catch the culprit. *I'd like that*, he thought. He stood and went to fetch Hu to photograph his discoveries and discuss the button.

"Well, it hasn't come off any of the victims," Hu said when Ethan showed her the button. They looked at each other.

Hu scanned the space to figure out how it might have torn off someone's clothes, spotting a section of railing jutting out nearby and moving closer to inspect it. "I suspect it snagged on this." She showed the edge of the rail.

Ethan came over and inspected a protruding sharp end with fibers stuck on it. "It's a fragment of clothing?"

"Yes. The button, and this, don't belong to any of the victims."

"We should keep this little discovery to ourselves for now," Ethan said, lowering his voice. "We need to check for anyone missing a button or searching for something. Do you agree?"

"Agreed."

Hu got her tablet ready and photographed what they had discovered. She then picked up the items and placed them in separate bags.

Ethan searched through the rest of the compartment but found little else of note. He left and opened the storage space but learned nothing there, so he returned to Hu, who was still examining the engineering compartment. "Nothing else that I can see, Hugo," he said as he entered.

"Is that a footprint?" Hu pointed to scratchings on the floor.

Ethan squatted. He got his flashlight from his pocket and turned it on to get a better view, casting the extra light along the markings. "Could be," he agreed. "It's from a small shoe."

"I agree. That discounts you. Your feet are larger than this. And the victims. The evidence is pointing to a female."

"I'll need to check the technicians' roster to see if any female technicians had a reason to come in here. Jake ..." Ethan choked as he said Jake's name, and the pain of his loss returned to him.

"That may narrow the list of possibilities," Hu commented. "Galena said she tried to contact Jezebel ... where is Jezebel?"

They exchanged a worried expression.

"Has she been hurt, too, or ...?" Ethan began but broke off — that thought didn't bear thinking of. He picked up his comm.

"Jade, can you track Jezebel down? Now. We need to be sure she's alright." He put the comm down and said to Hu, "Let's finish up here."

They returned to the cabin, and Ethan assisted Hu gather the evidence. She then hailed the ship's doctor to meet them and confirm the cause and time of death. His prognosis confirmed that Jake had died sometime not long after Galena had called him. They discussed where to store the cadavers and agreed to clean out a galley cooler store and store them there until they returned to Earth and could hand them over to the medical examiner at the morgue. The personnel the doctor had brought with him arranged for the removal of the bodies.

"We're done here," Hu said.

"Not a moment too soon," Ethan said.

It was well after lunch when they finished. "Want something to eat?" Hu asked. Neither of them had had breakfast.

"Not feeling hungry yet," Ethan replied with sadness. "I know it's early, but I could use a drink right now."

"That's a splendid idea. I'll fill in Apep. He doesn't need an excuse for a refreshment," Hu joked.

"And I might bring Jade."

"OK. It's just after one-twenty now. Let's meet at the bar at two."

"Sounds good."

They headed for the elevator and left the docking bay.

ETHAN AND JADE entered the bar together. Hu and Apep weren't there yet. Jade had just told him that Jezebel was alright. She had found her having a drink in the bar in a state of shock over the news of Jake's death.

"How did she know about Jake's death?" Ethan asked.

Jade looked surprised at the question. "I assumed Galena told her. Why?"

Ethan said nothing.

The bar was small, comprising a bench counter for ordering

drinks and offering some seating if desired. Jezebel was on one of the seats. Tables lay scattered within the room where people could relax. Ethan told Jade to sit at one of the tables while he ordered their drinks.

Ethan made for the bar where the barman greeted him with a cheery, "Must be a special occasion today. I don't usually see so many patrons this early in the afternoon."

"You could say that," Ethan replied noncommittedly and gave him his order. He then turned to Jezebel. "Don't see you here much."

"I guess I'm here for the same reason you are. It's such shocking news about Jake," Jezebel replied.

"It is. Who told you?" Ethan asked.

"Galena. I came here because I needed something strong," Jezebel said, facing him. "Jake was my friend, too." The words were not inappropriate, but Ethan noted that the tone was hollow, and her eyes could not quite meet his.

His own eyes widened when he saw the shirt she wore. Its buttons exactly matched the button he and Hu had discovered earlier, and the fabric looked like the fragment they had seen stuck to the railing. He tried to cover up his expression so she wouldn't notice. "I can understand that," he said as his drinks arrived. He glanced casually at her feet as he walked away, noting their small size.

The encounter shook Ethan's nerves as he returned to Jade.

"Is everything alright?" Jade asked, concerned.

"Yeah," Ethan said, distracted as he sat and pondered what he had just seen. No buttons were missing on the shirt Jezebel was wearing, but both the buttons and the fabric were distinctive. He doubted many on board had the same style. His mind had started connecting the dots when Hu and Apep entered.

"Hello, my wonderful friends," Apep greeted them, his usual exuberance replaced by a somber air. "I hear a terrible thing has happened to our good friend Jake."

"Yes," Ethan commented, his thoughts still far away, prompting the others to stare at him. Was this delayed shock?

When Hu and Apep headed to the bar, Jade turned to Ethan in frustration. "What's wrong, Ethan? You're a million miles away."

"I'm not sure yet. I just noticed something that's distracting me."

"OK. Do you want to share?"

"Not now. Let me make sure I'm right." Ethan drew into himself as he recollected prior events. *The sabotage of the connection cabling,* he thought. *I remember Jezebel looking nervous when she brought in the astatine for the test. I passed it off as nerves, her not wanting it to fail. But maybe she feared for her life. He could interpret her anti-social behavior as not wanting anyone to discover her intent. Galena mentioned Jake had gone to investigate the issue with the lander's reactor, Jezebel's field of specialty, and that wire was near the reactor's control panel. Now those buttons. I bet the torn shirt is in her quarters if she hasn't already tossed it.*

Hu and Apep came back from the bar with their drinks and sat. Ethan stood. "I'll come back in a minute. Hugo, can I talk to you for a second?"

They raised their eyebrows, curious over where Ethan might be going. Hu followed Ethan a few steps away. "Can you call me if Jezebel leaves here before I return?" Ethan asked.

"Sure, I will have a direct line of sight where I am sitting. What's happening?" Hu queried in surprised concern.

"Not sure yet. I just need to chase up something." Ethan left the bar, heading for the elevator.

He returned to the accommodation level and strode to Jezebel's quarters. After keying in the emergency open code, he slipped inside when the door opened. He felt uncomfortable looking through someone else's possessions, but he had to do it to test his hypothesis. He crept into the bedroom and searched it. It was tidy. He opened the closet and shuffled through the hanging clothes, but no similar shirts hung there. There was a set of drawers beside the closet, which he inspected next. His heart leaped when he slid open the bottom drawer. A crumpled-up shirt lay there. Ethan removed it. A button was missing, congruent with that discovered in the lander, including a scrap of torn-off material. Splatter marks of dried blood blemished one sleeve. Ethan closed the drawer and scanned the cabin to make sure that he had replaced everything. He took the shirt with him and headed for the entrance.

Ethan checked the viewer for anyone outside the cabin. The corridor was vacant, so he slipped out. He strode to his cabin and placed the shirt in a plastic bag, securing the bag in his safe. He returned to the bar, having retaken the pistol, concealing it in the small of his back. The diversion had taken twenty minutes, but he was now convinced of the culprit. Jezebel's motive was still a mystery to him.

"Hi," Ethan said as he returned. "Hugo, can I talk to you for a moment again?"

"Sure." Hu stood, and they withdrew a distance, where Ethan discussed with her his suspicions of Jezebel and the discovery of her shirt. Hu clarified minor points with questions, but she agreed with Ethan's analysis.

"What do you think?" Ethan asked in expectation. "Shall we confront her?"

"It's too much of a coincidence. Although I don't know how she will take your sneaking into her room if she is innocent."

"Let's worry about that if I'm wrong."

Ethan and Hu walked over to Jezebel at the bar playing with her glass.

"Lose any buttons of late?" Ethan asked as they approached.

Jezebel stopped her preoccupation and faced them, color draining from her face. "Why do you ask?" she probed.

"Three murders have occurred onboard, so we need to ask questions. When Hu and I investigated the murder scene, we discovered a button that looks remarkably like those on your shirt." Ethan pointed to her shirt.

"But this shirt has its buttons, and they're common. That button could be anybody's." Jezebel gave a look suggesting she thought she was off the hook.

"True, that shirt is intact. But I found another shirt with a button missing."

Jezebel stood in outrage. "You've snooped in my quarters!"

"I didn't say where I discovered it."

"That's where I placed ..." Jezebel began but stopped. She realized her act was up, and she had implicated herself in the murders. She tried to run out of the bar, but Hu caught her by the arm and held her tight as she thrashed to escape. Hu grabbed the other arm and pulled both arms behind her. She then kicked behind her knees, pushing her body, her knees bending, until Jezebel collapsed into a kneeling position. Hu pushed her shoulders forward, and Jezebel lay prone with Hu's foot pressing on the pit of her shoulders.

Ethan felt vindicated at invading her privacy but defeated and frustrated. "Why?" he asked.

Jezebel turned her head to face Ethan, malice spraying from her eyes, "I had to prevent you from getting to Iapetus early. Increasing the ship's acceleration made that possibility more likely, so I had to stop you. Even if you arrived first, you couldn't land on it. I couldn't fail my father."

"Your father?" Ethan said, still confused. "Who is your father?"

"He is the greatest businessman in existence. He deserves ownership of the deposit. It's stupid to let anyone share it for nothing. It provides so much wealth and power to whoever controls it. With it, you can control the world, you idiot, even the galaxy," Jezebel spat, the venom in her voice increasing. "I didn't want to kill Jake, but in the total scheme of things he doesn't matter."

"You're sick."

"And you're deluding yourselves. I won for Loki."

"You haven't won. You didn't know that I could fly a lander too. Not very well, mind you, but I can fly one."

"I can, too," Hu added.

Jezebel flushed with anger at the revelation and tried in vain to escape Hu's hold so she could attack Ethan. Hu just increased the pressure on her back. The bar manager had called the ship's security team, who arrived to investigate the problem and saw Jezebel on the floor. They looked at Ethan for an explanation.

"She's murdered three people. Is there a secure cabin to imprison her until we return to Earth?"

"We have a spot," one of them said as they took custody of Jezebel.

They led her away, but before she left the bar, she turned her head to Ethan and said, "It won't stick. Loki will get me free. You just wait."

"Good luck with that," Ethan replied with weariness and pity. He returned to their table, with Hu in tow, and sat again. "I definitely need a drink."

"So, are you going to explain now?" Jade asked, exasperated.

Ethan and Hu disclosed the whole turn of the day's events.

30

ARRIVAL

The shocks of the previous day had subsided, and calm efficiency had descended again on *Destiny*. Risking Galena's disapproval, Ethan slept with Jade, needing comfort for his torn emotions. He felt safe snuggled up against her sleep-warmed body, and he wanted to lie there forever. He had things to do, though. They would arrive at Iapetus late afternoon, and he had to prepare for any unpleasant eventualities. He tried, with no success, to slip out of bed without disturbing Jade. She stirred as he disentangled himself from her, so he gave her a kiss as she woke.

"Time to rise," he said into her ear as he nibbled her lobe.

"Mmm, so soon?" Jade complained.

"Sorry."

Jade opened her eyes and gazed at Ethan. "How are you feeling?"

"Much better, thanks."

"Good."

"Let's go get breakfast."

"A shower first?" Jade suggested with a twinkle in her eye.

"Race you for it."

"Who's racing? It's big enough for two."

"You're wicked."

They showered together, which was a pleasurable experience for them both, and dressed.

Hu and Apep were already eating and greeted Ethan and Jade with warmth. Galena was there too. "How are you feeling, Ethan?" she asked with concern in her expression.

"Much better, thanks," Ethan said, studying her face. "You look more ... relaxed, too, unless I'm mistaken."

"Yes, I am. I talked with Apep over a drink last night and that restored my spirits."

Ethan stared from Galena to Apep, who just shrugged, and back to Galena. "I'd be wary of Apep if I were you. He's as slippery as an eel," he joked.

"Speak for yourself," Apep said. Everyone had a good-natured laugh together and then immediately felt guilty for laughing. The specter of Jake hung over them.

"We have a busy day ahead of us," Galena said.

"Yes, we do," Ethan said. "Let's start with breakfast." He headed for the food bar with Jade.

~

After reviewing operations in engineering, Ethan went to the Command Center mid-afternoon. He wanted to check on progress and prepare for their arrival at Iapetus, scheduled for 5 pm. He walked into the Command Center when the elevator doors opened, and the approaching sight of Saturn and its moons stunned him. Saturn commanded center stage with its majestic rings sparkling in reflected but diminished sunlight that arrived eighty minutes after it had left the sun. He identified the larger moons on the planet's visible side. The scene was overwhelming to the senses. Titan and Rhea glistened as they were closest to him. Iapetus orbited behind Saturn, invisible to them at present.

"What's our progress?" Ethan asked the commander when he walked into the Command Center.

"The deceleration is proceeding to plan, sir," the commander replied.

"Call me, Ethan, please."

"Very well, si ... Ethan."

"Have you detected any unidentified objects here?"

The commander consulted the astrogator. "No, but we haven't looked either. We'll start looking for anomalous bodies. Anything in particular?"

"Yes. Another spaceship."

The commander raised his brow in surprise. "Spaceship?"

"Yes, another spaceship. I believe another ship is on its way or is already here. I want you to tell me the moment that you detect one."

"Will do. The astrogator will activate a routine scan to search for spaceships."

"Good," Ethan said as he sat in the command chair, bringing out the primary display from its storage position. He reviewed the main ship settings and current speed, which was 530 kilometers per second and slowing. They were six million kilometers from their destination. Everything looked excellent, and they should achieve their intended result — provided the other spaceship didn't show. It would be problematic if that happened.

Ethan searched through routine readouts and checked the external visual monitors to see if he could detect another ship, although he knew it was dreaming to believe that he could spot it from this distance.

Hu strode into the Command Center. She walked toward him and sat in the backup chair next to him.

"Can I help since we are two people short?"

Ethan considered her offer before he replied. "I'm occupied here, piloting for now, and then I will fly the lander to Iapetus. That means that engineering is understaffed, especially when we test the warp bubble drive for real. You can best educate yourself in engineering and the warp bubble drive. What do you think?"

"That sounds interesting. I can gain insights into alternative designs for our drive. Nothing like getting your hands dirty to learn how something works."

"That is so true."

"Sir ... I mean, Ethan," the commander interrupted, "we just detected an object that could be a ship. It's traveling on a vector headed for the opposite side of Saturn."

Hu and Ethan paused their conversation and looked at each other in apprehension. "OK. Keep a watch on it and tell me its speed, acceleration rate, etc.," Ethan instructed.

"Will do."

"What do you think it means?" Hu asked with concern.

"We have a race on our hands," Ethan said, whispering for Hu's ears only. "I'm worried about what happens when we reach our destination. How far might this guy take it? From what I know of him, we should prepare for ruthless behavior."

"Meaning?"

"I understand he is relentless in his business dealings and thinks nothing of destroying his competition if that is what it takes to get his way."

"Your point taken. His kind live in China, too. Given our experience of his manipulations so far, it's a fair assumption he has a contingency — if we threaten his claiming the mineral as his."

"Exactly."

"What maneuvering ability does this ship have?"

"Good, but it's not the ship that worries me. It's the landers. If he sees a lander take off for the moon, he might decide that taking out a lander is worth it."

"Why would he risk the criminal charges?" Hu asked.

"Maybe he's confident he can get any charges dropped with enough money or blackmail."

Hu pondered what Ethan had just said. "I think you're right. How can we protect the lander then?"

"I was wondering the same. There's something up my sleeve, but it needs me here on this ship, not piloting the lander."

"I can pilot those things. I'm sure that they aren't much different from ours."

"You'll be in a vulnerable position."

"Life is a danger. That's what makes it interesting."

Ethan gave Hu a bemused expression. "I didn't know you had the philosopher within you."

"You learn something every day. Can you tell me what you have up your sleeve to increase my confidence in survival?"

Ethan considered telling her, then decided against it. "Not yet. Let's see how this pans out."

"OK. I'll go get a 101 course in warp bubble drives then." Hu stood and walked to the elevators to go to the engineering level.

Saturn was getting ever closer, and they began their orbit around it to Iapetus. Ethan could see the moon now in zoom vision, but it still appeared minute. They were traversing to the northern hemisphere of Saturn. Iapetus had an orbit inclined to the equatorial plane, and it was now orbiting at its apogee on Saturn's northern hemisphere. The northern polar vortex with its hexagonal standing wave pattern came into view as they traveled further north. A giant storm was progressing around the planet, a third of the distance from the equator, its swirling motion obvious to the eye and resembling a mighty hurricane. Titan loomed to the side and slid away as the ship ventured north. Its fuzzy atmosphere obscured the sharp surface of the moon. Part of a cloud formation disappeared in its southern polar region.

Ethan pondered his conversation with Hu, wondering over the correct diplomacy for the looming confrontation with the spaceship's master. He didn't want to play his trump card unless he had no other choice, but no other options presented themselves to him. A sharing agreement wouldn't work. If the other party landed first, they would charge an astronomical price to supply the astatine. The arrangement would be unworkable. He had to land first. Then there would be no doubt about who owned the astatine since they had already signed the agreement. Also, if Hu, Apep, and Galena were on the lander, the three major powers would share it by default. *OK, we must arrive before them. Can we get there faster?*

"When will we reach zero relative velocity?" Ethan asked the astrogator.

The astrogator performed vector calculations with the clip on his screen. "We will hit zero velocity half an hour from Iapetus at this deceleration rate, sir. That's in three hours."

"What deceleration do we need for a stable trajectory around Iapetus with no maneuvering thrust required?"

The astrogator stared at Ethan with a 'you're joking,' expression, but seeing Ethan was serious, he returned to his screen and busied himself with more calculations. "Sir, a deceleration of 3.74g from five minutes' time will bring us into orbit five hundred kilometers above Iapetus. We need to adjust our vector by sixteen degrees when we decrease our deceleration to achieve the right trajectory. We'll shave twenty-five minutes off the time."

"Good work. See what you can do when you stretch yourself," Ethan said, encouraging him.

The astrogator glanced around, giving a sheepish grin.

"Make the adjustments."

"Will do."

"Where's the other object now?" Ethan asked. "Can you confirm its identity yet?"

"It is vectoring on a trajectory to intercept Iapetus. With our changes, it will arrive there twenty minutes after we do, sir. And, if it's not a spaceship, it's the weirdest asteroid I've ever seen. It has maneuverability independent of gravitational effects."

"OK, thanks." It'll be close, Ethan thought, but we might just do this. Nothing to do but wait now.

Half an hour away from entering the designated orbit, Iapetus loomed in their field of view. They could detect the differently shaded hemispheres by eye now, and the equatorial ridge was becoming visible. Ethan marveled at their achievement so far. No one else had seen what they were seeing with the naked eye. He sat and waited.

Fifteen minutes from orbit, the communications officer turned to Ethan. “Sir, that other object is requesting communication.”

Ethan stiffened with anticipation. “Is there an identification?”

“A Loki Mason, sir.”

“Wait.” Ethan got Hu on his comm. “Hugo?”

“Yes.”

“Can you get to the engineering station?”

“I’m sitting here now.”

“Good. Bring up screen 461.”

“OK, hold on a moment,” Hu responded, manipulating the keys on the keyboard. The screen displayed. “It’s locked with a password.”

“Alpha, Zulu, Foxtrot, Five, Two.”

Hu keyed the alphanumeric into the password field, and the display activated. “What on earth is this?” Hu asked in utter amazement.

A grim smile appeared on Ethan’s face. “My backup plan. How are you at arcade games?”

“I was a junkie. This will be fun,” Hu added with ominous amusement.

“Power them up and wait for me. I’m about to have a brief discussion with the other ship. I can fire from here, but I may be too busy. So be ready for target practice.”

Ethan turned to the communication officer, who sat patiently waiting for direction. “Channel a visual to my station.”

31

CHECKMATE

Loki sat on the bridge of *Loki's Lion* as it flew around Saturn.

"That other ship has slowed its deceleration rate, Loki," Carson said as he stood next to him.

"What does that mean?" Loki asked.

"It means, based on what our astrogation tells me, they will get there twenty minutes before us and go directly into orbit."

"Shit! Can't we duplicate that maneuver?"

"Not now. We've used up any lead we had. They have much more powerful drives."

Loki considered his options but realized he had very few left. He hoped that American Pie had caused a problem to prevent the others from descending to the moon surface. "How distant can we be to achieve a reasonable probability of a hit with our kinetic missiles?"

Carson made the mental calculations. A few moments later, he said, "We should be within striking range ten minutes out of them. The closer we are, the higher the chance of success."

Loki thought for a moment. If he fired a missile, it was go-for-broke. There was no turning back. He'd receive a backlash when they returned to Earth, but he'd own the deposit. He could sort out any political issues with his usual maneuverings, hoping they'd see sense and desist. "OK. Let me know when we're fifteen minutes away from them. I'll try talking to them."

"We'll tell you," Carson said.

"In the meantime, prepare the kinetic missiles for launch. I want you to fire a warning shot on my command if they're difficult. If they continue their obstinance, you're to aim for the ship. I will reassess the circumstances afterward."

"You think it'll come to that?" Carson asked, fidgeting in discomfort over the potential conflict.

"I hope not, but I'm not playing games."

"Let's hope that they don't want to play then."

"Let's hope."

Carson headed for the armaments station to prepare the missiles. The commander gave both Loki and Carson a worried look. He oversaw the operations of the ship and understood what Carson was doing. Loki stood stoically still, not letting his emotions filter through to the rest of the crew. He didn't want them to know that the adrenalin was flowing. He was in his domain now. Closing the transaction. Tightening the screws. This was his raison d'être. However it played out, it would end in either ecstasy or despair. There was no middle ground for him anymore. It never had been his entire life. All or nothing and no negotiation. In his books, that was the only means of preserving and increasing one's power.

"Fifteen minutes, Loki," Carson said.

"Hail the other ship with visual," Loki commanded the communications officer as he prepared for battle.

The communications officer complied and sent the call. Seconds elapsed. *What's taking so long?* Loki thought. *Are they trying to play mind games?* After a minute, the screen in front of Loki triggered. A young man appeared on it, displaying a nervous, anxious look. *This should be easy*.

ETHAN'S external comm screen came online with an image of a man radiating confidence and menace. They stared into each other's eyes, sizing up each other's intentions. Ethan knew he looked nervous, but he couldn't help it. He had faced bullies before when he was young, though, and had learned valuable lessons. You didn't get any mercy by capitulating. You had to find their weak spot and attack that. Ethan hoped that the person had weaknesses other than inferior firepower.

"Good afternoon, my name is Loki Mason of Mason Intersolar. Whom am I addressing?" Loki's voice resonated from the speaker.

"Good afternoon. You are speaking to Ethan Richards, Chief Engineer of the International Space Drive Project. How may I help you?"

"It is unfortunate that you have placed yourself in a position where you might land on Iapetus before I do."

"Is that right? Why is that?" Ethan's tone was sarcastic.

Loki glared into Ethan's eyes, trying to intimidate him. "Let's stop playing games. We both know a mineral of great value exists on that moon."

"It has worth to us, yes. What is it to you? Are you developing a star drive too?"

"This isn't a game." Loki felt his temper rising at the insolent young imp. "I intend to get possession of that astatine deposit."

"How do you contemplate doing that if I land there first?"

The elevator doors to the Command Center opened, and Jade, Galena, and Apep came rushing out of them. They had heard of the imminent confrontation and wanted to witness it. They took up positions where they could view the proceedings.

"You are to maximize deceleration at once and change your course," Loki said in a threatening tone.

"Or?"

"Or you may regret the consequences." Loki glanced in Carson's direction and gave a nod. Carson pushed the fire button to launch the first missile.

"Projectile fired from the other ship," the astrogator on *Destiny* shouted in alarm.

Ethan raised his brow as he glanced away from his screen to the astrogator. "Time to collision?" he asked, trying to stay calm.

The astrogator returned to his screen, and his face grew puzzled. "It won't come anywhere near us, sir."

Ethan looked back at Loki. "You have targeting problems," he said sarcastically.

"That's called firing a shot across the bow," Loki replied, fighting to contain his temper. "I promise the next missile won't miss. Now, will you change course?"

"No."

Loki glanced at Carson, who fired a second missile.

"Projectile outgoing from enemy ship, sir. Trajectory is for a collision course with ours. Impact in one minute."

"Watch it," Ethan said as he brought up an astrogation screen himself and took over the control of *Destiny's* drives. He altered the ship's course to a vector perpendicular to the missile's path. Beads of perspiration appeared on his brow. The others watched in alarm. The missile changed its vector to compensate. *Shit, it's got tracking sensors*, Ethan thought with alarm, but he didn't want to use his laser cannons yet.

The missile closed in, and Ethan kept instigating evasive maneuvers as it approached. "Brace yourselves." The projectile detonated, and the ship rocked as the explosive blast hit it. Ethan adjusted the course to the original settings. "Damage report," he ordered to no one in particular.

The commander reviewed alarms that had activated. "Indications suggest only minor damage ... slight damage to the warp ring, but nothing else is showing."

"Thank God for that." Ethan sighed in relief.

Loki was watching events unfold on the other ship with disdain. "Ready to obey my instructions?" he asked with impatience when Ethan faced him again.

"No," Ethan glared. The others in the Command Center stared at Ethan in alarm.

"Have it your way. Any deaths are on your head, not mine." Loki motioned to Carson to fire another missile.

"Another missile launch," the astrogator shouted.

Ethan brought up the laser cannon screen. A satisfied smile covered his face as he realized Hu had primed both cannons. He knew Loki could see his grin, and it was perplexing him. Ethan took control of the most convenient cannon and targeted it toward the approaching projectile. He locked the cannon's aim onto the missile, ready to shoot. "Time to impact?"

"Thirty seconds," the astrogator replied.

Ethan waited. "Time to impact?"

"Ten seconds."

Everybody braced themselves for another explosion. Ethan pressed the fire button, and the missile vaporized. Satisfaction appeared on his face as he turned back to the comm screen. Everybody else in the Command Center watched in confusion at what they were seeing on the primary screen, which showed the view outside the ship. The missile was there, and then it wasn't after a flash of ruby-red light emanated from their ship.

Loki's facial expression changed from predatory to bewilderment to alarm to determination in the space of a second as he understood what had just happened. He turned to Carson. "Fire at will!"

Missiles started erupting from the ports on the ship in quick succession.

How many does this guy have? Ethan thought. I must stop this. He contacted Hu again. "Want targeting practice?"

"Sure do."

"Take the far cannon. I need the other one."

"No problem." Hu charged up the allocated cannon, targeted the first missile, and fired. Light exploded across the screen as the laser vaporized the projectile. Hu smiled as she targeted the next missile for destruction.

Meanwhile, Ethan zoomed in on the incoming ship to locate the ports from where the projectiles had emerged. He located one by the flash as a missile left the port. He locked his aim into the hole, waited for the next missile to leave, and shot. It generated a massive hole in the ship's side where the laser hit. Seconds later, an explosion burst out of the hull as the stored missiles exploded. Loki rocked as the explosions tore at the ship. Ethan located the second port and fired again, with the same result. Missiles stopped firing, and Hu cleaned up the rest in flight with her cannon.

Loki sat confused over what had just happened. Unsteadily, he faced the still connected comm. "Touché. I believe that we have negotiations to conduct." Wisps of smoke floated across the field of view.

Ethan had had enough. He was furious. "There … will … be … no … negotiation!" he said, each word punctuated with a fist striking the desk. "You will end this now, or I will continue firing."

"Please don't do that. That's impressive firepower. OK, you win. I'll leave you alone. See you again another day."

Ethan grimaced. He knew it wasn't over yet. He was sure Loki hadn't finished with them, but he was relieved this confrontation had ended in their favor. The military support with their cannons was a godsend. He only wished Jake had been here to see it. He imagined with almost unbearable sadness how Jake would have high-fived his way around the Command Center. Ethan's emotions were tighter than he had ever known. He needed to relax.

~

~

LOKI ENDED HIS CONTACT, fuming once the link had broken. "How the hell did we not know they had armed themselves with such weapons?"

"They must have had military support, boss," Carson suggested, choosing his words with care because he knew Loki's temperament when in such a mood.

"Really?" Loki said sarcastically to Carson. "Well, it's not over yet."

Carson reacted with concern, detecting in Loki's eyes the same doggedness of other disastrous occasions, resulting in unsavory outcomes. "Are you sure? What else can you do? We have no firepower. We can't get there before them. What are you suggesting?"

"We can ram any lander that launches from their ship. That's what we can do."

"But we need a lander too."

"We don't need a lander. We'll smash it with our ship."

Carson scanned the bridge and saw the panic and alarm in the crew. He asked tentatively, knowing what could happen next. "Is that a good idea?"

Loki turned to stare at Carson with contempt. "I've never known you to run from a fight."

"And I won't now, but I want one I know I can win and live through. I'm uncertain we can win this one."

"We will win. Just follow my orders."

The rest of the crew stared at Carson for direction. He nodded, gesturing that Loki was boss and that they were to obey him.

"Make ready for full acceleration to any lander that launches from that ship," Loki ordered.

"Yes, sir," the commander said fearfully.

A SOLITARY CLAP sounded somewhere in the Command Center. Ethan couldn't tell from where it started. Before long, applause reverberated throughout the room, including from Jade, who rushed over to him and hugged him. "You did well."

"I might need to scrape brown spots off my seat," Ethan joked.

Jade laughed and hugged him harder, giving him a big kiss.

Ethan reddened. "I doubt it's over yet," he warned.

"What else can they do?" Jade asked, puzzled.

"I don't know. But believe me, someone like that guy doesn't give up without a fight. He'll be weighing up his options, and so should we," Ethan told her, sobering the merry atmosphere in the center.

The room calmed to the operational efficiency it had possessed before the conflict. "How long to orbit?" Ethan asked.

The astrogator reviewed the data on his screen and announced, "Five minutes, sir." "We had to adjust our direction and thrust afterward, but we're back to the correct tangential velocity for an immediate circular path around Iapetus."

"Thanks." Ethan beckoned Galena and Apep over to him. Ethan started the conversation. "We need to send a lander to the moon with haste. The other ship is too distant to land yet, but they will try if we waste our opportunity. What I don't know is what they might do when they see we've launched a lander. Galena, are you comfortable gathering the required astatine once the lander has landed?"

"Yes. The collection procedure is explicit," Galena said.

"Good. Apep, how would you like a joy ride? You can help Galena collect the rock."

"With pleasure." Apep looked at Galena with a twinkle in his eye, which made Galena redden like a young girl, something Ethan had never seen before. He fought hard to suppress a smirk at the thought of serious-minded Galena in a romantic relationship. And with Apep of all people.

"Good. You need to head to the docking bay and prepare for takeoff."

"What about you? Who'll pilot the lander?" Galena asked, confused.

"You'll have a special pilot — Hugo. She may be rusty, but she assures me she can fly landers."

Apep gave a hearty laugh. "This, I have to see," he said.

Ethan grinned in appreciation, and then brought their attention back to the nerve-wracking engagement in front of them. "Remember, I'm your insurance policy against that ship trying something else to cause us trouble."

The mood darkened again.

"I suggest you get going, or your pilot might leave without you."

Galena and Apep rushed to the elevator doors with Apep calling over his shoulder, "If Hugo leaves without us, she will pay an enormous price."

Ethan chuckled and directed his attention to contacting Hu on the ship's comm. The comm screen activated with Hu's face on it. "Well done cleaning up the missiles."

"I was just getting the hang of it. You could have let them fire more," Hu said.

"Sorry, I'll remember that next time," Ethan said with mock contrition. "I need you to prepare the lander for a moon landing."

"No problem. And you?"

"I'm staying here as your backup. Be prepared. I don't think our friend has finished with us yet. He'll try something when you launch. I'll be ready with the laser if he does."

"What more can he do? You took out his missile launch ports, and he has used no other weaponry. Although I agree, he will seek to stop us. He could ram the lander, but I can't understand how. A spaceship is less maneuverable than landers."

"Yes, he could. He could send a debris shower. That's much harder to dodge."

"It'd be tougher to destroy, too. I don't suppose you have a cannon installed in the lander?"

Ethan chuckled. "I wish. Although I'm not sure I would trust you with it. Well, we won't know until it happens. You'll have Galena and Apep joining you. They'll take the required samples when you land. And watch them! I think something's brewing between them."

Hu laughed. "Apep has always been searching for another companion after his wife's death. Maybe Galena is the one."

"They are heading for the bay now. They should get the gear together by the time you arrive."

"OK. See you on the other side of history ..."

"Hugo," Ethan interjected, with concern, "take care, be alert, and good luck."

"Thanks," Hu responded with appreciation. "I will. And I'll bring the two potential lovebirds back, too." The screen blanked.

Ethan reclined in the command chair and pondered his position for a moment. He heard, "Entering Iapetus orbit!" from the astrogator. The atmosphere buzzed with action and excitement as the impending significance of the moment descended on the crew.

Jade came over and rested in the vacant seat next to Ethan. "How are you feeling?" she asked.

"Tired. And the day isn't over yet."

"What can I do?"

"Nothing at present. Just pray the psychopath on that ship has acknowledged his failure."

"Yes. We can pray for that."

They sat in silence as Ethan contemplated the potential outcomes of the upcoming landing. He checked the weapons screen to make sure it was ready if he needed to use the cannons again. The drives had powered off now that the ship was orbiting Iapetus and relying on gravity to keep its position. His comm screen activated with Hu's face on it.

"Packed and ready to go," Hu said.

"Have you chosen a landing site?"

"Yes. We just discussed it after consulting a hologram of the moon. Galena has selected two potential sites."

"Good. Cleared for takeoff when you are and again, be careful."

"Thanks. Over and out."

"Now, we'll see if you'll cause any more mischief." Ethan called over to the communications officer, "Can you prepare to send a message to the other ship, please?"

"Will do."

Ethan studied his displays and the large holograph in the air in front of him that showed the view outside the ship. Everything was ready. He sat back, and moments later, he watched the lander leave and gather speed as it descended to the moon. He watched the other ship's movements on another part of the screen.

"Ship course change and at full acceleration, sir," the astrogator announced.

Shit! What are you doing? Ethan thought. "What's its heading?"

"Intercept vector with the lander, sir."

"Get a communications link to that ship," Ethan told the comms officer.

"Will do," he said. Time elapsed with no response. "Sir, I can't raise them."

"OK." *Have it your way, then. I warned you.* Ethan brought up the weapons screen and changed the power setting to one hundred percent from the prior fifty percent.

The lander descended and gathered speed. Loki's ship closed in on it fast. Ethan zoomed the targeting controls and locked the sights onto a drive. He pressed the fire button. A stream of ruby light flashed from *Destiny* to the other ship, hitting the targeted drive dead center. It detonated in a flash of explosive destruction. The ship started gyrating out of control as the destroyed drive unbalanced its thrust. Ethan sat back in joyless satisfaction.

"Try to raise the other ship again."

The officer sent the comm signal again, with an instant response, the comm screen displaying a scene of panic. Loki was ashen with fear. "OK. You win. We give up," he said, with perspiration dripping from his face.

"You should have realized that sooner," Ethan said without pity.

Loki turned to listen to Carson say something to him. He nodded as Carson spoke. He turned back to Ethan. "We have a problem. As you will be aware, we only have two drives and can't balance our thrust. We don't have the spares to repair the damage you just caused. We can stop our rotation and reduce our speed, but we can't return to Earth in this state. Our supplies on board won't last the trip," he said, adding sheepishly, "We were wondering whether you could help."

Ethan glared at Loki with disdain. "You have got to be joking." He left the communication in silence to make Loki stew while he contemplated his response. *I suppose I have to save them. I can't let the others die for this psycho's actions.*

Ethan returned to the screen and said, "OK. We have a tractor beam. We can use it to tow you into a stable orbit around Iapetus for now. I'll consider how far my generosity will stretch after that."

"We are grateful," Loki said and sounded sincere.

"Stay connected to the comm link to coordinate our activities. I'll be back when I have a plan." Ethan directed the comms officer to switch the screen to his own station and gazed at the hologram to find the lander's current position. It pleased him they were approaching the moon. Another ten minutes and they should land, with the stupidity ended. He waited, since he wanted the lander to land on Iapetus before he did anything. He opened a comm link to the lander. "How are things your end?" he asked Hu when she responded.

"Those were spectacular fireworks we saw. I take it you have resolved your conflict amicably," Hu replied.

"You could say that, although 'amicably' may not be the right word."

"We're fine. This lander is good to fly. I like it. We should land in under five minutes now."

"Good. I'll wait until you land before I go garbage collecting to tow the other ship back into orbit. I should return before you're ready to ascend to *Destiny*."

"Will we still have comms?"

"Yeah. We will be in comms' range."

"Good. Happy garbage collecting. I need to prepare for landing."

"See you soon." Ethan disconnected the link.

"Chart a course for the other ship," Ethan said to the astrogator.

"Will do," the astrogator responded.

A few minutes later, the lander settled on Iapetus. That pleased Ethan. "Let's go rescue this idiot."

Moments later, the *Destiny's* drives started, propelling into a vector heading for the stranded ship.

It took thirty-five minutes to reach it. It had stabilized its rotation by now and had slowed to a stationary position above Saturn. *Destiny* maneuvered close in front of it and secured its tractor beam onto the hull of the other ship, ready for towing.

Ethan gestured to the communications officer as he wanted the comms screen in his chair. The officer transferred it. "Are you ready for tugging?" he asked no one in particular.

Loki's face came to the screen a moment later. "Yes, we are ready."

"Have you shut off your drives?"

Loki glanced at someone offscreen and returned his attention to

Ethan. "Yes, they are shut off."

"OK. We will tow you to a stable orbit around Iapetus and leave you there for now. It should take an hour." He cut the comms back to the communications officer.

Destiny's drives fired up, and they started the return journey to Iapetus' orbit. It surprised Ethan that the ship was smaller than he'd first thought. He realized that it hadn't originally been designed as a star drive ship.

Just over fifty minutes later, they arrived in an orbital position around Iapetus. It was further out than Ethan preferred to be to pick up the lander. He didn't want the other ship anywhere near them, not with the lander in flight returning from the moon. The tractor beam disconnected, and *Destiny* powered closer to Iapetus, 180 degrees opposite Loki's ship.

Ethan's comm screen activated with Hu's face on the display. "We are ready for departure. Have you completed your little errand?"

"Yes. They're out of trouble for now," Ethan said. "How was the geology expedition?"

"It went well. Galena said the material was easier to collect and concentrate than expected."

"Good. I'm positioning the ship above you in a five-hundred-kilometer orbit, so the trip back shouldn't take long. See you when you get here."

"See you soon."

The comm screen blackened, and Ethan relaxed. Jade was still in the chair beside him, observing what he did. "What's wrong?" he asked when he saw her looking at him.

"Nothing. I was just watching you in command. Impressive. It suits you. I might learn to run the ship so we can shoot off to the stars together," she suggested with a dreamy face.

Ethan stared at her to check if she was serious or joking. Eventually he said, "That'd be good." He glanced at the hologram to confirm Hu's status. She had lifted off and was speeding back to *Destiny*.

Jade just kept looking at Ethan, appearing to be pondering future possibilities.

32

FASTER THAN LIGHT

The lander entered the docking bay thirty minutes later. Ethan and Jade waited until it had settled to the floor on its landing struts and the cabin door had opened before they moved forward to greet those returning from Iapetus.

Galena exited first, followed by Apep and Hu.

Hu grinned when she spotted Ethan and Jade. "Mission accomplished, despite having to chaperone these two," she told them when they came closer.

Galena and Apep gaped at her in shock and embarrassment.

"Nothing's going on ..." Galena protested, her face turning a crimson red.

"That obvious, is it?" Apep said with a shrug.

Everybody stared at each other before they burst out laughing.

When the laughter ceased, Ethan asked, "So, the astatine collection went well, I hear," directing the query at Galena.

"Yes. We found a concentrated deposit in lumps we could pick up, and we brushed the loose dirt off them. Little concentration was required. We just had to consider throwing rocks around in low gravity. It's only two percent of Earth's strength. A small throw went a long way."

Apep chuckled. "We almost had a rock fight."

"Oh, we did not!" Galena raised her eyebrows in mock exasperation.

"Well, let's get the samples stowed away and start preparing a feed for the muon generator," Ethan prompted.

"Yes, we had better," Galena said. "I'll prepare the feed canister. A fortunate thing our team members have overlapping expertise, with Jake gone and Jezebel out of action."

"Yes," Ethan said. "And it's good to be back together again. We took a hit, though. Current consensus suggests it's only minimal damage to the bubble ring, but we should check it to make sure. What do you think?"

Apep said, "That's an excellent idea. It may be minor, but we don't know whether it damaged a vital part that might give way when we want to use it. You must investigate it, yes?" The others nodded.

"Shall I suit up?" Hu asked.

"No. I should inspect it since I know the ship, and Jade should go with me," Ethan said.

They looked at him, surprised at the mention of Jade, including Jade.

Ethan chuckled. "There's a reason for my logic. Hugo and I shouldn't place ourselves in danger together. She is the only other engineer. And Jade is a fresh set of eyes and may spot something I miss."

"That sounds logical," Galena said.

"OK then. Let's get to it." Ethan gestured to Jade to follow him to the suiting-up room. The others returned to the lander and prepared to unload the astatine.

Spacesuits had developed substantially. They were no longer the bulky exo-skins you viewed on history holograms of earlier years. The protection layer clung to an individual's frame, with a slight space in between, so that air could circulate to remove heat and excess moisture from perspiration. The headgear was very similar but more advanced, with virtual displays of the person's vital functions and status of oxygen reserves and carbon dioxide levels. Necessary supplies of oxygen, carbon dioxide, humidity scrubbers, water, and nutrients sat on a person's back in a backpack with tubing to various locations in the suit, as required. The boots had magnetic soles that simulated walking in Earth-strength gravity, although some said it felt like plodding through syrup. There was a jet pack attached for maneuvering and a portable tractor beam they activated when outside the spaceship. This allowed the person to disengage from the ship's hull but stay within a specified distance of the ship. The further away you were, the stronger the attraction.

Ethan and Jade donned these suits, as they had during training exercises. He had worn one many times, but this was Jade's first unsupervised spacewalk. She looked nervous. Ethan could see that, so he piped up, pointing out into space, "Don't worry, I'll make sure you're suited and sealed before I let you go out there. I want you back inside safe too, you know."

"Shows, does it? Thanks," Jade accepted with gratitude. She continued with the procedure that she had learned.

Ethan finished first. He checked the vital supplies were functioning correctly and the suit was sealed. When a green light came on in the virtual display to show ready for use, he shuffled over to where Jade was and started checking the connections and seals on her suit. Once he finished, he gave her the thumbs up. "Easy, isn't it?" he said, encouraging her.

Ethan headed for the equipment locker. He pulled out two flashlights and gave Jade one. He then pulled out a tool belt he used often and strapped it around his waist. Afterward, he rummaged through the rest of the locker for another belt with fewer tools on it but ones useful for Jade to aid him with if needed. He gave Jade that belt, which she strapped on herself.

"OK. I think we're ready. Can you hear me, Jade?"

"Yes. Loud and clear."

"Good." Ethan switched to a different channel. "Are you receiving my communications?"

"Yes, sir. Loud and clear."

"OK. We're ready. Entering the airlock now," Ethan said as they entered the chamber and shut the inner hatch. Ethan pressed the evacuation button to equalize the pressure with the vacuum of space. They both checked their suit-seal lights were still green, which they were. Ethan opened the outer hatch, and for a few moments, they stood staring out into space at Saturn and its rings.

Jade gazed in wonder. “That’s so beautiful.”

“Yes.”

Ethan walked out of the hatch first and stepped onto the outside hull. Jade followed. They trudged back along the ship to the bubble ring, taking fifteen minutes. Once under the ring, Ethan adjusted the tractor beam range to its greatest extent to bridge the gap between the hull and the ring before being restrained. He advised Jade to do the same. They then used their jet packs to spear out to the ring and re-adjusted their tractor beams again to a closer limit.

They employed their jet packs to traverse the ring’s circumference, scanning for damage. Ethan had presumed it would be on the ring’s front, in the line of fire of the missile’s detonation. Murphy’s law prevailing, they had almost completed the full 360 degrees before they found the disfigured spot. There was a sixty-centimeter irregular gouge in the ring, forty centimeters deep. The damage looked minor.

They both used their flashlights to make a thorough inspection.

“The wiring looks damaged here,” Jade said.

Ethan shone his light to where Jade pointed. He pulled out a tablet with the ship’s design on it and identified the cabling. “That’s OK. It provides power to astrogation lighting. It’s not essential.”

“Good.”

They spent another half hour completing their inspection but found no destruction vital to the ship, so they packed their tools away and prepared to continue the circumnavigation of the ring. Just before they left the damage site, Jade said, “What’s that?”

“What’s what?”

“I thought I spotted something further around — over there,” she said, pointing in the general direction.

Ethan shone a light on the location and moved closer but saw nothing. “Maybe it was a reflection,” he postulated.

"Yeah, maybe."

They completed their circumnavigation and then jetted back to the ship's hull. They returned to the airlock they had disembarked from, entered it, and closed the outer hatch. Once through the airlock, Ethan closed the hatch, and they removed their helmets.

"How was that?" Ethan asked.

"Unbelievable!"

"Yes, I can remember my first spacewalk. It was one of the most memorable experiences that I've ever had."

"I agree. It's so exhilarating floating as just another speck in the universe's eternity."

They discarded their suits and re-dressed in their own clothes. It was late, so they ate dinner and retired to bed. Ethan had scheduled a meeting with the senior team at nine the following morning to confirm that everything was ready for powering up the warp bubble drive.

~

The elevator doors opened in the Command Center, and Ethan and Jade emerged. The conference room stood beside the Command Center. They walked to it and entered. It was just before nine. Ethan had slept well, which surprised him, as he usually found it hard to sleep before he undertook a major project event. He headed to a chair and sat, and then he stood again. He felt fidgety, wanting to start straightaway, and yet procrastinate, too.

Jade smiled. "Stay calm, Ethan. You're making me nervous."

"Huh, what? Oh, sorry. I do that sometimes when I get excited."

"So I see."

Apep and Galena entered the room next with contented smiles. The transformation in Galena amazed Ethan. She was a different person, a better one, having removed the world from her shoulders.

"This is a bright and momentous morning, yes?" Apep said.

Ethan grinned. "I hope so. You two had a sound night's sleep?"

"Yes, delightful dreams we ... I mean, I did." Both Apep and Galena reddened.

"I bet you did," Ethan said, eager to prolong their embarrassment.

"Did what?" Hu asked as she entered.

"Nothing," Ethan replied, silencing a retort. "Well, let's get started. We have a big and momentous day ahead of us," he announced, gesturing for everyone to take a seat at the conference table, which they did.

"So, I'll start," Ethan volunteered. "Jade and I inspected the bubble ring yesterday, and there was damage, but only superficial — nothing that will affect the ring's performance. We were lucky."

"That's good. And the spacewalk?" Hu said. "I'm sure it was stunning."

"Spacewalks are always awesome."

"Yes, they are. And romantic, too," Hu added with a teasing glint in her eye that Ethan chose to ignore. It was one thing for him to tease Galena and Apep but another to be teased himself.

"So, what is the status of the astatine feed canister preparation?" Ethan glanced at Galena.

"Ready," Galena said. "And it's amazing that it doesn't deteriorate out here. We must understand why, Jade."

"Yes, it's intriguing. We need to study the quantum stability of the whole phenomena. It could revolutionize everything we know of nuclear decay and the mechanism causing it. There must be an interaction between the baryonic and exotic particles we don't recognize yet."

"Hugo, how are you progressing in understanding the design behind the drive?" Ethan asked.

"The primary components are basic and standard. The engineering arrangement and integration are phenomenal. Pure genius. I'd like to meet the guy who designed it."

"He's here," Jade said.

"Oh," Hu said, grinning. "Not surprising. I've learned as much as I'm going to for now."

"Good. I need you in engineering looking after the drive when we fire it up," Ethan said.

"No problem." Hu nodded.

"That leaves just one question," Ethan said.

"Which is?" Apep asked on the assembled party's behalf.

"What should we do with our friends in orbit over yonder?"

"In the old days in Russia, we would have pushed them to Saturn and forgotten them, but those days don't exist anymore. More's the pity sometimes," Apep said. Everyone else chuckled.

"We have a choice," Ethan said. "Either we leave them there to find their own way home, in which case we might never bring them to justice, or we could give them a ride to Mars when we power up the drive. That way, we will get our friend Loki to pay for his greed."

"How is that possible?" Jade asked, puzzled. "And he's no friend of mine."

"Their vessel is much smaller than I thought it was. We can tuck it up next to us, within the enclosure of the bubble," Ethan explained.

"Won't it make the mass distribution unbalanced?" Galena asked.

"The bubble doesn't care what's inside it, so it doesn't matter if their ship is there," Jade said, warming to the idea.

Galena considered the proposal. "If it's possible, and they agree, it's the right thing to take them along with us. We can't morally leave them stranded there if we can return them to safety, as much as I'd like to watch them rot." The others agreed with Galena's conclusion.

"I'll contact them then. If they take up my offer, we will rendezvous with them and attach a traction beam to keep them close," Ethan said. "Is that it?"

Nobody had any other topic to raise. "OK then," Ethan said. "It's nine-thirty now. Let's be ready for the test at noon. That'll give us enough time and, who knows, we could be home for breakfast tomorrow."

The others welcomed the possibility of an Earth-cooked meal soon. The meeting dispersed, people heading to their separate duties to prepare to make history.

Ethan stayed behind to talk to Loki's ship in private. He asked the comms officer to send an invitation to Loki's ship and relay the link to his terminal. He had to wait five minutes before the other ship accepted and a video hookup could be established. Loki Mason's face appeared on the screen as the link stabilized.

"To what do I owe this pleasure?" Loki asked in a sarcastic tone.

"We are preparing to leave soon, as we have what we need for our test flight. We should approach Earth sometime this evening. I was wondering if you wanted to hitch a ride?" Ethan replied with forced benignity.

Loki's eyebrows rose in surprise at the offer and at how it might be possible. "I don't understand," he said, confused.

"We intend to test our FTL drive to take us back to near Mars. I have considered your ship's size. We can tuck your ship next to ours in a traction lock inside the bubble, if you prefer to return to Earth sooner, instead of later. Be advised we will impound your vessel as soon as we arrive," Ethan explained.

Loki thought for only a second or two before replying, "I'd rather get back. Who knows how long it will be to send someone to repair our drive? And I assume it's safe. I don't think you'd risk your lives otherwise. I'll take my chances with whatever legal challenge you may throw my way on our return. So, yes, I accept the offer. Thanks." Loki appeared grateful. "You can coordinate the traction details with my commander."

"Very well."

"Can we transfer to your ship?"

"Don't push my generosity," Ethan retorted.

Loki chuckled. "Fair enough. Would it be possible to transport one of your people to our ship, then?"

Ethan studied Loki's eyes before he replied. "If you mean your so-called daughter, Jezebel Liebmann, the answer is no. She is under arrest for multiple murders," Ethan forced out, trying to contain his emotions.

Loki reacted with genuine surprise and knew better not to ask about Jezebel's welfare. "OK. I'll see you near Mars then." He left, and the commander appeared. Ethan discussed the procedure when they attached the magnetic lock and the captain's needed actions once everything was locked in place. He then disconnected the link.

Ethan headed to the command chair and started the procedures to move *Destiny* to the vicinity of the other ship and attach a tractor beam onto it, so they could tuck it in near their vessel and inside the bubble ring. *Destiny* moved as the EmDrive started and vectored it toward the vessel. This took two hours. Ethan left the Command Center and told the commander he would be in engineering if they needed to contact him.

He walked to the engineering level and over to the equipment for the warp bubble drive. Hu was there, looking over the main control screen for the drive. "How goes it, Hugo?" he asked.

"Good. When are we set to go?"

"We'll be ready in two hours. Let's energize this, shall we?"

"Oh good. I get to play with your toys."

Ethan laughed. "Yes, you can play."

Ethan ran a quick check over the reactor, which was running in idle with the power generated diverted to the ship's main energy grid. He then checked the connections to the muon generator with Hu, showing her the important components, and explaining how they should behave. He provided similar explanations for the other items, confirming the units were operable and ready as he walked her through them. Heading over to the main panel, he reviewed the control settings. He needed to confirm that they were the same as when they had conducted their test on Earth. Everything was in order. Satisfied, he brought the muon generator and the muon wave resonator online, on standby.

"OK. It's set," Ethan said when he had finished.

"One thing I'm not sure of, Ethan, is how the warp drive generates the velocity to move faster than light," Hu said.

"We performed the test on Earth without the ring, so we didn't create any motion but a stable stationary bubble. The ring combines with the wave resonator and captures the muon waves, producing the forward thrust with a new bubble configuration. We deform space-time by adjusting the wave resonator, so the space-time at the front compresses and expands behind it. This causes forward motion. The greater the expansion and contraction, the faster the bubble's contents move. But everything inside doesn't experience acceleration or deceleration, or the velocity acting on the space-time bubble. The interior is stationary. So, we don't travel faster than light, only the bubble does. It's like sitting in a vehicle motoring along the highway. You are motionless, but the vehicle is driving at whatever speed you've set."

"OK. I get it now," Hu said.

"Good. It's time."

Galena came into the engineering room carrying the canister of astatine, aided by Apep. They had increased the container and slot size in the muon generator from the one they used in the test on Earth, to allow much longer periods for the warp bubble to exist. "Set," Galena said to Ethan as Apep and she placed the canister into the slot and locked it in place.

"OK. I'd better return to the Command Center and prepare to pilot us to Mars. We've located the other ship, too," Ethan said. "I'll let you get on with your duties here. Hope it'll be a boring trip for you."

"How long will it take?" Apep asked.

"Just over half an hour. We want to travel at 2c for our first run."

"Amazing," Apep said, contemplating the historic event.

"See you soon." Ethan headed for the elevator.

~

WHEN ETHAN ENTERED the Command Center, it was abuzz with people busily adjusting *Destiny's* position to accommodate the other ship and aligning the vessel with the traction lock. "How's it going?" he asked the commander on duty.

"Almost there ... Ethan. Another minor change and we'll be ready."

"Let me know when you are complete."

"Will do."

Ethan settled into the command chair and brought up the warp bubble drive and the astrogation displays needed for the test.

The elevator doors opened, and Jade strode into the Command Center, seating herself in the backup seat next to Ethan. "How's it going?"

"Almost there." He reviewed the settings on the screens.

"Is it alright if I sit here?"

"Yes, that's fine. You can bring up the warp bubble drive screen and help me watch the readings when we transfer to FTL."

"I'd like that." Jade raised the designated display and studied it.

Ethan completed his checks and reclined while he waited. *This is it*, he thought. *Our work's culmination for the past five years — for thirty minutes of FTL travel. You could see it as the project's end, but it's just the start of the biggest feat in human history. This must be what Christopher Columbus felt when he set sail for India, sailing west, only to discover America. With this drive, we can reach for the stars, spread throughout our galaxy, and explore its vast extent. It will be incredible ...*

"Ethan, sir," the commander called to Ethan.

Ethan emerged from his reverie, staring with vacant eyes at him until he recovered his concentration. "Sorry, what's the problem?"

Jade grinned at the comedy unfolding in front of her.

"Ethan, we are ready. You may begin at your leisure."

"Oh. Thanks," Ethan replied, embarrassed. "Well, I suppose everyone should prepare to create history. I should make a big speech."

"Don't you dare!" Jade threatened.

"OK."

Ethan called up the engineering room on the ship comm. "Are you ready there?"

"As ready as we will ever be," Hu, Galena, and Apep chorused.

"Let's do it then."

Ethan powered up the muon generator with the settings for the intended bubble size and opened the gate from the reactor to start the astatine's bombardment. Muons flared off the astatine in ever-increasing numbers until they established the required rate. They channeled through to the muon wave resonator and attained the correct frequency for the bubble's perfect resonance. Ethan checked it surrounded the entire ship, as predicted. He confirmed the load and saw that it was stable at fifty-six percent. "Here we go then," he announced. The tension in the air was electric. He diverted muons from the resonator to the ring, which changed the bubble's shape, and it, with everything in it, including the two ships, pushed forward in unison. He altered their vector so that it pointed them in the right direction and increased the muon flow. Muons from the generator replenished the resonator, and they moved faster as the muon density increased.

"0.5c," Ethan announced as the ship kept building velocity. The thrust yield was five percent. He increased the flow at a steady rate. The bubble's speed rose to 0.8c ... 0.9c ... 0.95c ... 0.99c ... 1.0c. "We are now traveling at the speed of light." Everyone applauded.

Ethan raised power again, but the ship started vibrating as soon as the bubble rose above 1.0c. Tension filled the air in the Command Center as people grabbed onto their armrests, knuckles whitening as they tightened their grip.

"What's happening?" Ethan asked Hu with deepening concern.

Hu came to the comm. "I'm checking. Nothing's abnormal, but we're losing muons somewhere, and ... wait."

The vibrations started building in intensity and severity.

"A secondary oscillation has developed, and it's emanating from a position 342 degrees around the ring," Hu told Ethan.

"The damage was there," Jade said. "That can't be a coincidence."

"No," Ethan agreed as perspiration appeared on his forehead.

"This is weird," Hu continued. "The muon loss is cyclic as if something is flapping."

Jade and Ethan glanced at each other. "That damage that I thought I saw. Could that cause this if we missed something?" Jade asked.

The ship bucked and lurched as the vibrations became more violent. They were so severe that they started throwing people not holding on from their seats. Ethan had to think fast, or their ship might vibrate to pieces. He attempted to reduce their speed but couldn't. A disturbance was preventing the muon flow from reducing. He realized now that the spot Jade had pointed out was outside the muon circulation toroids within the ring. There must be a segment flapping that tore when the missile hit them. It must have flapped open when Jade saw it first, only to flap shut again when they tried having a closer look. There were four toroids in total.

"I think there's a hole in a toroid," Ethan told Hu. "I'll try closing one at a time. When the offending toroid gate is closed, blocking its muon flow, the vibration should stop."

Ethan brought up the ring control screen on his display. He selected a toroid and closed its gate. The ship rocked. Personnel flew across the control room and panels sparked as electrical circuits failed. He reopened that gate, and the reverberations eased to the earlier level. *That wasn't it*, he thought. "Hold on," he said over the comm. "We might get more of those." He chose the second gate and shut it, resulting in the same violent effect. He reopened it and closed the third, still the same. *Murphy's law would have to revisit us*, he thought as he shut the fourth toroid's gate. As soon as the gate closed, the vibrations abated and, within a few seconds, ceased. Ethan gave a gigantic sigh of relief as he wiped the perspiration from his brow with his sleeve.

"That was close," Jade said, permitting herself to breathe again.

"Yes, it was," Ethan said. "How is the generator behaving now?" he asked Hu over the comm.

"Everything is returning to stable, thank God," Hu replied with relief.

Personnel in the Command Center picked themselves off the floor or prized themselves away from whatever they hung onto, several with injuries from hitting panels and equipment. Ethan called the doctor to tell him of incoming casualties to treat, as people were helping the injured to the elevator to transport them to the medical bay. Others collected fire extinguishers to deal with the fires that had started, although these were few and minor.

Ethan waited to allow his heart to quieten to a healthy pace. He checked the status on his screens and watched them return to normal. He let the drive stay like that for over five minutes. Looking back through the velocity trace, he noticed the bubble velocity had been oscillating between just below and just above 1.0c, with ever-increasing amplitude at one stage, as if it was in positive feedback. He noted they needed to investigate the phenomena further when they returned to Earth, as it should not be possible. He realized it was why he couldn't reduce the speed. The feedback was feeding on itself.

Satisfied that it was stable and in control, Ethan tried increasing the power again. The bubble velocity increased to 1.1c. Nothing untoward happened. He raised the speed ... 1.2c. Steady. Feeling confident, he raised it until he reached 2c with the thrust at twelve percent. "2c," he announced as the atmosphere in the room returned to normal. He remained alert for the rest of the FTL phase of the trip back.

Forty-three minutes after starting the bubble movement, they neared Martian space, and Ethan decelerated. Within two minutes, he had slowed to below light speed, and as they did so, a rush of photons and particles rushed from the bubble surface, dissipating into the surrounding space. They had collected the stowaway particles on the surface as it traversed the space-time between Saturn and Mars.

As their velocity reduced to EmDrive capable speeds, Ethan shut off the warp bubble drive and brought the EmDrive online. He gave the controls over to the commander to steer them back to Earth.

Ethan requested a comms link to Martian Control, and the operator at the other end came on the video screen. "*Destiny* returning to Mars from Saturn in forty-three minutes," he announced, "completing its first FTL flight. If you will excuse my theft of the words, that's one small step for a man and one giant leap for mankind."

"Congratulations," the operator responded. "I'll pass your message to the authorities. Have a safe passage to Earth."

"Thank you. See you next time," Ethan concluded as he broke the link.

"Piece of cake," he quipped across to Jade, who was beaming beside him as he sat back, looking pleased with himself.

"Hah! You were terrified like the rest of us," she protested, giving him a soft punch on the arm.

"Maybe," Ethan replied with a coy grin.

"What was with the quote?"

"What is today's date?"

"July 20, 2069. Is that significant?"

"One hundred years ago today, man first walked on the moon."

"Oh. I see. Neil Armstrong said that when he first stepped on the moon."

"Yes, or at least that's what he was supposed to say."

Jade looked at him quizzically.

"He wrote the line, but when he stepped onto the moon, the 'a' in 'a man' wasn't heard, so to this day people think he said 'man' and not 'a man'."

"Does it matter?" Jade asked, perplexed.

"It does if you care about the English language. The first step related to a particular flesh-and-blood man, Armstrong; the giant leap related to 'man' or 'mankind' — or, as we would say today, 'humanity'. Get it? 'Man' and 'mankind' mean the same thing. So, it came out sounding like he was talking about humanity — twice."

"You really are a know-all nerd, aren't you?' Jade said with a grin that took the sting out of the words.

"Yep," Ethan said happily. "Get used to it."

"I guess I will."

Hu, Galena, and Apep walked into the Command Center a short time later to a congratulatory welcome.

"That went well ... finally," Hu said.

"Yeah. Sorry for the bit of turbulence in the middle there," Ethan replied with characteristic understatement.

"That was frightening," Galena admitted.

"If nobody needs you, Ethan, we should retire to the bar and celebrate," Apep said.

"What a great idea."

"Sir, you have a comms signal from the other ship. Do you want to take it?" the communication officer interjected.

Ethan sighed. “I suppose I had better. Put it through to me.”

Ethan’s comms screen activated, and Loki appeared.

“That was impressive.”

“Thanks,” Ethan replied, affronted by Loki’s audacity in playing on his good nature.

“So, what happens now?” Loki asked.

“We are decelerating toward Earth and will get there around seven tomorrow morning. We’ll keep your ship locked in traction during transit. Once we arrive, I’ll hand you to the authorities to prosecute.”

“That’s it then?”

“Yes.”

“Are you sure that’s the right approach?” Loki persisted. “Or we could make another agreement profitable to us both?”

The people with Ethan rolled their eyes in disbelief.

“Yes, I am sure, and there won’t be any arrangement,” Ethan retorted, his anger rising. “I don’t negotiate with psychopaths who try to kill me and my friends.”

“Come, now. That’s exaggerated, don’t you think? I wasn’t trying to murder anyone.”

“You fired missiles at our ship, and you say that you weren’t intending to kill anybody?”

“You weren’t seeing reason. Besides, you fired at us, too.”

“How dare you! That was self-defense. You intended to destroy our lander.” Ethan now started raising his voice. “And what about your so-called daughter killing *three* of our crew?”

“I didn’t ask her to do that,” Loki said blandly.

Jade rubbed his shoulder.

“We shall see how others perceive it then,” Loki concluded with a mocking smirk.

Ethan heaved as he tried to restrain himself from reaching through the screen to throttle Loki. “Yes, we will,” he said and pressed the disconnect button. “What a nerve!”

“Calm yourself, Ethan,” Galena said. “He was trying to make you doubt the legitimacy of your actions and press his political influence over you while he could. Two can play that game. You may need coaching in the art of diplomacy and political tactics before you're through with him."

Ethan calmed and saw the wisdom of Galena's words. "Yes, I see that now. I've never been good at politics. I just want to do my job and let others play their games."

Galena sighed. "If only life were that easy."

Ethan became thoughtful. "I'll have to plan out my accusations beforehand and put in place contingencies for any countermoves he might have."

Galena laughed. "Spoken like a true schemer. We'll make a politician out of you yet."

"I'm thirsty," Apep said to everyone's amusement.

"We'd better fix that," Ethan said. He rose from his chair and led the others to the elevator and on to the bar.

33

LAST RESPECTS

The *Destiny* arrived in orbit around Earth just after eight the following morning, and Ethan and Hu piloted a lander from it to the spaceport at JPL with Jade, Galena, and Apep on board. Three others, who wanted to rejoin their loved ones urgently, filled the vacant seats.

They released Loki's ship from traction and handed it over to the authorities once they explained the circumstances. Security transported Loki and the crew to Earth and detained them for questioning. They transferred Jezebel to a holding cell on Earth for processing, awaiting trial. Hu gave the evidence that she had collected to the detective in charge of the investigation. Jezebel was still hopeful Loki would find a way to have her released, but it was evident to everyone else now, including Carson, that Loki was only thinking of himself.

They took the dead to a morgue in Los Angeles for autopsy.

Hu and Apep booked into the Hilton in Los Angeles, although Hu was unsure how much time Apep spent there as he was always unavailable. Galena retired to her residence and took a vacation to recuperate from the voyage's rigors. She, too, wasn't contactable on most occasions.

Ethan and Jade returned to their respective residences but enjoyed the time together, their relationship deepening. Ethan scheduled a few days at an ocean resort near San Diego, where they lounged and swam.

Lying on the beach one day, Jade suddenly sat up as a thought occurred to her. Turning to Ethan, lying beside her with his eyes shut against the brilliant sun, she asked, "Did you ever think *I* might be the saboteur?"

Ethan pretended he hadn't heard.

"You did, too!" exclaimed Jade and threw a handful of sand in his face.

Sitting up, spluttering, Ethan defended himself. "Well, what was I to think when a beautiful girl like you showed an interest in a nerd like me? And it was only for a nanosecond."

"I don't know whether to kick you or kiss you," Jade replied.

"May I suggest the latter?" Ethan said, and they both started to laugh.

~

THE FAMILY ARRANGED Jake's funeral for a week after they landed. He had come from a small ranch in Jeddo, near Austin, Texas, where his parents still lived. They had asked to return his body there for burial at the local cemetery. The entire team attended the funeral.

Ethan had so many emotions running through him on the day. Jake's death saddened him and filled him with regret that their friendship had lasted such a short time. But when he thought more deeply, he felt honored that he had known Jake, and he remembered the good and fun times he had shared with him. They were memories he would always cherish.

The eulogy and interment were traditional and typical. The family invited the mourners to their family residence for refreshments afterward, and Jade, Ethan, and the others attended.

"How are you feeling?" Jade asked Ethan as they walked up the path to the front door of the house with her arm wrapped around his to give him support.

"OK, I guess. The funeral was positive. It gave me finality. I've said my goodbyes, but it hasn't sunk in yet that he is gone. He was a treasured friend, a ratbag sometimes but a friend, and I will always remember our good times."

They arrived at the front door, where Jake's parents met them and gave them each a hug of gratitude for their friendship with Jake. Mrs. Bodie said in a Texan drawl to Ethan, "So, you're the famous Ethan that Jake kept lauding whenever he called us. You were special to him, you know. He looked up to you always."

Ethan struggled to contain his emotions at these words. In the end he just said, "Thank you. He was incredibly important to me too," and pressed her hand in mutual support. He did the same with Mr. Bodie.

"Well, we'll have a toast to Jake afterward. We will, you and I," Mr. Bodie said.

"I'll hold you to that." Ethan smiled.

With a stream of mourners behind them waiting to offer their condolences, Ethan and Jade walked inside to mingle.

Jake's siblings offered the guests refreshments and talked to whoever they served.

His brother Tom made a point of introducing himself to Ethan as Ethan stood with Jade. "He was a wonderful brother," he told Ethan, even if we got into scrapes together."

"Brothers do that."

"Yeah, they do. He talked about you often. He said you were the only person who understood engineering. He said you saw the practical side of machinery. Most scientists and engineers didn't know their head from their ..., sorry, ma'am. I shouldn't talk that way, I suppose."

Jade laughed. "That's OK. I can hear him saying that, too. He was a great guy and didn't mince his words."

"Well, he liked you, and what he did, and Ma and Pa were proud of him and his achievements. A tragedy what happened."

"I promise you that those responsible will pay. I'll make sure of that," Ethan said.

"Anyway, what's your poison?"

"Jade?"

"I'll have a beer to honor Jake."

"I will too."

Tom left to get their drinks.

Ethan caught sight of John trying to be unobtrusive but wanting Ethan's attention. Ethan considered what he should do. He pointed the general out to Jade. "There's someone I'd like you to meet," he said, walking in John's direction.

"Hello, John. Glad you made it for Jake," Ethan said, when he and Jade had reached John.

"Hi. It was mandatory to pay my respects to one of my close acquaintances. And who is your lovely companion?"

"This is Jade. She's the project's quantum physicist and more than a colleague."

"Oh!" John said, raising his brows in conspiratorial surprise. "It is a pleasure to meet any friend of Ethan's. I'm General John O'Conner."

"It's good to meet you, too. Ethan never mentioned that he knew any generals." Jade replied, looking at Ethan with curiosity.

"It's nothing," John reassured her. "We chat occasionally. And by the way," John turned his attention to Ethan, "would you contact me when you return to Los Angeles? We need to discuss the future."

John's dropping so much information in Jade's presence surprised Ethan, but then he realized John wasn't being careless. If he divulged the intelligence, he had a reason to, which Ethan would discover when he was ready to explain himself. "Yeah. OK, I'll do that."

"I'll see you later," John said with an enigmatic smile as he walked off to circulate.

"That sounds clandestine," Jade said, probing. "What did he mean by Jake being a close acquaintance?"

"Nothing. We just know him." Ethan changed the topic. "Shall we meet Jake's other friends?"

"We haven't finished this conversation, but yes, let's mingle."

Ethan and Jade conversed with the crowd for the rest of the afternoon.

LIFE RETURNED TO NORMAL, as far as normal goes, after the funeral. They resumed work and their duties, debriefing on the voyage, and discussing what they learned about the warp bubble drive and improvements that they could make.

I wonder what the future holds for us now, Ethan wondered while relaxing with Jade and watching the sunset on a warm summer's evening at the end of an exhausting day. *Humanity has come a long way. What direction will it follow? There is one thing I know: we'll always devise ways to achieve our dreams. We keep proving it again and again.*

The End of Book 1 of the Reach for the Stars series.

You can continue reading about Ethan's adventure in Centauri. Click below.

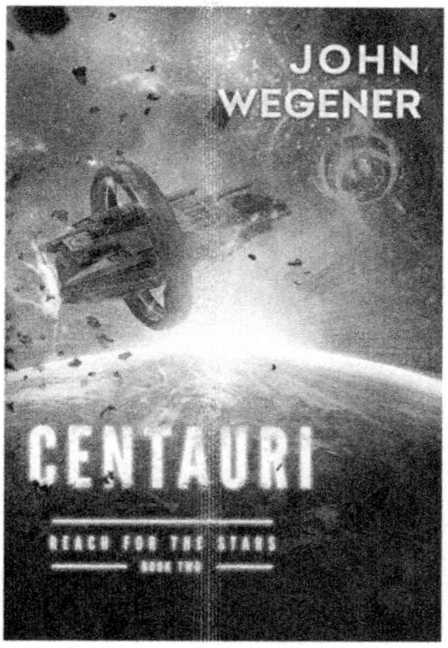

Thanks for reading this book. If you loved the book and have a moment to spare, I would appreciate a short review on the site that you purchased the book from, as this helps new readers find my books.

Subscribe to my Newsletters and receive three free episodes of The Chronicles of Gatacus Todd.

Click Here

ABOUT THE AUTHOR

John Wegener grew up in the Adelaide Hills of South Australia. He has decided to express his imaginative dreams and start engaging in writing after a 34-year career as a Chemical Engineer in the steel industry, which has taken him to many countries and allowed him to experience many cultures. John currently lives in Wollongong, Australia with his wife and children.

Click on johnwegener.com to find out more about him or to contact him at his website and blog. Subscribe to my emails for more stories and information. I would love to read what you thought about the book.

ALSO BY JOHN WEGENER

Books

Reach For The Stars Trilogy

FTL

Centauri

Ceti

Zodiac Series

Scorpius

Libra

Halwende's Legacy Series

Halwende's Redemption

Halwende's Resurrection

Halwende's Reincarnation

Other Stories

The Dark Ages

SAGI

Short Stories

The Love Particle

Printed in Great Britain
by Amazon

39013312R00165